W9-ACG-198

Also by Gerald Seymour

HARRY'S GAME

THE GLORY BOYS

KINGFISHER

A NOVEL

GERALD SEYMOUR

SUMMIT BOOKS · NEW YORK

Copyright © 1977 by Gerald Seymour
All rights reserved
including the right of reproduction
in whole or in part in any form
Published by Summit Books
A Simon & Schuster Division of Gulf & Western Corporation
Simon & Schuster Building
Rockefeller Center
1230 Avenue of the Americas
New York, New York 10020
Manufactured in the United States of America
1 2 3 4 5 6 7 8 9 10

Library of Congress Cataloging in Publication Data

Seymour, Gerald.
  Kingfisher : a novel.

  I. Title.
PZ4.S5192Ki 1977   [PR6069.E734]   823'.9'14   77-15584
ISBN 0-671-40015-0

To Gillian, Nicholas and James

1

News of the arrest spread fast.

There had been nothing about it, of course, in the Party newspapers, or on the radio, or on the television news programs; but then, they were not the tried and tested sources of information. The news moved in a different and more circuitous way; traveled as a bird carries a wisp of branch for its nest, as a fly takes a germ and deposits it on food—a constant and fast process of dissemination; and so there was knowledge of what had happened. In the queues they heard of it while the sun was climbing high over the monuments and parks and lofty buildings that were the achievement of the regime. Queues waiting for the buses; queues at the food store, where there was a delay in the arrival of the day's fresh-baked bread; queues at the bank before it opened.

The talk of the arrest was neither loud nor furtive. Just a subject of conversation among bored and tired people, so that it rippled their lives momentarily—passing a few wasteful seconds of time; relieving the tedium of the day that was to come a little less harshly; easing the personal load because of the sure knowledge that somewhere in the city there was a being who was in great trouble. Someone who had a problem more real and more acute than any which the mass would face that morning, or that afternoon, or that night. And the thought of it sent an eddy of apprehension through those who knew.

Some had seen him taken. Seen the cruising black car of the militia come to the sudden halt in the midst of the traffic lanes of the wide and central street of the city; seen the rear doors snap open and the avalanche of men in the pale brown uniforms weave a path for themselves in front of and behind the other cars till they were at the sidewalk and sprinting for their quarry. He had been walking casually, unaware of the risk, till they were on him. The one at his legs and pitching him forward. Another to spread out his arms on the coolness of the pavement, so that if he had a gun secreted on his person, hidden impossibly beneath his trousers or his light summer shirt, he would not be able to take advantage of it. The third had stood above him, looming and huge, right arm extended with the cocked pistol aimed into the small of his back, the ultimate warning that he should not resist. And then he was gone, even as the crowd, unsure and hesitant, circled to watch. They bundled him toward the car, which now idled at the curb, its rear door open and spanning the gutter; dragged him so that his torso was far in front of his feet, which scrabbled and scuffed at the ground in an effort to find a grip and control that were not permitted him. There was no siren, no flashing light, and the curious waited till the accelerating car was engulfed in the traffic and lost. Others had looked as the vehicle spun hard, tires fighting for a grip, into the shadowed entrance of the militia station, the noise attracting them, and because of the loss of speed of the car they had had the opportunity to notice for a carved fraction of a second the face half buried among the uniforms around him. A face that was white, with the eyes staring, and with the hair already disheveled. That there was fear in the boy was clear for all to see, however short the opportunity to watch. Deep animal fear—that of the rabbit trapped by the wire snare; that of the fox whose leg is fractured and held in the teeth of the gin trap. Profound terror, and the word of it had passed through the city that night and spread further the following morning.

There were some who conjectured and said that they knew why he had been held. Those who knew of the shooting, those who had heard of the wounding of the policeman far out in the industrial suburbs to the west across the river.

The principal headquarters of the militia security police in Kiev, capital city of the Ukraine, is a formidable construction. Built close to the seat of power, which it can watch over and protect. Adjacent to Party offices; within a short walk of the administration center. There is a wedding-cake decor on the front facade, columns and gently sloping steps and statues all maintained in a bright and soft-colored stone by the water jets that banish the clinging residue from the city's chimneys. It is the legacy of the Stalinist postwar rebuilding of all that

German bombs and Russian shells had destroyed. But the interior does not match the finery of the visible facade. Behind the walls, no allowance has been tolerated for aesthetics; a purely functional honeycomb of rooms and corridors and narrow staircases, and deep in the basements are located the prisoners' cells.

At the far end of the buried passage, devoid of natural light and behind a door numbered "38," Moses Albyov now lay. He rested on a mattress of straw held together by rough farm sackcloth which rustled and protested with each shift of his weight. A slightly built figure, with a pinched and concerned face and dark, straight hair that had been thrown haphazardly in all directions and that needed the attention of comb or brush. They had taken his shoes and his belt, and his hands, from which the veins protruded in relief, held the waist of his trousers—not that he was about to rise and move, but simply for some vague fantasy of protection because a man feels defenseless unless his trousers are secure and will not fall. Gone too were his glasses; left on the pavement where they had spilled from his face at the moment when they had taken him; probably broken in the short scuffle, certainly abandoned. Without them his sight was reduced, blending the hard lines of the wall and floor and ceiling angles, causing them to be softer, less cruel.

Not that there was much for him to focus on. A door to the front, steel-faced and scratched where others had attempted to achieve a pathetic immortality by carving their names and the date, fearful perhaps of entering and leaving the cell in total anonymity. Only a spy hole, small, circular and reflecting the light of the room, interrupted the smooth, complete surface of the door. No natural light was permitted to enter the cell; illumination was from a low-powered bulb recessed into the ceiling and covered by what he presumed was toughened glass embedded with wire mesh. The floor was of roughened cement, as though the workers had wished to be rid of their job and had hurried their work, leaving it pitted and lined like a plowed field when the winter frosts have come. Nothing to call furniture—no table, no chair, no cupboard, no shelves. Only the mattress and the bucket, which he had moved away to the farthest point from him because of its smell, the odor of vomit and urine and feces. It was not far away that he could put the bucket: perhaps seven feet, in the corner behind the door—not far enough to divorce its presence from him; not far enough to shut out the taste that swelled in his mouth.

For company, only the cockroaches. They came fearless and exploratory, and because of the quietness of the cell, the distance that he was removed from the activity of the building above him, he believed that he could hear their feet, their legs, their antennae, whatever they were, brushing in a gentle and sympathetic and caressing passage across the floor toward him. He had thought that the light which burned through the night would have frightened them and could not believe that creatures so devoid of intellect could recognize his helplessness, but some instinct told them that they had nothing to fear from him. Once he had brushed two away with his hand, and his whole body had trembled in the aftermath of the contact. He could not touch them again, and they had come, sometimes singly, sometimes in their cohorts, to examine him, to ponder the visitor. And as if bored and uninterested they had gone on their way. It is because there is no food, he thought.

His right shoulder still hurt, ached where the bruising had now won through and discolored the pale skin into a kaleidoscope of blue and mauve and purple and yellow. On the final flight of stairs, and he had not been ready for it. Already down two flights, while they held his arms above the elbows, tight grip, squeezing and firm, and then on the last leg, without a warning, the hands were gone and the knee was in the small of his back and he was away, arms flailing in the vacuum, seeking to break his fall against the cement steps that rushed to meet him. Toes in his ribs, a fist in his hair, and he had risen to walk the rest of the passage, stayed on his own feet while they produced the keys to the cell door, made his entry without interference and stood stock-still in the center of the floor as the door had shut behind him. That was all the violence they had shown to him. Just the once, reckoning in their trained minds what was sufficient to impress a message, insufficient to harden his resistance. The footsteps and the casual conversation of the guards had faded, become immersed in the silence around him, and since then, nothing. Nothing for him to hear. Not a door slammed, not a raised voice. As if he were immured, cemented away, removed and forgotten.

He could understand what they were doing. Simple if you examined it, thought about it, applied logic. The process of vegetation: that was what it was all about. They wouldn't talk to him yet; they would wait until they had assembled the dossier, hardened the evidence, examined the files. When they were ready and not before, that was when interrogation would begin. Stupid if they rushed it and showed him they had not taken time for their homework and background. So he knew what they were at, why they were taking their time and not hurrying themselves. And he knew what they would be asking of him when they had prepared themselves. Because it had been decided in the group that he would be the one; because it had been he who had drawn the short twig.

His hand had been shaking, and the pistol barrel waving, dancing and cavorting in the air. And all the time the fattened and elephantine form of the policeman had convulsed as, semistunned, he had tried to rise from his knees and make good an escape. Bewilderment and pain etched on his features, struggling to construct reality from the previous moments of racing confusion.

All four had known their role in the attack. Rebecca from the front asking the question of direction and fumbling in her bag for the map, holding his attention. David from behind with the hammer blow of his clenched fist pounding onto the tunic cloth of the policeman's right shoulder and felling him. Isaac springing from the shadow, his hands thrusting at the holster flap to prise away the precious pistol—the speed of the rapist at the virgin's protection; drawing it clear and throwing it abruptly to where Moses stood.

When the gun was in his hand the others had faded, clearing the field, deserting the stage. Just Moses there, because he had drawn the short one; just Moses and the policeman who strove to rise. Strange in his hand, foreign in its feel, unfamiliar; such a small thing. The first time, and they had chosen him, they had chosen Moses. . . . And when he had looked down myopically at the barrel, fascinated by its movement, tilting his head to see it, then the identity-protecting stocking cap had slipped and obscured his vision, and he pulled at it, ripped it across his face, over his head, clear of his hair. A distant and retreating scream from David for him to hurry, in concert with the sharper growl that was Isaac. When he fired, the policeman was gazing at him, the trained bovine mind conjuring the description that he sought to remember, conning the facial features even as the bullet struck with its tumbling velocity into his upper chest.

From the way the policeman fell, he had known it was not a fatal shot. That was the moment when he had needed to stand, needed to root his feet to the pavement and finish what he had started. But he was running and panting and sobbing to get air into his lungs, frantic to create distance between himself and the man whom he had failed to kill. The others were at the corner, where it was dark and sheltered and safe, and when he had come they had all run together till they had not the strength to sprint further. It was only after he had heaved the early supper his mother had prepared for him, spewed it behind the bus shelter, that he had felt in his pockets, one after another, and trying not to create alarm among the others, realized that he no longer had the cap.

The importance of the loss had been demonstrated to him with brutal clarity within minutes of entering the militia headquarters. They'd sat him in a chair, in a room at the back and on the ground floor, and a man in a white coat had come forward from his desk with a shined and scrubbed steel comb, and had run it through his hair and looked with pleasure at the debris that he extracted. There would be a match: they had the skill to do that. It would be no problem for them to marry what they found embedded in the wool fiber of the cap with the hairs that lay between the teeth of the comb.

The man in the white coat had said nothing, just placed the comb in a plastic bag. Too simple, and damning, confirmation of an involvement, to be added to that which they had obtained from the bedside, the identification by the policeman. Sitting in his bed, he'd be with the men around him who make up the photographic imitations of the people they are hunting. Moses' face would have been circulated, the policeman's memory of it, and the militiamen who had come from behind him as he walked must have seen the features which the experts had re-created and assimilated them sufficiently for them to act. When they'd walked inside the headquarters with him, they'd shown their pleasure in the knowledge that there was no mistake, that they had taken the one they wanted. Before, they had been in the realm of belief; now they had the evidence to swing their opinion to certainty. Two follicles of hair—that was all they needed. Two. strands: nothing, till there was a microscope. But they would have a microscope, and scientists to use it, and a laboratory for them to work in.

Too easy, Moses. Too facile to rely on their luck or their genius, whichever. Too simple. Go deeper, boy; hunt for the source of identification, the factor that isolates you from among the mass of youths who parade the streets of the city. Remember the stocking cap: remember the campus shop at the north side of the University; remember the label. They would have stored the information, gloated over it while the bedridden pig put together the description that could be circulated. Then salivated over the two.

You did it for them, Moses. Performed their work. A student with features that matched the description: what more could they have asked of you? So forget the crap about photo fits and laboratories and the magnification of hair roots. There was nothing that should mitigate his stupidity. Had given it to them. All they needed for suspicion. Left them only to supply the proof. And their technology would be massive, equal to that, hugely excessive for the task.

So how many hours more; how long till the report was typed and the knot tied, till they were ready for him?

It was cold in the cell, and the memory of the warmth as he had been walking in the street, wrapped in his own thoughts, was fading. There was a chill and sort of dampness that he could not identify, as the white-painted walls showed no rivulets of moisture. As if water had once been there and had, strangely, found no route of escape.

There was no escape. And he sat up sharply, disturbing the orderedness of the straw underneath him. What would they do to him? Didn't know. Be easier for him if he knew. Understand then whether he could counter it or not. But he had no answers; all outside his experience. Drugs: perhaps they would use drugs. That would be painless and would remove the stigma of confession, not dent the virility of defiance. But what if it was to be pain? What if that was the instrument they would use? They'd break him—not because he was special, not because he was different; they'd break anyone with pain . . . David and Isaac as well, and Rebecca quicker than them. They'd all break for pain. Everyone has a barrier through which he cannot pass, and they'd push you right through it till you were screaming, till you were shrieking, till the names came tumbling out so fast that they couldn't write them down, and the addresses and the rendezvous. Everything they wanted and much more, only stop, stop and no more. Please, not again, please.

He was stirring on the mattress, squirming with his body, compressing the flesh. Pain was what frightened him, because he knew it would destroy him, the pain of a beating from the truncheons, the pain from the electrodes they would wire to his limbs. And they'd have a place to do that, somewhere in the building; that too was a certainty. If it was to be drugs, then you were helpless, unable to summon resistance, couldn't find an antidote to the chemist's technology. But what was the antidote to pain?

Moses tossed and heaved now, his mind taking control and drifting him along a course from which he could not turn aside. Perhaps it was courage. Not really important for how long. For a few hours; a day, perhaps. To give the others time to go. Had to give them time to go. And what if they didn't know that he had been taken? He wondered how long he had been in the cell, the sense of time lost after they'd taken his watch. Would have heard by now, wouldn't they? Must have. And they should be running and dispersing and separating, because he wasn't strong, wasn't ready for the pain, could not give them much time.

He sagged back, flattening the harder lumps of the straw, and turned his body so that he lay on his stomach with his face buried in the roughness of the sacking, and with his arms clasped around his head to shut out the incessant light that beat at the back of his neck. There were tears that he could not control, that came without noise and that ran a little way over his upper cheek before falling on the sacking, staining it momentarily, then disappearing.

Opportunity now to think and to reflect and to consider. Just what they wanted him to do. Needed him to put it all together in his mind, sort out where it had started, and why, and what were the aims and intentions. Quicker for them that way—they'd get their answers faster; and be easier for him too—he'd suffer less. Make it easier, Moses; that way it doesn't hurt so much. Have it all ready for when they come for you; then they won't need to hurt so much. The awful fear of waiting—but this would be only the start of it. First the waiting for the time when they were ready to take the confession. Then the waiting for the trial. And after that, more waiting. Waiting for sentence, waiting for execution. Be from a cell like this that they'd take him out. Still dark before the creep of dawn, and floodlights playing on the high walls, and somewhere in the yard they'll trip you over, Moses, then jerk you down to your knees, and there will be a hand to hold your head steady, and then the grip will loosen from the hair and there will be the noise of the pistol being cocked. That's what you're going to wait for, Moses; that's the future; that's eternity.

They'd grown up together, the four of them. The war long over when they were born, and the fighting finished, but nothing changed in the lot of the Ukrainian Jew. Second-class people, on the outside, without benefit, without recognition. Didn't live in a ghetto, that was not the way housing was allocated, but learned to fall together because that was survival in an alien world. Taught to be quiet, taught not to answer back, taught not to risk a provocation, taught to ride a jibe and an insult; taught to be better and fitter and stronger and more able because those were the necessities of equality. That was the message handed down from their parents, who were now bowed and humbled people.

When they were children David had been the leader among them, the one who knew the answers and understood the struggle. It had been he who told them of Babi Yar, and none of them then past eleven years of age. Not a place their fathers and mothers spoke of, not talked about by the rabbi; but David had led them to the ravine on the edge of the city's suburbs and told them of what had happened there, told them of the machine-gunning of the Jews, told them there was no monument to commemorate the place because those who had died there had been Jewish.

They had listened, Moses and Rebecca and Isaac. David had pointed to the places where the Germans had set up their machine-gun tripods, marked the spot for them, explained how the columns of the condemned had come without thought of flight or resistance, spoken of the meek and pallid acceptance of the order to wait patiently, to file forward, to kneel down, not to move, not to obstruct the soldiers' aim. Then he had shown them the refuse of the suburb that had been tipped and thrown into this place—the bottles, the cans and the plastic bags and the fire ash—and walked with them to the broken jars in which the brave placed flowers at night, when they were safe from view, and which were destroyed in the morning by the shoes of those who walked past to the trolley cars and buses.

In the way in which the young learn the facts of reproduction from their friends rather than from their parents and their schoolteachers, so had the trio listened as the one they trusted above all others, David, explained their position in life, their heritage. For a boy of his years he knew so much, had the patience to tell them when they wanted to play the games of children the matters with which they should concern themselves.

The group had become inseparable. At school they had sat together; at home they had worked together, because David said they must be cleverer, with better grades, better diplomas than those they sought to emulate. But they were being prepared for a life of conformity and inaction, inevitable in its way, until the day that David had come to Rebecca's house with the radio set. Teen-agers now, but isolated from the outside world until the radio flitted into their lives. The Voice of America; the World Service of the BBC, Radio Liberty, broadcast by an émigré staff in Munich and beamed from a massive transmitter across Central Europe. The curtain was pulled back, a shaft of sunlight brought in. There was a contact with the forbidden, teeth ripped into the fruit, excitement and stimulation at the illegality of it all. David said he'd bought the radio, and smiled. They knew it was beyond his means, and he'd also said they had no need to learn more of its acquisition, only to listen and to understand.

It became a secret thing, special and precious with its expanded shortwave band, an access door through which they followed the June War of 1967, and the War of Atonement of 1973. They heard of the tribulations endured by those of their faith who sought to emigrate from Russia to the State of Is-

rael, were told of the trials of those who were not permitted
to leave the Motherland they wanted to forsake. They knew
of international protest at the lot of Soviet Jewry; they suckled
themselves on what they believed to be the strength of world
opinion. Desperate and heady and intoxicating drink for the
four students.

And David was their leader.

Nothing had ever been formally decided. It had never been
talked over, but the time had come when he made all the
decisions for the group. At first there had been discussion,
followed always by the inevitable agreement to David's point
of view, till within the last two years the pros and cons were
no longer argued. David announced what they would do and
there was immediate concurrence. And as he assumed command, so the personality of David seemed to grow, and he
took on a mantle in the minds of the other three of new
strength, new influence.

And when Moses submitted to the men in khaki, with their
instruments and their drugs, when he gave the names, then
David would follow to an identical cell, a geometric imitation
of the one that Moses lay in now, and his future would be as
strongly etched as was that of Moses. The torture would be
the same as he would have endured, and the culmination
too—perhaps the same dawn, perhaps the same prison yard.
All of this would be David's if Moses talked when his interro-
gators came for him; all of this, and an equation of betrayal.
Was David any more fitted, better equipped, to confront
them in the interrogation basements? David of the smiling
face, who could transmit the passion in his words, communicate the life in his eyes. Did he possess a higher threshold
that would protect him from the fear and terror of pain? And
Moses realized that he had never known David to experience
helpless and uncontrollable stress, had never seen the moments of pressuring anguish screw at his cheeks, never in all
the years known him to exchange the comforting confidence
for confusion and hurt.

A chilling and winnowing shudder hastened through him:
what if David were no better, no stronger, no more resolute
than he, Moses, the follower? Clasped his arms across his
chest, digging his uncut fingernails through the fabric of the
shirt. Hurt gouging, penetrating his defenses. What if the

leader were no better able to withstand the pigs, had no defiance, no arrogant obscenities? That would be betrayal, to expose him to them, open the zipper of his trousers, leave him
weak and vulnerable and screaming.

How many months ago it had been that David had found
the woodsman's hut in the birch forest near the "dachas"
north of the city, Moses could not remember. Time had traveled fast since then; much had been squashed and distorted
into the days till they had seemed to run together without
shape and pattern because of the new stimulus of what they
called the "program." Moses had allowed his work at the new
chemical factory near his home to become subordinate to the
meetings the group held inside the darkened and damp
shack, which they reached separately, making their own way
at David's behest. Bare walls, only the rough-cut timbers to
shield them from the spring rain that followed the snow and
that preceded the summer heat and the flies. It was here that
David had talked and the others had listened.

The irony was, and it was not lost on them, that the doctrine he preached was available for all in the Ukraine to find;
there were histories, tomes of them, of the partisan warfare
against the Germans who had occupied the area, and trea-
tises on the tactics of Guevara, and for those who had stored
them and who had not thrown them away when they were
suppressed, there were the works of Mao, and there were the
thoughts of Giap, who had conquered the invincible Americans. That was what David talked to them about.

On one fundamental only did he depart from the text and
bible of the guerrilla fighter. There would be no "first stage,"
there would be no "infrastructure period," no creation of an
"indoctrinated population base." Took too long, took too
many people, and the circumstances in which they found
themselves could not be translated directly to the paddy fields
of Asia. The Jews of Russia have spoken of the ills too long;
they have no need for more words, only for action. If the
action was successful, then his movement would develop as a
sapling does under the spring light; but first there must be the
root, deep in fertile soil. He told them of the revolutionary
warfare that would hit back at the oppressors of the Jewish
people. "Like a fleabite at first," he had said. "But a flea that
cannot be found, that cannot be hunted out, that comes back

and wants more. That turns what is first an irritation to an anger. When their anger is aroused, then we know that we are hurting them, then we know that we have vengeance. There has been a great wrong here, too great a wrong for us alone to erode. But it is a gesture that is needed. How many walked in submission to the German shower chambers? How many now walk in submission to the camps at Potma and Perm?"

David had indeed been persuasive, but there was no necessity for it. All in the group knew the fighting ground, knew of the trials. Isaac said that he had met a youth who had met once with Yuri Vudka, who had had seven years at Potma in which to think over his application for leave to emigrate to Israel. David had chimed in, not allowing him to finish, but then he seldom did and it was not resented, "Vudka from our own Kiev, and seven years to think of his city, and his crime that he had wanted to leave, that he had written things down, that he had books from the West and in the Hebrew language."

David had talked of the new Jews in Israel, hardened and fashioned in their own sun by the rigors of their own land and their own freedom. He called them "sabras," men who had washed away the placidity of the former generation that had marched to the cattle trucks with a whimper and not an arm upraised. So how placid, docile, unquestioning were their people? Enough evidence to make him believe it; enough that he had heard to verify the belief that they were supine, without the ability of self-help. But often they had wondered whether there were other groups that met in bare and shadowed rooms, that came to darkened and pathless woods, that sought shelter in the same anonymity and that talked of a struggle and a hope and revenge, however trivial.

David had heard on the radio of the bomb that had detonated on the Moscow Inner Underground; would tell them of protest and disobedience among their people in Novosibirsk and in the main square at that, and of a man who was executed in the prison at Tbilisi and who had set off six explosive devices. He had heard it on the radio, where the word carried biblical validity. Not all were Jews, he had said, and smiled to encourage them, but at least others, of different faith and aspiration, were creeping and crawling and burrowing at the edifices, chipping and hacking. Others who rejected the required submission as totally as they, and who stood back from the flyswatter resistance of the press conference, and the smuggled letter to the West, and the complaint to the Foreign Power.

"Words, words, stupid and ineffective," David had said. "As valuable as lying in the sand in the path of the steamroller. It is action that will change them, action that will achieve something."

They had wondered how great was their island, how many other tribes shared their jungle and ate of the same fruit. They had no road to the knowledge. As the group became more daring and more cohesive, so too was augmented their dread of breaking the precious security. There was no consideration given to widening the cell: too dangerous, too hazardous. Heighten the walls, strengthen the locks, repel recruits even should they be found. An island, aloof in a battle sea: that was how they had decided they should remain.

They had followed David through each step as he prepared for the movement that would lift their course from the level of conspiracy to action, accepting every stage of his logic, not disputing his argument. Moses thought of the long weekend days and the midweek summer evenings they had spent, the four of them, in the hut. How they had talked of what they would do, sometimes all shouting together and laughing and hanging on each other's shoulders and imagining how a grateful people would bow to their courage, acknowledge the standard-bearers, feel a pride in their bravery.

Then David had deemed them ready, and none had queried him, only quieted in the elation of knowing that the moment had arrived. They had talked in closed voices that evening, subdued to the droning harassment of the mosquitoes, and clung to each other before the time to go to their homes, and memorized the route to the rendezvous the next evening. Wonderful for Moses as they had held each other close, the male smells unable to counter the softer, more gentle trace of the girl's scent. So much strength, so much power; nothing they could not do, because they were together, they were segments of a whole.

Later had come the chilling loneness for the boy, when he left the warmth of the group, when by himself he walked on the dusk-ridden forest path toward the road. David had said he would be the one to kill; Isaac had disputed him; Rebecca had found the compromise. None should claim the privilege by right; in the cell they were as one, she had said, and she had seemed to mock at David. The leader rejected her, demanded it for himself, the prerogative of the front-runner, and Isaac would not yield. Rebecca had spoken again, chided David. Were they not all capable? It was a simple thing, was it not? She had opened the door, gone to the gloom of the evening for a minute, not more, and when she returned there were four bark-roughened twigs in her fist, their tips arranged in line, their length hidden in her closed palm.

David had drawn first, expressionless, watching and waiting; then Isaac, with a smile lightening his features because his was shorter; Moses third, and the winced sigh of disappointment from the other two men when they saw the stubbed, abbreviated length of the one that he had chosen. A protest from Isaac; a taunt from Rebecca that already they were trying to divide themselves—officers and men, commissars and proletariat; a shrug from David. No remark from the boy himself.

Again and again in his mind, Moses had worked over the plan, digesting the part that he would play, remembering the detail. The first blow they would strike, and Moses Albyov had been chosen. Not David, who was their leader; not Isaac, who fancied and believed in his fitness; but Moses, the last of the recruits to arrive before the structure of the cell had been sealed. To curse Rebecca or to love her for the chance she had wished on him? He had not known the answer as he stumbled from the closing tentacle shadows of the wood to the roadside.

But his hand had shaken, and the wool had drifted across his eyes. The mistakes of Moses Albyov. Errors that the others would not have made. And if he now collapsed, if he buckled, then all would pay the penalty for the faults that were his alone.

If there could only be someone to speak to, or just the sound of a human voice, however distant.

No food, and his belly aching with the deprivation and his bowels grinding with the remains of the last meal, God knew how many hours before.

Pray God let it finish.

Those were the thoughts of Moses Albyov, bouncing centrifugally fast, at neutron speed, off the walls of the cramped cell. And they stayed with him till the moment they were dissipated by the sounds of keys turning in the lock of the door and of the bolt being withdrawn from its socket.

Four men for the escort. Not gentle, yet not brutal. Guiding him uncomfortably down the barely lit passageway. Arms pinioned and their fingers digging hard down into his muscles, and the manacles that they had put on his wrists set tight so that the encompassing steel bit into his flesh. But he was classified as "political terrorist," "enemy of the people," one who had sought to kill a guardian of the state, and Moses knew that there was no possibility of sympathy for him. No words as they moved, and their feet were rubber-shod, so that the party—more like a cortege, he thought—went silently on its way. That was why he hadn't heard them, but they must have come, every few minutes, must have come to the door to spy on him, only he had not been aware of it.

Fear now. The caught and trapped and guilty fear that slows the reactions of the legs, that compresses the muscles of the stomach, that dries the throat, that brings sweat to the nape. A horrible clinging terror, something that was new and that he had not experienced before.

More doors and more guards and more keys. Out into a brighter corridor where men sat at a low wooden table with a radio playing light music, men who interrupted their card game to stare at him—the look that men have for the fellow creature who is not one of them, who is contaminated, condemned. Fit and strong men who were taking him, not tolerating his weakness of step as they bustled their way up the flights of stairs and down the lengths of the passageways. Another door, another lock, another staircase, and they were half pulling him with them. His lagging was not a conscious decision; if anything, he wanted to please, like a dog that is about to be beaten and that nestles against its master's legs. But he could not follow at their speed, and so they dragged and pushed him to maintain their momentum.

The cold of the cell was gone, replaced by the warmth of midday, a fierce summer's day. Sweat too on the faces of the men who took him, struggling on the corners of the staircase landings, with their only respite as they flattened themselves and their prisoner against the wall to allow free passage for a senior officer in his pressed trousers and tailored tunic and with the medal ribbons of his service on his chest. Seven flights they climbed; then a closed and polished door in front, and the respectful knock of the "starshina" with the stripes on his arm, and the command, distant but impatient, for them to enter.

One at each arm, one behind and the sergeant in front. Through the outer door and across the outer office, then the inner room, and the door open. Moses could see three men at a desk facing him as he was propelled forward. Trousers sagging and held up by his hands, stockinged feet bruised and chafed from the stair surface of concrete and stone. Cold eyes, looking at him, boring into him, examining and stripping him. The sanctum of the enemy. There was a breeze now on his face, soft and careless against his cheeks, playing on his hair, cooling at his chest. On the left, the source of the draft: an opened window, double-glazed for winter, but pulled back now to permit the free flow of air. No bar, no impediment.

If they saw him look at it . . . if they gauged his intention . . . These were the ones who would bend and break it out of him. Who would make him tell them of David and Isaac, and Rebecca with the black hair and the dark eyes and the breasts that he was afraid of and the waist that he yearned to encircle. . . . Moses' eyes were riveted to the front, locked on the man who sat in the center chair at the table.

The guards, preoccupied with delivering their charge to such august company—a full colonel of militia, the KGB major and the major of police—did not detect the flexing of the arm muscles, the bowstring tightness of the legs.

Moses Albyov closed his eyes, closed his mind at the moment that he catapulted himself the seven feet from the place where he stood to the windowsill. There was a delay as he scrabbled, impeded by the handcuffs, to swing the weight of his torso out into the void, and for a brief second one of the guards was able to claw onto the trousers now flapping and loose at his knees. If his ankle had been held, that might perhaps have been sufficient to arrest his fall, but the fingers of the guard were clamped only on the cotton cloth of the trousers; it was not enough for him to grip at when he took the full weight of the diving Jew.

At the time that he was falling, there was a sudden clarity in the mind of the young man. There was an image of a group, of young faces that were laughing together and smiling, and their arms were all around him, and their voices pealed like bells for him. . . .

All ended by the sledgehammer impact onto the tarmac of the headquarters car park.

Hot water into an ants' nest. Men running and shouting and reacting to orders, forming excited, shifting patterns around the broken figure in their midst. From high above, the Colonel of Militia surveyed the chaotic panorama, sharing the seventh-floor vantage point of the window with the police major. Alone among them, the man from the KGB remained at the interrogation table.

It was he who broke the shocked silence of the room.

"Dead?" he asked. The voice of a man who has seen a catastrophe and is relieved that the responsibility for it is laid elsewhere.

From the window the reply, muffled because the head was still craning outward: "There is no possibility of survival, not from such a height."

"And no preliminary interrogation, no initial questioning?"

"There had been none, and it was as you requested. As you had asked. Just the forensic on the hair and the photograph. You were specific; there were to be no questions until he had cooled. Not even his name and his address, not even why he did not carry the card. You were specific."

A nodded head; enough of the games, enough of the point scoring. Wouldn't bring him back, didn't matter now. The KGB man waved a gesture of dismissal to the four guards: time for their sheepish, failed exit.

"So we had just a photograph. No address, not even a name. . . ."

"You had said there should be no questioning."

"I am aware of what I said. So we return to our starting point. We have the photograph. He is" . . . and the dry smile, the suggestion of humor . . . "he was Jewish. Forensic confirmed that the hair textures matched. It becomes a job for policemen. It will not be difficult to identify him—many ways; and once we have achieved that, the associates will be easy. We shall have them in a few days. It will take that time, a few days, but less than a week, and then we shall have the little bastards. And we have saved ourselves a bullet. Perhaps that is the way we should look on it: we have saved Mother Russia the price of a bullet."

Out in the car park, the bone-shattered body of Moses Albyov was being lifted by many hands onto a plain brown canvas stretcher.

2

Early that morning, many hours before Moses died at the militia headquarters, his mother had taken her bicycle and pedaled to David's home. It was a long journey in the fast-forming heat for a woman suffering the first pangs of untreated arthritis, and the fact that she attempted it indicated her anxiety about the overnight absence of her only son. They had talked at the front door, David blocking her from coming into the crowded interior, determined that she not meet his own parents once he had heard the germ of the news she carried.

"He had spoken of having some food in the city, then going to the library; then he said he would be with you and with the others, with Isaac and the girl Rebecca. He had said that he would not be home late. His bed is not disturbed, and he has never before been out through the whole night."

David had half-listened and half-wondered to himself what had delayed the boy. He was aware that only Rebecca and Isaac had joined him the previous evening; remembered the talk there had been among the three of them as they wondered where the last member of the cell was.

"He has always come home at night. And when he went out yesterday he didn't take his police card; it was at home. That is wrong; that is not allowed. And without it, if he is in trouble, if he is in a hospital and hurt and cannot speak, then how will they . . . ?"

So he had acted as David had instructed all of the group. Carry the cards only when you need them. His mother, curious as a sparrow, must have rummaged in his drawers looking for a clue as to his whereabouts, and found no satisfaction, only the card in its cellophane wrapper with the head-and-shoulders photograph and the official stamp set across it. Moses had acted as instructed by David. Acted as he had told

26

them they all should. But never explained the motive for his order. Left them to think on it for themselves: that if they were taken in, and casually, without the link's being forged between their activities and the police inquiry in hand, it would be easier to explain the absence of identification as a careless lapse. It was usual for them to pick the Jewish boys off the streets, if they found them out late, if they were in a group, if they just cared to exist. But if the pursuit was hot, if the pace were steaming, then the lips could be sealed and the identification stalled, time gained and inquiries delayed. The mallet-head power of the militia could be slowed if they did not have the card as access to the files and folios of the index systems.

Not that there had ever been talk among them of questioning and arrest and imprisonment. Not a subject that David would have tolerated: too chilling, too personal, too fist-clenching; and therefore it was not considered by the others, a silent and forgotten realm that was outside the necessity of argument. Impossible for it to happen if they were careful, and they had been careful, except for the stocking cap; only the cap and the policeman who had not died. Isaac had noticed, with clarity, impervious to feelings, abrasive in his accusation, as soon as they had gathered again with their breath still coming in a streaming torrent, and while Moses had hung his head, and while David had quieted him. And it was outside Moses' nature to be away through the night. A steady boy, not likely to panic, not one to sleep in the park, not a one for the girls, and David knew all their friends who were outside the cell.

". . . without his card, if he is injured no one will know to tell us . . ."

"I'll see Isaac and Rebecca and I'll ask them what they know," said David. He was kindly in the pitch of his voice and reassuring, sufficiently to mask from the old lady the rising fever that he now felt. Not fear—nothing as defensive as that—and not as strong an emotion as excitement: just a feeling that at last real battle was joined. The skirmishing was over. The patrol cars would be out. Guns issued, semiautomatic to augment the usual side arms. Control rooms perspiring with the effort of pursuit. The beast had been angered and sought to retaliate. The wounds had gone to the quick, as

had been intended. But it was not the time that David would
have chosen, and his jaw was stiffened, and he sought to hide
the quivering of his mouth and to play again the role of command and competence. Little to practice his mood on. Only
an old woman who showed fear and confusion and who had
come to him for help. Whose darned stockings were twisted
and sagging, and who had missed her place in the queues to
seek him out, and who did not know where her son was.
From his own instinct he had already decided that Moses had
been taken, arrested, even as the woman had spoken, his
thoughts fueled by her very apprehension.

He sent her on her way, and closed the door after her, and
told his own mother that it was just a friend who had called
and that he was going out to walk and that he did not have to
be at the plant for the afternoon shift. Needed to be alone,
needed to think and needed to have a plan to put before the
others. It was expected of him now, that he could produce an
instant solution, but the initiative was absent. Perhaps it was
they, the pigs, who held the high ground. Not a dimension of
the battle that he had considered before; but what if they
were consigned forever to the valleys, if the fortresses of advantage for the enemy would always dominate the skyline?
Immaterial. A battle there would be, and he must be alone,
needed the opportunity to think, must have a plan to put before the others. It was expected of him now that he could
produce the instant decision—but how to regain the initiative
that had been lost if Moses was being held? He must consider
the strategy and shut from his mind the face that was near to
tears of the old lady with the roughened cheek and the thinning and gray and wispy hair, who was frightened because
she did not know where her son had spent the night.

No sidewalk and an unpaved road to walk on, rutted and
pitted from the winter's ice, ignored by workmen in the summer. Never finished adequately when they had built the
apartment houses. Farther out of town than the show blocks
of the Khrushchev days, when accommodation rose to impress the people that they were at last remembered. But that
was not where the Jews lived, not in the apartment houses
that were filmed for television; not the ordinary ones who
failed to qualify among the minimal few who held positions in
the offices and bureaucracy of the administration. Mean little

premises these that he walked past, where the rent racketeering was fiercer than in the capitalist West that he knew of from his radio. When you were Jewish, how to get your name high on the housing list, that was the problem, and when you couldn't then you were in the hands of the landlords. Life was a shared kitchen and a shared bathroom and a shared toilet. Inside what passed as the privacy of a front door were three rooms, and his mother and his father and his three sisters to share them with. Nearer into town there would be flowers in front of the small houses, but nobody bothered out here; seemed no point, seemed unnecessary, and they would be covered with dust when the bus came down the road, suffocated, and the water pressure was too low to run a hose . . . and for what, anyway? Take more than flowers and color and the scent of pollen to brighten these homes.

So perhaps the bastards had Moses. Down in the city was where he'd be. Didn't have his card with him, which meant he'd have to talk for them to know who he was. And when he told them that, then the shortcuts would begin: names of associates, addresses, rendezvous locations, dates—all falling into place. And why would they have taken him? Obvious, clearly reasonable to any but the deluded few. Because of the pig whom Moses had said he only wounded, and the blustering about the stocking cap and the shame in the boy's face. Identification: not a difficult task, not for a body so efficient as that with which they had joined conflict. How soon would he talk? That was the only question that he should answer now. How soon? What was the boy made of? How much spunk, how much balls, how much courage? The same courage as Israel had when the Syrians were traversing the Golan? Did Moses have the courage of the Israeli tank commanders? But it was one thing to fight with your friends around you, your own equipment, on your own side But what did Moses have now, in a damned police cell with the electric wires and the batons and the impatience of the questioners? David shivered in the fierce sunlight that bounced back into his averted eyes, reflected from the brightness of the dried-out gravel and mud of the road. Not much that the little guy would have going for him. Just loyalty—and what would that mean when the pain was intense? How many minutes, how many hours of pain to equate on the graph with loyalty?

Isaac coming toward him up the road. Hot and red in the face. Stains under his armpits. Had been running. Shorter than David and not so well muscled, face strained and the sinews of his neck bulging. Hang or shoot them all, that was what the bastards would do, once Moses talked. Moses and Rebecca and Isaac, who was panting and who had speeded his stride, and David too. Just took Moses to talk. Perhaps they'd shoot them, perhaps hang them; didn't matter, though—not important how you went. No consolation to those who went to the pits and had the covering of lime whether their necks were broken or their brains blasted out. Made no difference to them. Only one thing mattered: that you kept fighting, that you didn't make it easy for the bastards, didn't put it down there on a plate for them.

And Isaac was beside him and blurting incoherently, so that David embraced him and quieted the boy and told him to get his breath and to begin again.

"It's all around the University. I heard it first in the canteen before classes, then again in the lecture room before the professor came. Everyone is talking of it. They say there have been attacks on policemen, and that last night the militia took a man, right in the center of the city, and they say he is a Jew. One of the chemistry students, his uncle works there, in the files section, and he told the boy's mother last night, and there were celebrations last night in the headquarters— vodka in all the offices. And you remember that Moses didn't come to the hut last night."

"He didn't come home at all last night. His mother has been here and asked about him."

"Has nothing been said on the radio?"

"Nothing. How would they?—it is not their way."

"What to do, David?"

"To be calm and to think and then to fight them."

"With what, David? How can we fight them? They will do things to Moses, things so that he will talk and confess, and then they will come for us. In the darkness of the morning they will be at our homes. How long will he last, if he can resist them at all? Not longer than this evening—and that's a whole day, a whole twenty-four hours—and they will come."

Isaac had no more to say. Through all the time that he had run from the bus that had carried him away from the University, the thought of the four-o'clock awakening, the time the militia always came, had buffeted and pummeled him. The boots, the guns, the hammering, the axes crashing through the door, the bedclothes wrenched back. Now he could wash it from his system; he had demonstrated his fear, exposed it in the street to David.

"Where is Rebecca?" David asked.

"Still at the University. Botany starts later than chemistry. She will not come out till eleven, perhaps late if she has work in the library."

"Get her," said David. "Meet her and take her to the woods. To the hut. We will meet there, at two . . . you can get there by then . . . and don't be late." And then the smile that the others so coveted. "And don't worry. They won't touch us. Moses hasn't talked or they would be here by now. We have some time yet."

He slapped Isaac on the back, sent him off as a father does a child when he wants an errand run. He turned back toward his home, but the smile that was for his public face was wiped off now, and there were the deep creases of concentration and worry on his forehead, and his eyes were down, staring at the stones and debris of the road. A mystery, and a confusion for him. If Moses had been taken, why were they not here yet? How much more time could the boy buy for them?

Only one certainty. They would none of them be lying in their beds waiting for the police to come, rubbing the sleep from their eyes as they pulled on the bare essentials of clothing at gunpoint. Anything rather than that.

But if they ran, how far could they go, and was there anywhere that was safe?

And if they hid, for how long, and with what future?

Rebecca and Isaac would come to the hut in the afternoon and expect him to lead them, would anticipate that he knew the solution. How could he explain there was none, that he was incapable of providing the inspired answer? They would choke on what they had bitten off—because of a youth's carelessness, because of a lost winter garment. Rebecca would not see the weakness, would follow where she was taken, but Isaac would see, would strip away the camouflage. And there was nothing in Mao, or Giap, or Guevara—nothing that offered solace, nothing that was of relevance. David watched

Isaac's long walk, rolling and round-shouldered, away down
the street. Perhaps was puzzled that the other reacted so
completely to his apparent calmness and control. A lone figure that skirted the few parked cars, that gestured once to a
passing cyclist. David regretted his going, resented that there
was no opportunity for Isaac to stay longer, to talk, to discuss,
to share.

But you knew it would happen like this, David.

Not so soon, not at this time.

If anything, it has been slow in coming, David.

But we are not prepared.

If you shoot policemen, David . . .

We are in confusion; we do not hold any initiative.

Did you expect them to wait for you to be ready, David?

With long strides, adrenaline-spurred, he ran toward the
shabby front door of his home.

At first the road followed the west bank of the Dnieper.
That was the route out of the city. Then a left turn and the
wide tarmac ran far and straight across the agricultural plain,
passing by the occasional clusters of homes for the collective
workers till the cultivated ground gave way to the forests. A
dozen miles later was the bus stop to which they made their
separate ways. From the roadside they walked along the dirt
fire path through the woods to the place where David had
first taken them many months before.

The path led to the dacha complex. Neat log cabins built
after the war for the Party bourgeoisie as they became attracted to the legitimacy of possessions. The homes fronted
on a small lake, idyllic and beautiful and unlike anything the
group had seen before; another world opened to them after
the pretentiousness and preposterousness of the new buildings in Kiev.

The hut was short of the complex, reached only on foot
and from a diversion from the main path, five hundred yards
along an overgrown trail. Too far from the summer resi-
dences for the children of the privileged to stray upon it while
at games of exploration, and the undergrowth too thick for
the adults to push their way to it in search of a remote picnic
spot. Because of the density of the trees and the saplings and
the bushes, it would have been easy to walk right past the
single-story building and not notice it, such was the way that

it blended into the forest, dappled with the shadows that fil-
tered through the upper leaves.

There was no latch on the door, just a piece of wood that
they propped against it and dug into the ground as a buttress
to prevent the weather from forcing a way into the interior.
David kicked it clear when he arrived—a savage and impatient gesture. First there, as he had wanted, and the others
not due for ninety minutes, perhaps more.

This was where they had put the policeman's pistol, up on
a shelf and in a cookie tin, but closely wrapped against the
damp in a plastic bag from the vegetable market. David paced
across the lone room, his feet easing down on the boards,
and reached up for it, extracted the bag from the tin, the gun
from the bag, and checked the mechanism to be certain
there was no bullet in the breech. Satisfied that the gun was
safe, he removed the magazine from the butt. Only six
rounds there. There was also the second magazine, placed
separately in a paper bag; thoughtful of Isaac to grab that too:
seven more shots. Thirteen shots in all, and a pistol with an
effective range of twenty meters. Should not have allowed it
to be Moses; himself or Isaac—only they would have been
capable. The girl had willed it, and he had listened to her,
and he did not know why. Should have ignored her, should
have followed his instinct. Wondered why she had called for
the game of chance to determine who would be the one: to
give herself the possibility? You, Rebecca, you wanted it?
Sought the medal? And now catastrophe.

No plan yet, only the unfamiliar feeling of helplessness, of
near despair, that they had no power and that such an awe-
some strength was gathering its weapons with which to strike
them. He thought of Moses—a cheerful, honest boy, a follower, without a mind of his own, who craved the compan-
ionship and the strength of the others, who had been asked
to do one thing himself and who had not succeeded at it.
A weak link in the chain he had set himself to forge, and
when the chain snapped how long till the dogs were barking
and the cordons were sweeping and the sirens were crying in
pursuit?

Isaac was next. He had traveled on the same bus as Rebecca. He in the front, she in the back, not acknowledging
each other. He had hurried along the path closely flanked by

the tall trees; she had dawdled. Twenty-two years old, studying chemistry at the University. Quick, logical in his approach to problems; a good student, his professors had said
when they offered him a place, with a future in a government
laboratory if he could achieve the right marks at the autumn
examinations. He was pleased to be in front because that en-
titled him to hurry, and he was anxious to reach the destination because he believed he knew the solution to their problem, thought he had determined the answer. He had carved
and chiseled it against his own self-appointed objections
while scurrying across the white stone flags of the University's
central precinct. Concerned himself as he approached the
hut, using the codes of habitual caution and wariness, with
the reaction he would gain from David. Rarely that he was
listened to. Not that it was David's fault, only that he seldom
offered his opinions. Stepped on a dry branch, and as the
noise cracked in his ears, cursed the momentary carelessness.
It was a good plan and carried the possibility of success. But
he would not be the first to speak; he would hear what David
had to say. He would evaluate that, and then if his own equation seemed better he would offer it. He was pleased with
himself and hoped that others would be too. Not that he
minded an existence in the shadow of David, not that he felt
the requirement to assert himself; just that on this occasion
and after his street meeting with David he had thought on
the options, had weighed them and was satisfied.

Rebecca came more slowly. Her flat soft-soled shoes were
unsuitable for the pitfalls of the path, and her print dress
caught at the brambles which trailed across the way that was
so rarely used. But when the thorns caught at her she had
little regard for them; there was an enormity about it all now
that dominated her thinking. Her thoughts too were of Moses
and the place that she presumed him to be in, and it was an
effort and a struggle for her to while away the walk along the
path, such was the vividness of her image of the surroundings
in which her friend was held. And he had been the nervous
one, the last who would have wanted to shoot, and he would
have fulfilled his wish if she had held her silence.

Dark hair swept back at the sides of the high-boned face,
and pulled to the back by an elastic band before spilling pony

style to below her neck. Attractive lines on her body, small but firm breasts developed beyond the point of adolescence, narrow waist, hips that swung as she walked, but all masked by the cut of the dress from GUM. But it had been cheap, and money mattered more than appearance, and since she had met David and also Isaac and Moses, it was not appearance that was important. Vanity that, and frippery. When David had found her the Voice of Israel on the radio and she had listened to the programs from the kibbutzim, she would think, The stupidity of dresses with raised and lowered hemlines, and flowered prints, and waists that hug and hips that fall in flared lines. Do they need those to drive a plow across new land, when they break the virgin and arid dryness of Sinai?

A quiet and solitary person she had been before the spell of David wove close around her; slight in knowledge and deep in fervor. He had taught her much, she believed, of the nation-state of the Jews, leaving her unaware of the vacuums of her learning. No word of those who went from Russia to the railway stations of Vienna and Amsterdam and Rome, who had won their freedom with a promise that they were traveling south to Tel Aviv and instead headed west for the new frontiers of the United States. That there were Jews who left Russia and who then refused to make the final journey to Israel would have dumbfounded her. That emigration from Israel was a subject covered by rigorous censorship laws passed by the Knesset in Jerusalem would have confused her.

Sheltered and suppressed, devoid of the trappings of sophistication. A product of the undrawn but actual perimeters of the Kiev ghetto. Twenty years old, and she like the others a Jew without the faith of Judaism, taking only that part of the heritage which imbued the separateness of the race, the pride of a wandering people and the stubbornness not to falter again as in the past. She did not attend the synagogue for the Feast of the Tabernacles, or on the Kol Nidrei night. Too great a burden her people had stumbled under, she thought, for there to be a faith that she could follow.

David had taken her from the botany classroom, transported her to a battlefield where she herself could fight alongside her kith from the kibbutzim, and it had seemed brave and worthwhile, and the danger had seemed distant, remote.

It had hurt her to squash a spider on the kitchen floor, swat a
fly on the plaster wall above her bed. She could not have
endured the misery of the sight of a snared rabbit. Yet he had
turned her, shaped her, molded and sculptured and guided
her arm, caused it to rise, rigid and clamped on the pistol's
handle, and influenced the squeeze of the trigger finger as he
lectured her in the mechanism and technique of their one
weapon the afternoon after they had taken it.

A terrible and beautiful and desperate secret he had given
to her; a secret to be shared by only three others. And he had
nurtured and nourished her strength, watering and feeding it
over the years, till she was capable of participation. No boy,
either with love or with lust, could hold her as the other three
had in the hut before they went to search out the policeman.
Impossible to match and measure any sensation against the
supreme shared orgasm of the cell at that moment of firing.
And never a conversation, or a moment, or an occasion
when she believed she had taken the supreme step over the
abyss. Just a logical progression.

Then Isaac, standing outside her classroom door, stopping
her as she hurried for the next lecture, waiting for her, waiting with the news unspoken. But in his eyes the message that
there was catastrophe.

All of them together now. Sitting cross-legged or sprawled
on the bare boards of the floor that were damp in winter and
spring, dry and musty in summer. And David was talking.

"We must continue the fight; we must not give way to
them. Whatever they do to us, we must not allow them to
destroy the group. If we have to go underground, then that is
what it shall be. If we have to try to go abroad, then we must
attempt it, through Czechoslovakia or Rumania. We must
not lie down. . . ." Rebecca had not heard him talk in this
way before; realized that he had no plan, nothing to offer,
and that it was a new situation which confronted them.
There was a strain in his voice, and he spoke louder than the
tone to which she was accustomed, his words coming staccato as if only through speech could he believe in himself.
And Isaac was fidgeting and moving on the floor, unable to
hide his frustration and his dissatisfaction.

"We have not the wherewithal to fight, no equipment,"

said Isaac. "They would hunt us, pursue us till they ran us down. Always they would be after us. We could not strike back."

"Is it certain they have Moses?" from Rebecca, quiet but reedy in her voice, seeking the consolation that would come if there was hesitation in the reply, and knowing from the way David ignored her that there could be none.

"We cannot just surrender," said David. "Not just because they have taken Moses."

"Fuck Moses, forget Moses, obliterate Moses. In his cell now, and screaming to them, and he the one who lost his clothing, he the one who did not hold the gun . . ." Isaac shouting, and David shouting louder, their words lost, melted, mingled.

"You cannot say that. How can you say that?"

"Because it is true. Because he has no further part to play with us. Because it is as if he had never been part of us." Isaac steadied, swept the control back through himself. He had no wish to launch his idea in controversy, wanted the receptive minds, sought attention. "We could fly out." He spoke with great deliberation. "We could take a plane. We have a gun. It has happened before . . ."

"Impossible, we could never . . ."

"Where would we go to . . ."

". . . and it has been successful, and . . ."

"How to get aboard; you cannot just carry guns . . ."

"We have no time to plan . . ."

". . . we could do it. Don't you see the possibility, don't you see the opportunity?"

They had all shouted together, each seeking to denounce the words of the others. Stick in a wasps' nest, and now their minds were racing with objections, clarifications. And then silence. Isaac, his mouth closed, but smiling and knowing that by accident he had chosen his moment well. David blinking and trying to think through the turmoil of his mind. Rebecca shuffling her bottom on the boards, wanting to speak again, not knowing what to say.

When Isaac spoke again it was still slowly, demanding no interruption, asserting his right to be heard out. "We can take a plane. Fly it out. To the West. Then on to Israel. All of us together we can go to Israel. We don't have much time, and we would have much to do in preparation, but it could be done. And none of us has another thought, another prospect."

It seemed an age to David since he had listened to the ideas of another member of the group. He was strained, choked with the words that were hard to enunciate, and bowing his head in a gesture of deference.

"We're listening. We want to know what you have thought of. Tell us."

There was a hesitation; then Isaac began to speak. Quiet around him. He had pitched the life belt into the water; could they reach it, could they grasp it?

"We have to take a plane. Divert it from an internal flight, because it is easier for us to buy the tickets for a flight inside Russia. We have to find one that has the range to take us to the West. To West Germany, or to Greece, or to Italy—it is not important. There are many places. Once we have landed and we are beyond their reach it does not matter. From there we can go to Israel. We should not fly directly there. Two reasons. It would be hard to find a plane with the necessary fuel, and we would spend too long over our airspace, and that of our friends and comrades." Sarcasm and confidence; Isaac blossoming at his opportunity of holding the ring. "First to the West, the nearest frontier, the nearest landfall—reach it while they are still confused—and there we will find fuel and friendship. We already have the gun, and one gun is enough if it is in the cockpit, if it is beside the pilot. They cannot risk anything, not with the passengers to think of; they must follow our instructions. And we must go tomorrow. It will involve other people. All our parents have their savings, and we will need those. We must have that money for the tickets. They are all good people—David's, Rebecca's, mine . . . if we ask they will not question; they will know there is necessity; they need not know the reason. David, it was you who said we cannot just remain here, sitting on our asses, waiting for them to come for us. We are agreed on that. We have to go, and this is the way to go."

"I have never been in a plane," Rebecca said. And the two men laughed at the innocence of the remark. It served to fracture the tension.

"We must have tickets. There is no other way," Isaac went on. "I have flown from the Kiev airport twice to spend holidays on the southern coast. It would not be possible just to run to a boarding plane and climb aboard. Too many guards, and all are armed, and there is no access to the place where the planes are parked. We would have to board as normal passengers. No other option. But there will be no problem, not if the destination of the plane is far from the frontiers. And if there is suspicion, then the bribe will see us through, the folded rubles that open the door."

There was a confidence and an assurance about Isaac, winning over the skepticism. "We let the plane get airborne, let the pilot start his journey; then we rush the cockpit. After that it is simple." He paused, looking from the face of David to the face of Rebecca; stared hard into their eyes, burning the doubt from them. "That is my plan. And what else can we achieve? Surely this is the gesture, on the grand scale, beyond the life of a mere policeman. Beyond the lives of a hundred policemen. All the people in many countries will know that the Jews of Russia are not a dead and lifeless people, that we have something left to offer."

"We would need more guns," said David, pensive now and faraway. The primary decision had been taken, and he was seeking the answers to the questions of detail.

"We have only one gun." Resentment from Isaac.

"We're not attacking you, Isaac." David was quick to calm him. "I think I know where, and without risk. But we must have more. Tonight I think I know where it is possible."

"In the West they have checks and searches, we have heard that on the radio. Because of the Palestinians they take precautions that people do not carry guns onto the planes. And it is the same here." Her first intervention, and Rebecca hacking at the artery of the plan, where Isaac had shielded it because he did not possess the answer.

"They have checks," Isaac conceded.

"How do we get past them?" Logical, female, destructive.

And Isaac said, with aggression pushing out his jaw, hardening it, "I don't know. I have not had time to think of the small points."

David smiled, as if he were the old one among them, as if solutions were simpler to him than to the others. Not that there was any significant age difference—just that he was used and accustomed to taking control; and the uncertainties of the last few minutes were banished. "There was a report on the BBC many months ago. One of the planes, a British one, was taken by the Arab terrorists. There had been great security at the airport, all the passengers were searched with thoroughness, and yet they had their guns when it came to the moment of taking the plane. The way they did it was simple. They had a friend, a friend who worked at the airport and was therefore outside suspicion. It was he who placed the guns on board and hid them, all long before the passengers boarded. What did the Arabs have to do? Only to go to a prearranged seat and find the bags. It was all on the BBC. And there is a man who is known to us, isn't there? Yevsei Allon—isn't that the name of the boy, Rebecca? In your class in ninth and tenth year. He is at the airport at Kiev . . ."

"But he is in freight and cargo. He would not have access to passenger cabins." An interruption, as if she were willing the dampening of the project that was so fast assuming shape and reality and proximity. Out of the fantasy stage now and welling into something sharper, keener, more dangerous.

"He will have to find a way, Rebecca, and it is you who must persuade him. You are the one who knew him best. You are the one he will listen to."

"We rely on you, Rebecca." Isaac was close beside her, hand on her shoulder, where it had not rested before. "And we must rely on your friend. Otherwise we will not board the plane, and if we do not then we shall be taken. Night follows day, that is certainty; so also is that unless we go they will take us."

David rose from the floor, dusting the dirt from the seat of his trousers, pushing away the coil of hair that had slipped onto his forehead. "I will try for the guns tonight, and Rebecca, you will see Yevsei. Don't hurry yourself, don't rush him—and put him in debt to you. Do him a favor that he must repay, and set a rendezvous again tomorrow morning. Isaac, you must go to the Aeroflot booking center, the big one on Kreshchatik, where they will be busiest. And a flight tomorrow afternoon that goes far into the interior of Mother Russia. We want a four-hour flight, not less, so that we have sufficient fuel for our purpose. It is for you to decide where we go and how you will purchase the tickets. But it must be in the afternoon—if that is not too late."

"Where do we sleep tonight?" Rebecca asked.

"You, I don't know," David said, laughing, and there was a twist in his lips, in the lines at his mouth. "Isaac and I sleep here, and this is where you will come when you have finished with Yevsei. If they have broken Moses, then they'll come in the morning for us—to our homes. Rebecca, you understand what confronts us here? You know what the future is if they take us? It's the basement cells and the interrogations, and they'll shoot us or they'll hang us, as the will takes them. There is no mercy, no clemency to those who seek to kill the pigs, not if one is on his back in the hospital and may die. Yevsei is important to us, don't forget that. If you want to grow old, if you want to bear children, to see the sky, see the fields, if you want to know the breadth of Israel, then . . . then, Yevsei must help you."

They were all on their feet and moving toward the door. He put out his arms and took her, lightly holding her shoulders and urging her toward him, so that her forehead was against his mouth, and he kissed her gently and just below the hairline for the first time. "Tomorrow night we will sleep in the West. Do not forget that. Tomorrow we go."

The two men watched her as she broke away and went down the path toward the track that would take her to the main road. She did not look back, and her shoulders were hunched except when they straightened and rose in small convulsions, the action of one who was crying. Then she was gone, lost in the trees.

Neither boy looked at the other, both avoiding a meeting of their eyes and feelings. They had chosen the easier road, both of them. Had given themselves tasks that were not comparable to hers, and felt a clutch of guilt that was shared and unspoken. The clinging, creeping silence of the forest spread across them when her footsteps had faded. A brave girl, Isaac thought, if she will do this for us; a brave girl. Not that he'll have an easy time of it, old Yevsei; not that the winning and wooing would be simple, painless.

"Will it work, Isaac?" asked David, staring beyond him into the undergrowth, watching the pirouettes of a butterfly that had freedom at its fragile wing tips.

"There is no alternative. This way offers us a chance. Not a good chance, but something. Without it we are condemned."

It was two years since they had given Charlie Webster an office of his own. He hadn't really known whether to be flattered or grateful or what. It gave him a certain importance to be able to turn a key in the door when he went off for lunch, leaving an empty desk behind him as he headed for the elevator and the fifteen-floor descent in the tower block that overlooked the Thames. Not that many of the "Firm's" deskmen enjoyed the privilege of only themselves for company. Trouble was that he could never quite satisfy himself as to whether the private office was a recognition of the work he now did, or simply a reward for past services rendered.

Foreign Office, Charlie called himself to those who asked but who did not know him. Well, not exactly Foreign Office, his wife would say, but something like it; to do with foreign affairs, anyway. Fact was he never went near Whitehall—too public a place. You couldn't be certain there wouldn't be some of those bloody agency photographers hanging about waiting for an ambassador or something, and he didn't want his photograph plastered all over the front pages just because he happened to be following a Venezuelan or a Zambian diplomat into the edifice. But since they came under the Foreign Office wing, and that was where the undersecretary who now headed the Department had worked before his transfer, it was most convenient for members of the Secret Intelligence Service to bracket themselves with the herd of diplomats and civil servants who ran the public side of Britain's dealings with overseas governments.

Charlie worked on the Soviet Desk. Nine of them in all, answerable to Cecil Parker Smith, OBE MC, and most of them concerned with things military. That put four in the same office, where they fiddled in one another's hair and didn't get much done, and thought they were the cream for the cat. Two more on politics—the heavy fellows who spent their time reading the speeches of the Kremlin men, poor buggers. One for economics, and he had an office to himself, and needed it; kept him going flat out, flogging his way through textbooks and brochures and progress reports. Then there was the one they called the Real Estate Man; he was the speculator, and his job was to predict long-range changes in Soviet attitudes and postures; worked to the letter of his brief and kept his thinking right in the far term, to the extent of sitting most of the day with his pipe in his mouth watching the pleasure boats negotiating Lambeth Bridge.

And there was Charlie, the ninth.

Last Christmas party, all a bit drunk, they'd christened him
Double Diamond, seen it as a hell of a laugh, and he'd looked
blank, and they'd explained: DD; those were the initials for
his work. He'd still looked vacant and wondered why grown
men always spent the last two days before the holiday dropping everything to gum paper streamers together to drape
across the ceiling, and they'd shouted, "Sub-Desk Dissidents." All thought it hilarious, falling about over themselves.
No knowing with these public school fellows; different to the
rest, really; strange chaps. But that was his charge—Sub-Desk
Dissidents.

There was something to find out. Couldn't doubt that.
There were groups, cells, sections, call them what you
wanted, that were alive and well and kicking faintly inside the
womb of the big Red monolith. Not as many as there had
been a decade before, but certainly some still there. Problem
was that Charlie's job was to put them in perspective, extract
any relevance from them.

Much of his material came from émigré groups in London
and scattered across the cities of Western Europe. Hopelessly
unreliable people who would have you believe the whole
bloody place was on the point of mass insurrection if you
could only drop a Hercules load of Stirlings and FNs and grenades into People's Square, Novosibirsk. You had to weed
and prune. Use the cosmetics to brighten the facade and
then search the cross-references and the files. Slowly, patiently, that was the way you touched on the subtle signs that
pointed the way to the trends so beloved by his masters.

Ukraine was usually fertile. There were bits and pieces
from the Baltic; quite a little set-to they'd had in the Department over the Russian warship that tried a flit to Sweden and
that took a hammering from its own air force and turned
back shot up. Sub-Desk Military said it was theirs; Charlie
claimed it too. Parker Smith sat for half a day on it while
nobody spoke in the outer offices, then did his Solomon and
gave it to Sub-Desk Military. Followed by appeasing Charlie,
told him he was doing too much valuable work for him to
mess about working on something that was common knowledge to every European NATO setup. Quite a ripple they'd
had over that one. Bit of activity last year down in Soviet
Georgia; Charlie had liked that because it came right out of

the blue. Hadn't expected anything on that sort of scale, not a dozen bombs; quite excited him. He'd wondered what sort of devices they used, where they'd learned the trade. Realized that it was the technique, the string and tape, the timers and detonators, that absorbed him. Should have been ashamed really, and he supposed to be an analyst.

Interesting work in its way, but Charlie had to pinch himself from time to time to make sure that it was actually important. He'd done enough in his life that was classified as vital, in the "national interest." Cyprus had been special, because attitudes were different then, and he was younger, and public opinion accepted that young men would go abroad and die in the sunshine for the preservation of something or other. Aden too, though nastier there, and the last of its type, and people beginning to bore at the concept of "our lads overseas"; but a serious place, where survival took skill if you did Charlie's work. And Ireland wasn't pretty, not in Dublin, and you had to know what the Provies were at, and you spent your nights low down in cars outside the pubs watching for who went in and who came out, and who was talking to whom and had he done it before. That was important, all right, if you wanted a man to be able to take his missus for a Friday-night jar in the local in Birmingham, or Manchester, or Glasgow or Guildford. Had the '74 campaign and the '75 campaign, and the bombs taking off arms and legs, and the glass scything the faces, to show for justification of spending his evenings watching the Paddys at their booze. But hard to convince himself that what he did now was of value. Nice to know, of course, that Big Brother was having difficulties as he sat all serene behind his watchtowers and minefields and barbed-wire fences. Nice to know that the gnats were out and nibbling, that he was scratching a bit, that he'd be turning over in his bed and cursing.

And there was the material that had come in that day. Hadn't gone through the files yet to find out what the pattern was—whether it was new, whether it was ongoing. But he'd do some typing after lunch, string it all together for Parker Smith's In tray. Sort of material the Minister liked to have; when he was having a hard time at those conferences, it made the man feel that at least he had something up his sleeve. Gave him confidence, Charlie supposed, when he was in for a good kick in the crotch from those humorless bastards. Wouldn't want anything too long; ministers never did: about half a dozen lines. But a policeman shot and nothing in the Kiev press—that was out of the ordinary. Straight criminals, then there would be no shortage of newsprint. But nothing on this one, not a public whisper; that was why it was different. And someone else thought it interesting; otherwise SIS (External Services) wouldn't have noted it, and the paper wouldn't have been duplicated and categorized that it might find its way to Charlie's desk. Showed there was a bit of life in the old system after all, if they could pick up pinpricks like that. So perhaps there was something going on, something for him to think about.

Quite interesting, really, if you had the time to look into it; and Charlie Webster had the time.

3

David had known the source of semiautomatic weapons for some months, but had not revealed it to the others in the group.

It was a particular knowledge that he treasured, and that he wished to keep only to himself. The decision not to spread the information had come a long time before, when he had made the resolve that if ever there was the possibility that he would be cornered, then he would sell his life, and well. Not something he had ever spoken of, because that was the diet of weakness. But being taken alive and put through the courts and the due process of law was an obsession for the young man, something that he told himself he would never accept, whatever the feelings of the others, whatever they would do if the cordon closed tight around them and the squeezing began. Never come out with his hands high, never. Take a few of the pigs with him.

He had come across the old man by accident. Meandered into him in the forest and then been aware of the frightened, trapped, primitive eyes that had peered through the trees at him. Faint and sparse hair that was tousled, clothes that were torn and patched and torn again and were too heavy for the summer weather but were needed for the winter cold of the forest. Hands that were shaking and gnarled and clawlike and that rose to protect the head of the man lest the intruder strike him. A hermit, one who had put himself apart. The bearing of a woodland recluse who had forsaken company, believed that it brought only danger. And David had talked to him and smiled and used soft words and broken down the resistance to conversation. On his visits to their own hut, some three miles away, David would come earlier than the rest, so that he could take food and fresh clothes to the old man; the food would be eaten, the trousers and jackets and woolens ignored. In protracted and desultory conversation, David had learned of his history and his situation and what kept him hiding. The more he learned, the more the old man's worth increased to the plans that David was fashioning for the four-strong cell.

It was a far journey old Timofey had traveled. Only he'd been young then, and strong, and whiplash-fit, otherwise he would have been dead long before. He was from the farmlands south of Moscow that had lain behind the German winter line of 1942 which ran from Zhizdra through Orel and on toward Kursk. His town was Sevsk, and in that spring a man named Kaminski had come with a letter in his wallet that bore the signature of Generaloberst Schmidt, commanding the Second Panzer Army.

Kaminski became the local governor of all the towns round Sevsk. His authority took in the communities of Navlya, Dmitrovsk, Dmitriev and Lokot; he had the power to appoint civilian officials, and most important of all, he was answerable only to Generaloberst Schmidt.

Timofey's collective was one of the first that Kaminski "liberated." The land was divided, the animals apportioned along with the farm equipment and food, and in return the workers enlisted in the local militia recruited to fight the Communist guerrillas with an expertise that was beyond the alien German troops. It had been Generaloberst Schmidt's brilliance that he had possessed the foresight to realize the potential of a man such as Kaminski, and using the carrot before the donkey of individual land ownership, he had derived the benefit of this unexpected source of manpower that could be mobilized against the partisans who till then had ravaged the extended supply routes to the Eastern Front.

Prior to Kaminski's time, the farmers like Timofey had watched with apathy as the guerrillas came at night to replenish their food stocks from the yards of the collectives. Now they were directly affected; they were losing that which had been made their own. The life of the guerrilla became harder, his reception at the darkened farmhouse more hostile.

The next step was logical enough. The new militia were formed into fighting units for patrolling and ultimately for hunting down the guerrillas. As a tactic it was a great success for the Germans. Their allies were self-sufficient in abandoned Soviet weapons, antitank guns, machine guns, mortars. They became military formations and safeguarded the access routes. Timofey had a position of rank, commanded a platoon-sized group, was a noticed man.

And then the line to the north sagged, and there were bulges and salients before the Germans were gone, pushed back toward the distant Polish frontier. The Red Army reoccupied the towns where Kaminski's word had ruled. There were many now who could name those who had collaborated. Timofey's picture was displayed in the square at Sevsk; there was a reward for his capture.

Three submachine guns and a rifle he had taken with him as he had foot-slogged south, moving at night, keeping away from the roads and the towns and the villages all through that long summer of 1943. He had entertained a vague hope that he might assume a new identity in Kiev, that the confusion of war would allow him to reappear without questions, without the necessity of explanations.

There had been many times when he had thought that the time was ripe for him to throw off the bonds of this solitary exile in the forests and make the break from the past. But it would have been a great step, and he could never quite bring himself to it. Five, six, perhaps seven times he had stood on the edge of the tree line of the great road that ran toward Kiev and braced himself to step out of the sanctuary of concealment . . . but he had never been able to accomplish it. And the years went by and the task of self-rehabilitation became ever harder, till it was impossible, till he had made permanent his prison in the forests.

Thirty-five years he had been there now. Through the discomfort of sores and bruises and spreading scabs, the pain of his ailing teeth, the frustration of his fading sight. Paid a few kopecks by the dacha owners, who asked nothing more than that he watch over their properties in the winter, and a few more coins for the wood he brought them for their fires in the spring and the autumn. Not that he had use for their money. And they left him to himself and his memories and his hatreds, seeing him only as a harmless, pathetic and sometimes laughable figure with a marginal usefulness that was his protection against denunciation.

David whistled a warning of his approach when he was still a clear hundred yards from the old man's hut. Stood stock-still as always and listened after the harsh notes that Timofey had taught him, and heard the answering call; a sort of game it had been at first, but that was before the talk in the group had been of action. After that, a difference. New justifications and seriousness for the precautions. David had not told him of the program—just prodded his memory, vague and fading, leading the old man to the days in the woods around Sevsk when he had stalked the partisans. Technique, procedure, maneuver, tactics—all those Timofey could teach him. "Be careful. Be on guard at all times. It is when you relax that they take you. The knife in the back, at the throat; the single shot. Always the same epitaph. That you had relaxed, that you had not been careful. A silly thing to bury a man for, that he was casual," Timofey had said.

The hut was not as large as the one the group had found. Big enough for a woodsman to spend a night in when his search for dried and fallen branches that were needed for the fires caused him to stray far from his home. Table inside, and chairs, and a mattress on the floor; all had been thrown out from the dachas and disappeared overnight from the rubbish heap. Rabbit snares on the wall, neatly in line, the coils of steel wire suspended from nails: a source of food.

When they were inside, David said, "Timofey, I don't have much time, and I have come to ask something of you. It is of the greatest importance that you give me what I ask for. You have suffered greatly, Timofey, at their hands. If you give me what I need, you will have the chance to hit them in a way that has not been possible for you. I want guns, Timofey. Not a rifle—I have no need of that—but the machine guns. Two of them, certainly, I must have."

In the half-light of the room David saw the eyes opposite him glint together, closing with interest as the old man's attention was captured by the request. Desperate to know what I want them for, the old fox, thought David. Give his right arm to know.

"Timofey, it is not a criminal act, not robbing a bank, not for money. It is against them, the system; it will hurt them whether we succeed or fail. It will punish them for what they have done to you, and done to us."

"What have they done to you?" And his voice was strangely hoarse, the legacy of so great a silence.

"They have hunted us in the same way as you. Only the weapons have changed. They are our enemies as they are yours."

"You have a house, you have clothes, you have work, you have money. How are they your enemies as they are mine?"

"We do not have the same opportunities; we are second-class citizens. We are not permitted to be part of their world. They reject us because we are Jews."

"We saw the Jews go in the war. We were on the side of those who exterminated your parents and your relatives. Perhaps we even approved . . . it is difficult . . . it was a long time ago . . . we did nothing. How many millions of your people was it who died then? And now you wants guns, and guns mean death, and you want to kill people to get a better place in the sun, so you can climb from the valley onto the high ground. Is that reason enough? We killed so many of each other at that time. What you now talk of seems a little matter. Perhaps because I am old, but what you seek for yourself seems nothing . . ."

"I don't have the time, old man."

Timofey rose from his chair. "When you have guns then you will go to war. That is the time when you must learn the wisdom of patience and calm, or you will end as nothing and the worms alone will welcome you. With the strength of the gun beside you your haste must be tempered, even your haste to be clear of an old man who asks nothing of you, nothing but a few words that can be lies or truth, immaterial." He went stiffly, because the damp had long been in his knees and movement was hard for him, toward the hanging sacking that marked off from the rest of the room the place where he slept. When he emerged again, it was with an aging knapsack colored the steel gray of the wartime German forces. He placed it with deliberation on the table and unbuckled the straps that held down the top flap. There was pale green mildew on them, and the buckles were dark with rust. He saw the way the young man looked at him. "Have no worry. Inside it is dry. Weapons do not age, not if they have been cared for, if they are cleaned. These have been." Then the bundle of oilskin—a mustard-brown camouflage ground sheet—and that was laid on the table, and there was string to be undone, and finally the guns were revealed. So small, David thought. The tubular-steel shoulder rests folded down the stock, magazines separate and detached; just barrel length basically—insignificant little things such as the children play with when they mimic the television pictures of the Red Army at its maneuvers. But clean, and shining, and as worked on as any of his mother's mantelpiece ornaments.

"The ammunition too I have cared for. It would not be wise to fire a test, but I tell you, my boy, that they will function. They are adequate to kill any who are keeping you as a second-class citizen." And he laughed, and the hoarseness gave way to a raven's croak, and his face cracked with the humor of his remark, spilling new lines across the log-brown face.

"I need two, Timofey."

"So there is more than one of you. You have a follower, perhaps an army, and you will be the general."

"There are no generals; we are together."

"We all say that when we are young. But do not listen to yourself. When there is danger, when there is risk, then there must be a leader. You cannot fight by committee; even they found that out. And are you that leader, David? Are you the one with the resolve? Can you take your friends forward? When you have the guns it is changed, you know. You must discover that before you begin the course, whatever it may be, that you have chosen. Later is too late; there is not time."

David did not reply, and Timofey silently took one of the guns in his hands.

For half an hour he showed David the workings of the weapon until the lesson was learned to perfection. Showed him the safety mechanism; showed him how to arm it, how to load the magazine, how to attach it; explained the drift of automatic fire, high and to the right if more than five shots were fired in a burst; showed him what to do if he suffered a jam.

At the door, the load he had come for in a plastac bag, David said, "What is the call that you taught me, told me to use when I approached?"

"The call of the kingfisher."

"Why? Why did you choose that one, that bird?"

Timofey pointed past his hut into the tangle of trees. "You cannot see it from here, but there is a stream, where no one comes, and where I sit. There is the nest of a kingfisher there, and I hear her call, or that of her mate when he has need of her. It is rare for people to see that bird. Most of these swine who live here through the summer would never see one, let alone hear her. So I say that if I hear that call, and I hear it from the path that you use, then it will be you. Another bird, and I could be mistaken, or I might hear it too often. But the kingfisher is the rarity, a princess among them."

"I have never seen one."

"Because you are from the city. She is fast and swift, and she holds the initiative in her world. None can catch her; few even see her; she is devastating in her attack. She is a lesson to the guerrilla. She is what you must strive after."

"It is a good name, old man. It will be heard. Many will hear of our kingfisher."

They were walking now, close together because of the narrowness of the track, and the old man was shorter than David, bowed and shriveled in his age.

"Will you come again?" he said, and his eyes were looking up.

"I will not come again. However it goes, there will be no return."

No farewells, no hands shaken, no words of comfort or encouragement; just the blunt moment of parting as the old man turned back to his hut, and David hurried down the track, his right hand holding the weighted package, his left shielding his face from the low, sharp-cutting hazel branches.

Remember what David said went again and again through Isaac's mind as he stood in the center of the huge marble-veneered floor of the Aeroflot main offices. A bustle of people coming and going around him, and queues at the ticket counters. Just the way they had wanted it. And when it comes to the booking, choose a harassed girl, one with pressure accumulating on her and a short temper and a willingness to be done with the business. They didn't want a girl with time to waste and questions to ask. Incredible, really, in a society like ours, how people had so much time to ask questions; fear, he thought, fear is what it comes to, fear of being held responsible if there was error, retribution. A whole society so consumed with curiosity about the legalities of their fellow citizens' lives.

He had already taken the state airline's timetable and leafed through it till he came to the map that boasted the extent of the international as well as domestic routes. Take the North Sea as the outer limit, going due west. Have to be somewhere inside that orbit that they must put down, and still be left with a fail-safe quantity of fuel in the tanks. Must look at it analytically: that was the way he had been trained at school and the way they were teaching him at the University. Take a problem and search out the solution. So where to? Where to buy a ticket for?

Leningrad—no good. Equivalent distance to the center of East Germany, and he wasn't to know how much spare fuel they would carry. Would get them to Turkey, but that wasn't safe, not a fascist military regime; same sort of people as the party here, hard to tell the difference, and run the risk of being shipped back. Red fascists and black fascists, not much to choose between them. Needed the "liberal democracies," as David called them, where they followed the fortunes of Israel with concern, did not genuflect to the Arabs and their oil. North Europe the answer for the refueling stop, and the sense of frustration that these decisions were being made now, as he was brushed against and pushed and disturbed by the loudspeaker announcements—plans that should have molded days earlier and would now be rushed and pressured.

Yalta—too short; same for all the Black Sea resorts. Plenty of flights, but not enough aviation fuel.

Tbilisi—nearer, but who ever went to Georgia, and they must not have to explain the reason for their journey. Miserable, tight bastards down there, and everyone in Kiev knew that. Have to explain if he wanted seats to Tbilisi.

He poised the map between his open hands again, running a finger farther north. Tomsk and Novosibirsk.

Novosibirsk—opportunities there. God knows why anyone goes there, but that's an intellectual base, Science City. Perhaps a chemistry student could be going, and Rebecca with her botany, and David with his working chemistry. The indicator board carried the daily arrivals and departures, covering a whole wall, the flights of the week. Nothing to those two cities for Wednesday. No to Tomsk, no to Novosibirsk, blank, nothing. Disappointment, and back to the map.

Tashkent—a flight to Tashkent tomorrow. Flight on Wednesday. Sixteen hundred hours, the sort of time they wanted; could have finished their preparations by then . . . but if they had three hours to play with, if Moses gave them that long . . . and he'd sworn and cursed at Moses when he should have prayed for him, prayed for strength for him. More than two thousand miles to Tashkent, way beyond the distance they needed. Fuel for more than five hours; take them into Europe, into the West. But down into Tashkent, that was where the flight was routed, what papers would you need for that? Didn't know. It had been his plan, his idea, the whole thing, and the others had accepted it, and he didn't know the answers, and had no way of finding them, only at the counter, only at the ticket counter. Cannot apply logic to regulations; either know the answer or you are ignorant.

He joined the queue to one of the central counters—heavy traffic, more than at the extremes of right and left. Funny how people sought the center, where the delays would be greater. Conformity. Five, ten minutes slipping by and time for him to gauge the girl in the dowdy blue uniform, two-piece—only one a year issued to her, but should have been able to make more of it than she had. Customers in front of him being satisfied, queue lengthening behind him. Then one more man in front—heavy suit of a Party worker. Perhaps he wasn't, but Isaac reckoned all of them who wore heavy suits when it was hot were Party workers—status in showing they had the clothes, and sweat running down his neck onto his collar to show for the gesture of superiority.

An argument. He wanted Moscow. She said it was full for two days. He showing his papers and his documentation and his cards, and she saying it made no difference, that everything was full but he could go to the airport and try his luck. Isaac realized that the man couldn't be that important, didn't qualify by his rank for the tickets held back for senior Party officials on all flights. Everyone knew about that.

The girl was flushed at the cheeks, looking around her for support when she caught Isaac's eye, and his wink, the lowered lid, was acknowledged. Saw her stifle a giggle and return her gaze to the man whose voice was now raised.

There would be trouble for her, a complaint to the responsible person. His department would lodge a protest at the highest level. What was her name? Blatant obstruction of an official. And he left his place at the counter.

Isaac said, "I'd like to book three for tomorrow, to Tashkent, student fare, coming back fourteen days from tomorrow. I'd like to go on tomorrow afternoon's flight, return two weeks from Wednesday. If it's possible?" And he smiled, boyish, intimate. "Silly old man that, and you handled him well; you won't hear from him again." His right hand had moved from his hip pocket, clutching the fifty rubles, and his fist opened among the papers in front of her—tickets, timetables, price charts—and without taking her eyes from him she covered the bills, faded and worn, with her booking pad. She didn't reply, just picked up her desk telephone—computer not working again—and was talking into it; Isaac waiting for the verdict.

Still holding the phone, she asked for the names, and when they had been given to her repeated them into the mouthpiece, spelling them out letter by letter; it seemed to take a lifetime. She said, "Priority" and grinned at him; not badlooking, Isaac thought, but someone should do something about her teeth. He smiled back.

"Confirmed," she said, and started to make out the tickets themselves. Not much to fill in—not like an international ticket. When she had finished, she set to work on her calculator. "With the student reduction, and the fourteen-day-stay reduction, and the special rate for the ballet festival in Tashkent, you're lucky on that one . . . five hundred and twenty-two rubles for the three. You pay over there, on the right at the cash counter—if you haven't a voucher, that is."

"Our parents have the money," said Isaac. "Keep the tickets there beside you and I'll be back with the money."

"I'm not supposed to do that, to make out tickets that aren't immediately paid for."

"I'll be back. I know when you close. Keep them on one side. I'll be back."

So the flight was booked, and he found it difficult to walk when he was out on the street again. How damned easy. It was going to work. The whole damned thing was going to work. He wanted to shout, yell the message. David and Rebecca and Isaac, they'd show the bastards, show them how it happened. Show them all, in spite of the Jews who kept their peace—show them that the spell was broken.

Isaac's mother was waiting, as he had told her to be, outside the savings bank that was nearest to their home. A small, sparrow-sized woman, with the lines on her face that were devoid of relief. And the boy had not explained, given her no reason for her presence there, just told her to bring the passbook. A hard and suffering time she had had, with money not easy to come by; it had been grafted for, and worked for, and collected with a miser's hand. And he had said he would need most of the deposit which had increased at such a pitiful pace over the previous thirty years. Had said that David's mother and Rebecca's mother would repay her in part, and she had thought that she barely knew these other persons who were of the families of her son's friends. But there had been that in the boy's looks which denied her the right to remonstrate, and so she now stood at the outside door and waited for him.

When he came, Isaac clasped her arm and kissed her on the cheek, and they took a place in the line and started the shuffling movement forward toward the teller. A bright, airy interior. Lace curtains, and flowers on the table where the customers could sit and prepare their paperwork. Even Lenin, in his wall portrait, seemingly content as he looked down the length of the bank to the photograph of the Ukrainian General Secretary of the Party. At the counter, like a ventriloquist's dummy, his mother spoke while Isaac, a pace behind her, primed the old lady's ear as to how much she should withdraw. It was time-consuming, but without difficulty, and they maintained a punctilious politeness to the teller, for she could delay and hinder them if they antagonized her in the slightest. And they were Jews, and it was easy to offend. The papers were inscribed, with carbons for green copy, pink copy and white copy.

When the money had passed from the teller to his mother, and on to Isaac, he said, "I can't tell you why, but you will know by tomorrow night, and you must have courage, the courage of our people. Whatever happens, you must be brave. Do not bow to them. I will not be home tonight; don't ask why. Be brave."

The old lady displayed no emotion as they stepped back out onto the street. Feelings masked, no indication given of the confusions and anxieties she felt for her son. She walked away with a brisk and sturdy step.

And he had the money in his pocket. A tight wad of rolled, crisp, mint-fresh banknotes, and he was hurrying for the bus that would take him back to the center of Kiev and the Aeroflot office. So he had done his part; they could board the plane that would lift off in twenty-three hours. But did David have the guns? Would Rebecca secure the access for them to the plane? And when would Moses break, when would Moses talk, how long till the dogs were unleashed? But all was gone from his hands now; he had done his part. It remained only for him to hurry to the rendezvous with Rebecca, tell her the flight they would go on and look for her smile, her gratitude.

Yevsei Allon could barely believe his luck.

First the call by telephone to the freight office, and his being told by the Under Manager that there was a personal message for him, and not to take long because the line carried official business. The voice of the girl whom he remembered from school, and who had been too haughty then to acknowledge him; the suggestion that they meet and talk about the old days in the classroom; the little laugh that mingled with the static of the poor connection, and Yevsei thinking of his night classes and not daring to mention them. They would meet at the subway entrance that was near the small church of Saint Sophia.

Before he left the airport at the end of the day shift, Yevsei had spent ten full minutes in the washroom, scrubbing his hands and lathering the hard public-utilities soap on his face. He wetted and then combed the short hair on his head till the parting was straight and exact, and he had looked at himself in the mirror, and the man who waited behind him to use the basin had quipped, "You'll need more than soap and a comb to please her." He'd blushed, crimson over his whitened face that rarely saw the sun, and mumbled an answer and run for the bus.

There had been coffee after they met, sitting at a table away from the bar where the voices of other customers were reduced to a background drone. The girl listened to him as his confidence grew, and she asked him about his job—what he did at the airport—and they talked of their teachers in the low voices of conspiracy, and of their friends, and demolished them all. Her white teeth flashed when he made his jokes, and she threw back her head, so that the long black hair trailed away from the slightness of her neck. He could see the shape of her breasts and the outline of her waist till there was a tightness and a sweat inside the ill-fitting trousers that he cursed himself for having chosen to wear that morning when he had risen. Too much, really, to believe in. He stumbled, banged his foot against the leg of the table, rattling the cups, drawing attention, on his way to the toilet, and scrabbled in his pocket for the kopecks that he needed for the machine, for the packet he would want when the light faded.

She took him in the early evening to the sandbanks of the Dnieper, and they swam in the great river that flows from north to south through the city. She was prepared and wearing a one-piece swimsuit that had been concealed under her dress; he was in blue underpants, which bulged and heaved in spite of the cold drift of water around his lower belly. When he touched her in the water, trying to pretend it was accidental contact, she did not move away, as the other girls did, and when she laughed it was with him, not at him. There were others there, naturally, because it was a warm evening and the authorities prided themselves on the cleanliness of the river, the way they had been able to stave off pollution from the water artery of an industrialized city of more than two million inhabitants. But she seemed oblivious of them, allowing no intruders in the private oasis she was creating for the man who worked at the Kiev airport and who had access to the tarmac and the planes.

The parks were numerous in the city, putting those of London and Paris and Frankfurt and Rome to shame. Some ornamental, with laid-out flower beds, where the elderly went; others little more than enclosed spaces of bushes and trees where the grass had been permitted to grow, and there were paths that could lead far from the noise of voices. It was to such a place that they walked after the river. His trousers showed a dark and damp stain at the seat from his sodden pants, and she hid the shivers she felt still encased in her wet swimsuit. But her trembling was not from any sharp wind, but from what must happen in order that the guns would go on board the plane; and he mistook the shaking of her hand for an excitement that he believed he was responsible for.

The place they found was remote and distant from the life of the city, hidden and enclosed by undergrowth, and she said to him, "Don't look, but I can't stay in this swimsuit. I'll catch my death if I keep this damp thing against my skin." Twisted away from where he sat and turned her back on him, and reached behind her to pull down the zip fastener of the dress till it was clear of her shoulders. More contortions and the garment was hanging, straps free, at her waist. Hands now under the skirt of her dress, and the wriggling before it was free and she reached up again to pull the dress back into position. But the zipper remained open, and he could see the knotted outline, suntanned by the weather, of her backbone.

"Why don't you take yours off?" she said, matter-of-fact, as though it were everyday, nothing special, habit.

Though he could feel the clamminess of his pants against his skin, he said, "I'm all right. I think they've just about dried." There was a huskiness in his voice. The sort of thing the men at work talked about in the canteen during lunch break, and it was happening to him, to Yevsei Allon.

She laid her swimsuit out on the grass with neatness and care as if to prevent it from becoming creased, then fell back onto the ground, her arms stretched above her head. "I love it here. So peaceful, so beautiful, so quiet. It makes you forget everything else." It was a lie; her thoughts were far from the leaves and the cool grass. What would they do to the boy if he did as she was to ask? That was what passed through her mind. What would be his punishment? Perhaps they'd think that he was one of the group, and if they did, that would mean the firing squad, or the execution shed. He'd have to work hard to prove that he wasn't. If he was lucky, it would be the cattle trucks to Moldavia and the camp at Potma. The Jews had a hard time there, especially from the fascists— there were still fascists there, from the war days, but they were the "trusties" and now ran the camps and took their revenge on the newest source of prisoners, on the Jews. Perhaps he would not be linked to them, but that was unlikely; they were thorough people, those pigs, and how could poor Yevsei be warned to cover his tracks? Poor Yevsei. God, he wants to kiss me, and there's spittle at the side of his mouth. How many hours since he shaved? And the spot at the side of his nose by the right nostril, ready to break and burst . . . Lucky if he just went to the Labor Camp. He'd be a casualty of the breakout, but there had been casualties before. Six million casualties in the war, and how many since then? And what war was ever won without the ignorant and the innocent standing up in the crossfire and dying with disbelief on their faces? Isaac had the tickets; there now remained only for David to get the guns. They'll give me one. One of my own to hold.

"I don't think you should do that," she whispered, and smiled bravely. His hand was at her kneecap, and his fingers, cold and small and bony, were skating patterns on her lower thigh.

"I don't know," he said, and he was panting and his mouth was very close to hers.

"I don't really know either," she said, and looked into his eyes. Was there a squint or not?—couldn't be sure. God knew he was heavy.

Never done it before, she thought. Hadn't an idea, but neither had she; couldn't claim the virtue of experience. Could have with David, but . . . One hand climbing her thigh, the other pushing between her breasts, seeking a nipple to squeeze and hold to, and finding it and not knowing his strength till she cried out, and he believed she was encouraging him. The hand higher, searching and brushing gently at her and trying to prize her legs apart, and the one that had been at her breasts gone and the motion of rolling activity as he struggled to release something from the buttoned-down pocket on his buttocks.

"Oh, my God," she blurted. "The time, it's so late. And I haven't said I'd be out late tonight. Yevsei, I have to go—I really must." In his confusion she could straighten and sit up, disengage, disentangle. But was it too fast, too hurried? Had she merely wound the elastic, and in releasing it would she explode in him an anger, a teased fury? Out of her orbit, out of her experience. No necessity for the casual evenings with stranger boys and a few kopecks in their pockets now that her life was with the group. The anxiety showed in her eyes, the fear that she had damaged the work of the evening. She flitted a hand to his wrist, withdrawing it but consoling. How far along the path must she walk? How deep was the submission required to guarantee the passage of the guns? Hideous, the thought that she had failed them, David and Isaac, that she could not prize apart her thighs for the love of her friends. And Yevsei hovering over her, weight on his knees.

"Another ten minutes, just ten minutes." Pleading, and knowing he had lost as she smoothed her dress down her thighs.

"I want to. I desperately want to, Yevsei. But I can't tonight. You've made the time flee. Tomorrow I could come back. I could come tomorrow evening. If you want me to."

Yevsei Allon nodded, bewildered by all that had happened to him. But that was a promise, and he had done nothing wrong, had not upset her. Only the tightness and agonizing frustration to tell him how close he had been to the most triumphant success of his twenty-one-year life, and burning in his hip pocket the prophylactic he had bought from the coin machine in the café.

When they were walking back along the path to the road and the bus stop where they would part, she said quickly, "Yevsei, you're in freight, is that right?"

"Yes." He wasn't proud of it. He'd told her earlier what he did; she had telephoned him there. What was the need to ask?

"And you go to the planes to load them?"

"That's done by the ramp men. Rebecca, what time tomorrow—what time will I see you?"

"But you could go to the plane yourself—if it was necessary?"

"Of course. The same time tomorrow, and I'll bring my swim trunks."

"The same time, Yevsei. But I have something to ask of you. There's a friend of mine who's going to Tashkent tomorrow. He is of our faith, of our people, and he has to take a package with him. There are some books he can't put into his bags in case they're seen. I want you to put them on the plane for him, Yevsei." She had linked her arm through his, and walked close to him, her hip bouncing against his. "I want you to tell me where they're placed so that he can collect them during the flight. When he gets off at Tashkent there are no searches and he can carry them off."

Still the suppressed, flattened pain fighting the coldness of his pants; but tomorrow there would be only liberation on the pressed-down park grass. It was a promise. She had promised. He said, "Is it dangerous?" Was ashamed of his reaction immediately as she smiled and shook her head.

"We wouldn't ask anything dangerous of a school friend, much less of one of our faith, one who worships with us." He could not remember that he had seen her at the synagogue which he visited with his family each week, but she had pushed his arm that encircled her waist higher, so that his hand could cup her breast. "Which flight?"

"The flight to Tashkent. The one that leaves at four o'clock."

"Bring the package to me at noon when I take my lunch break, at the outer door of the freight offices. Then you will need to phone me at three—the same number you used today. I'll tell you what seat your friend should take so that he can find his books. I can do it for you."

She kissed him on the cheek, and did not fight when he swung her mouth to his and explored behind her gums and teeth with his tongue. He saw that she still smiled—a deep, radiant, consuming smile.

Parker Smith was never at his desk before ten in the morning, claiming with a shrug that he could never survive the stampede of the rush hour, but he stayed late to clear his In tray, load the Out. He let it be known among the men who worked for him that he was most receptive to discussion and exchange of viewpoints after formal office hours, when the telephones had stopped ringing, when no secretaries were left on the premises to harry him.

Around seven in the evening he would put his head out through the door to his office and see if anyone was waiting in the outer section. It was a house rule that after five o'clock nothing short of the death of Stalin, chopping of Khrushchev, declaration of war between the Union of Soviet Socialist Republics and the People's Republic of China should cause him to be interrupted before he indicated his willingness to receive visitors. Parker Smith was keen on rules, had learned them in his army days and not forgotten when he transferred from Intelligence Corps, Ministry of Defense, to the civilian wing of the government's espionage service, the SIS.

With his jacket left in his own office, and his tie loosened, collar button undone, Charlie Webster was waiting, far back in an armchair, idling through the previous day's *Financial Times*. Not really the type we're used to, and more's the pity, thought Parker Smith. The totally committed man, and with more experience up front than the rest of the Section put together. He'd noticed the way the others kept their distance from Charlie Webster, didn't mix with the older man from the different background, put him on the outside. Hadn't read his personal file, had they? Would have treated him like a king if they had.

"Come on in, Charlie." Liked the way the man straightened in his chair, left the newspaper folded on the coffee table, pushed up his tie before entering the inner sanctum. "Take a chair, and what can I do for you?" It was a good office for talking. Parker Smith had the rank and the Civil Service grading to be able, within a stipulated budget, to choose his color scheme—kept it soft, a gentle sky blue and a rich cream. Full-length net curtains; two quietly abstract paintings; a sprouting philodendron in the corner. None of your prints of HM in Garter robes, or any "Myself Meeting Winston Churchill" photographs.

"It's this, sir. Something or nothing, I'm not sure yet, but could be amusing, could be interesting. I put in a 'B' category to you this afternoon, about Kiev. Perhaps I shouldn't have bothered you. It's just that a policeman has been shot, and there's silence in the local rags and on the wireless. External picked it up and pushed it in my direction. If the Soviets had been trumpeting it, I wouldn't have been bothered. But they haven't, and that's what made it a bit unusual to me. Seemed it could mean there's something political there."

"I read it," said Parker Smith. "What's the source evaluation?"

"Not bad. One of the businessmen's pickups from a longtermer, passed on by the handlers. We've had this chap's stuff before, and not had reason to doubt it, cause to prove him wrong."

Parker Smith bowed his head faintly in acknowledgment. One of the crosses the Department had to bear was that its hard news came more often than not courtesy of the active wing of SIS that occupied floors below.

"There's not much to add to the report I handed in, except

that a bit more has come in from the Moscow end. It's a bit convoluted, but it's moved fast. Seems a British student on exchange postgrad studies at the University got into a bit of a panic, left his passport on a bus in Kiev and rang into the Embassy in Moscow for guidance. Seems he told them that the talk there was of truckloads of militia moving into the city late this afternoon and that there had been attacks on policemen. It's very fresh, this; he was only talking to the Embassy a couple of hours ago. He said all this was mixed up with a rumor running the rounds at the University, and only a rumor, that a Jewish youth had been taken into custody. The kid said that the students were saying all these three factors were related. He's just an ordinary student, nothing special, not one of ours. But it all comes at the right time to go with the other stuff."

"Interesting, Charlie. But still doesn't top it up to 'A' category."

"Be pretty hard for anything the bloody dissidents do to manage 'A' quality, sir."

"But it's nice to know. Nice to know the bastards have their own little bit of Belfast. I don't envy the little blighters up the sharp end if they get their hands on them."

"That's not really why I wanted to see you this evening. It's just that if what we have already is genuine, we could be into something much deeper." Parker Smith was listening. It was what he wanted to hear, what the Department existed for, drew the Treasury funds to discover. "Ever since I came to work here it's struck me that one day the Soviet Jews are going to get lively. We've been through all the primary stages—press conferences, hunger strikes—trying to stir up the pot to get themselves shipped out to Israel; the botched-up job of the Leningrad hijack when they didn't have a gun between them and were riddled with informers and didn't even make it onto the plane before they were picked up. We've had all that kind of thing, but that was the older generation at work. It's the same the world over: all these things start with the thinkers and not the hard boys running the show, and they're too fragmented to have any unity, and there's failure. But there comes a change, when the toughies get involved. I've damn all of nothing to base this on, but if you have, and it's only an assumption, but if

you have a specific target shooting, and you have troops coming in—paramilitary, anyway—and you have a Jewish boy
picked up, then you have a pattern. There's a load of 'ifs'
about the whole scene, but should there be the connection
that I'm drawing, then things could get very interesting,
could all warm up a bit."

"I think that what you're saying, Charlie, is that it doesn't
really matter how the Ukrainians and the Georgians and that
crowd up in the Baltic spend their evenings, but that if it was
Jewish, then the flavor would be richer, the spices would be
in the pot. We'd have an international scene, wouldn't we,
Charlie?"

"Something like that, sir. And I thought you'd like to know."

Anyone else and Parker Smith would have given him more
encouragement, but it didn't work like that with Charlie
Webster. Always at his best when he had to convince people,
and seemed to lose interest once he had. Strange chap, not
really part of them, but a bloody good man to have around.

Charlie let himself out and walked back to his own office to
collect his coat and his briefcase. The bag had nothing in it
beyond the morning paper, and he'd long since done the
crossword, but his wife liked him to carry it, had the EIIR
monogram on it, and she liked that to be seen. Couldn't take
any of the office papers home, all classified and restricted,
but he liked to humor her. He'd be in time for the eight fifty
two from Waterloo.

4

A deep and leaden silence hung over the forest; caused David
and Isaac to soften their voices as they talked in the hut. No
other human being sleeping within miles of them, except
only old Timofey. No shuffle of feet through the sun-dried
leaves, no disturbed dead wood to protest and alert them.
Enough to startle them, the grating cough of a vixen fox or
the lamenting wail of an owl; but those were intrusions, and
the creatures of the wood rested, thankful for the cool of the
darkness and the possibility for rest that it brought.

A tin of stewed meat, sliced open and the contents eaten
cold and messily with the dribble on their shirtfronts, and a
loaf of bread were their food as the two men waited out the
night hours, a liter of beer to wash it down and deaden the
taste but which they would not finish. Need for a clear head
in the morning, David had said, and Isaac had nodded, and
watched as the screw top was replaced on the bottle. But the
beer had been good, and had cooled their bodies and soothed
the throats that were sore from the incessant talking of the
day. Like talismans they had laid out, where both could see
them, their achievements of the afternoon. Close to David's
right hip, the sacking bundle in which he had brought the
guns, the protective wrapping artfully pulled back so that the
metal shapes could be watched, admired and doted on. By
Isaac's crossed ankles was the thin paper envelope that bore
the insigne of Aeroflot and in which were secreted the wisps
of paper, printed and pen-scrawled, that were the tickets to
Tashkent. Worthy of studying, both of them, comprising the
power and the subtlety that were necessary for the escape.
And what awaited them now was nothing as tangible as what
they had accomplished, just a promise—Yevsei's promise.

The meal taken, the quota of beer consumed, and the boys
left with nothing to succor them but the sight of each other's

faces, the sounds of each other's words. Many times Isaac looked to the door, as if anticipating that it could open without prior warning, that the girl would be back with them, spilling out her success. Irritating to David, who preferred to keep his own company, willing himself a protection from the cruel and slow-passing hours; he sat quite still, breaking the mood only once to reach for the empty tin and throw it to a darkened corner, far in the shadows from the single spitting and declining candle.

"How long do you think, how long till she comes?"

David shrugged, noncommittal.

"Can she come at night?"

"You know the bus times as well as I do. There is no other way she can reach us."

"It's just the damned waiting. Everything we've done today, and not knowing whether it's meaningless."

"There is nothing to do but wait."

"Doesn't make it any easier." Isaac laughed, nervous, cramped.

"Why should it be easy?"

"I didn't say it should be easy. I just meant . . ."

"There is nothing in a fight such as ours that can be easy. If it were, there would be many like us. We would not be alone."

The elder boy spoke almost in a drawl, his eyes closed now, seeming to ignore Isaac.

"Is that why you began, it that why you started—because it would not be easy?"

"Someone had to, after everything that our people have gone through."

"But that's a slogan, David."

"The fight had to be started."

"Another slogan."

"If you didn't believe in it, why did you come; why are you a part of us?"

"Different from the words you use, a different reason. Revenge perhaps, revenge for what had happened."

"We are no different. We are of the same mind, the same body. We hate with the same depth."

Isaac shifted himself, mindful of the nails in the board floor that were poorly hammered and whose heads bit at his buttocks. Pushed a hand through his curled and dank hair that was bereft of parting and shape.

"What was your vision of victory, David?" He saw the other man start, the eyes flash open, the warning curl of anger at the mouth.

"What do you mean?"

"A campaign must have an aim, it must have an ultimate, there must be a possibility of victory. If we are to fight them . . ."

"We have hurt them; isn't that enough?"

"Never enough, just to hurt. We could go on hurting them, hurt them for weeks and months, and the achievement would be nothing."

"You think it is nothing that we have achieved? A policeman shot, an organization formed, a commitment forged, and you call that nothing?" David intense, staring, chin jutting, spitting his words.

"It was a start to something." Isaac seeking to catch the tone of reason and rationality. "But it could not be the end. You must have thought that what we did would develop, that it would lead on. I can't find the words for the expression of what I want. I say again, what did you hope for, what did you expect?"

"You say to hurt them is not enough. Isaac says we have achieved nothing. Well, who else has hurt them? Tell me that. Who else has filled their coffins for them? Who else has wounded and angered and insulted them?" Rasping, staccato sentences, the leader roused and baring his organs, his lifeblood. "What would you have us do? Send another telegram to the President of the United States? Call a press conference for the foreigners to attend in your home and tell them of our problems? Sit down in the street and wait for the militia to carry you away? Does that hurt them? Has anything changed in the years of the passive people, the clever people, those who go under the banner of 'nonviolence'? Have they won any battles? What has altered for them? Do the visas flow because their names are broadcast on the outside radio? They win nothing, these people. Only a mindless and valueless hour of attention before they're forgotten and taken to rot in the camps."

Startled and quieter, fearful of the passion that had been

laid before him, Isaac said, "But you knew, David, you knew that it could not just continue. They have organized themselves; they will sense they have a target. You yourself have said that in all probability they have taken Moses. If we cannot escape, they will close around us . . ."

"They would never take me."

"But is that what you foresaw? Damn it, David, is that what you thought would happen—that one morning they would surround us . . ."

"They would never take me."

Isaac shouting, changing his voice, believing he had secured the truth. "It's a goddamned death wish. It's the martyr you want to play. Spread out like a damned hero, and your name on the song sheet. Is that what you wanted—a tree on a hill outside Jerusalem . . ."

"I don't want to die."

". . . and a crowd of people to come each Shebat, and stand in silence . . ."

"I don't want to die."

". . . the weeds will grow over you. You'll be nothing, just a damned symbol. Is that what it was all for, to satisfy your goddamned death wish?"

"The door, Isaac. It's behind you. You can open it, you can walk through it, you can walk away, make your own path."

Isaac looked into his face, blinked at the old unmoving eyes of the friend he had known since he played with a tennis ball in the dust of his street. Saw that the composure had taken root again, would not falter whatever provocation was offered.

"I'm sorry, David. I mean it, I'm sorry."

Just a whisper, competing with the light wind in the high trees. "If you think it has been easy, Isaac, it is because you have not listened, you have not watched."

For many minutes neither spoke, content to let the candle gutter, and the darkness settle and increase its spread across them. Both faces in shadow so that neither could sense the brooding mood that gripped the other. When would the damned girl come? thought Isaac. How much longer? Would she come in the darkness and in secrecy or in the public light of dawn? They would read it, written over her, whether she had succeeded them or failed them; would not need words and explanations: would see it in her mouth. David had won his battle, had found the guns, and Isaac had fulfilled his task. Was she capable, the girl, of meeting her commitment?

Hours and hours he had spent with her over the last years, and yet he hardly knew her, understood little about her. Just the facade, the face and the clothes; not why she was a part of them, not why she had cradled the gun in the brief moments she had handled it, not why she had declared her intention to execute a man who was unknown to her, not why on this evening she would be wheedling her sexuality on a stupid, oafish youth.

What did she owe them, this girl, that she risked her life to be part of a strange and demented crusade, a witness to the death wish of David, an accessory to the vengeance of Isaac? He'd noted that she kept silent when David spoke, seldom joined the others in questioning, seemed in fact to float with them, a piece of driftwood in the cell. Would be different and straightforward if she were David's girl, but the moments, hidden or open, of gentle affection were not present. Not that he had seen them, anyway: never entwined fingers, never the hidden jokes and intimacies of lovers, nothing to tell a tale. But she was not relegated to the role of follower, there to provide the boys of the group with the services they needed; she was an equal, as much a part of the "program" as he, Isaac. And now they depended on her, their hopes rested with her, there was no flight without her, no salvation. If she failed them, it would be the police cells and the beginning of David's yearning for the martyr's lime pit, and the end of Isaac's possibility of vengeance.

Pictured her in his mind. The awkward and ungainly chopping stride that would have been too long for a girl who cared to draw attention; the teeth that were too prominent in the front, aping the rabbit; the hair that was not tended; the clothes that were husbanded. Difficult to imagine her in David's front line, fighting his battles, setting out for combat where the intellectuals of their people had lost their way.

Come back to us, Rebecca; come back with the light wreathed round your face. Come back, girl, with that damned promise. What would they do, the pigs; what would they do to them in the police basement? What would they do if the smile was not on her face, if she had not won Yevsei, if there was no escape?

It was a hot night, but Isaac shuddered, and hunched forward with his body as if to draw toward himself the fragile heat of the shrinking flame.

Rebecca was haggard with exhaustion by the time she reached the hut in the woods at the first light of morning. Wednesday morning, and the day they had chosen for the breakout. No sleep during the night. Too late, by the time she had ditched Yevsei Allon, to get the bus that went far out of the city to the forests; too dangerous to go home in case the police and militia should come. So nothing to do but walk the streets, fearful of passing cars, anxious over the sound of footsteps behind her, shrinking into shadows and finally collapsing in a dazed and nervous rest on a park bench. Had taken the first bus of the day out, and then stumbled the long walk through the trees to the hut which had been silent and had seemed deserted till she had knocked softly and said her name and heard the movement inside that told her Isaac and David were there.

The relief had swept over their faces when she had said flatly, "It's all right; he'll do it. Someone, it had better be me, has to take the parcel to him at noon. He thinks it is books he is handling. But you have the guns?"

David had unwrapped them and laid them out on the board floor, and she had seen the killing weapons, and her face had screwed and compressed with the certain realization that the moment for turning back from their chosen course was now gone.

"Isaac and I will have these," said David, handling the submachine guns. "We understand them. For you there will be the policeman's pistol. It is enough for you."

"Where did you get them?" Rebecca asked, and there was wonderment in her voice, built from the uncertainty she had felt through the evening and the night that even if Yevsei agreed to handle the package there might be nothing to give him.

"There is a man I know. In his own way he fought the pigs, but many years ago, and he is now old and has no need of these things. He would want them to be used for the purpose for which he once had them. He gave them to us."

"And I have the tickets," said Isaac, pride on his face, ignoring the fact that he had told her his triumph the previous evening. "I thought there would be difficulties, and there were none, and the seats are confirmed. We are going to-night to the West, Rebecca. Tonight we sleep in peace, Re-becca."

And the three stood together in the center of the small room and held each other close and kissed each other's faces and there were tears that ran on their cheeks, and they clung hard to each other's bodies, willing the strength they needed to invest them all.

"But we were four, we must not forget that," Rebecca said. "We must not forget Moses. Wherever he is, whatever they have done to him, we must not forget Moses. If we weaken now, we betray him."

She had changed their mood, brought a somberness to them all, and the hugging excitement of a few moments ear-lier had evaporated. Like abandoning the wounded in battle, thought Isaac, to leave their friend. But what alternative had they? It was turning their backs, though, however they dis-guised it, papered it over. David said, "Rebecca, you must sleep now. If you don't, you will be useless to us, and half awake. You have time—three hours, four hours—before we go to the airport."

On the floor she tossed and turned the minutes away, striv-ing for comfort on the uneven boards, and her dreams were of the guns, and of the bullets, and of the blood that they could spill. She was alone while she slept, unaware that the others had gone, surreptitiously and with care, to their homes and to hers and that they had collected their personal-iden-tity cards, which David decreed should not be carried on their persons, but which they would need at the airport. Work and school and the morning shopping rounds had emp-tied the houses, and they came and went unobserved by their families.

It was Isaac who had remembered that they must produce the cards at the check barriers at the airport.

Luigi Franconi had lost his suitcase. Or rather, the porter's desk at the Hotel Kiev had lost it. All the baggage of the dele-gation had been put outside the room doors as requested and had been taken downstairs on the service elevators; all had appeared again beside the main swing doors, to be loaded onto the airport bus—all, that is, except the suitcase belonging to Luigi Franconi.

Outside on the street, the bus revved its engine, and the driver sounded his horn with impatience. The Party representative who acted as the delegation's guide, interpreter and way-smoother attempted to assure the unfortunate Franconi that if he traveled to Tashkent without his bag it would be sure to be found and would be sent on to him on the next flight. A totally unsuccessful effort, as the Assistant to the Foreign Policy Committee of the Partito Comunista Italiano was not to be budged with mere promises. Not till the other eight members of the PCI delegation touring the Soviet Union had joined in the angry chorus was there a sudden and exultant shout from the far side of the cavernous lobby area which signified the discovery of the errant piece of luggage nestling among the bags of the Rumanian football team that had just arrived.

There were more delays for a last rechecking of the baggage, and by the time the laden bus was on its way to the airport, it was running late. The members of the delegation were, to the distress of their guide, in poor humor, and Luigi Franconi, sitting alone in a window seat, was not one to show gratitude that his problem had been solved.

Edward R. Jones, Jr., and his wife, Felicity Ann, had been more circumspect in their travel arrangements and had left the Hotel Kiev on schedule a full twenty minutes before the Italians. But then, when you were on a free trip, and they always traveled on free trips, you went when the car came to collect you. His Russian hosts at the Cultural Section of the city's Party Administration had been puzzled by the use of the word "Junior" in his name and had found it strange that a man represented to them as a distinguished American poet with more than forty years of writing behind him should bother with such an appendage. That Edward R. Jones, Sr., had died in 1937 was known to them, because it figured on the visa applications that the couple had filled in; why this aging son should insist on using what they regarded as a child's title was confusing and baffling.

Edward and Felicity Ann had realized many years before that the best way to travel the world and enjoy their summer vacation was to spend their winter firing off letters that begged in their reply an invitation, and they had found their ploy remarkably successful. Leningrad, Kiev and Tashkent this year. Budapest at the invitation of the Hungarian Socialist International Writers Conference the year before. Two years ago an expenses-paid summons to a poetry seminar in Warsaw. Not that the hotels were especially good, and the restaurants were slothful and lifeless, but it was at least a plane ticket across the Atlantic and a month away from the suffocation of New York in high summer.

As the taxi made its way through the outer suburbs of the city, Felicity Ann mopped her forehead with a scented square of cotton. "I hope the plane's on time, dear," she said.

"If it is, it'll be the first one we've had, dear."

He did not seek the conversation with his wife. Talk was only a distraction from the task at hand: jotting the iambic pentameters of an ode on the back of a postcard. When it was completed, he would type it out on the portable Olivetti he always carried with him and post it to Valery Guizov, who headed the Department of Cultural Studies in the Ukraine. He'd found on earlier journeys that his hosts were quite touched by such a gesture and sometimes printed the work in a Party periodical.

On the last stretch to the airport now. The fifth-year schoolchildren who packed the bus had had the noise and argument bounced and melted out of them by the 225-mile drive from Lvov, on the Polish border. Silent and slumped in their seats, for which their teachers were grateful. Six hours, with thirty-eight children, they'd endured through all the usual gamut of threats and cajolery, and at last the little ones had succumbed to the jerking motion of the bus and the sun that pierced the curtainless windows. Ahead of them, an hour and a half of fractious hanging around at the terminal and then the tedium of the flight to Tashkent. More delays there, inevitable, before there was another bus to take them into the Kazakhstan city.

"If any of them have the strength to appreciate ballet, it will be a miracle," muttered the Headmaster, balding, sweating in his dark suit, bright tie knotted high, to his neighbor from the Art Department.

"Well, if they sleep right through it, at least the little monsters won't be fidgeting in their seats from halfway through the first act. Remember the ones last year. . . . But you wait and see; they'll sleep on the plane and be as awful as ever by tomorrow morning."

The Headmaster grimaced and settled once again into the pages of *Pravda*.

Other passengers for the 16:00 Aeroflot departure to Tashkent were already at the check-in counters: toeing their baggage forward; inching ahead with cloth-wrapped bundles, string bags and rope-fastened suitcases through a confusion of noise and objections and rancor.

David and Isaac among them.

Nervous, both of them, and sweaty. Nothing strange in that; nobody in the queue able to keep calm and avoid the perspiration that the minimal air-conditioning system did little to counter. Taking in the scene round them, looking with half-detached interest at the passengers who would share the plane with them, watching their stress and their push as they struggled to get nearer to the counter, another stage nearer the aircraft. Wry smile on Isaac's young face, and the whisper in David's ear: "Wouldn't be shoving so hard, not if they knew where they were going."

And for a reply, just a hushed "Shut up, you fool!" that telegraphed to Isaac that David was frightened and fighting to keep his control. Surprising, really, thought Isaac; wouldn't have expected that of David—nerves, yes, but not fear. Would have expected him to button it down, shrug off the pressure. Last night that was how he'd thought that he himself would feel now—frightened—but he wasn't. A little tense, fingers stiff, voice hoarse, tight in the guts, but nothing else; sort of distant from the whole thing. Not that he was worrying about David; he'd be all right once they had started, once they were in operation.

Isaac wondered how it would be there, what Israel would be like. Just a place that people talked about, dreamed about, but he'd never met anyone who'd been there, nor anyone who had achieved the exit visa. The way they spoke on the foreign radio you'd imagine anyone who applied could get the visa: just filling in a form, filing a piece of paper, packing up and going. As if they didn't know how many were refused, how they weeded out the ones they wanted to stay and how, if they turned you down, the pressures and persecutions built on your shoulders. Didn't know in the West; didn't know what it was like, the reality of Soviet Jewry.

And why was it important, this place, Israel? Different things to different people—that's obvious, Isaac. Well, for the old ones, for them there was the faith; just a chance to stand at the wall in Jerusalem, stand there and pray to their God. For others it was a place where a man could work and earn his money, and live his life and have no fear of the Party commissar and the Party spy. But for you—what does it mean for you, Isaac? A sort of freedom, that was what he was seeking; a freedom of choice. Not that he wanted a society of anarchists: just the freedom to join the system if he wanted to, an end to compulsion. So, he didn't really know. He'd have to find out, wouldn't he?

"Get the tickets." David close to him, and hissing the instruction, and his face set, controlling the mouth muscles. "The tickets; come on!"

"Where's Rebecca?" Isaac said as he pulled them from the inside pocket of his lightweight jacket.

"Coming from the far side, from the telephone. Give the girl the tickets."

Isaac could hear behind him the strident voice with its American accent, cutting across the other tongues. Not that he could understand the words—science at school, not languages. And beyond, and just surviving the drowning emphasis of the American, was a further babble, European and could be Spanish or French or Italian, but he could not gauge which.

The girl at the counter said, "Where's your baggage?"

Heads sagged. Something they hadn't thought about; so little time, and so much to think of, they hadn't considered the need for baggage. Who goes on a plane with no baggage? With a fourteen-day excursion ticket. They had gone home just for the identity cards, and not thought to empty a wardrobe, to throw clothes into a suitcase. People pushing behind them, and the American voice brimming with complaint, the girl waiting for an explanation.

"Our friend took it," said Isaac, with David still lost and

unable to conjure an explanation, "when he went earlier in the week." First thing that came into his head, first thing he could think of saying.

"For three of you? Hope he paid the excess." She ripped off the top coupon of their tickets, one by one. Gave them the boarding cards. Small and sparse scraps of thickened paper, flight number scrawled on them. "Gate Four you want. Through the departure door, then the security, and you wait in the lounge till they call you."

"Is the flight on time?" David asked.

But her attention was gone from him; he had lost to the succeeding client. She shrugged, didn't know.

The American couple took their places at the counter. Red trousers—well, red with a white check in them—and a faded cream jacket. The woman in mauve, her hair a delicate blued tint that caught Isaac's eye by its unfamiliarity. Why do they wear those clothes?—straight out of the cartoons in *Krokodil*.

Just security now, and nothing for them to find. Clean. Not a germ among them. Scrubbed and shining and polished, that was the way to go through security. David was talking to Rebecca, arm around her shoulders, heads near to touching, and she was showing him a piece of paper. Must have worked; must be where the guns were.

"There's time for coffee. At least ten minutes till we need to go through." David led and they followed over to the bar. Not that any of them was thirsty; not that they wanted to drink. But the process of ordering and paying and waiting for the coffee to be brought to the table, and then drinking—all that would use up time, time which they had no use for, time which had to be exhausted. Should have told our parents, Isaac thought; should have said something to them. They should know what has happened, and why it has happened, before the time the police arrive. He excused himself and rose from the table and went to the small shop where there were magazines and newspapers, postcards and cigarettes and souvenirs of Kiev. He asked for some notepaper and an envelope, but the man insisted on selling him a whole pad of notepaper and two dozen envelopes because that was the way it was packaged. There was no option, so he paid for them all and took them back to the table.

"I think we should write something to our people. It will be long over by the time it reaches them." There was agreement, and for five minutes, silence, no talk at the table, all writing their farewells and justifications.

> Esteemed and respected Father and Mother and dear Sisters,
>
> By the time you read this you will have heard of our actions. You must forgive us the danger and hurt they may cause you. We have taken this course because of what we saw as the persecution of our people in this land. If we had stayed the police would have taken us, and for what we have done there is only one sentence, and there would have been no possibility of mercy. Our air tickets have been purchased with money from Isaac's mother, who paid for the three of us without knowing for what reason her money was wanted. From the family savings please send her one hundred and seventy-four rubles. Rebecca will request her family to do the same. We hope to be in Israel very soon. We hope it will be possible for you to join us there.
>
> There is much to say and little time. All so difficult to explain. We started because we believed in our actions, but we did not know where they would leave us. We still do not know.
>
> Be brave.
>
> Your loving son, who will not forget you,
>
> David.

After she and Isaac had written similar letters, Rebecca took the three sealed and addressed envelopes to the post-office counter for the stamps while David and Isaac stayed at the table waiting for her. When she came back, the three of them walked toward the departure doors, leaving the almost full pad and the twenty-one envelopes beside the coffee cups which had remained untouched while they wrote.

Abruptly Rebecca tugged at David's arm, pulled him closer to her as they crossed the concourse.

"What will they do to them, when we have gone?"

He didn't look at her, fastened his gaze on the doorway ahead. "I don't know." A lie, and he could not meet her eyes.

"Will they be punished for what we have done? They have punished others. . . ."

"What they will do to them will be as nothing to what will happen to us if we stay."

"Do you care what happens to them, David?"

"I care more what happens to my parents than you are concerned with the fate of Yevsei Allon. Think of that."

Her hand flew from his sleeve, leaving him free to walk on unimpeded. If Isaac had heard, he showed no sign of it; stern-faced, regular stride. All three of them making their way across the tiled floorway.

Beyond the doors there was an airline official, bored and uninterested, who checked their tickets and the boarding passes and matched their names written there against the plastic-coated identity cards, not troubling to compare the photographs with their faces. Farther on, the high arch through which passengers had to pass and which showed whether they carried metallic objects in their pockets. This was the realm of the Frontier Guards, with pistols hanging on their hips and wearing clean uniforms with wide-peaked caps. The man in front of them was stopped when the small green light which the guardsman watched changed abruptly to flashing red, and his body was searched till a cigarette pack was retrieved from his trousers and he was shown the foil wrapping that had activated the detector. Isaac said to himself, Thank God we carried nothing. Then it was their turn, and the light stayed green, and they walked past the guard, and on.

All of them braced, shoulders stiffened as if to ward off a blow, as if expecting the shout from behind. But there was none. Just a sun-filled lounge, with the ashtrays overflowing and paper on the floor, and dust and grime, and children running and shouting between the wooden benches, and a teacher's command. Across the room from them were the windows through which all could see the tidy, painted profile of the Ilyushin 11 18V turboprop airliner, due to depart for Tashkent in thirty-five minutes.

In a tight phalanx the little group approached the forward steps of the aircraft. All of them sweating from the slight exertion of the walk across the apron. The captain to the front, straight-backed, gray hair thinning, uniform pressed, rank connoted by the gold stripes sewn to his tunic sleeve, carrying his cap carelessly in his hand. A pace behind him the navigator, with his briefcase filled with the maps that covered the air routes of the southern area of the Soviet Union over which they would fly to Tashkent. Alone, not seeming to wish to engage in conversation with her male flight-deck companions, was the copilot. Anna Tashova, skirt riding high on her knees as she maintained their pace. She felt once at the knot of her thin black tie; unnecessary and unfeminine she thought it, but if it was decreed that it should be worn, then it was her obligation to make certain that it bisected her collar with precision. The two flight stewardesses, acknowledging they were not a part of the cockpit club, came last, flight bags on their shoulders, talking of men, and prices, and hotels, and the boredom of it all.

At the bottom of the forward steps the captain waited, a fixed smile on his face, for the young technician in coveralls to hurry down the stairs. The boy should have waited for them, should not have obstructed and delayed their boarding. Seemed in a rush, and bounced against the captain's shoulder. No apology, just something mumbled from behind his teeth.

"Dirty little bastard," the captain said. "Soap and water, but perhaps he's never heard of them. That's all you need for a face like that."

The navigator laughed cheerfully, all the more for the sneer of distaste on the copilot's small mouth as if the retreating, jogging boy had left an odor behind which would contaminate all of them.

"We'll be off on time today, sir."

"Well, don't blame me for it. Accidents happen even to the best of us."

More smiles, and a moment of gallantry from the men. Stepping aside that Anna Tashova and the stewardesses should be first on the steps.

The major of the Committee of State Security—KGB— worked from a smaller and less imposing building than his colleague in the militia security police. The address was not listed in the telephone directory and was known only to those civilians who had a need for the knowledge. The major was a frugal man who seldom took more than thirty minutes for his lunch, but since the arrest of Moses Albyov and his subsequent suicide he had not left his office, sleeping the previous two nights on an army bed that graced one corner of the room.

At half past three the gray telephone on his desk, the direct line that bypassed the switchboard, rang out. A short message and from militia headquarters.

The Jew had been identified.

Quite clever, really. The photograph they had taken of him showed indentations at the sides of his face from the earpieces of eyeglasses—recent enough, but not worn when he had been brought in. One of the patrolmen from the car had said he might have been wearing them when he was taken; and the wounded one's description on which the arrest had been made, that had included glasses. They had found them in the gutter where the street sweeper had pushed them, and the luck was that the lenses were still intact. The major had been kind enough to say that it would be police work that would identify the boy, and that was what it had been. A photograph of the glasses, an analysis of the lenses, a photograph of the boy and twenty-five detectives touring the city's eye clinics. Faster than doing it with the teeth—fewer eyeglass wearers than those requiring extractions and fillings.

And now they had a name and were cross-checking with the dossier of the statutory civil authority. Moses Albyov, residing at 428B Avenue of the First of May. He was told it was a workers' quarter in the northern suburbs; was informed also that there was no previous record of violence, and that two cars had left for the address and would be there within a quarter of an hour. Smash the little bastards, he thought; smash them till they screamed like the rats they were. Not long till they'd have their hands on them; the Albyov parents would tell of the associates; they would have them all in the cells by the pencil line of dawn.

No delays on the departure of Aeroflot flight 927 to Tashkent. On time, on schedule. The passengers walking in untidy caterpillar file out across the tarmac, the hundred yards to the plane. Heat streaming back at them from the great open surface, burning through the soles of their footwear, driving their eyes together, with everything beyond the middle distance dissolving into a heat haze of obscurity.

"The seats run ABC down one side of the aisle and DEF on the other," David said to Isaac. Near the plane now and walking to the rear exit, where the steps had been wheeled up and there was an angle of shade thrown by the single high tail structure. "Yevsei told Rebecca the package would be on the right-hand side, level with the nineteenth row, and would be under the blankets—the blankets they store in the luggage shelf at the top. We must get on the plane quickly, before the herd, so that one of us can sit in that row. I'll try and see that it's me. When I take the package, I'll go to the toilet at the back to assemble them. Give me two minutes; then come and knock at the door. We'll go quite soon—after ten minutes, when the seat-belt sign is off."

David was the first up the steps, Isaac close behind, Rebecca separated by a dozen passengers. He climbed steadily, taking the steps one at a time, his speed dictated by the pace of those in front. To any passenger who glanced casually among his fellow travelers, David would have aroused no particular interest, the inner tensions successfully masked. He seemed confident, relaxed as he ducked his head through the low doorway and hesitated for a moment, sizing up the long cigar interior of the plane with the robin's-egg decor and green-backed seats that stretched away from him to the distant cream-painted door that was half ajar and through which he could see the silhouettes of the shoulders of pilot and co-pilot. Isaac nudged him, and he walked down the aisle, noting the row numbers. Row 19, aisle seat C. Isaac opposite him, row 19, aisle seat D. The package would be above Isaac, and the boy hadn't looked for it, was settling in his seat, fastening the belt, and with his back in the cushion at the top. Rebecca stooping into her place, four rows in front, but not turning to see them, and then he lost sight of her as intervening passengers surged the long length of the cabin in a steady clamor of excitement and protest. It was what he had heard, that people always suffer stress before takeoff and before landing; makes them raise their voices, and push with aggression in a way they would not contemplate if their feet were grounded. David fastened his seat belt and looked across at Isaac.

"Courage, my friend," he said.

"Not courage. It is the time for luck now." Isaac closed his eyes, waited for the motion of the plane to tell him they were taxiing.

Five minutes they'd been in the house. Time enough for them to recognize the stark terror on the faces of the father and mother of Moses Albyov before the truncheon in her lower abdomen and the pistol whipping across his face had delivered them the names of David and Isaac and Rebecca. One policeman stayed in the living room covering with his drawn pistol the woman who cowered in the covered chair and clutched herself and moaned and the man lying still on the floor with the blood running from the head wound and laying its trail across the baldness of the linoleum surface. Another had gone to his car to radio to headquarters the fruits of the visit. Six more, packed close together, were speeding toward the home of the one called David, the one the woman had said she had gone to visit the morning before to ask the whereabouts of her son.

Some hundreds of yards short of the address of David that they had been given, the driver of the police car silenced the siren that he had used to clear a path through the traffic, and when they staggered to a halt, his foot hard on the brake pedal, there was a swift and often-rehearsed routine for them to follow. Two running for the back, jumping the wire fence, then crouching low, their guns aimed at the rear door. Two more at the front, and behind the car, to give themselves cover. The remaining two, an officer and one who was brave, chancing their luck at the door. "Shoot him if he has a gun. Without hesitation. Remember what Albyov did, and remember this is one of them."

David's mother alone in the house, answering the hammering at the door. Younger children still in school, husband at work, without protection as the officer forced her against the old wooden sideboard that had long since lost its varnish, knee hard against her thigh so that the carved angle bit into her side. There was no reason to strike her; she talked without resort to violence. Too much for her, after a year in Treblinka and not knowing why she was never called to the showers; no resistance left, not to a man in uniform who carried a gun, and who shouted and who wore boots that reached to the knee. She had submitted before and would do so again: nothing changed; renewal of a nightmare. She told them of her son's friends, showed them which was he in the family photograph, said he hadn't been home the previous night.

At militia headquarters they believed in the power of routine. Three names; photographs that would chase them when the cars came in from the homes and when Central Records turned up the files. All standard and routine. Just as it was routine to call the airport with the names, and the principal Aeroflot ticket offices, and to send descriptions to the railway station and the bus terminal by the square with the granite war memorial. All routes of exit from the city were notified with Priority messages. And because the computer of the central Aeroflot offices was repaired and functioning, that was the source of the first hard information. The message rattled back over the teleprinter—three names, three tickets, flight number, takeoff time, destination. All being controlled from the second-floor operations center of the militia headquarters, fast, quiet, efficient: a trained team that was good at its work, and was producing a scent, and believed that the kill was close.

A call to the airport, routed through the offices of the Frontier Guard control point, to the commander of the unit who had responsibility for all matters affecting security. A second call to the control tower.

"Aeroflot flight 927 to Tashkent has been airborne nine minutes, close to ten," the Frontier Guard commander reported back to the control room. Verified by the tower.

"Then tell the control tower to radio the pilot, order him to return. Tell him the passengers should be informed there is a technical difficulty. When the plane lands, I want every man you have around it. Nobody gets off, not till we arrive."

"Do you want the pilot to be told that this is a security matter?"

"Why not?"

Down in the yard, the black Moskva car had been alerted; it waited with its engine idling for the sprinting figure of the Colonel of Militia.

They were climbing in light cloud when Yuri Zibov—eighteen years an Aeroflot pilot and most of them on the lumbering Ilyushin 11 18V, and before that Yak bombers in the air force—received the recall order. He motioned to his co-pilot—young, feminine, petite, a hint of lipstick and as many flying qualifications as her male equivalents. Had she understood the message? A nodded head. Zibov turned to the navigator, sitting behind. He also had understood. Into the microphone that jutted out from his headset and that rested three-quarters of an inch from his mouth, he said, "Bolt the cockpit door. Just a precaution, but fasten it; then we'll swing."

The navigator started to intone the statistics that would govern their change of course.

David was groping with his arms into the recess of the shelf where he could not see, even as he stretched upward, reliant on the touch of his fingers to tell him if the package was there. Fumbling among the softness of the blankets and the pillows, scratching with his fingers and seeking for the hard shape. Not there, not above row 19—and in a driving and frantic motion his hands spilled out to right and left, and he was high on his toes, and the passenger who had the seat beside him was staring and wondering and was interested. Almost at the moment of panic when his hands locked onto the ungiving shape of the parcel. Must have slipped backward because of the takeoff angle, he thought. Right over row 20, and low-voiced apology to the seated neighbor who was leaning back in his seat with his legs bent sidewise to give David room. He lifted it down. Just as they had wrapped it, right down to the knots in the string; not tampered with. Package under his arm and lurching a way through to the rear, to the bolted security of the lavatories, and a half-turn to be certain that Isaac was watching him; the gleam of recognition that told him Isaac was ready, coiled, anticipating. Had to push past the two stewardesses—blue uniforms, crumpled shirts, hair wisping from buns, minimum of makeup—preparing the food trolley and drinks. No alcohol on board—mineral water and orange juice and coffee. Reluctant to step aside and let him pass, an obstruction when they were trying to work, seeming to say why couldn't he have gone in the terminal lavatories?

He slammed the door shut behind him. Ran the catch across. Began to tear at the paper and the string binding; pulled at the cardboard that had given the parcel the rectangular shape, had made Yevsei believe it was indeed a mass of books that he had handled. The parcel spilled open, pitching the handgun onto the floor beside the toilet, where he let it lie while he unwrapped the further protection around the two submachine guns. Lovely babies. Sweet, keen, pretty things, but already taking on the ugliness of their trade as the barrel symmetry was broken when he fastened the magazines right-angled to the bodies. One at a time, and take it slowly; remember the drill with the old man, with Timofey. Never hurry in the preparation of weapons, he had said. The loud rasping of the cocking mechanism—devastating how the noise reverberated inside the confined space; then check that the safety is on. Same for the pistol when he stooped low; arm it, then ensure its safety. No accidents—not in a capacity-filled airliner; not when the pressure of the cabin will soon be in jeopardy.

Abruptly he lunged to the side, cannoning into the wall-fitted basin, knee ramming against the rim of the toilet seat, thrown off balance by the sudden shift in direction of the plane as the pilot banked to begin the long turn that would bring the aircraft back to Kiev. David's mind was razor-sharp, honed by suspicion, and he was still regaining his balance when there was Isaac's voice muffled by the closed door; dispute with the stewardesses, and they retorting angrily that the seat-belt signs were illuminated again, that he should return to his place. Over the intercom, which had its own loudspeaker in the lavatory: "This is Captain Zibov, your pilot. Sorry, but we seem to have some minor technical problem that necessitates our return to Kiev. It is nothing that should concern you, but we must land again and the fault must be repaired. Please fasten your belts again, and no more smoking. I hope the delay will be short. Thank you." Warning bells, cymbal-loud. Not good enough, you pigs. Has to be wrong, phony; too controlled, too much coincidence. Must not land, not at any cost.

David pulled the door open. Submachine gun in each hand, pistol in the belt of his trousers, he careered straight into the gray-metaled drinks trolley; heaved with a desperation to free himself from the obstruction; saw the faces turning, the necks twisting, the saucer eyes that were below him and that repeated into the infinity distance of the cabin; and

was clear and sprinting. Isaac in front of him, standing, waiting. Shared anxiety; had read the same message from the
pilot's announcement and the tilting of the plane. Ready to
receive with outstretched arm the weapon that would be his.
Drumming feet as they ran down the thinly carpeted aisle.
Unaware of everything now, of the passengers, of cabin crew,
everything except the damned door of the cockpit. David
rammed his right shoulder into it, expecting it to give. His
face wreathed in amazement as it flung him back. The old
David, the man of decision and fight, who had brought them
together, armed and aimed them. The old David who should
have told Rebecca to go and scratch herself with her damned
twigs, who should have vetoed the use of Moses in the attack.
The old David, whom Isaac, two paces behind, would follow
as far as he was led. Submachine gun held low and away from
his body, and the flash and explosion that drove at their ear-
drums as he fired into the center of the door.

"Open or it's machine-gun fire! Open or I kill the whole
fucking lot of you!" Voice at screaming pitch. "Open the
fucking thing!" There was a hesitation, seemed endless, was
in fact little more than three seconds, and the bolt was withdrawn, the door opened.

So small in the cockpit, a tiny space, like the lavatory, like
a box room, and three persons already strapped and har-
nessed in their seats. Saw the pilot, saw the copilot. A
woman—David noticed that because she was the one who
had turned her head toward them. Then his eyes were riveted
to the mass of dials and buttons, the instrument boards. Find
the altimeter, that was the first thing. Had to be certain they
weren't losing height; had to climb, had to get up . . . after
that the time to set a course.

"Take the damned thing up," he yelled, and pushed sidewise with the gun barrel at the pilot's shoulder; aware there
had been no response; still staring at the bewildering array of
controls, searching for the magic of the altimeter.

Isaac said, and his voice was very quiet, like a desert wind
that murmurs and that can be felt but scarcely noticed,
"You're wasting your time, David. No point shouting at him.
You've killed him."

David stepped back, peering at the pilot held upright in his
cockpit straps. Witnessed the neat expertise of the drilled

hole at the back of the skull where the circumference showed clear against the short-cropped graying hair, and the river path of blood that had traversed the short slope to the uniform collar and the white shirt. He arched his body round toward the expanded exit hole where the woodwork had been forced out from the door by his bullet. Eyes rolled back again and via the instrument panels to the copilot. The noise and venom gone from him, replaced by a vague aloofness, like a schoolmaster in a laboratory talking to students.

"What's your name?" he asked, almost conversational, polite interest.

"Anna Tashova, pilot officer."

"You will ignore all instructions. Get the plane up now, get it high, and a course to the West. We want a course to the nearest frontier of the West. And know this. I do not know about flying; I have never piloted an aircraft; but I think I would know if you deceive me. If you seek to trick us, Miss Anna Tashova, then I will kill you, and if you die then so does everyone on board the aircraft. We are Jews, Miss Tashova, and the days when we could be told that we were going for a warm shower to shed ourselves of lice are long gone. Do not test us, Miss Tashova; today we are a harder people."

She did not fight him, forbore to play games, recognized her responsibilities. "The tower is talking to us. They are directing us to return to Kiev. What do you want me to tell them?" Calm, with a brusqueness in her voice, as if in a committee meeting, secretary taking a note.

"You say nothing; you ignore them. Let them shout and let them bluster. They can do nothing."

He watched her hands, moving with a nimbleness and deftness over the scores of buttons and switches in front of and beside her, never allowing herself a glance toward the dead captain. Saw the preparations until she was ready to move her hands, both together, onto the control lever in front of her knees; heard the navigator who was beside him calling his lists of numbers and figures that represented a path through the airways. And there was the sensation, felt through his feet and the angle of the floor, that they were climbing.

Possible for him to look now, without the courage to stem the curiosity and fascination. Possible for him to gape at the occasionally lolling, drifting head of the first man he had killed. And he had bickered with Isaac that first evening, snapped at him because the boy had used the word "easy." What was more facile than this? Not a moment's thought demanded, not an intention, not a program, not a plotting. Just the tightening of a finger knuckle. Nothing more. A man dead that David might go free. A life ended that David might live. The pilot officer involved in the work he had set her, the navigator concerned and stretched by his task. Only David and the captain who had no immediate function. But it had not been intended—not to kill him, not that he should die. He does not listen, David. He does not heed you. He will not turn to hear your explanation. He is removed from your apology, your regret, David. Now you must live with it, David. Coexist with the rolling scalp. Live with it, lest he destroy you.

Soaring, heaving upward, the Kingfisher bird escaping her enemies. Full power given to the four Ivchenko Al-20 engines, reaching for her operational altitude of twenty-seven thousand feet, fuel tanks loaded to a capacity of five thousand two hundred imperial gallons, offering a range of minimally less than two thousand miles with the cover of one hour's clear reserve.

Rising as she banked, and finding her new course, the Kingfisher of old Timofey, far below and unaware in his forest retreat.

5

In the control tower that dwarfs the low-slung, white-painted cement of the airport terminal buildings, the traffic controllers were quick to observe the change of course of the Ilyushin. For a full minute the Frontier Guard commander demanded of the man who wore the headphones and who had been talking to the crew of Aeroflot 927 that he continue repeating the instruction that the aircraft should respond to its order and return to Kiev.

The controller did not turn to his superior, hovering at his shoulder; just repeated, because that was all that was required of him, "There is nothing, sir. No response. They are ignoring us. Nothing since the second pilot reported the shooting, that the captain had been hit and incapacitated."

"But the plane is still operational; it is not flying on automatic controls?"

To men of lesser importance than the Frontier Guard commander the controller would have been scornful of such lack of knowledge, but he answered with politeness, "There can be no question of that, sir. The maneuvers it has made are not those of a plane flying remote. It must be the copilot who is handling the aircraft, and she is working now to orders; that must be the assumption. The planes are dual; she would have no difficulty in piloting on her own—only if she has to land by herself, and if she were tired and under stress."

"What is the course?" The Frontier Guard commander could feel the initiative slipping from him; he was losing whatever tenuous control he had once had on the aircraft; the umbilical was breaking.

"Toward southern Poland, and climbing. Ultimately such a line as they now hold will bring them into the airspace of West Germany. Perhaps two hours' flying time." He was the uninvolved one, in the easy and comfortable chair, cocooned from responsibility and in the grandstand seat to watch what his betters would make of it.

"And again, what was the last message?"

"As I told you, sir. They reported the bolting of the door. They reported they were responding to instructions to return. They reported a shot being fired at the door, that the bullet penetrated the door and struck the captain—that is Captain Zibov. They reported the impression that he was killed instantly. They reported that they were being threatened with machine-gun fire unless they opened the door, and they reacted to that threat. There is no option; you must understand that, sir." As if fearful that the military would have no knowledge of the reality of an aircraft cockpit, and the weight of the burden of the lives of a cabin full of passengers. "Not when you have such a confined space as the flight deck; the damage could have been very great. Since the opening of the door we have had vague shouts, which I could not distinguish. That will be on the tapes, but to us they were not clear; perhaps you will be able to decipher them. Pilot Officer Tashova has identified herself to the hijackers, if that is what they are; she has told them that we are talking to her and requesting her to return. There has been nothing since that."

The Guard commander finished the scribbled note. He reached for the desk telephone and dialed militia headquarters. Operations Room patched the call through to the telephone in the back of the car that was bringing the militia colonel toward the airport. The situation was relayed, the number of the nearest direct line to the Guard commander was passed on, the call was terminated.

The communications of the Russian internal security services had long been a source of justifiable pride, much admired by their opposite traders in the West; the colonel was able to reach within seconds a senior official of the Ministry of the Interior in central Moscow. He was connected directly to the Minister—one of the four most important personages in the Soviet Union, and the one who at that moment had the power and the full authority to make decisions on the future flying of Aeroflot 927. The colonel's role in the immediate course of the incident was completed. During the subsequent two minutes, radio and telephone conversations were activated from the seat of government to the air-force base

that lies close to the small town of Chernigov, due north of
Kiev. The order for the moment was short, spring-water
clear. The Ilyushin 11 18V should be forced to land within
Russian territory.

In a flight of four, the Mig-23s lifted off. Two pairs, match-
ing and racing each other down the runway till they had
achieved takeoff speed and in an explosion of aviation-fuel
fumes, and with sheets of flame spewing from the rear engine
vents, were airborne. These were not the low-level ground-
support aircraft with the North European Theater camouflage motif, but the silver-fuselaged altitude interceptors that
were held far to the rear of the Cold War front.

Closing into diamond formation as they climbed, capable
of eighteen hundred miles an hour in flight, code-named by
NATO planners "Foxbat" and an unmerciful over-match for
the lumbering, hesitant, stricken, clumsy airliner to which
those same planners had given the title of "Coot." Four
sharks that had the scent of blood and offal and were hunting, thrusting their way into the upper atmosphere where
they would poise themselves, bide their time till ground control gave them the precious radar bearings that they would
need, so that the instrumentation could be locked onto the
quarry. Young men at the controls, little older than David
and Isaac, but the elite of the society they served, on whom
money and expertise and time had been lavished that their
effectiveness would be guaranteed. The sun burnished a reflection off the cropped, sharpened delta wings as they
banked to take up the level flight that meant they had
achieved the necessary altitude, in excess of forty-five thousand feet, that when they came for the airliner they would be
diving. Cannon belt loaded in the wings, and slung below the
heat-seeking snap-down missiles. Lethal and vicious, with no
morality of their own, without an opinion on their orders,
and now responding to instructions, feeding the information
into their transistorized computer workings. Beginning the
search for a creature that by comparison was unworthy of
their strength, a lamed and limping prey.

David was still in the cockpit.
With the barrel of his submachine gun, Isaac shooed the

stewardesses back toward the main passenger cabin, gesturing them toward vacant seats, telling them to sit and to fasten their belts. Time now to see whom they had on board, to evaluate the passengers. Stunned they seemed, most of them; all staring at him till he caught the individual pairs of eyes, which then looked away as if terrified by what they saw and unwilling to recognize the reality of the moment.

He shouted the length of the cabin, that those at the back, seventy-five feet from him, might hear and understand and have no doubt as to his intent. "All your hands on your heads. If you do as you are instructed, then no harm will come to you. But you must obey our orders, and without hesitation. All hands on your heads." And he felt a curious thrill at the depth of his voice that echoed back at him, drowning the monotonous roar of the engine power. Some reacting immediately, some so confused that they had to have the instruction repeated by those who sat beside them. Old hands that were weatherbeaten and vein-ribbed and on which there were heavy gold rings, hands that were used to manual work and which showed calluses and worn skin as they were lifted. Hands that were manicured and had no bruises; hands that were young and pink and undeveloped. The small hands of the children reaching up to the well-washed hair of their heads. That was how he was first aware of the school party. Hadn't seen them before, not to register, hidden away behind their seats till their hands came up, with the popping eyes and the wide-opened mouths.

Surprised in a way that there wasn't more hostility on the faces, but not once he'd thought about it—not he they were frightened of, not little Isaac, not a student, with a hole in his shoe, and underpants changed once a week, and the shirt with the collar button off. It was the gun in his hands that brought the submission and the obedience and the respect for his orders. Not for yourself; kick your balls halfway to Khabarovsk if you gave them the chance. The gun, that was his protection.

Isaac moved warily down the aisle, Rebecca walking backward behind him, covering the passengers who could have turned to face his retreating back. About sixty of them in all, he reckoned—not an exact count, but good enough for his needs. All of them waiting on him; all of them waiting for the explanation that would clarify the gunshot, and the lurches in the direction of the plane, and the sight of the young man with the curly hair and the shabby clothes who carried the submachine gun at his hip, whose thumb was on Safety, whose forefinger was abreast of the trigger guard. The full length of the plane he walked, sometimes reaching with his free hand to steady himself as the aircraft pitched and fell away. His arm then close to heads that shriveled away from him. Checked the lavatories; both empty, bar the one strewn with the paper that had wrapped the firearms. A good precaution—necessary to make certain no hero of the Soviet Union was hiding there looking for a Red Star to be pinned posthumously on his coffin. Clean at the back of the plane. All passengers and crew in their seats and where they should be, neat and tidy and packaged. Called Rebecca forward, so that she could stand in the stewardesses' province, away from the passengers and close to the rear exit door. He pulled the soft-drinks trolley across the aisle where the rear row of seats ended and the galley area began. Gave free space for Rebecca to stand, and a degree of protection if he left her there. Made a barricade for her to shelter behind, the bottles rattling and chinking together in protest as he moved the obstacle into position.

"You're going to be at this end, Rebecca, and for much of the flight. I'll be at the front with David—him in the cockpit and me mostly watching the passengers. If they turn round to stare at you, order them back, to look to the front. Don't talk to them; don't start speaking to them—nothing at least till we're over the West."

"What's at the front? David was shouting."

"Nothing now. The shot that he fired to get the door opened, it's killed the pilot. The copilot is flying now."

"Oh, my God, oh, my God . . ."

"He didn't mean to; it was an accident." Her head was down on her chest. Eyes bagged and sacked and exhausted, all in, beaten. And David half out of his mind and screaming up there in the front. On your own, Isaac, and where to turn to for the reinforcements? "Take a grip, Rebecca." He snarled the words at her. "Remember why we're here, what we came for, and if another of the pigs gets in the way, tries anything, attempts what the pilot did, you shoot him. You know that, you understand that." Saw his failure, and the unreasoned rejection of what he said. And then more gently, and with the smile: "It's not long from now; just a few hours, two or three, and then we land. Then it's the refuel, and on to Israel." He took her left hand, closed it in his own, small and buried and cold and without response, trying to impart his own strength, trying to hide his own fear, then walked down the length of the aisle again toward the cockpit. Forty-eight paces, that was the length of their castle, battened down and with the hatches fastened, wondering again how was David. He turned to face the passengers.

"Ladies and gentlemen, you have nothing to be afraid of from us. We are taking this plane to the West. We will be there soon, and then you will be rid of us, free to return wherever you may wish. I must tell you that my friends and I have no life left inside the Soviet Union—we have nothing to return to except a death sentence. I must tell you that because you have to know that we will die in this rather than return to Kiev. If there is any resistance, any attempt to disarm us, we will shoot and that will endanger the safety of the aircraft—and of you, of all of you. Later in the flight we will tell you more. For now you must remain seated, remain with your hands on your heads, and you must not talk. That is all." Another speech, Isaac, another audience. It seemed so inadequate, so divorced from the wood hut, and the faint light of evening when they met there, and the plans to conquer the system that they hated. But then, there were so many things that had not been prepared; freewheeling, really, with the engine disengaged, but the hill was steep and there was no braking now.

No murmur greeted his words—not of appreciation, not of condemnation; just soaked them up like so many sponges as they stayed in their seats, hands static on their heads. Nothing to please him, nothing to anger him. Nothing.

A brisk little face she had. Pale, and smooth-skinned, with a pittance of makeup, and severe bobbed cut to her hair. Eyes that flitted over her instruments and that were sharp and a deep honey brown. When Anna Tashova smiled, the lines at her mouth were clearly drawn, without byways and meanders. Not a smile of pleasure, or of satisfaction. A smile of triumph and of victory. David saw it, saw the way she half-turned to her right, and broke his steady concentration on

the half cloud and the hazed horizon to the front, turned
instead to follow her glance to the starboard cockpit window.
They were flying very close, the Migs. The nearest, some fifty
feet from the outer point of the Ilyushin's wing, had crept
forward with a stealth that had deceived him, and beyond the
closest of the fighters another, in such proximity that the two
seemed nestled together. United, close enough for him to see
the pilots, to identify the numbers of their machines that
were painted on the slender noses, to witness the menace of
the rockets hung beneath the wings.

The pilot officer pushed the microphone mouthpiece away
from her lips. "They are on the other side as well. They have
come to take us home."

David could see the gestures of the pilot on the port side,
the motions of his gloved hand, that they should turn, retrace
their path toward Kiev.

"They will have orders," Anna Tashova said. "They will
bring us down if we do not comply. What do you want? Is it a
plane full of dead passengers? Does that serve your cause?"

The lead portside plane, the one whose pilot had made the
arm movement, inched its way forward. Strange, really, and
the effect upon David was hypnotic, compulsive, the way it
could move so delicately, a beast of such power yet held to a
fingertip control that permitted it to nudge, foot by foot, into
the airspace almost immediately in front of the Ilyushin.

"He will slow now, force me to lose thrust and altitude if I
am to avoid him. It is an accepted procedure." Jet interceptor
and airliner, the gap closing between them. An inevitable
course they were following—collision course, midair, frag-
mentation, breakup. Fascinating for him to watch, crawling
toward the impact. A distant shrieking bending through his
ears, like wind in the roof eaves in a storm, and Isaac was
beating at his shoulder.

"David, what are we doing, what are you telling the pilot?
The Migs have come."

A deeper, more general noise from behind, which took him
a moment to understand and then was clear as the hysteria of
the passengers. Predictable, and he knew the course he would
take.

"You fly on"—flat and without emotion, speaking to the
pilot officer, ignoring Isaac.

"Then you have collision; is that what you want?" Strain bouncing in her voice. The first time. Turning hesitantly from the cockpit window and the great shape that masked her view to the pallid closed features of the young man at her back, with the gun loose in his hands.

"There will be no collision. Fly on. Remember your responsibilities, and they are your passengers too." He turned to Isaac now. "They are trying to force us down, and we will not respond. I believe they will not risk more, and soon we shall see." So close now that both could see the huge chasm of the interceptor's rear exhaust, blackened and flame-charred. And the distance narrowing the whole time, second by second, foot by foot, and the pilot officer's hands beginning to waver above her controls. "Do not touch them. Touch them and I shoot."

"If they have orders to bring us down, that will be sufficient. They have rockets, you can see for yourself, and they will have cannon. They can bring us down if—"

"Who is listening on our radio? Who can hear us?" The luster was back in his voice; he too was rejoicing in the power he had accumulated, as Isaac had done moments before, drinking deep in the new sensation of achieving the kernel of events.

"Half the world can listen to you when you talk from an airplane cockpit." The moment of triumph lost, dissipated by her assessment of the man with the gun, and of his madness, fanaticism, determination. At the briefings in Moscow, the antihijack briefings, they had spoken of two types—those seeking a ride out and those yearning for a wider audience. The second grouping, they had said, was the one to be feared, to be nervous of. "At this speed, we collide; ten seconds more—that is all. I must reduce speed. I have to—"

"It will be they who increase speed. I want to use the radio. I want to speak." Radio silence so far, he had noted that much; not even talking to the navigator. No conversation with the airliner from the jets—serve to make it all public, wouldn't it? Confirmed what she'd said, that half the world could hear him now, half the world listening, and wondering why a plane was off route, out of the lanes and of the corridors. One hundred and fifty feet in front and fractionally above was the tail of the lead Mig, and the escorts closer to the wings, crowding them, hemming them, boxing them in, and at three hundred and thirty miles an hour as they flew four clear miles above the Russian plains.

Headphones pushed down into his hair, microphone across his mouth, and instructing her to activate it, and all the time the barrel of the gun close to her side and his finger by the trigger.

"This plane is now under the command of a Jewish Resistance Commando. We have taken Aeroflot Flight 927, Kiev to Tashkent, and we go to the West. Our final destination is Israel. The pilot of the aircraft is dead, and his colleague, Pilot Officer Anna Tashova, is flying. I hold a submachine gun to her body. We have an escort of Mig-23 fighters who are trying to make us land. We have told Miss Tashova that if she follows their instructions then we shoot her. We are prepared to die, and if we shoot her then the plane will surely crash. There are many passengers on board. We call this flight the 'Kingfisher'—that is our name for it. There will be no more broadcasts from the aircraft until we are beyond the borders of the Soviet Union and her Socialist allies." Short and staccato sentences, but the whole spoken slowly, mindful of radio operators bowing over their sets in many countries, ensuring that the message was clear, understood.

The Mig immediately ahead abruptly surged clear of their path, climbing beyond David's vision, and the wing-tip escort banked away.

"They are not finished," Anna Tashova said. "They are maneuvering to shoot at us."

The screaming in the passenger cabin behind David and Isaac had not lasted for many seconds, stifled by the very helplessness of those who had no role to play but as witnesses. What point in pleading when there was no one to answer? The girl was far back at the rear of the plane, and none dared turn to see her. The man, the short one, the one who had addressed them, hovered half in and half out of the cockpit. The other man was long gone from view and busying himself with the direction of the aircraft. Those at the windows had the best view of the gleaming Migs, and they saw from the gestures of the pilots that this was a time of crisis.

Luigi Franconi had won the courage to ignore the instruc-

tion that his hands should be on his head. They covered his
eyes as he crouched low in the seat, shutting out the fantasy
nightmare of the killing machines that cruised so calmly and
that so ostentatiously displayed their rockets. Knew what they
were for, and knew also the determination in the young
man's face, the one who covered them with the gun, always
watching with the gun, always ready, as if some ludicrous intervention were possible. A test of wills, that was what they
were caught in, and though the young man might at some
time submit, this was not the hour, not when he had the
whiff of freedom playing at his nostrils; the mere presence of
the fighters was insufficient. That was the reasoning of the
Italian; that was why he buried his head from it, and thought
of his wife and his children and the flat on Via Aurelia. At
home, he reflected, the officials of the government did not fill
the cells of the Regina Coeli with the terrorists they held at
Fiumicino; they shipped them out by military aircraft, un-
mindful of whether there was a decent lapse of time between
arrest and release. Their concern was with the safety of the
Alitalia fleet, and the avoidance of reprisals; the Western
world called them cowards for it. Franconi could only surmise, as he peeped between the fingers clenched across his
scalp, that the Russian approach would be different, and that
his life was as irrelevant as the safety of a wooden chess figure—a humble pawn—to the generals and senior politicians
who would make their decisions in deep-set operations rooms
and bright office suites.

Edward R. Jones, Jr., and Felicity Ann understood their
future less dramatically. She too had removed her hands
from her thinly waved hair, and they operated the couple's
Agfamatic 3000, the camera that they took on all their travels
and which aided him in his notes for the lecture tours of the
Midwest that followed the summer journeys. His own hands
still embedded in his winter-white hair, he called the stop
changes to his wife as she alternated between interiors and
film of the fighters through the porthole. A fortune to be
made, and what an auction! Associated Press against United
Press International for the world exclusive rights. His optimism about the immediate outcome was not based on any
specialized knowledge of Russian thinking, rather on a lack of
it. American, and conditioned to reading that the pilots of his
own country had orders to fall in with hijackers' demands, he

could not conceive that the interceptors had any role other than one of bluff.

The schoolchildren, whose ages spanned their eleventh and twelfth birthdays, had had too sheltered and cloistered an upbringing to realize the dangers to which their young lives were now exposed. Most rigidly obeyed the instruction to keep their arms raised, only a few grumbling at the discomfort to those who sat beside them. No question, the headmaster thought, of querying the order, not with the girl and the two men so preoccupied. Necessary to maintain a calmness among these people, and any interruption, however trivial, however well founded, would only lead to anger, would only harm the position of the children. He kept silent.

Twenty-five others. Some praying through closed eyes and clenched hands, some stolid and still and defiant and gazing straight ahead, some fascinated by what they saw beyond the reinforced windows, some crying quietly. Even the baby, halfway back, snuggled in a mother's shawl, was hushed.

Wandering with his eyes, restless, Isaac fastened on the two stewardesses, sitting together, holding hands, watching him, following his movements. The pretty one in the center seat, with the red hair, smoothing her skirt down her thighs. Isaac winked at her—just a flash, just a trace—and saw her blush and twist her head away. All of them sitting there, inanimate, straining away the minutes.

Would the jets open fire? Be quite a way to go if they do, Isaac.

From Moscow the orders were transmitted to Air Force Headquarters, West Ukraine, and from there relayed to the major who had the senior rank among the Mig pilots. He led the formation, four planes in line, separated by a half mile, across the path of the Ilyushin, spitting long bursts of cannon fire two hundred yards in front of the airliner. For pilots trained as these were, it was a simple maneuver. Climbing again and leaning back across the space of his cramped cockpit, he radioed that there was no apparent deviation of the Ilyushin. Once more, he was told, he should fire across the nose, again with the cannon, but closer. If that was not successful, he should return to station and await further instructions.

Inside the cockpit and the passenger cabin, hemmed in by the hermetically sealed fuselage, the noise of the cannon fire was considerable. A deep and guttural roar, so that none could be in doubt that this was the next stage of the play-acting. Isaac had joined David in the cockpit and they stood together, huddled in the limited space, as they watched the contortions of the fighter planes. Dive, level off, pull out. Vicious hammering of fire from the wings. So close that it made them draw back and wince, instinctively and involuntarily, seeking safety from the threat. The slipstream of the jets jolted and tumbled the Ilyushin, and both men clung to the back of Anna Tashova's seat.

And then they were gone, and the airliner was still on course, and it was as if there had been nothing, except that David's knuckles were white as he held himself upright and his face was drawn and old beyond his years, and Isaac saw that there were tears in the pilot officer's eyes which she fought to suppress. She thought they were going to kill us, herself as well, and all in the back; that was what she would have preferred; that was the depth of her hate for us.

The navigator, in his seat behind them, broke the silence. A forgotten man, who had stayed quiet and unobtrusive since they had swarmed into the cockpit, contenting himself with plotting their course, identifying their position on his maps. "We have perhaps half a minute to turn. The next time it will be the missiles. They know they cannot damage us sufficiently to force us to land but still permit us to land successfully. If they damage us we crash, and so they will make it fast for us, they will destroy us in the air. The pilot who tried to land the Libyan plane that the Israelis fired on, the Frenchman, he tried and he failed. A passenger liner cannot withstand any damage, not at this altitude."

"We fly on," said David. "The Kingfisher bird is on course. They will not come again."

"Are you blind to it, you crazed fool? Can you not see the signs with your own eyes? That was the warning, the final warning. The next time it is over." Anna Tashova's words lapped around David, rippling and eddying at him, but without the conviction to strike him, leaving him unmoved. Isaac put his arm around the taller man's waist and hugged and pulled their two bodies together. "I did not know it would be like that," David said. "I had no idea . . ."

"But you found the strength to fight them," encouraged Isaac.

"Never again, not like that . . . never again," David whispered, and he trembled, his whole frame consumed by the convulsions as Isaac held him. And he no longer stared out through the small cockpit windows, but was again magnetized by the captain's slowly moving head, its inverted pendulum motion.

"He is still fighting me . . ."

"Don't be so stupid. You couldn't know. It was only one bullet; you couldn't know."

"He is still fighting me . . ."

"Keep the plane on course," said Isaac wearily.

Radio chatter among the Migs.

"Eagle 4 to Sunray. What do they want us to do now?"

"Eagle 3 to Sunray. We cross the Polish border in under a minute."

"Eagle 2 to Sunray. Do we shoot to bring them down or not?"

"Sunray to Eagle Flight. You hear the orders as I do. The order is to wait . . . they are checking something out. Maintain course."

"Eagle 4 to Sunray. What is there to check out?"

"Eagle 3 to Sunray. Did you see the children at the windows? Quite clearly you can see them."

"Eagle 2 to Sunray. There is the man in the cockpit. I saw him . . . with the gun."

"Sunray to Eagle Flight. Stop talking. I know where we are; so does Ground. I have eyes too—I have seen the children—I have seen the man. They will be checking the passenger list. They want to know who is on board."

"Eagle 4 to Sunray. If there is no one important, we shoot: is that why they want to know who is on board?"

"Sunray to Eagle 4. Keep the airwave clear. Keep your opinions to yourself. Observe the order."

The Migs overflew Polish airspace for two minutes, then peeled away.

Three years previously, a hijacked aircraft had mysteriously disappeared from the radar screens of Western military forces stationed in Germany and was presumed to have been shot down. That Aeroflot flight 927 was permitted to continue its progress was determined by the composition of the passenger manifest. The matter of the children on their way to the ballet festival at Tashkent did not sway the issue, nor did the question of the survival of the Russian adult passengers and the Russian crew count in any degree toward the final decision. It was the knowledge that among the passengers was the delegation of the Italian Communist Party, all of them senior men and belonging to a party with which the Soviet Union was trying to heal ideological rifts, that carried the day. Luigi Franconi and his comrades ensured the safety of all on board. If the only foreigners to have taken the Tashkent flight had been Edward R. Jones, Jr., and Felicity Ann, then the Ilyushin would by now have been a mess of wreckage, burning and disintegrated, scattered over a half-mile square, scorching the summer stubble of a collective field. Perhaps the Italians would have been flattered had they known their lives were held in such esteem, but their ignorance of the reality was total, as too was that of David and Isaac. Both stood in the cockpit above Anna Tashova as the plane powered on, content in the belief that their determination, their power had won them a great victory, that their greatest test was behind them.

The defining of the problem and the taking of the decision not to shoot down the Ilyushin had involved two of the Soviet Union's most senior officials in a bitter and protracted argument fought out over the telephone lines between their respective ministry buildings. Defense was for the strong arm of physical prevention of the aircraft from leaving Russian airspace. Foreign Affairs held out a calmer option and pledged a massive diplomatic campaign by telephone hot line and teleprinter to dissuade all governments in whose territory a landing might be attempted from offering the terrorists either refuge or succor for their onward journey to Israel.

From the moment that David had broadcast over the aircraft radio that the group was Jewish, he had played into the hands of those who saw, with sharp clarity because they had only bare minutes in which to reach their conclusion, that a great diplomatic coup was offered for the taking should the three be returned to Russia to face trial. The discussion had ultimately been three-pronged—Defense, Foreign Affairs and the all-powerful Secretary General of the Party, who would ultimately influence events—and the argument of the Foreign Minister had been the most persuasive to the ears of the ruler of the country.

"If we destroy the plane in the air, we have achieved the aim of the Jewish terrorists. We will highlight what they call their cause. The whole world will talk of our brutality. We will make these three into martyrs, and no one will remember the crimes from which they are fleeing. Problems from Italy, problems from the PCI. All this can be avoided. It is the suggestion of this ministry that we let them fly to the West and that we precede their landing by messages to the heads of government in all the countries in which they might come to rest that we expect the immediate disarming and return of these people to face the charges that can be brought against them."

There was more that he could have said, but insufficient time. The Migs were in the air, pilots' hands close to the triggers that would release the cones of cannon fire and the projectiles that would seek out the heat of the Ivchenko engine exhausts. The airspace was being eroded as they talked.

"And among the passengers, whom do we have?" The Secretary General seeking time before his decision.

"We have children. We have a delegation of comrades from Italy, from the Central Administration of the Party, and the effect there could be catastrophic. Also to be considered is the fact that they have broadcast from the plane. In the West it is now known what has happened. The incident is no longer confined inside our own frontiers."

"We are all agreed that the plane could be brought down only over our own territory. You have very few seconds to make up your minds." The final intervention of the Defense Minister, certain by this stage that he had lost the day. Certain too that the time of the hard men who had mobilized the great wartime defense of the country, whatever the cost, was now a thing of the past.

"Let the plane fly on." The order of the Secretary General. "And the message that goes to the foreign governments, I will want it read to me before it is released. It will bear my name."

• •

Three o'clock and a London afternoon. Charlie Webster at his desk and with precious short of nothing to entertain himself. Usually like that after lunch. Worked fast enough in the morning to clear his desk; didn't space it out like the others who seemed to have something to get round to, to keep them busy, all eight hours that God gave for working. Too hot, and the bloody air conditioner still up the spout. Typical, really: put them all in a damn great tower block with all that glass to soak up the sun, and not a window that could be opened in the whole place. Must be some sort of breeze flying about this high up, if only the window could be opened and we could tempt the little blighter in.

Trouble is, Charlie, you're not really an inside man. Never were and never will be. Not the temperament, not the patience, not any of the things to believe shuffling paper is worthwhile. Wrap it, Charlie; becoming a grumpy old goat in your senility. Stop worrying about yourself; worry about what happens to old soldiers too ancient for anything useful and too young to fade away.

He'd changed from the Cyprus boy and the Aden boy, when he hadn't cared, when he was with Military Intelligence, not thirty, not married, not a doubt to trouble him. Ireland had been the undoing—the grayed, opaque fight, the tedium of procedure and rule books. The danger, too. Something he hadn't thought of before, hadn't concerned himself with.

Not worth getting your arse shot off, Charlie, he'd told himself. Not worth getting blasted into a gutter in Monaghan or Clones or Ballyshannon. Not worth bumping across the churchyard with the Union Jack to keep the sun off the box and eight blanks to give the rooks a fright. And so he had said that he would like to come inside, and everyone had seemed very pleased, and said he'd be a big asset to the team. He'd told them he didn't want anything connected with his previous work. Wanted a change, and pointed to his Russian-course qualifications: taken it years ago on National Service before he'd decided to go for Regular. So out of Military Intelligence he'd popped, demobbed, bought a gray suit—nothing special, and off the peg—and they sent him over to SIS, Soviet Desk. Probably bloody glad to see the back of you, Charlie.

One of the chaps from Sub-Desk Military coming in without knocking. Didn't do that normally; observed protocol. A flimsy in his hand and couldn't keep it to himself, not till he reached Charlie's desk.

"There's a hijack, Charlie. Over Russia. All hell broken out, fighters up and everything."

Daydreams gone. Feeling-sorry-for-self time over. All attention. Charlie said, "Out of Kiev, is it?"

"How do you know? How did you know that?" Looked blank, stopped in his bloody tracks, puzzled.

"You mean it really is?" said Charlie. "Really Kiev? Just a guess and something we were talking about yesterday. Let's have a look."

Eight teletype lines, and telling him all he needed to know. Aeroflot internal, pilot dead. Jewish group, broadcast from the aircraft, unsuccessful attempt by air force to turn it round, shots across the nose, now over Poland, still escorted at a distance. Too good to be bloody true, thought Charlie; they'll have me down as fortune-teller at the next Christmas binge.

"Any more?"

"Well, that's not bad for starters. There's something coming through. The Russians are putting out a long screed. In essence it demands that the plane and the passengers and the hijackers be returned to them forthwith after landing. It's pretty hard stuff. They're saying it was only for humanitarian reasons and in the interest of the passengers that they didn't shoot the aircraft down. But they want them back; say they're gangsters and attempted to murder a policeman."

Bloody amazing, Charlie. "Boobed it, though, haven't they?" he said. "Shouldn't have dropped the pilot. That's not the way to earn a nice jolly welcome, not when there's blood sloshing round the joystick. Someone's going to have a packet of trouble when that little bird runs out of fuel and has to land."

"Fuel isn't the immediate problem. It's a long-range Ilyushin 11 18V, and well tanked. It was on a run to Tashkent and was lifted straight after takeoff. There's enough juice to go anywhere in Europe, including here. Anywhere they want, except Israel—that's off limits to this plane, out of fuel range. But they can take their pick round these parts."

"All the makings of a very cheery scene." Charlie thanked him, then sat alone in his office. All a bit confusing when he started to think about it. Terrorist hijack or freedom fighters' breakout. Square pegs in round holes. What did you greet them with at the airport—bouquet and a speech of welcome, or a Saracen and a pair of handcuffs? Been rabbiting on long enough, hadn't they, our political masters, about the state of Soviet Jewry, so what were they going to do with this one? Only one thing to do, he thought. Pray God it doesn't come here.

6

While the big Ilyushin purred its uninterrupted path across the airspace of Poland and the German Democratic Republic with its now more discreet escort of Migs that had scrambled from more forward Warsaw Pact airfields, frantic meetings were being convened throughout Western Europe.

All of the Continent's countries can now call on the services of "crisis committees" of politicians, civil servants and senior police and army officers who are on call to advise the heads of government on what course they should take if confronted with a major guerrilla action. It is the task of these committees to evaluate the threat and the implications of involvement with the new breed of warfare that since the start of the decade had proved so costly in terms of money and prestige to the Old World. The lesson of preparation had been learned the hard way, with cabinets ill briefed and security forces poorly trained to do battle with the new militia playing by their own new rules of warfare who descend in their capitals and airports with the AK-47s and RPGs and who spread mayhem and disgrace and disfigurement with minimal discrimination.

Meetings in Bonn, in Copenhagen, and Stockholm and Oslo and Helsinki. Ministers and officials hurrying to their chauffeur-driven cars in Brussels, Paris and The Hague. Policemen being called by telephone to the Cabinet offices in Madrid and Rome and Lisbon and Bern. In all the capitals, as in London, it was recognized that speed was of the essence, that a policy must be formulated and agreed upon and authorized before the Ilyushin attempted its inevitable landing. Dominating the discussions was the Russian note, now being studied in a dozen languages, none of which could succeed through translation in blunting the harsh message that the Secretary General of the Soviet Communist Party had intended should be conveyed. They have something in common, the politicians of Europe who are answerable to an electorate; the constant factor is the determination not to lay their backs open to the rod that can strike and wound them. To permit the plane to land when it had fuel to fly on, that was only begging for difficulties and diplomatic furor and dangers in the high echelons of international relations. Those countries most keenly affected, in that their airports lay within easy striking range of the present flight path of the Aeroflot airliner, had the least discussion time available to their committees and reached their decision first.

In Bonn the advice to the Chancellor was without equivocation. Under no circumstances should the aircraft be allowed to land. Any airport the Ilyushin approached should immediately be closed; if necessary, trucks should be driven across the runways to prevent their being used. A drastic solution, that was agreed by all who took part in the evaluation, but so also were the alternatives horrifying. Let the plane land and offer yourselves to the whim and hazard of a full-blown hijack siege; there could be no question of allowing the airliner to refuel and fly on in the face of the Russian demands, and no possibility, with the pilot still warm in his seat, of offering safe conduct. Far better to skirt the issue and pass the problem outside the Federal frontiers. The embassies of West Germany were instructed to pass the government decision to other interested parties, including the Soviet Union.

It was Isaac who stayed close to the navigator watching the pencil lines that he drew across the green, heavily overscored map surface on the small pullout table that acted as his workbench. Slow and painstaking, the plotting of the course. A few more minutes and they would have crossed the dark and shaded line that marked the barricade between the cultures of East and West. Just a line on a map at that height, and hazed squares of toned brown and yellow beneath them. Nothing to demonstrate the wire, and the mines and the watchtowers, and the fear and the clinging helplessness that the frontier meant twenty-seven thousand feet underneath. Soon the descent would start, and the ground shades would sharpen, and then it would be over, and they would have achieved the impossible. Escape, something that could not have been contemplated two short days before. And now it was achieved, bar a few miles, a few minutes' flying time.

"We are nearly there," he called softly to David. Why is the man still so tense? Why is it necessary to hold the gun so close to the girl? The Migs have gone, defeated, seen off. "It is over now, friend. We have beaten the pigs, hammered them, destroyed them. Relax, David." Still the stress etched across David's face, still the suspicion there, nothing to show that he was convinced of their victory. Impatience now from Isaac. "Can't you see, David, we are there?" He pulled the map from the navigator's table and thrust it close and with frustration and aggression under David's face. "It's over, we are there. What was it you called it? The Kingfisher flight? The Kingfisher flight is over. The breakout of the Kingfisher, and we have done it."

David declined to speak to him, but said quietly, with strain eating at his voice, to the pilot officer, "Which airport should we land at?"

Indifference on her face; not her concern. She jerked her head back in the direction of the navigator. "You should ask him. He is the one who will tell you that."

"Which airport do we go to?" David asked his question of the navigator, still the concern in his words, and the man in the blue uniform with twin rings of gold braid on his wrists waved away the question. "I am talking to the ground; they have contacted us. They say they have a message for us and are awaiting the responsible person who will read it. The nearest airport should be Hannover; that is the civil airport. Also in that area are many of the military bases of the NATO forces of the British. It's unlikely they would permit us to use an Air Force field. There are many options that are open if they give us permission to land. But you must be quiet, because I do not have much English, and that is the language they will use to me. The pilot officer has very little, insufficient to talk to the controllers. The man you killed, he was the one who spoke English."

"How far are we from the border?"

A momentary calculation by the navigator, a deviation from his main task of awaiting the message from the ground, pencil and ruler on the map. "We are there."

Isaac turned away from the cockpit; walked past the forward exit door and the lavatories and the closet space for the winter coats; came to the entrance of the passenger cabin, machine gun still at the ready, held low across his thighs. Looked at the faces; saw only the drained and exhausted stares that faltered back at him. He realized the ordeal to which they had subjected this passive, muted collection of strangers; only one thing in common, all of them: that they wanted to sleep tonight in Tashkent. Time to relieve their misery, put an end to the persecution, and time, too, to demonstrate the power of three young Jews and what faith could win.

"Ladies and gentlemen, I have news for you that I hope will prove welcome. We are now crossing the frontier between the two Germanys. We are awaiting the instructions of the West German Government as to which airport they wish us to use for a landing. You should be aware of our descent very soon. It has not been our intention to cause you any hurt, but you must stay in your seats and observe our orders. That is all." And as an afterthought, and he laughed like a child when he said it, "Perhaps some of you would care to leave the plane with us?" His humor was drowned by the sad, tired, worn eyes that offered no flicker of response.

Separated from him by the full length of the cabin, half hidden by the drinks trolley that was her protection from the rear passengers, Rebecca, flagging in her strength, was leaning on the trolley top for relief and showing the pistol. He smiled to her, saw her return the greeting. Funny girl, he thought, but she'd done well. There hadn't been the time, not the opportunity to talk to her of Yevsei. The little guy must have been on a hope and a prayer to have put the guns aboard, but he wouldn't have made it, would he? Not if David wasn't getting it . . . no chance for Yevsei. If she wasn't around David so much, then there could have been the opportunity . . . roll of drums for Isaac. Didn't understand, David; too busy with his war games to see what was there on a plate. But she couldn't have kept her legs crossed all night; must have let old Yevsei get his hand in somewhere. Stood to reason, if he was going to take a risk like that. Take a girl to persuade a man to put guns on Aeroflot, only a girl. . . .

David tugging at his shoulder, pulling and wrenching at him, heaving him backward and off balance as he was swung toward the cockpit. "Shut up, you fool. Shut up and come in here." A moment to see the relief sucked from the faces of those passengers closest to him, and David had dragged him too deep for them to follow his whispered words. "The Germans say we cannot land. They forbid us to use their airfields."

"It's a bluff . . . like the Migs" was Isaac's reaction, but even as he said it the cold sweat that comes from chronic uncertainty, comes when the mast is broken, when the ladder slips, was spearing its way across his stomach, into his groin, an awful chill. "They don't mean it . . ."

"How do you know they don't mean it? They say they will prevent us from landing."

"Perhaps it's just an airport official, someone who had not been notified about us. Do they know who we are? Do they know we are Jews?"

"They know everything about us. They know we are Jews. They know our names. They know we have passengers on board. They say that they know we have fuel, and they say we must fly on."

"Which is the nearest airport to our present position?" Isaac snapped at the navigator, seeking to regain command.

"Still Hannover."

"Tell them that we are going to Hannover. Tell them we are going to land at Hannover." Isaac was shouting; they were coming to the West, they were coming to freedom, they were coming to the democracies. "Tell them that, and hold the course for Hannover."

"Only one person who can give orders in the cockpit, Isaac, and that is me." David, animated, creased in anger.

"Well, give some orders, then. Take the plane down to Hannover."

"Take the plane to Hannover," David told Anna Tashova. The transfusion of his fury was short-lived, seemed to crumple again, the belief in the outcome slipping. Her hands moved to the instruments to make the changes and deviations that were called for by the navigator. Checking altitude, checking airspeed, asking him to seek a talk-down into the airspace, and with her face set tight as he shrugged and said they would give no cooperation, that they could only repeat the message already passed to the airliner, that they were sorry.

"How long?" David asked the navigator.

"Ten minutes and we will see the airfield. I will tell them again that we are coming. But you should know that they were very definite. They said they would prevent us from landing."

Because he was a big man and sat high in his seat, Edward R. Jones, Jr., had seen David pull Isaac back toward the entrance to the cockpit. All the passengers, adults and children, were susceptible to the changes of mood in their captors, studied and examined and analyzed them, because they had little else to do and because these were the only clues they possessed as to the future of the flight. Every spark that flashed, every smile, every furrowed forehead was noticed and evaluated as the passengers sought for information. It was as if the act were mimed, because the voices of David and Isaac were far removed, and were lowered, and the yowling of that damned baby obliterated any possibility for even the keenest ears to eavesdrop.

But Edward R. Jones, Jr., was not totally disappointed by his inability to hear the words that were spoken; his eyes had not betrayed him. They reported a new mood, a new urgency, a new tension at the front of the aircraft. He and his wife were sitting far to the back of the plane, among the last rows of the cabin, while the mass had herded toward the front because they had not read, as the American had, that the only possibility of survival in an air disaster is to be sitting in the rear. He and Felicity Ann always sat at the back, and it was that which put him in easy conversational range of Rebecca as she stood, with the gun still unfamiliar in her hand, watching her charges and as ill informed on the cockpit situation as they were.

"Miss," he said, hands still on his head. "Miss, do you speak English?"

"You have heard the orders; it is forbidden to speak." Clipped, hostile, shunning the contact. But the answer in the language that he sought.

"Forget that crap, miss, if you'll excuse me. The question was do you speak English, and the answer was that you do."

"It is not permitted for you to talk." Her English was halting, and styled by school classrooms, but she could understand what he said, reply in a fashion.

"It strikes me, miss, and I'm only a passenger here, but it strikes me your friends up front have a problem. You get that impression?" She ignored him, wondered what else she could do. Couldn't shoot him, not just for talking. Couldn't hit him, not without coming from behind her barricade; couldn't call David and Isaac because they were at the cockpit, and she had seen what the American had seen, and they had looked anxious. "Perhaps the problem is, miss, that no one is that keen to have you. Have you thought of that? That there won't be a red carpet down there waiting for you."

"We are Jews; we are persecuted. We are fleeing from a system of intolerance, and so we go to Israel. In the West they are the enemy of the Soviets—you tell me they will not help us?"

Edward R. Jones, Jr., turned full toward her, eye to eye, face to face. Quite a pretty girl, really, if she did something about her hair, bit of makeup, little eye shadow—not a beauty, but presentable; awful dress, but they all wore things like that over here.

"Have you thought, miss, that it could all be a bit harder than that, that people this side of the line might not be quite as cozy, quite as friendly as you thought they would?" A sort of rhythm in his voice, a monotony like the drip of a faucet that needs a new washer, hypnotizing in its way, and dulling and wasting. "When the Palestinians fly the planes into Arab countries they get locked up now, you know. No more garlands and a big villa to lie around till the heat cools. They shove them into cells. Times move on, miss."

"We are not Palestinians; we are not terrorists. We are Jews and we have been oppressed, we have been persecuted, and now we have fought back . . ." She too had now raised her voice, the last of the group to do so, but responding in her own way to a strain that was becoming intolerable, crippled all the time by the isolation of her position, divorced from the others, wanting comfort, reassurance.

"They all say that, miss. All reckon that their God is on their side, that He looks with a friendly eye on their cause. You're not the first to join this merry-go-round, miss; there are plenty before you. All kinds—Weathermen, Puerto Ricans, Tupamaros, Zeepa, Provos, Baader-Meinhof, Eta 5, PFLP. They're all in your line of business. And they all face

one problem: they need somewhere to go, somewhere to
sleep, somewhere where they aren't going to be hunted. Rest
houses are short on the ground, miss. If you can't put this
bird down in Tel Aviv, you're lost; you'll be like all the other
lepers and pariahs. No one will want you."

"We are going to land; Isaac told you so. Isaac told you we
were going to land. And the plane is now descending."

Close to shrieking, and the words carrying the length of the
cabin, enough to rouse Isaac from far away so that he ran the
distance of the aisle, and when she pointed to Edward R.
Jones, Jr., she could not speak because the tears choked in
her throat. The American seemed to dare the boy, seemed to
want to taunt and anger him in the very defiance of his
steadied, aged eyes. Not even the hands raised in self-defense
across his face, not his body turned away that a blow might
be warded off. Isaac swung the barrel of his gun in a short,
chopping arc onto the top of the American's skull; one blow
to submerge it under the protection of Felicity Ann's arms,
and there was blood on her dress and the sound of the distress of an old man for protest.

"Rebecca, it will be over very soon. We are nearly there.
We are losing altitude. Courage for a few more moments.
Courage."

Isaac's was the only voice in the great hushed cigar of the
cabin. But he had not told her of the message from the
ground, had not thought to. Flaps moving and arresting
the progress of the plane, causing it to yaw, thrust sound
changed to a higher pitch, and the rumbling of the extraction
of the undercarriage.

The movement of the plane made it difficult for David to
stand in the cockpit, but there was nowhere else for him to
go. The pilot officer in her seat, the navigator in his, and only
the captain's place with the strapped-down body that was still
tall and erect available to him. Couldn't bring himself to
touch the man. Different if they'd meant to kill him, if he
had been an enemy and his death had been reached by decision. But it had been just an accident, an empty and hollow
accident to a man whose status represented no threat to
them. Not like killing the policeman. And so the captain kept
his seat, his head rolling with the motion of the aircraft, and

the blood trail was congealed and darkened and no longer held the warmth and freshness of the moment of wounding.

"We are talking again with the tower at Hannover. They repeat that we are not permitted to land there. They call it a blanket order for the whole of the Federal Republic. They are emphatic that we will not be permitted to land there." The navigator seemingly calm, unaffected by the bowstring tension around him, repeated his messages as if uncaring as to who heard them, and all the time interrrupting his recital of instructions from the ground with the minutiae of course adjustments that the pilot officer required.

"Another few seconds and we will be through the haze; then we will see the runway. Then we will see if they mean to stop us or whether as your friend says, it is just a bluff." She had had five years, three more before that at the training school—sufficient experience solo for her to be able to handle the Ilyushin on her own. Too senior, really, for her to be flying copilot, especially a ship like this, but the rosters were not logically drawn and did not always recognize her logbook of flying hours. They taught you how to pilot an aircraft and gave you lectures on emergencies; but those were concerning the technical problems that might be faced—fire in an engine, undercarriage that would not retract, fracture of pressurization, loss of flap control. They did not know how you would react if there was a submachine gun at your rib cage with a thirty-round magazine attached, and a class of schoolchildren that you must bring to safety. No way they could know that when they gave you command of an aircraft. Lectures and courses, but this . . . impossible to simulate.

"There is the runway." She snapped it out and was peering high over the bottom lip of her windscreen at the dun-colored strip of concrete thousands of feet beneath her. City laid out like a toy town farther away. Neat gardens, high chimneys of the factories, rising office blocks. But closer, and this held her attention, the shape of the airfield, runway placed straight ahead for her by the skill of the navigator.

"There are vehicles across it. See them? Fuel tankers, armored cars. Suicide, suicide if we go down there." Without the order from David that had preceded her every previous move, she had pulled on the instrument column and was scrambling to complete the job she would have shared with her captain, to reset the mass of dials and switches that were necessary if the plane was to climb again. David had seen it all, seen it as she had. Recognized the impossibility of a successful landing. Every three hundred meters the variation between the yellow-and-white fuel trucks and the green-and-olive armored cars, clear and silhouetted against the background of the tarmac. A hammer blow to the pit of his stomach.

"Don't answer any calls for us from the ground, and circle the airport, low enough so that they can see us." David moved out of the cockpit, the first time he had left it in more than two hours; stepped into the corridor, the passageway between the flight deck and the passenger cabin; reached forward to pull the curtain across so that the watchers might not observe him as he spoke to Isaac. Quiet and sombered voice, and a resignation about him that unnerved Isaac, and the great shoulders shrunken by the enormity of the problem. "What do we do now? In God's name, Isaac, what do we do now?"

"We can tell them we are coming in to land, and see what—"

"And if they don't move the trucks, and if we are committed to landing and cannot climb again—then we are dead."

"We were dead if we had not left Russia."

"But we have to live. We did not do this to die. To die well is no different from dying badly. To die with heroism is no different from walking in submission, craven, to the burial pits. We came here to live."

"Perhaps it is because they know we have fuel."

"And how many countries will follow the lead of the Germans?"

"If we crash the plane, that is by our hand. They know how much fuel we have; they know when we can go no farther. It will not be at our hand, David." Isaac spoke feverishly and searching to build again the momentum that had taken them to the flight. "When the gasoline is expended, what government will refuse us permission to land when they know we have children on our flight? This is not the crisis; this is not the ultimate. Time for Masada, time for suicide—that's later. If we have to die it will be, but that time is not yet, and when we have landed, then it will be different." Again Isaac had his arm around him, squeezing, the gesture of friendship and support. "David, you are down, and that is how they would wish you. They would want us to dispute with each other; they would want your depression, because that helps them. We have known that it would not be easy, that it would not be simple. There are other countries we can reach, many others. Not all are like the Germans. We too have friends, David."

"Less than two hours now; that is the fuel we have. After that it will be settled for us."

As he went back into the cockpit, David wondered at the new turn in their fortunes. Realized that he was bemused that they should meet with opposition at this time, and after they had won so much. It was like a betrayal; he felt as a boy feels when he knows his father has told him a lie. He had not known that Isaac possessed such inner reservoirs of stamina; they would come to lean on him, both of them, Rebecca as much as himself. He felt such a great tiredness now, just a longing to be shed of it, to walk again on the ground, escape this box of confusions that he did not understand, would never comprehend. The joy of walking again on grass, and of not running, and of not listening at night for the footsteps that might follow. He repeated it over in his mind. Lean on Isaac; lean on him till his strength returned. Could any of them understand the awful, wearying, endless conflict in the cockpit? The pilot dead, the shape that would not respond, would not forgive. The fighters—modern, technolgical killing soldiers that he had stood his ground against and beaten. The cool, iced proficiency of the pilots. He had stood against them. He, David, had stood against them and seen them off. But it was sapping and weakening, and now he should rest on Isaac, let the boy carry the load till he was ready again. And the boy was good—better than your expectations, David— and there was comfort there, the sole succor in the blackness.

"Give me a course for Holland," David said. Again there was a suspicion of request in his voice. Again the Ilyushin banked and began to turn, roused by the new thrust of power, searching once more for the Kingfisher's landfall.

The airport at Hannover is categorized as "international," but the traffic it handles is not considerable—minor in comparison with Frankfurt or Munich or Cologne/Bonn. So the groups of delayed passengers and crew and idled airport staff were sparsely scattered on the concrete terminal roof. Clusters of multinational businessmen, a party of British war veterans who had come again to relive the triumph and the misery of 1945, some Scandinavians in search of fresh hiking pastures, mingled among the Lufthansa men and girls.

All could see the Ilyushin, proud and alone in the azure late-afternoon sky. Watched with arched orbiting heads its flight around the far perimeter of the airfield, occasionally stealing a glance at the rock-steady armored cars and trucks that were the runway obstructions. A transistor radio chattered a report from a local broadcaster who described the scene and could tell of no more than their own varied eyes could take in. It was the only sound to compete with the low-pitched, incessant drone of the engines set far forward on the wings from which the Aeroflot flight's markings could be read by those with clear eyesight. Neither limping with fatigue nor impatient with frustration; no sudden banking or acceleration; a voyeur who had made a visit, and who sensed an atmosphere, and would therefore not intrude.

And the watchers realized that the plane would not come, that the confrontation was not sought. They saw the new course set and watched the diminishing silhouette and were left with a feeling of emptiness and inadequacy, because they were a part of something that would not be completed. Only when the plane was telescoped to their vision, small and now hard to see, and its engine noise was faint, did a new sound spring forward, powerful and dominating, as the armored cars and tankers revved their engines and started to move clear of the tarmac.

There was a woman from Stockholm who cried, and said again and again, "I don't know why. I don't know why." And her husband was embarrassed and gave her his handkerchief and tried to shield her from view as she dabbed her eyes.

The tolerance of the men with dark suits and attaché cases and schedules to maintain was waning. Much checking of watches and loud discussion as to how long it would take to get things moving again, to fly them on to their homes or belated meetings.

The ground staff were first to leave the roof, beckoned by

the work and organization that now awaited them; the businessmen hard on their heels; the hikers needing to make up lost time if they were to reach their chalets by nightfall.

The old army men stayed on. They had no need to hurry; it was known where they were; they were confident of being called when their flight was ready. Men in their sixties and seventies, at the fading of their lives, who for a week had recalled "machine-gun platoon," and "mortar platoon," and "Monty," and "knocking the Hun for six." A great deal of wine and beer and sausage and reminiscence they'd been through in the last few days, and they did not seek to end it by returning more quickly than necessary to the polished cleanliness of the Departure Hall.

"Should have come on in, shouldn't they?" Cyril from Mechanised Infantry.

"Then there'd have been the risk of pranging her." Bertie, HQ Staff.

"If you're to win in that sort of game, you have to take a few chances, like it was when we crossed . . ." Jim, Pioneer Assault.

"They won't have come this far if they haven't taken some risks. You don't knock an aircraft off and get this far without chancing your arm a bit. I wouldn't fancy doing what they've done." Herbie, Armoured Corps Maintenance.

"Cyril's right, though. Whatever they've done up to now, they chickened this time. Should have come on in, like Cyril said. The Hun always buckles. Pressure him enough and he buckles." Dave, General Staff, batman.

"What do you bloody know about it, Dave? You were so far back, they never even bothered to give you a rifle. Never even saw a bloody Hun with a gun in his hand, you didn't." Harry, Airborne machine gunner.

And they all laughed, and Dave looked pained, and they slapped his back. "Time for another beer," someone said.

Harry Smith had been a sergeant when they'd all been in uniform a lifetime ago. Para, too, and they admired that. Gave him the sort of leadership over the rest, that and his Military Medal, and the fact that he now had a sweet shop in Kilburn and was self-employed. "I heard a bit of what the chappie said on the radio, picked up a bit of the language when I was here. They're Jewish boys up there. I don't know whether that makes it all different. But it's not for us to call them cowards. We had a bloody great backup scene behind us. Stores, supplies and orders, some other bugger to tell us what to do. So what have they got? Sweet Fanny Adams, not much else. If they're Jewish, they'll have thought it all over by the time they reached here. Thought they were home and dry. Think of it as they'll be seeing it now; think of it and you'll know why that bird over there was crying."

"They're still bloody terrorists, Sarge," said Dave.

"If you say so," said Harry Smith. He stared hard into the lowering light, searching through his glasses for the aircraft. But the haze and mist of distance had wrapped around the Kingfisher flight, lifting it beyond his reach.

Had David but known it, the West German "crisis committee" had anticipated that an attempt might be made to land the plane in spite of the precautions taken. The fuel tankers and the armored cars all had members of the green-uniformed Bundesgrenzschutz at their controls. If the word had come from the tower that the Aeroflot plane was on irreversible landing approach, the order would have been transmitted to the cabs of the vechicles to drive onto the grass margins of the runway and allow the aircraft to land without further hindrance. In the second-floor offices of the Federal Ministry of the Interior in Bonn there was much congratulation and backslapping among the team of politicians and civil servants who had directed the operation as the news was brought to them that the plane was climbing and had taken a flight plan that ran to the south of Hamburg and to the north of Bonn, Cologne and Düsseldorf. A bottle of Scotch whisky was broached. It was the opinion of the aviation experts that the course was for Schiphol Airport, Amsterdam.

"I had not thought," said the Minister, "that we would accomplish the plan so easily."

"It was a new tactic for these people. Their protests have been verbal before; they have not attempted anything of this intensity. But it is surprising, as you say, that they could be so easily deflected. I think we will find when the business is completed that they were very young." It was the contribution of the senior police officer present, who had been on the ground in the chaos of the Munich police ambush of Black September at Fürstenfeldbruck air base, who had laid out the bodies of nine Israeli athletes and coaches and who never wanted to be part of a similar confrontation again. "But even though they are young, and even though we have turned them away—that does not mean that the problem for someone else is in any way diminished. What we have done is to temporarily depress them. My forecast is that this setback will, in the long term, serve only to harden their resolve."

The policeman spoke with distaste, unimpressed at the enthusiasm with which the unresolved problem had been shuffled elsewhere.

Parker Smith had left in a hurry, his departure preceded by a confusion of ringing telephones, summoned messengers with paperwork and shouting through opened office doors. Just time to push his head round Charlie's door. Excited and not caring who saw it. Call from the Big Boys, call from Whitehall, beckoned to the Presence, to attend the Emergency Group meeting. He might send for Charlie later, and would he have his files at hand and be ready to bring them if it was required that he should come? Charlie noticed he hadn't cared to comb his hair, a mess without the ruler-straight parting, and that was unusual for him; he bothered about his appearance. Meant the flap was building.

"Getting a bit nervy, are they, sir? Our masters?"

"Decidedly so, Charlie. You've seen the Russian note, and it's very tough. You've seen what the Hun's reaction is. Pass-the-parcel games from now, so it's with the Dutch next, and FO are trying to establish what position they will take. If they don't come down in Holland and they keep going, then we're next in line, and not much fuel to play with. If we send for you, look snappy."

"I'm not a counterhijack expert, sir. Home Office do that." Caution from Charlie. Long time now since he'd been involved in anything fresher than stacking paper.

"Course you're not. But you're supposed to know these bastards. That is what we'll be requiring from you—every damned little thing about them. So don't shift off that telephone."

Parker Smith was gone, not finding the time to close Charlie's door, lost in a welter of shouted farewells. And the word

that the section was involved spread through the offices like a
dry-grass fire. Huddles in the corridors, and voices raised in
anticipation, and pleasure that the Old Man had been sent
for. Charlie went to his steel-gray cabinet and fished in his
pocket for the keys, discarding those of his front door, his
car, his office door, his garage. Unlocked the cabinet and began to rifle through the buff-colored folders. Charlie kept a
good system—something he'd learned in his old army days.
Extracted seven—two of them marked with a red sticky-tape
X diagonally across their length and breadth that connoted
the classification of Secret; five with blue tape crosses that
simply connoted Restricted.

Time for some fast reading, Charlie.

The helicopter that carried the Israeli Prime Minister had
left the Golan Heights in a swirl of choking, rasping dirt, sat-
urating all those who had gathered at the stone-cleared landing pad to see him off.

His tour of forward positions on the Syrian front that overlooked the ruined and war-broken city of Kuneitra had been
scheduled to last for three more hours, but the radio transmission from Jerusalem had caused it to be cut short. He had
enough to be concerned about without the burden of new-
fashioned crises; in his mind he was attempting to obliterate
the problems of the perpetual argument between Defense,
which sought more planes and more missiles and more antitank weapons and more cement for fortifications, and on the
other side Finance, which bleated at every Cabinet meeting
at the cost of it all and the effect on civilian morale of the
creeping taxation that was the corollary of sophisticated and
modern firepower. Shut it out, block it, as the helicopter staggered off the ground and hovered before seeking its route.

The Prime Minister had been a military man before entering politics and prided himself that he had spanned the gulf,
that he understood both points of view, but that in itself
made it no simpler for him to bridge the chasm between the
two lobbying factions of his government. Three devaluations,
and that inside the last nine months, and no change in the
precariousness of the national budget, and still the army demanding more hardware and showing no interest in where
the money to pay for it should come from.

The visit to the Golan and its strongpoints was long planned and was supposed to have been a sweetener to his generals. He was to have walked around behind the sandbags and the barbed wire and laughed and joked with them in the slang they had used when they were all together as lieutenants and captains, and look serious and understanding when that was required of him, and sympathize with their complaints and shortages, and make promises that would be vague and that would not sustain analysis, but that would mollify and placate here on the battlefield sheltered by the minefields and tank regiments and artillery batteries.

And now the effect of the day was wasted.

The summons had come from his offices on the hill in Jerusalem that he should return forthwith, and there had been no time for explanations and excuses, just the opportunity to shake the hands of men who showed their disappointment and who had the look in their eyes of soldiers who do not trust the commitment of their political leaders.

An hour and twenty minutes he sat in the helicopter. They'd brought in an Alouette from Rosh Pinah to ferry him back—a maintenance problem, fractured oil-feed pipe, denying him the use of the faster, more comfortable Sikorsky in which he had made the morning journey from the capital. Room for only three passengers once the army fliers had taken their seats—ADC and a bodyguard. No one to talk to, and he'd left the majority of his party on the bare stripped ground of the Heights; they'd follow by car. There was a radio in the helicopter, but that must be kept clear for operational messages; effectively he would be out of contact for the duration of the flight. Little enough information to consider at this stage. Russian aircraft hijacked, internal flight, was on its way to the West; that the involvement was Jewish; that the Soviets would take a hard line. Not much to chew on, little enough to react to.

No contour flying, not with the Prime Minister on board. Up to three thousand feet, where the sharp winds that gathered on the hills behind Tiberias buffeted and pitched at the helicopter, causing him to steady himself in his canvas seat and feel for the safety harness that he wore. Not a time for thinking, or for reflection; not a time for weighing alternatives. Dead time, lost time, that would accumulate till inevitably the pressure on the decision makers would increase. Not the way it should be, but the way it always was. Always the decisions that had to be taken in the moment of duress, never with the luxury of consideration and reflection. The penalty of living in a country perpetually in a state of war.

Flying south of the hills and towns and villages where the Palestinians liked to work, the settlements close to the Lebanese border fence. The targets the Palestinians sought out. Hard, fanatical killing teams who came to Israel to test their puny muscle against the might of a modern and sophisticated society, and who were broken on the rack of gunfire and grenade explosions, and who kept coming. Regarded by a majority of the peoples that scratched and suffered a life on the world's varied surface as the new freedom fighters, not as the murderous terrorists that the Prime Minister spoke of them as in his interviews for the American newspapers and television correspondents. This was the ground they came to, bright in the harsh sunlight below him; to the little communities that nestled close to the cultivated fields and the orange groves that were burned and dry in the heat. Men who traveled in their groups of four, having let their blood run together in the symbolic farewells in the Fatahland of South Lebanon, and who died horribly and brutally at the hands of Squad 101, the elite of the Israeli army, the counterterrorist storm squad. Terrorists they called them in his country, could find no other title for them, shunning the acceptance of such words as "guerrilla" and "commando" because that would bestow a certain fractional legality on their actions.

He was musing to himself; not thinking with the speed and clarity of which he was capable, just blowing and wafting the ideas in his head as the helicopter powered its bumping way toward Jerusalem. And what was it Qaddafi said? Muammar el-Qaddafi, President of Libya, paymaster of the assassins, organizer of their plans, harborer of their escapes. Qaddafi said there were terrorists and freedom fighters; that if the cause is right, then so too the action is justified. Any action against the State of Israel was justified; any attack could be supported if it bore the name of Palestine—that was the message of the Libyan. And the response of the Prime Minister's government had been fierce and consistent: that the international community should provide no succor to the gangs and cells of

armed men, that there should be no condoning of the terrorist, that he should be fought and brought to justice. There
must be no weakening.

The helicopter yawed its way down the scale of the altimeter, dropping sharply and without ceremony into the city with
its familiar skyline broken by the sun's flat beams splintering
light onto the golden Dome of the Rock. Was a Jew with a
gun held to a pilot's head a different flower, to be nurtured
and watered and husbanded, from the Palestinian weed that
they chopped and hoed when he took his grenades and explosives to the cockpit of the El Al plane? Did the Jew fight for
freedom or for terror? Principle or self-interest? And cruel,
vicious, wounding, the dilemma. No precedent to take comfort from. The decision of Entebbe had been easy by comparison; the decision to loose the killer squads in Europe to seek
out their Palestinian counterparts had been simple. But this
was dangerous and fraught and hazardous. Principle and expediency, principle and emotion; all bouncing and cavorting
inside him as the machine lurched the final feet to the
ground.

He hurried to the gray-green Pontiac with its curtained rear
windows and chassis that strained low under the weight of the
armor-plated body. Men around him with unshielded Uzis
and walkie-talkie radios, and police who saluted him and who
wore pistols at their belts in holsters of which the top restrain-
ing flap was unfastened. And why were they all there? One
reason, one reason only. Because of the threat of the small
groups, the men who stood apart from the shouting, chant-
ing, abusive crowds of protest. Four hundred yards from the
helicopter pad to his offices, and an elevator to the third
floor. More men in slacks and light summer shirts which they
wore outside the waists of their trousers so that their hand-
guns would be concealed and not frighten the stream of foreign visitors who came to pay their respects and tell him how
his government should conduct its affairs.

The Security Committee was waiting for him, gathered
around the table by the window, opposite his wide-topped
desk. Piled in front of the chair that he would use were the
papers that would tell him the story so far gathered of the
hijacking, what was known of the participants, the statements
of the Russians and the decisions that had been made by the

West European governments in whose territory the plane might attempt a landing. Somber reading, no light in the darkness, no crack through which optimism might worm a path.

He shuffled the paper together, waved his colleagues into chairs, understood the pain of their faces and knew they had read all that he had seen. Fools, he thought; three idiots wallowing in their own stupidity.

"One decision at least can be made," the Prime Minister said. "We cannot condemn and we cannot condone. The world will be watching for our reaction—our friends and our enemies. We cannot support these three, not publicly; at the same time, we cannot be seen to be abandoning them. Our movement must be seen through the passive channels, through suggestion."

"But that does not confront the issue." It was the senior civil servant of the Ministry of Foreign Affairs, still in his thirties, with the aggression of youth and the high brow of intellect. "The Russians are asking for the return of these people once they have landed. They are telling the Europeans that these three are criminals and must be sent back to stand trial for murder. They are accused of shooting a policeman in Kiev, and we hear now that the pilot of the aircraft has been killed. The penalty for those offenses in the Soviet Union is death. There are many in our country who would believe in such a sentence if the roles were reversed. For any Western government to permit the plane to land and refuel and facilitate its onward flight is unthinkable; that is why the Germans refused to become involved. The country in which the plane lands must disarm these three and then will have to think of its options; will have to decide whether to send them back, to their executions. Whether we do it privately or publicly, this is the issue on which we must clear our position."

"You have preempted me," said the Prime Minister. "I too see the problem. You are not alone; you do not have a unique capacity to identify the kernel of the difficulty. All of us can see it."

"We have spoken much in the past of the need for solidarity to fight the aerial warfare of the Arab groups—"

"You say the obvious," interjected the Prime Minister wearily, his ears still ringing with the hammer of the rotor blades. "We know that; we know what we have said. So what do you ask me to do? Do you ask me to tell the British, or the Dutch, or the Danes, or the French . . . do you ask me to tell them to disarm these people and put them on a flight to Moscow? Is that what you ask of me?"

The silence of the room was broken by the scraping of chair legs on the tiled floor. All except the Prime Minister pacing and searching for clarity, and the smoke rising in gray-blue columns, and coffee being poured, and each man wrestling and grappling, but unable to grip and hold the quarry.

The evening of the Middle East comes fast, running across the sandstone houses and the cement towers and the grayed roads; but it was many minutes after the shadows had infiltrated the room before the chandelier lights were switched on. That seemed to change the mood and break the stillness in which all present had cocooned themselves, emphasized the passing of time when none should be lost. The Prime Minister rapped the desk top with his pen.

"When the plane lands, we must offer our services to the government concerned. We must make an offer to help in all ways possible to ensure that there is no further bloodshed, no siege. Perhaps we could send one of our own people to talk to these three youngsters, to persuade them to surrender. We would demand one thing in return, and require a solemn promise on this: that the three should be tried in whatever country they land in for whatever offenses they have committed. There are no death sentences in Western Europe. We would accept a period of imprisonment . . ."

"And in Western Europe who has the greatest sway?" The skepticism of the Minister of Defense. "Is it we, or is it the Soviet Union? What if our appeal is rejected?"

"What is your solution, then?" Anger that his reasoning, so carefully arrived at, should face challenge so soon.

"I have no solution, as you call it. Perhaps there is none. But we must be clear in our minds what we seek for. When the French took Abu Daoud, we called for his extradition. We made noise and we flexed what muscle we possessed. It is irrelevant that it was not sufficient. On the same basis, the Soviets will want the return of these three, but that is something that we cannot permit, that is unthinkable. There would be the deepest shame on ourselves and our people if we failed to use every artifice available to us to prevent their being sent back to execution. I accept, of course, that we cannot associate our government with their actions; but at the same time I say that we cannot disassociate ourselves to the extent of permitting them to go to their deaths in a Soviet prison."

"What would you have me do? Fly the paratroops again, re-create our Entebbe? Lift them from whatever airfield they land at?" Laying on the sarcasm, the Prime Minister struck back.

"I say that we cannot hold our heads high as the representatives of the people of the Jewish state if we tolerate the sending back—"

"What do you seek to tell me?"

"For years now we have fought and struggled to rid our people in Russia of the yoke of persecution. We cannot allow, must not allow them to be sent back; the humiliation would be unacceptable."

"What, then, do you think I am suggesting? Do you believe I look toward a craven retreat? This is why I offer to send a man."

The divisions of the politicians stripping themselves of the garments worn for public consumption. The civil servants taking notes, walking clear of the storm clouds from which no advantage could come.

He broke off, tailing away, seeming to keep the last for himself and thankful for the softened knock at the door that precluded further argument and would only take them deeper into the labyrinth of confusion. A single sheet of paper, and while he read it the sound of the door closing behind the messenger. A deep sigh, from far down in his chest. Then the Prime Minister, irritated, shrugged his shoulders as if to throw off the constriction of a burden.

"Gentlemen, there is little time now. Slight opportunity only for further semantics. The Dutch government has informed our embassy in The Hague that they have decided, and they say it is with regret, that they have made certain conditions which must be met if the plane is allowed to land. They must have the word of the three that they will disarm themselves and surrender. I note that our Ambassador makes no mention of what would happen to the three should they comply with the instructions. But it would seem that the question is irrelevant. The demand has been rejected; the plane is flying on. They will be over the United Kingdom in less than three-quarters of an hour; they have enough fuel to get there, but not for a further diversion. It seems it is the British with whom we have to deal."

The Defense Minister leaned across the table, his hand outstretched and reaching for that of the Prime Minister. "I agree to what you propose. It is right for the first step. We must win more time to talk of alternatives. You have my support. You have my word."

There was a pale moon of gratification at the Prime Minister's mouth. He said, "You must find a man whom you think well of who could talk to the three; someone young; someone they will have admiration for, who can convince them. A man of our strength, of the strength of our people." And then he added, as an afterthought, half to himself and yet not caring who heard, "I would rather it had not been the British."

7

The closing of Schiphol Airport, Amsterdam, represented a huge task to the dozen air-traffic controllers on duty in the tower. All flights on the ground indefinitely delayed; simple enough, that, and only passengers' fury and carriers' frustra-. tion to contend with, but harder and more complex to handle the fifteen aircraft in various stages of final approach. Diversions to Brussels for those closest, and to Rotterdam for those which came from the north, and for those which were farther afield there were requests for information on fuel loads and suggestions that they put down at Lille or Charles de Gaulle and Orly, on the outskirts of Paris. Short-haul flights coming from North Germany and Britain's Heathrow were advised to delay takeoff until the situation had clarified. Within a matter of minutes of the order's being given, the intricate and complicated process of planning the controlled flights of some scores of aircraft across northern Europe was in apparent chaos. In the terminals there was confusion; passengers struggling into queues at the check-in counters, where the abused staff could neither accept their baggage nor award them boarding cards.

Out on the runways of Schiphol, Dutch troops had taken their lumbering tracked armored personnel carriers which are permanently stationed there on antiterrorist duties. Blue-uniformed and booted men of the police airport squad with steel helmets and M-1 carbines drove their jeeps alongside them to augment the effect of the APCs. The blocking maneuver that had been successfully used by the Germans was admired and aped till the runways offered no scope for landing, only for disaster.

But the Dutch Government faced greater emotional problems than the Germans had needed to tackle. Ever since the Yom Kippur war of 1973, when the support of the Netherlands for Israel had been unqualified through the clouds of bitter invective from the Arab oil producers, the small nation had acquired a reputation of providing a solid staff on which the Zionist state could lean and rely with confidence. For this reason, the Dutch Cabinet, in emergency session in The Hague, had felt the necessity to offer landing permission to the Ilyushin, but had attached such sufficiently deterrent riders that they felt confident they would deflect the Aeroflot's route beyond their airspace, beyond their responsibility.

It was by now academic what line the Cabinet would have taken in response to the demand of the Soviet Union that the three be returned to Soviet jurisdiction. The plane had circled the airport twice, watched by huge crowds of transistortoting passengers and mechanics and ground staff, before heading toward the dikes and the seawall and the cold evening waters of the North Sea, still chilled as if in defiance of the long day's summer warmth.

Like a bird that was lost and uncertain and afraid.

Although on their circuits of Schiphol, David and Isaac had been able to identify the faint and indistinct shapes of the blocking vehicles, their feelings were much changed from those above Hannover when they had first realized that the West was reluctant to play host to their errant migration from the East.

The navigator had provided them with the piece of paper on which was written in his neat hand the brief message from the Dutch authorities that listed the conditions of landing. They had studied it, read it perhaps three times each, trying to win the nuances of the carefully prepared government statement of policy, and known, both of them, that they would fly on.

"Where can we go to?" David had asked the navigator, quietly and with respect for his knowledge, as if accepting that in spite of their guns and their loaded magazines and their proven willingness to kill, they had need of the man's expertise.

"We can go south. Try Belgium, perhaps, or the French. We can go north toward Denmark, or back into the Federal Republic. If we continue we will reach Britain. But if they make us circle, if there is more waiting, then we have no further alternatives. We would not be able to regain the European continent. If we go to Britain, that is where we must land." The pilot officer supported him, wordlessly pointing to the quivering fuel counters which now edged past the vertical toward the wing of the measurement arc and which hustled closer to the red warning line.

The navigator waited for them to determine their next move. No interference, sensing perhaps that at this moment they relied heavily on him and that in their dependence on his skills he might exert, subtly and imperceptibly, an influence. If he antagonized or disputed with them, then the cotton-thin relationship could be destroyed. He knew that at this moment there was no possibility of abject surrender, that the time was not ripe for him to begin the gentle and clandestine process of wearing down the resolve of the two men who shared the cockpit with himself and the pilot officer; knew that that time would come later, when the lives of the passengers were not at such direct risk.

He was just past his twenty-seventh birthday, tanned from his holiday on the Bulgarian coast, engaged to be married and flush with the confidence that came from the knowledge that he did his job well, that he would advance. The men who stood behind him and looked over his shoulder at the air routes and tried to decipher the meanings of his lines and paths and to assess the distances he talked of and weigh them against their scant knowledge of the different implications of reception in the north, in the south, or the west, were only a very little younger than he. Similar to the people he saw in the streets of Moscow and Leningrad and Kiev when he was on layover. A great ordinariness about them, he thought; nothing to distinguish them from the wallowing, compliant herd of the mediocre; nothing in their faces, their hands, their clothes, nothing to make them stand out . . . only the guns.

He suppressed the slow smile: their only claim on him, on his interest, his attention, his curiosity . . . the guns, and the fact that if they were fired then a planeload of people would perish. But such ordinariness surprised him, and he wondered how they could have chosen this course, and why, why they were there, why they had started, just why.

"We will go to Britain." David speaking, evenly and in his own voice, calmed now. "I want it made clear that this time we land. You must tell them of our fuel position, but not till we are near their airfields, till they cannot move us on, bundle us up, send us elsewhere." He was going to say more, but clamped on his tongue; had to talk to Isaac more, had to have consensus, had to draw again on the syringe strength of his friend.

Again the nose of the plane rose, climbing once more. The Kingfisher soared, but there was a tiredness now and the engines no longer throbbed with the exultation of freedom.

Out in the passageway between the cockpit and the passenger cabin, where there was storage space and the closets and the forward toilet and privacy, the two men huddled together. David facing the flight-deck crew, Isaac the passengers, both studying their charges, speaking from the sides of their mouths, bodies close, and still the guns aimed and pointed as if a danger that had yet to materialize itself was possible.

"I had thought it would be finished by now," said David.

"They have made it difficult for us. They will not change now."

"I did not think it possible . . ."

"And we do not make it easy for them. It is not they alone who can hurt, who have teeth."

"You have heard the stories of the Arabs on the radio . . ."

"It will be difficult, but they can be made to soften."

"They give in to threats."

"We have to take the philosophy of the Arabs, David."

"And we have hostages, and we must use them."

"If we want to see Israel, David."

"If we are to force them, if they must bow to us . . . but then it will be a long road . . ."

"It has been a long road already that we have come from Kiev."

"You know what it means, Isaac? If we are to go on, if we are to succeed?"

"I know what it means. I understand."

"We must use the passengers . . ."

"I understand that."

How docile they sit, how quiet, and they do not know what I have talked of, what David has accepted, what I know. Like the Jews of old. Do not know they no longer count as human beings, that their destiny has forsaken them, nameless and unidentifiable, pawns to be toppled and levered and pushed, casualties that will fall if our will does not rise supreme over that of the people that we will face.

Expendable . . . and how many of them? How many to be taken off the board before we convince the people on the ground that we are traveling to Israel? One? Perhaps the Italian, the man who sits in the middle of the front row of the group, who cannot look at me, who has the capped teeth and the silk tie; would he be enough to convince them? Perhaps the schoolmaster; perhaps we will need two. With his glasses that do not hide the way he stares back at me, not because he is brave and has courage but because he is afraid to lose face in the presence of the children. If we kill him as well, will that bend them? Take a third, and why not? The American with his bleeding head and the handkerchief that his wife has wrapped around it, who seems like a farmer now in the field with his hay, who must stop the sweat from dropping from his scalp to his eyes. Why not him also, if they hesitate, if they wish to test us? And the children—what of the children, Isaac? A wave of nausea rising through his stomach, creeping upward and clawing at his throat. A terrible shame and ignominy, a humiliation that the thought should even come to him. He had made David say it first, led him to the cliff face, nagged him, pressured him, forced him into a defile, till they had come together to the ultimate—the children. And what if their will is stronger than ours, if they do not bend? How many do we kill to find out the temper of their resolution?

He seemed to shrug to himself, disengaging from David. It will not be so; we will have the fuel. They will give us the fuel.

A full-measured, slowed, leaden-paced hour since they had last come to the back of the plane to see her. Only the seat tops to look at, and the hands that were on the heads, and the occasional stolen glances over the shoulders to see that she was still there—that the pistol was in her hand. Hatred on some faces when they looked back, something they would not dare when Isaac was watching them, not since he had struck the American. But that was an hour back, and they looked differently at Rebecca, because she was a girl, just a girl, and had no right to be feared.

But they do not come and talk with me; they leave me here, isolated, ignored, searching the length of the plane to lip-read their whispers far away as they meet in the corridor outside the cockpit. Because I screamed—is that why I am not to be trusted? she thought. Have I less strength than the others, and is that the only currency they value—strength, whatever that may be; man's strength; their stupid, ignorant puerile virility? David has screamed too, and I have heard it, heard it the length of the plane, heard it with all the passengers and seen their heads jump up like those of jerked marionettes and subside cautiously again when calm returned to the cockpit area.

They loathe me, these people; they would want to stamp and kick and pummel the life from me, beat and beat till each bone is broken; that is the revenge they seek, and only the gun prevents it. Only the squat and polished security of the gun holds them back, because that is what they fear.

The headmaster's hand was raised.

Like all the teachers she'd ever known. In his best clothes because he was taking the children somewhere; would have polished his shoes, selected his best shirt. A compilation of Soviet virtues, preaching the Love of the Motherland, Industriousness and Frugality, Friendship and Comradeship, Love of Studies and Consciousness. Teacher's hand raised. Ludicrous, the classroom table turned.

"The children want to relieve themselves, miss."

Of course they do. Don't we all?

"The children have been very patient, miss. They have waited a long time."

Just like the American. Called her "miss" because she had the gun; would have put his sharp bony knee in her crotch if she hadn't had the gun, and kick her, and kick her, and kick her. Looked for Isaac, but he was lost from sight again. Lost in the bloody cockpit, where, with David, he spent all his time; time when he should have come to the back and told her what was happening, what the descents had meant, why they had not landed, why they had flown on. Was it as the American had said? That there wasn't a red carpet, that nobody would want them. What was the word he'd used? Pariah, that was it. A being that fed off the scraps, that turned people's noses; an outcast; something set aside. Could have called her a Jew, couldn't he? Same thing, what he meant, but nobody said what they meant, not while she held the pistol.

"Miss, the children have been very patient, most patient. There can be no harm in their going to the lavatory."

No sign of Isaac, and anyway, what harm could there be from it? That was what they had left her there for, because they had problems to wrestle with in the cockpit. It was not out of choice that they had left her there, but for a reason. David must have had reason; Isaac too. She was being stupid, playing the idiot, and they had left her in charge and given her responsibility. Above the droning power of the engines that permeated the insulated cabin she shouted her answer to the headmaster.

"They can come in threes. Just the children to start with. They must come from each block of seats at a time, and the next will follow only when the previous has finished."

She pushed the soft-drinks trolley end on to the aisle so that there was a gap through which the children could pass, and the first three rose and hurried toward her, relief written on their young faces.

"Thank you, miss," the headmaster called to her from his seat, craning around, watching the procedure, watching her.

Disciplined children. The product of the system and the Pioneers, taught at school to conform and to show respect, bobbing their heads with acknowledgment as they passed her on their way to the three rear toilets, and another conveyer-belt expression of gratitude when they came back into the cabin and moved to their seats. Bright faces, scrubbed with soap, and short hair for the boys, neat ribbon-tied pigtails for the girls. A few years back and that was what she had been, not different, not separated—until she had met David; before she had known Isaac and learned the power of a policeman's pistol, the pistol that was in her hand. They regarded the gun as they passed by her, but were too well mannered to stare at it, too well schooled to give it more than a glance. Eleven years old most of them, twelve a few, and now regimented and able to hide their fear of the gun under the umbrella of childish curiosity. Doing what they had been told to do.

The headmaster was out of his seat and walking toward her loosely holding the hand of a child, leading him and coaxing him toward the gap between the trolley and the galley wall.

He said quietly, in a voice that would not embarrass and attract attention, "This one, miss, he has a kidney problem. There is equipment under his clothes, and I must help him."

She let him pass, didn't consider it, scented the damp perspiration of his body under his suit as he pushed through the narrow entrance that was available. She turned to watch them disappear inside the toilet door, saw the "Occupied" sign light up and twisted herself back again, easy and relaxed so that she faced the front, dominating her passengers.

She was not aware of him as he came close to her back; had no sense of his proximity; was concerned only with the woman holding the mewling baby who was rising from her seat far to the front; understood nothing of his plan till his hands were on her.

The baby crying, always that bloody child crying . . . and then the sudden, panic-stricken fear, coming alive, blossoming in a single spring moment. One hand across her mouth and fingers squeezing against her lips so that she could not scream, shoving the ends with the clipped dirt-tasting nails between her teeth so that she could not bite, and the other hand clawing for her right wrist and seeking to break the grip that held the gun. Had to get the hand from her mouth, had to scream, had to give warning; tumbling through her mind the need to arouse the others who were at the front, and all the time the fingers in her mouth choking at her, denying her air, and the grip on her wrist was vise-tight and closing so that the blood could not pass, her muscles not respond. Others in front of her, coming from their seats, gigantic, looming and fearsome, and she was falling . . . another of the schoolmasters, one whom she took for a farmer—and a boot caught her hard on the shin, causing her to buckle and collapse to the carpet of the aisle.

It was the fall that broke the headmaster's grip on her arm. The jerk with which her body collapsed was not anticipated; the sudden shift of her balance and weight was too great for the pliant fingers not used to physical action. When she hit the floor, the gun exploded in a blast of noise and cordite fumes, and she winced from the flash burn to her chest that seemed to sear a way through the fabric of her dress. Hands all around her now, pummeling and driving to reach under her body to where the gun was, pulling at her thighs, at the slight softness of her breasts, frantic in their haste now that the noise of the discharging bullet had sounded the alarm.

And then there was no one. Liberation. The hands withdrawn. She pushed back the hair from her face and looked up. Saw the feet that were edging back from her, moving away. Tilted her head farther. Their hands were on their heads again, faces of guilt and fear, the boys found out, and halfway down the aisle was Isaac with the submachine gun at his shoulder, and far past him and guarding his back was David. Just the droning pull of the engines and the fractional swaying in the air currents of the plane on steady course; no words. The men who had left their seats making their way back, ashamed, caught out, a girl to disarm and they had failed, and now they faced the wrath of the young man with the chill in his eyes. He would not have made the mistakes that she had, and their faces showed their concern at the retribution he would exact, the toll that he would take.

Deep throbbing pain in her leg where the man had kicked her, and an aching through her shoulders where a knee had pressured downward against her spine, and a place on her forehead where there would be a bruise from the impact against the metal stanchion of a seat support.

Interrogation in Isaac's voice. "Why were they out of their seats?"

Difficult to speak at first; had to get the air back into her pinched lungs.

"They said the children should go to the toilet; they said there was one who needed help, who was ill; that was how they came behind me."

"Nobody was to move." Cold of a tundra wind.

"But they said the children wanted to go—"

"You were given an instruction. You disobeyed it. You jeopardized the whole damned scene."

"But the children have to pee, Isaac. It was not . . . How was I to know?"

"If they want to pee, they can use their damned pants. You nearly destroyed everything, the whole plan, and you alone could have destroyed it." No anger, not the burning in his eyes, but something else that was inanimate, had the haunt of death as if the passion had been quelled and replaced by deep ice-bound winter. She had never seen him like that be-

fore, not with the contempt turning the lines of his mouth
and the reddened patches on the high points of his cheeks,
and the hands that were white and bloodless in their grip of
the machine gun.

"Which one was it? Which one attacked you?"

As if in a limbo of loyalties she hesitated, the struggle war-
ring inside her as to whether she should identify the headmaster. What would Isaac do? Would he kill him? Had she
the power to sentence the man, to cause his execution? He
was closer to her than to Isaac, with his head bowed, and she
could see the bald top of his scalp, and the places where the
gray hair still grew, and the places where the revealed skin
was blotched and discolored, and . . . and he had tried to kill
her, that man; that was why he had struggled with her, to kill
her and to kill David and Isaac.

"It was the one in the aisle seat, four rows from you, on the
left."

"Louder," said Isaac, but his voice was hushed and low,
competing with the aircraft's power. "Don't be afraid. Don't
believe that these people will save you. They'll cut your
throat, your little white throat, Rebecca, bleed you like an
animal. If they could they would have bludgeoned you to
death—if the gun had not fired, if I had not come. Which
one was it?"

"It was the one in the aisle seat, four rows from you, on the
left." She looked away as Isaac advanced down the aisle between the avenue of passengers, no heads turning to watch
him, just the shuffle of his canvas shoes on the carpet.

"Listen to what I say," Isaac said to the headmaster. His
voice as in a conversation, a tone of muted friendship, bi-
zarre to her and obscene. "The Germans have prevented us
from landing, and the Dutch too. They have driven trucks
and armored cars across the runways of their airports to make
it impossible for us to land. And now we are going to England. We have fuel to get there and no farther, and they will
let us land for that reason.

"But we have not come this far to finish in England; we go
to Israel. Perhaps we will have to show the English that we
have the will to fly to Israel, that we are not as the Jews were,
that we are a new generation, as the sabras are. If it is necessary we will shoot you, one by one, to prove to the English

that we have determination. If that should happen, then I make a promise to you, a promise that I shall keep. If anyone dies on this plane to convince the English of our will, then it will be you. You will be the first; you will be the one we call for."

Isaac walked on till he reached Rebecca. Held out his hand for her to give him the pistol; checked the mechanism, made sure there was a bullet in the breech, that the gun was live. "The mistake must not be repeated, Rebecca." He turned on his heel and strode back up the length of the passenger cabin. And the Ilyushin pursued its course across the smooth, unruffled waters of the North Sea toward the coastline of England and the Kingfisher's landfall.

The news that the Dutch landing conditions had not been accepted was sufficient for the summons to Charlie Webster to attend the Emergency Committee meeting in the offices of the Home Secretary in Whitehall.

The Home Secretary was in the chair. With him were one of his junior ministers; two civil servants of the Department, both with the grading of principal undersecretary; a lowly Foreign Office minister, in order that the deliberations of the two giant bureaucracies could be dovetailed through liaison, and the Commissioner of the Metropolitan Police from Scotland Yard. At the far end of the polished mahogany table at which they sat, and directly opposite the Home Secretary, was Parker Smith, whose suggestion it had been that they call for the man in his section who specialized in the study of Russian dissident groups. Windows open because it was a warm and windless evening, with the murmur of the London rush-hour traffic faintly audible from the courtyard onto which the Minister's office faced. Coffee cups on the table, and filled ashtrays, and the paraphernalia of the meeting— torn-up scraps of paper; others crumpled and discarded, some with the artistic and intricate doodles of the Foreign Office man; briefcases and maps; a telephone on an extended cord at the Home Secretary's elbow.

A messenger in the blue livery of the Home Office had been waiting in the wide and high-ceilinged lobby for Charlie to arrive. He hadn't bothered with the formality of signing him in, and together they had taken the sweeping staircase two steps at a time till they were on the second floor and walking briskly along the central corridor flanked by the un-cleaned oil portraits of the Minister's predecessors in office. A brief knock and the messenger opened the door. Charlie spluttered involuntarily as the wall of smoke hit him, befogging his nostrils and his eyes.

"Mr. Charles Webster, gentlemen."

The Home Secretary waved him toward a seat, the only one vacant and halfway down the table on the right-hand side. Interest on the faces of all except Parker Smith. Different type of fellow from the ones the politicians and civil servants of rank were accustomed to doing business with: suit not as sharply pressed, and shirt looking as though it had done service the day before; the shave wearing off because he had not slipped into the men's room at lunchtime as these more public men customarily did.

Parker Smith sitting easily in the company, anxious to put Charlie at ease and overdoing it, sounding patronizing, sort of speak-up-boy-they-won't-bite. "Charlie, I've told the Minister and his colleagues here of your background. Told them of your experience overseas and in Dublin, and I've sketched through the work you do now, with emphasis on your predictions of last night."

The Home Secretary cut him short.

"Mr. Webster, the Aeroflot flight is perhaps a quarter of an hour off our coastline. We can keep it circling for a bit, but there will not be much opportunity for equivocation. We are advised that it has enough fuel for perhaps a further forty minutes' flying time, three-quarters of an hour at the most. It is our intention to put it down at Stansted in Essex. We do not have the luxury of our European colleagues of being able to pass the buck. The buck stops here; the fuel load of the plane determines that. We will obviously attempt to persuade the hijackers to surrender without recourse to needless and stupid further bloodshed, but we have to know right from the time that the wheels hit the ground what sort of people we are dealing with. We want you to put some flesh on them, Mr. Webster. I don't mind conjecture, provided that it's based on very sound background, but what you tell us may have to be acted upon very quickly, so I'd prefer caution in your analysis."

Civil servants and junior ministers with their sharpened pencils and gold-plated pens poised; only the Home Secretary and Parker Smith looking at him. And what do they want to hear? What can you give them, Charlie?

Tell them about the kids. Without a dollar or a pound or a piaster or a peso to their names. Kids who hate the system, want to break it and smash it and have learned that you don't walk through Hyde Park shouting anymore; you get yourself a nice shiny Armalite and shoot a copper in Belfast; you get dished out an AK and blow a Brit squaddie to kingdom come in Crater; you get an RPG and cuddle up to an airport fence to bag yourself an El Al jumbo. They're waiting for you, Charlie. So go slowly, and don't use long words.

"There have been two confirmed hijack attempts out of the Soviet Union in the last few years. A family took a light aircraft to Turkey. Insignificant, and a one-off incident. Then there was the Leningrad plan that aborted and never got off the ground—a group of Jews who wanted to take over a plane, unarmed, and fly it to Finland. It was a short-haul flight, and the whole thing was a disaster, the group hopelessly infiltrated by KGB. All arrested at the airport and some still inside.

"There is a third incident, but it's less hard and we have fewer details, even through 'I' channels: Israeli announcement that a hijacked internal flight was coming out, and it never came—'74 or '75, I think. From the East Bloc there have been a series of chaps jumping a plane and coming over, but not Russians. There hasn't been a major Russian one before, so that's the first bit of new ground. Now the second one: those people up there are apparently Jews. In the past the Jewish dissidents have for the most part contented themselves with media protests, clandestine interviews, press conferences, civil disobedience where they'll be noticed by foreigners and it will get reported, trying to put pressure on the local authorities and most of their efforts beamed at the United States. Chief contention has been emigration either to Israel or to the West generally, followed by complaints of ethnic discrimination. That's very broad and very brief, but probably sufficient."

There was the click of a cigarette lighter, the noise of nibs scratching on paper.

"These people, however, are different," Charlie went on. "We've had a policeman shot in Kiev—wounded, apparently seriously, and nothing in the media. That indicates it was neither criminal nor casual. The one thing that would really concern the people over there is if they consider this a target shooting, an attempt at a gesture, though a botched one for all that. A gesture equates with conspiracy and organization. That would concern them. There have been terror attacks put down to minority nationalist groups, but nothing that we have been able to identify as internally aggressive and specifically Jewish. As I said, we had the shooting of the policeman. We've also heard rumors round the University area that a Jewish student was arrested a few days ago and that militia reinforcements were seen moving into the city. Perhaps he talked—the one they picked up—and the assumption has to be that the security people were on the point of staging a large-scale arrest sweep. And then we have a hijack."

Charlie paused. Not for effect, just to clear his mind again; didn't make speeches, not in his line of work. The difficult bit starts now, he thought; where we lose the facts; where we start jogging along with the theory.

"There are two types of hijacking or hostage-taking operations. When the Palestinians do it, along with the people associated with them, it's usually what we call a leverage operation—designed to get some of the comrades out of prison, and usually an Israeli prison. Doubled with that is the publicity factor of attention being turned on their operation, with all the attendant explanations as to who they are and what their grievance is. That was Dawson's Field in Jordan, OPEC in Vienna, the Air France to Entebbe. All well documented.

"That's one type. Then there's the other sort—what we call a breakout job, which is what I think this one is. Kids who felt that time was running out at home and were looking for the fastest and most successful bolt they could manage. Difficult place to go underground, the Soviet Union, especially if it all starts falling round your ears quickly. You'd need months to set up an underground situation, just for the paperwork of changed identity. They didn't reckon they were capable of that, so they've tried the bunk. I doubt if it was planned more than a few hours before takeoff, and their major success was very simply to get the guns onto the aircraft. They're probably young—early twenties at the most, naive politically by the standards that we are familiar with; and by this stage they'll be frightened and dangerous."

Waiting for someone to interrupt, get him off the hook, but nobody did.

"Keep going, Mr. Webster," and the gentle rebuke from the Home Secretary: "Please remember that if we have any advantages at this stage, time is not one of them."

"I say dangerous because they will have believed that they would be permitted to put down anywhere in the West. They've tried twice now, and as you explained the fuel logistics, this is their last chance. They'll know that if they're still to get to Israel, then they've a fair amount of shouting to get through first. You have to be prepared for them to shift from breakout to leverage, if and when they discover that the fuel wagons aren't going to be beside the plane and filling her up."

"There is no possibility that the plane will be permitted to fly to Israel. Both from the diplomatic side and the question of principle involved, that eventuality has not been considered." The basic approach had been agreed long before Charlie had arrived, relayed to the Prime Minister at his holiday retreat in the South of England, sanctioned by him without dispute. So that's the policy, Charlie—taking a hard line. Easy to be tough with this one, he thought: one-off job.

"I cannot be definite," Charlie said, "but I would expect these people to go hard once they find that things aren't that rosy. They'll know the case histories of previous hijacks: they can take in BBC, VOA— plenty of radio sets that can pick up that kind of thing in the Ukraine; no problem of jamming now, reception's not difficult. I wouldn't think they'll have a stamina fallback; they won't be able to keep up the pressure for long—forty-eight hours or so; but in the meantime, expect them to play it rough."

"Will they be intelligent?" The undersecretary with responsibility for coordinating and implementing the decisions of the Emergency Committee. The high pitch of the public school and private means that Charlie detested—but it was a good and important question.

"Academically they'll be bright. They'll have an ideology, at any rate, that will stem from their breeding, their position in Soviet society. Committed people. Probably they'll believe they are prepared to die for it all provided the moment isn't too close at hand. They'll be similar enough to all the other groups. When you get down to it—start trading, that is— you'll find them the same breed as the Palestinians, Baader-Meinhof, Tupamaros, Monteneros, Provies. They'll be speaking a different language—that's all you'll notice."

"Do you call the Provos intellectuals, Mr. Webster?" queried the undersecretary.

"You asked me a different question. You asked me whether these people were intelligent. You don't need a university degree and marks at school to be good at this game, but you have to have intelligence, be sharp, know your way round and keep your thinking cap on. I say again, these people have done bloody well to get this far; it takes a bit more than luck, you know."

"Is there anything you'd like to say in conclusion, Charlie?" Parker Smith was filling his briefcase with assorted papers; cigarettes stubbed out; pens removed to inside pockets; ties straightened.

"Only this. They've come a long way, these three. But they think they've a fair old mileage still to come. Don't underestimate them. Take them very carefully to start with."

Charlie sat back in his seat, sank his backside into the upholstery, felt tired, hadn't the old resilience. The man next to him—there had been no introductions and Charlie didn't know his name—pushed three photographs across the table to where Charlie could see them. Snapshots, and they hadn't traveled well on the photofax machine from Moscow to the Foreign Office. Blurred and creased from the printing apparatus, but still the recognizable features. Names printed in Russian and English across the bottom of each picture. Straight out of the bloody Bible.

"Mr. Webster, I'm going to Stansted now by car. I'd like you to accompany me."

The Home Secretary had risen; gestured to Charlie to lead through the door; follow him out to the corridor and the rear staircase that led to the car park. The Minister's black Humber waited there, with a chauffeur and his personal bodyguard, and a three-liter Rover, with its engine idling, that would drive behind them. Three in the back they managed— Minister, undersecretary and Charlie.

Out into the traffic, swinging east from Whitehall toward the City of London, where the building faces shaded from the falling sun were already darkening. End of a routine commercial day, and the pavements thronged with the last shifts of commuters heading for main-line stations, bus stops and underground trains; only hesitating for their evening papers, succumbing to the luxuriant propaganda of the billboards with the compulsion of the headlines . . . OUR HIJACK ALERT . . . BRITAIN PREPARES FOR RED HIJACK CRISIS. They'd be there after the plane landed, Charlie thought; no chance of avoiding that. The Ilyushin would be at Stansted when they arrived, and Charlie pictured again the three faces that they'd shown him. Stupid little bastards and don't know what they've bitten off, and'll wish when this is over they'd stayed at home and played kids' games.

And now you're deep down in the pit, Charlie, and after you'd said you didn't want to see the ladder anymore and wanted a desk job. Should have been franker, Charlie, months ago, told them that you were sick of the killing, sick of being a guardian of the right of the middle-aged, middle class middlebrows to sleep in their beds at night. Should have spoken then, and you didn't. Kept your speech till tonight, till you impressed the big men, and they wanted you as part of the team, want you to help screw these three, help con them—help kill them. Stupid little bastards.

"Too slow. Too slow. What do you think they'll be doing— sitting around chewing betel, smoking hash? They'll be ready for you. They know what time we come, can set their watches by it. Always we come at dawn. They know and they are ready for you, and you must be quicker than they. If not, then it is you who are dead, not they."

He stood watching the soldiers as they trooped sheepishly back to their start line, which was the top of the cement staircase. Eight soldiers, all of them crestfallen at his condemnation of their work, and the air was choking heavy with the reek of fumes from the flash grenades they had thrown and the blank cartridges they had fired.

"You must remember that this for us is a rehearsed drill, simple and straightforward. You will have experienced it many times, so that it has no strangeness to you. But for them it will be the first time. However ready they are, if you are fast enough you will have the time. When you hear the machine-gun fire outside, then you must explode, you must go. You have to be faster, or you are feed for the worms. Again we do it."

Thirty-one years old, Arie Benitz, and wearing on his denimed shoulders, black against the olive green, the insignia of lieutenant colonel. He commanded the most specialized force in the Israeli armed services, the antiterrorist storm squad. Akin to both his predecessors, who had died leading their men on operations, he was a draftee from the Parachute Brigade. One who had held the rank had died in the assault on the beachfront Savoy Hotel in Tel Aviv after Palestinians had sprinted with their hostages to the top-floor rooms; the other, from a random sniper round during the mopping-up stages of the Entebbe rescue mission. Any new commander will insist that the training of his men bear his own hallmark, his own stamp, especially when the expertise called for is the ability to prize out dedicated and determined fighters from the cramped rooms where they have chosen to die, and die if possible in the company of their hostages.

The building that Benitz and his front-line section used for training was a three-floor block of disused sleeping quarters in the big army barracks on the Beersheba road out of Ashdod. They were working the top floor, because that was where the vermin usually sheltered with their prey of terrified and hushed civilians, where the space for movement of the attack force was limited, the opportunity for varying the direction of assault was minimal.

Hand on his stopwatch. Blast on the whistle clamped between his teeth. The long, hammering chant of the outside machine guns that would be aimed for the windows of the last bunker the Palestinians would creep to. High fire aimed to pass into the rooms and then impact against the ceilings— fire to make a man hesitate in his desire to win courage, to force him to the floor where he would cringe, to gain the precious seconds the attackers must have.

At the first echo of the firing, he screamed at the top of his voice. "Go, you bastards! Go, you buggers!" First man raking the door, flattened against the wall that was adjacent to its hinges. Number two crashing it with his weight, a fraction of a second after the firing stopped. Number three with the grenade pins already pulled and hurling them into the opened space. Fourth, fifth, sixth and seventh and eighth, bullocking through the smoke in the moments after the explosions and firing for the corners as they entered each room, where the man who already knows that he is doomed will hide for an illusion of protection. When the next group came from Fatahland, Arie Benitz would be fourth in line, fourth man, but the first through the door. It was traditional that the commander led from the front—not in practice, when the men worked on the drills, but when it was real: when there was the smell of the Palestinians who came from the camps with their filth and their hate and their Kalashnikov rifles.

"Better," he said, as they emerged. Smiles now from proud men who valued his accolade. "Better. Three and a half seconds from the machine-gun fire to the grenade explosions. Seven seconds till the last of you was inside. At that speed you have a chance—perhaps only two hairy asses shot off." Low murmur of laughter from the squad. Hard, battle-tested young men all of them, born and raised inside the State of Israel. Helmets covered in camouflage cloth and netting; denims not encumbered with any webbing that might hinder the rush forward; on their backs a weird and apparently incomprehensible series of fluorescent strips in varying patterns, each different from the others, which told the trained soldier which man was in front of him, what was his job—essential in the half-light in which they would fight.

"We will go in one more time."

He went inside the rooms beyond the flapping and damaged door that creaked with a widow's sigh; rearranged the target dummies of beaten straw wound about with sacking and adorned with the grotesque masks that his men had fashioned; put them in different recesses and corners from where they had been the last time, under beds, behind chairs, deep in shadow; lit a candle in the inner hallway that would serve as the only illumination for the soldiers. This was the way it was learned, the killing game. None of the long-range-marksman crap that the Germans had tried at Munich; close-quarters work, body to body, point-blank range, near enough for the nose to find them, the eyes to see them, the ears to catch the sob for mercy as you fired. Time to loosen the muzzles again, slip the leashes, send forth the pack.

When he came back out of the apartment and slammed the

door shut behind him, he saw the stranger among the troops. Not one of the unshaven, dirt-smeared soldiers gangling and lolling in apparent semisleep that was deceptive, but a ranking officer in office uniform. Could have cursed the damned men: not one of them stiffened, not one of them erect, not a salute among them. No recognition of the deputy commander of the barracks. Because they were paratroopers and had now been elevated to antiterrorist standby, and the outsider was just an admin man.

"Colonel, my apologies for the interruption. There are men from the Ministry of Defense, from Tel Aviv. They are in my office to see you."

"We have one more run; then we're through. My respects, and I'll be with them in ten minutes."

"I do not think, Colonel, they would appreciate such a delay."

Pleasure on his men's faces. Knowledge that the shouting and hectoring was over for another day. Time for a shower and something to eat, time to get out of the sweat-sodden fatigues they had worn through the day and half the night.

"Don't look so damned lively," the colonel snapped at them as he followed his escort to the stairs. "Tomorrow we're back here, and all day, till we lose at least a second off the entry time."

But awaiting the men of the storm squad stationed in the Central Military Zone of Israel was a long sleep—no early call in the morning, no immediate repetition of the assault techniques. From a briefing by two Military Intelligence officers and a senior official of the Foreign Ministry, Colonel Arie Benitz was driven to an Israeli Air Force base. Under the mantle of the bare, starlit darkness he was strapped into the navigator's seat of a Phantom fighter-bomber and flown at many hundreds of miles an hour to the Royal Air Force base at Akrotiri, Cyprus. At the cemetery-quiet airfield, denuded of activity by successive Defense White Papers, he was transferred without formality to a VC-10 of Support Command. He sat far to the rear of the aircraft and separated himself from the small groups of service personnel and their families. During the five-and-a-half-hour flight to Brize Norton, the transport base in Wiltshire, he would have a chance to mull over, to evaluate, the direction that had been given him, to concern himself with the role that the Prime Minister of his country had asked him to play. No passport, only his IDF identity card, and the uniform still splendid with the twin flashes of fluorescent light on the back. At Akrotiri they'd assured him that he'd have five minutes in the washhouse at Brize Norton before the helicopter flight to Stansted— enough to change into borrowed and begged clothes that would rank as less conspicuous.

At the time that the colonel was flying out of Israel, Aeroflot flight 927, scheduled for Tashkent, was beginning its final approach to the Essex airfield of Stansted.

The original course plotted by her navigator had taken Pilot Officer Tashova toward Heathrow, London's principal airport and one of the busiest in the world. Paris, thankful that the ultimate responsibility was not hers, had guided the plane in accented English along Green One, leading her to the fan markers, the radio beacons that drove a high, shrill whistle into her earphones and flashed sharp lights at her control panel. Paris signed off, with gratitude, offering as final consolation the London airways frequency of 128.45. The Ilyushin should begin to call for further instructions.

That the navigator had brought the plane south before beginning the short drop across the English Channel was not out of error but deliberate. There was a determination that whatever authorities now had jurisdiction over the plane should have no doubts from their calculations that the fuel tanks were drying out and parched, that the flight time was exhausted. From the cockpit on the eastern approach to London they saw the distant hazed lights of the lit-up city that merged into the ink-dark horizon, and then the instruction had come for the diversion to Stansted, an airfield that neither Tashova nor her navigator had heard of. No reason why they should—not an international strip, but dealing with the trade of holiday charters and offering facilities to virgin British Airways pilots and crew on their takeoffs and bumps.

Incomprehensible to David the instructions on flight level, squawk ident, course-degree numerals, VOR locations. A foreign tongue, a foreign science. Not possible for him to know that Stansted had been chosen as the airfield in Britain most suitable to receive a hijacked airliner—that the studies had been made by Security and Board of Trade a full three years earlier. It was remote, could easily be sealed, and if it had to be shut down because of an alien parked presence on the runways, disruption of the massive traffic using British airspace would be minimal. A nice and cozy and intimate and private hitting ground—that was what Stansted was designated for.

As the Ilyushin headed away from London, its red indicator lights flashing the message of its traverse over the Essex countryside, three companies of the Third Royal Regiment of Fusiliers were beating a path down the country lanes from Colchester, the barracks town to which they had returned thirty-six hours earlier from four months' duty in Londonderry. Leave abruptly canceled, and orders to the commanding officer to provide a military cordon. The fusiliers traveled in the high-powered, whining Saracen armored cars and in the clumsy three-ton Bedfords; men disappointed in the cancellation of the reunions with their families, but for all that thrusting the zany adrenaline through their bodies at the prospect of seeing for themselves, watching, guarding over, the plane. The plane that had come from Russia, the plane that dominated the television news. . . .

Farther away, but closing with greater velocity on Stansted, a formation of Puma troop-carrying helicopters, bringing a Special Air Service detachment from their distant camp on the Welsh border. These were the men specifically trained in antihijack operations, and the lack of talk among the eighteen being ferried across southern England reflected their frustration at being summoned late, due to arrive only minutes before the airliner—little time for reconnoitering, preparation, before they slipped to their planned and practiced positions.

From Divisional police stations in the county, FN automatic rifles and Smith & Wesson pistols were distributed to men of the Regional Crime Squad. Uniformed police were dispatched to set up roadblocks on the approaches, on the roads from Saffron Walden and Thaxted and Great Dunmow and Bishop's Stortford. Keep the rubberneckers back; hasten the arrival of the various agencies, civilian and military, now speeding toward Stansted to greet the arrival of the Ilyushin.

David knew none of this; just watched the cold, unspeaking

skills of Anna Tashova as she alternately cudgeled and ca-
ressed her controls; followed her instructions that came from
over her shoulder. Knew nothing of the guns and the armor
and the tensions that were amassing and that would await
him.

Flaps moving again, change in the engine pitch, deep-
throat rumble of the undercarriage dropping, and the passengers were craning at the cabin windows, searching out the
lights on the ground.

It would take more than a blow from a gun barrel to depress the inherent cheerfulness of Edward R. Jones, Jr.; and
besides, his wife had managed a picture of his head and the
blood-stained handkerchief, right after she'd attached it,
when the blood was really red, before the wound dried out.

"Hey, miss," he said, turning again in his seat, looking back
to Rebecca, "and you don't have to get that gorilla to belt me
this time, but is this it? Are we really going in this time?"

She did not understand the American with his bright plum-
age and his bravado; could not come to terms with the man;
and she said nothing.

"Have it your way, miss. But I hope you know where the
ball game goes from here. It could be awfully disappointing,
miss, awfully messy."

Still no response, and he smiled at her, two and a half
thousand dollars' worth of capped teeth, and turned back to
the window.

The Italians talking fast and excitedly among themselves,
tightening their seat belts, leaning sometimes forward, sometimes backward to spread their conversation among the
whole group.

The children subdued in their seats because they were tired
and hungry and had not been taught by their teachers what
their reaction should be to this situation and who looked for a
lead and received none. Unable to digest the new noises of
the engine and approaching lights of the farmhouses and villages below.

Alone on the plane, bound in his own deep and introverted
mood, the headmaster. No one had spoken to him since his
attempt to disarm the girl. Like an animal in the bamboo that
is crippled and will surely die and which is avoided by all its

species, he was shunned by all those who had not matched his one unreasoned moment of courage.

As the aircraft dipped and the pressure levels changed and the engines throttled their power, so too increased the fevered screaming of the baby, unnoticed, irrelevant to all on board as the ground slipped and staggered and lurched toward them.

8

Remember that she'll be close to exhaustion, nerves frayed on a hacksaw, that she doesn't understand English; everything must go through the navigator. Nurse her down, not condescending, not patronizing, but take it so gently. Those were the instructions given by telephone from London to the air-traffic controller in the Stansted tower who would talk Anna Tashova onto the runway. Encourage them to query anything, make it a hundred percent certain, hundred and one. No risks, not at this stage. Policemen, army officers, airport manager, senior air-traffic supervisor all crowded into the shadowed, dim-lit space behind the young man who was now in direct contact with the Ilyushin. Full runway lights blazing out in the half-gloom of the evening, marking the tarmac that stretched three thousand yards beyond the battery of red lineup lights upon which she would straighten trim, make the final calculations.

"We'd like you to tell her that everyone here is with her, that everyone thinks she's done very well, that it's nearly over."

"Roger, I will explain to her what you say." Voice of the navigator booming inside the glass-encased tower.

"About a hundred too high. She should drop twenty knots. Otherwise she's fine. We'd like to see her landing lights."

"Roger. She is making the adjustments you require." Pause. "The pilot officer apologizes for the lights."

Just like they are in the books you read, thought the controller. Not an iota different. Formal, correct, like it's a training run, like there isn't a submachine gun six inches from her. Apologizes for not having switched her lights on. Pilot dead beside her, or on the floor somewhere; planeload of people to think about; three mad bastards with guns, and she's saying she's sorry. Bloody incredible.

"Just tell her not to worry. She's doing fine. We're all with her." Pause again. Silence in the tower, all eyes scraping the sky for the lights. "No wind problems, surface westerly fifteen knots, you'll be landing right into them. There is no other traffic. Nothing else to concern yourselves with. Still a little high; drop the speed down ten. Call at the outer marker."

"Roger, thank you, 927 outer marker, inbound. Your instructions are very clear. We appreciate your help."

"You're not going to need them, but there are emergency services ready. Everything is prepared."

The controller wondered what it must be like in the cockpit; checked the flight plan they'd given him; saw the takeoff and mentally equated it with the British time difference. Five hours the girl had been flying the bloody thing now. He knew about the Migs, knew about Hannover and Schiphol. Poor little bitch, must be like having a guardian angel all dolled up in halo and wings and white sheets hovering alongside to have a sympathetic voice talking from the tower to her. Not that she'd know what he was saying; just get the feel, the togetherness. . . . Could see the lights now, the men behind him pointing out to his right. He looked away from the green-tinted radar screen from which he had been working, turned for a moment from the bright grass-green blip that was the Ilyushin. Two huge and powerful beams scything into the night from the elevated angle of the aircraft's approach.

"Nine-two-seven, we can see you, and you're doing very nicely. Take it calmly. No problems. Speed's right, height's right, line's right. Doing very well."

Nothing more to say now. Time just to watch and pray that the tiredness of the girl did not force her into error. No reason why it should; only male chauvinism that made him worry, he thought. Chance of a woman flying a plane in the West, next to minus nil. One or two of them, of course, but so extraordinary that they had their pictures in the papers each week; nothing like the Russian system that he'd seen in the aviation magazines where the girls had the same opportunities as the men. Wondered what she'd look like. Funny not being able to talk to her, only the distant voice of the man who sat behind her, and who switched off his radio each time he relayed the instructions to his pilot, like he didn't want anyone else to hear the backchat of the flight deck. Meant you couldn't evaluate her state of mind, didn't know what her condition was.

"Trim's right. Height right. Speed right."

"Roger."

"No problems, take it steady."

"Roger."

Don't give anything away, the buggers.

The shape of the plane eclipsed the lights at the far end of the runway, and in the tower they heard the roar of the reverse thrust being applied which meant she was down, the big bird had made her landing. The tower's rotating searchlight caught the Ilyushin halfway down the runway, flooding the white and red and silver of the fuselage as it began to slow its landing speed for the taxiing run, and in a moment, as the beam moved on, the plane was lost and there was only the noise and to the front the lights that shone ahead by which the men in the control tower could follow its progress.

All eyes were gripped on the plane.

Like men who have seen a topless sunbather for the first time and stare and are unashamed; voyeurs like the Soho blokes—that's what we are, thought the controller. Bloody fascinated by it, and it looks no different from any other plane—not from the scores he talked down each week. But they stared at it, as if hoping by their very persistence to see men with guns, or the passengers, unwilling to accept the shroud of night and that the Ilyushin was a full six hundred yards from them. They'd plotted on the airfield map where they wanted him to direct the aircraft to take its stand. The position had been carefully worked at—not for this flight, but years back when the hijack plan for Stansted had first been rehearsed.

"Turn her through one eight zero, and back the way you came. Two hundred yards up on the starboard side you'll see a "Follow Me" van, with yellow lights. He'll take you to the stand. And well done to the pilot officer. Pass that to her, please, from all of us in here."

"Roger."

The controller saw the plane turn in the distance and begin a sedate progress back up the runway toward where the truck with the flashing amber lights waited. The searchlight on its pass picked out the two Saracens that crawled in pursuit, but that were hidden from the vision of anyone on board.

"I'll stay with them till they douse the engines; then it's your problem, gentlemen." Half a minute more, and wringing in sweat and knowing he'd slipped half the procedure rules but feeling that for once in his life he'd achieved something, the controller eased out of his chair.

The Assistant Commissioner of Police for the county had taken his place beside him, looking warily at the equipment. Too bloody right, he thought; now it's our problem—till the heavies get down from London.

Three green-and-white fuel tankers parked close together and forming a half-moon barricade. A little to the right of them a squat single-level concrete building. Close to here that the Ilyushin should taxi and come to rest. Simple and logical, as all military plans should be; cover for the troops close to the aircraft, offering no risk of detection. Ten of the SAS team here, with their control radio set, their chests heaving slightly from the exertion of running to their hide with their equipment as the plane was readying for its approach. A hundred yards from it, perhaps less, certainly no more. They wore no badges of rank; were dressed in dark blue boiler-suit coveralls and had covered their faces with the newly developed lotion that suffused the brightness of their skin into an indistinct mess. Stirlings, rifles, machine guns, an antitank Carl Gustav rocket launcher, a crate each of the incapacitating CS gas canisters and smoke grenades—all were available to the unit. Via his elaborate radio net, Major George Davies, 22nd Regiment of the Special Air Service, learned that the first stage of the planning blueprint had worked as hoped. But he was not a man who suffered from self-delusion, and he could recognize that this was a small bonus, trivial.

Out beyond them, quiet, hidden, silent, the cordon of armored cars and the prone and crouching soldiers of the Fusiliers.

A great and spontaneous burst of applause was the passengers' reaction to the successful touchdown. Shouts in Russian and Italian, and one in English, and all carrying the same

message of admiration for Anna Tashova, a desperate gratitude for her skills and stamina. As the plane slowed, some
gave way to tears, noisily and silently, publicly and in the
privacy behind clenched fingers. Others hugged those who
sat next to them, total strangers embracing and pressing their
cheeks together, and there were smiles on the faces of the
children, who took their cue from their elders and realized
that this was a moment of celebration.

The experts who have studied the subject of hijacking, and
who sit in the offices of the Secret Services or Defense Minis-
tries of those countries which regard the problem with care,
would have said that this was a totally predictable emotion for
the passengers to be showing. They would point out that the
morale of men and women and children who have traveled
for many hours at gunpoint and at risk is a very fickle matter,
that they are constantly seeking for the sign that their ordeal
is over. On Aeroflot 927, the feeling was abroad that their
troubles were now gone, a past episode. They had forgotten,
because they wished to, the words spoken by Isaac in the passenger aisle a bare hour earlier.

Silly, helpless, laughing tears on the face of Luigi Franconi, something they would never have believed in his office
in Via Botteghe Oscure; not little Luigi, not the little silent
one. Found he could barely talk, not with coherence; felt the
muscles of his stomach slackened; felt his legs lapping hopelessly together. The arm of his friend around him, the comfort of Aldo Genti, who supervised in Party headquarters the
realism of economic affairs, and who was from Sardinia and
who was a man who chose not to show his emotions.

"I did not believe it possible."

"It is not finished yet, Luigi."

"It cannot be worse than it has been. They will see reason
now, these young people. The worst must be over."

Farther back toward the rear with his dreadnought confidence, Edward R. Jones, Jr., swiveled his backside in the
confines of his seat, once more to face Rebecca.

"What now, miss? Where do we go from here?"

"We refuel. Then we go to Israel."

Involuntary reply, and she knew that she was not supposed
to talk, and hated herself for the weakness and loathed the
moment because there was no one with whom she could

share the joy of the landing that was all around her. An outcast, her link with the general pleasure severed.

"Might not be easy, miss. As I said earlier."

She bit at her tongue, stifling the desire to argue with his
pomposity. Who was he to tell her what would happen?
Sneering at her, contemptuous of her.

"What happens if they don't give you the fuel? What happens then?"

She did not reply, only stared back at him, trying to outlast
his clear and unwavering gaze till she accepted defeat and
focused again on the long length of the cabin, unable to look
back at where he sat. Heard him say to his wife, his voice
loud and unrepentant, "They haven't an idea in hell, these
kids. It's what makes them so damned dangerous. If they
were a bit more pragmatic about it all you could assess what
they were going to do. But they're out of this world, don't
know what it's about, and Christ only knows what they'll do
when the truth sinks in."

The art teacher leaned over from his window seat toward
the headmaster, sandwiching the boy who sat between them.
First time anyone had spoken to him, punctured the ostra-
cism of fear—first time for a life-span; and his face was haggard with the strain of the silence, lines at his eyes, age at his
mouth.

"Headmaster, we will support you. We believe in what you
did. It was right what you attempted." What they would all
say. But who had joined him when he needed their strength;
who had come to him with anything more than a medley of
desultory kicks at the little bitch? Held their ground, hadn't
they? Waiting to see the outcome, fearful of committing
themselves till they knew who would vanquish, who would
stand condemned. Tardy in their words of comfort.

Forward in the cockpit, Anna Tashova sat immobilized in
her flying harness, head flopped onto her narrow and barely
defined chest, eyes closed as if she were asleep. A very great
tiredness she felt, and a desire only to immure herself behind
any barricade that would protect her from the talk of the two
men who had dictated her route and from the eyes and fingers of the dials and switches that peered back at her from
the control panels. For her too the flight had seemed an infi-
nite nightmare of darkened turnings, chased and harried by

endless closing pursuit, with the only sedative to block out the images found in the mechanics of the aircraft, the occupation of controlling the insensate instruments. Like the American passenger whose existence she did not know of, she too wondered what would happen next. But unlike him, now that she had shut down the four Ivchenko engines, she cared not a damn.

The navigator—he had been briefly introduced to her before takeoff by the captain because they had not flown together before, and she had forgotten his name—was shuffling his papers and maps into an ordered shape—methodical, a tidy man—and putting them quietly into his briefcase, as if they might be of further and future use. The scope of the maps was long since exhausted. To the border of West Germany, and everything after that on instruments and from the chorus of ground controllers who had passed them on, like a ship that flies the yellow flag and cannot find welcoming port.

Both of them in their various ways ignoring the presence of David. The pilot officer, who had not spoken since the landing, and the navigator, who did not meet his eyes and who busied himself with trivia to avoid the contact that otherwise would have been inevitable. And the captain too. Not a movement from him. Five hours dead now, and not a wavering of his posture; the ultimate act of defiance, sitting there, trapped there, head bowed down. Face whitening to the sheet pallor of death, the mouth clamped fast as if in determination not to show the pain that would have come too fast for him to know it.

Isaac back behind him at the end of the corridor, the mouth of the cabin, studying the passengers, relentless and with total concentration after the attempt to overpower Rebecca. Suspicious and hostile and watchful, seeming to crouch his body as though among the facing mass of people there were a missile or weapon that could damage him if he presented a broader target. He stood out in the center of the aisle where all could see him if they stretched up from their seats and take note of the rock-firm grip on the handle of the submachine gun. The passengers would know that the inhibitions of the pressurization of the cabin had now deserted him. The plane was on the ground. He would have no hesitation in shooting.

"I am going to talk to the tower on the radio. I want all the people to remain in their seats. None are to move, not for any reason."

Isaac did not look away, eyes still ranging like a prison-tower searchlight; nodded his agreement. It seemed natural that David should resume the initiative, take the leadership up again. David waved, an afterthought, to the girl at the far end of the cabin, caught her attention and waved again and stayed long enough to see the thankfulness on her face.

"When you're ready, Isaac, take her place; she has been away from us too long."

Inside the cockpit the navigator made way for him, but David declined the small, low-set seat, not wishing to box himself in, seeking freedom of movement from which he could dominate. Held the gun in his left hand now, away from the pilot officer and the navigator, and with his right began to pull at the headset that was fastened to the ceiling of the flight deck.

"You're wasting your time," the navigator said. "Unless you speak in English there is no one there who can talk to you."

Saw the disappointment cloud over the young man's face, the surprise for the jab to the jaw. So far, so much at stake for him, and no one to speak his language. Half a smile from the crewman, little more than a suspicion and covert, as David backed out of the cockpit, petulant anger rising.

He strode down the corridor, almost marching in his speed when he reached the passenger-cabin aisle. For many of them it was their first clear glimpse of the man they took to be the leader of the group, the man most directly responsible for their position. Good-looking, those who could be re-motely obejective would have conceded, but they were few, and from the majority there was only loathing hidden in the turned-away faces. Edward R. Jones, Jr., took a surreptitious picture but doubted whether it would expose well in the dull, artificial interior light. David strode all the way to Rebecca, pushing past the drinks trolley, till he reached her and took her slowly and with gentleness into his arms—the greeting of a brother, of a friend, not a lover. An arm around her shoulders, and the other, the one that held his machine gun, pressing her head against his chest, and the gesture was awkward till he sensed the intensity of her response.

David felt the ripple of her breath playing on the skin of his neck; heard her say, "Are we free now, David? Is it over—is it finished?"

"The crewman says there is no one there yet who will speak in our language. You speak some of their English; in a moment you must talk to them."

"How will they be to us, after the Germans and the Dutch; how will the British be?"

Found that all he wished for was to hold the girl, keep her close, continue the contact. Her words now a distraction, turning him away from the sanctity of the moment.

"Why should they be different? Why should they not think the way their friends in the West have thought?" Sensing the softness of her body, the pliant pull of her weight.

"Was it a great crime, the shooting of one policeman, and he not dead? They know why we fight; they have told us on the radio of their sympathy. Does the wounding of one policeman outweigh all their statements?"

Tighter, closer, pressing her frailty against him. Silly, stupid idiot girl. Lovely girl. Squeezing, hugging, binding her to him.

"You forget, Rebecca; you forget the captain in his cockpit. You have put him from your mind. But they know of it. They knew at Hannover and at Amsterdam, and these people here will know of it. I have killed the captain, and to these people he will be the martyr and we will be the animals. One shot— that was all I fired. One shot. It was I who fired it, not Isaac; it was I, and the panic was there and running fast, and the door would not open, and I fired. I did not angle the gun, Rebecca; I did not fire for the floor. I killed him, Rebecca, and to them it will be a murder."

"You are wrong, David—too tired to think."

"Where can there be rest now?"

"You must calm yourself."

"I should have been calm when I fired at the door."

To the girl he seemed to sag, forcing her to grip at his waist to steady him. A terrible pain she read in his eyes, a great hurt. He hung on her a full minute, then jolted and awoke himself.

"You are the one who speaks English; you must come and talk to them." But he made no move to loosen her, just stood close, rocking slowly, eddying the feel of her body against his own. Frightening to the girl to see him so weakened.

The words of the navigator barked over the loudspeaker system of the tower. Volume turned to maximum, and the listeners knew from the sound of his breathing that the Russian was whispering.

"They are all out of the cockpit now. There are three of them. The two men have submachine guns. There is also a girl, but she is always with the passengers and we have not seen her. I think they have gone for her, because they do not speak English, the men. I have said there are no Russian speakers. Sometimes they are calm, sometimes they shout. They believe they will get fuel for Israel, and . . . They are returning."

Nothing more from the loudspeakers. Opportunity for the second tape recorder to be switched on, while the spool of the first was lifted off and hurried for transcription. There had been shorthand notes, but every word spoken from the flight deck and from the control tower would be recorded. It was the way in these matters.

"A very switched-on boy, that one," the Assistant Chief Constable said. "Be a star hanging on his chest when this lot's over." He'd done the courses and seminars Home Office organized, and attended the Special Study Groups, because Stansted was in his "manor," and if the fiction became reality he was designated as having a part to play. Fancied he knew his subject, and liked the fact known. Put him a cut above administering CID and Regional Crime Squad and investigating the corruption allegations.

"The fact that there's only three of them, and that one is a girl, where does that put things?" The question was from the Fusiliers colonel—familiar enough with urban guerrilla fighting across the Irish Sea, inexperienced in this most particular field.

The Assistant Chief Constable warmed, reveling in the deference shown him by the army officer. "I think the fellow knew what we wanted to hear. Took his opportunity well and gave us the bones of it. Didn't mention explosives. On the Middle East jobs they try and booby-trap the doors, but he didn't say anything about that. Could be that he just doesn't know, but if they haven't, then it has to be easier for us if we go heavy. The fact that there are three means it's not likely to last long. Should be quick. But I didn't like what he said about the shouting; infinitely more dangerous to everyone if they become unstable. Then anything can happen." A hurried smile, warmed by the nods of agreement to his analysis.

There was much more he could have said, a longer and more elaborate assessment. But the voices finished him, and the bustle of activity behind him, and the drift of the attention that he had held veered toward the door. The features, familiar from the television screen, of the Home Secretary, who grinned thinly at the stiff salute. A man at his right shoulder whom he had not seen before, not present at the weekend courses—worn, pale, autumn face, and bagged eyes, and none of the confidence there. There were handshakes and he caught a name—"Webster, Charlie Webster"—no explanation of rank, department. Had they started talking yet from the plane? And he'd scarcely begun to answer before the newcomer was in his seat and close to the extended microphone and was gathering together scratch paper and drawing a ball-point pen from his pocket. Wouldn't say that he was unhappy that someone else had come to do the chat, but he'd like to have been asked, like to have known the pedigree.

Charlie slid his jacket from his shoulders, slung it over the back of the seat rest, loosened his tie, settled himself to wait for the contact. Sort of been drawn into it, hadn't he? Never really been asked; his willingness had gone undiscussed. Just expected of him, taken for granted. Charlie Webster, terrorist hunter back on the job, keeping people safe in their beds, letting the great unwashed fornicate in peace, and by the by chopping a few kids who'd been sold some crap ideology and thought they could change the world on the strength of it. The transcript was placed in front of him. He read it briefly: three to chop this time. Shouldn't be too difficult, Charlie, not unless they played stupid.

The Parliamentary Private Secretary was at the cabinet doling out the ice cubes, pouring the gin.

"Plenty of that, and not too much tonic." The Foreign Secretary always said that, and it didn't affect the same weak mixture always surrendered to him. Had hated the drive back from Dorneywood, quite detested the speed, should have been one of the privileges of his rank that he didn't have to submit to those bloody siren-paced races up the M4. Generally able to instruct the driver that he wanted a steady ride, forty-five miles an hour, but events hadn't waited on him that evening. The Russian would be waiting outside, in the anteroom, but time first for a stiff one—not that it would be. Some of the blighters you couldn't talk to, the Russians; not a spark of contact, dead as the Sahara. But at least this fellow was out of the ordinary—quite human, and good enough English to ditch the interpreter, which always seemed to smooth the way. Downed the drink in a single heave, leaving the ice unmelted and the lemon slice unsullied, and handed the glass back to his PPS; the man knew the drill, put it out of sight in the cabinet and closed the doors on the array of bottles.

"Let's have him," the Foreign Secretary said.

Decent-looking chap, in his way; hair well cut, and not a bad suit. Those had been the first impressions of the Foreign Secretary at the entrance at the far end of the forty-foot office of the Russian Ambassador to the Court of St. James's. Now he offered him a seat on the sofa and took his own place in the armchair at the side. PPS behind them both with the scribbling pad and the pencil. Not really form, not having an FO man in there with them, but the Russian hadn't brought anyone either. Times for an official minuted record of a meeting, times when it wasn't suitable; he judged that neither of them sought to preserve their conversation now for historical posterity.

"I would like to say first," the Ambassador began—flawless English, marginal accent—"that my government sends a message of gratitude to the British Government for permitting the Aeroflot flight to land." With a gesture of his hand the Foreign Secretary acknowledged the formalities. "But I think, Mr. Foreign Secretary, that we both understand that we have reached a most difficult and complex stage in the handling of this criminal incident. I am informed by my government that prior to the murderous hijacking of the aircraft this gang of thugs had attempted to kill a policeman in the city of Kiev. For this they were being sought at the time that they took over the Aeroflot flight from that city to Tashkent and by doing so endangered the lives of many innocent passengers. During their capture of the aircraft, which had no armed security men on board, they killed the captain at his seat in the cockpit; we have been told by the young pilot officer who successfully flew the plane to Britain that her captain was executed as the assassins took over the flight deck. All of this you know, Mr. Foreign Secretary. Also, you will have had by now the communication of my government, personally issued by the Comrade Secretary General of the Party and sent to all heads of government in the countries in which we thought it possible that the aircraft might land."

He had the admiration of the British politician. So many of them would have taken half an hour to get to the point, to rupture the hymen of abstraction; but they were already there, and the first cigarette in the Russian's hand not half smoked.

"My government cannot look upon these three as political refugees, but as murderers and criminals. We regard them as you regard the terrorists of the Irish Republican Army who bomb your cities. When you arrested the men and women of Birmingham and Guildford, the terrorists of your Central London campaign, you put them through the courts and you sentenced them as your law permits. I venture to say that if those men had taken refuge in any European country you would have sought their arrest and extradition. We cannot believe that the British government would contemplate the refueling of the aircraft to facilitate its onward flight to Israel"—there was a nod of acquiescence from the Foreign Secretary—"and after your authorities have disarmed these people, we will require that they be sent back forthwith to the Ukraine to face justice in the city of Kiev. I am also informed, and this may help you when you arrive at your final decision, that the position of the aircraft at the moment when the captain was shot places the crime within the jurisdiction of the courts of that city. That is what I have been asked by the senior personalities of the Soviet Foreign Ministry to pass on to you, in addition to the communication of the Comrade Secretary General. I have also been asked to furnish some indication of the attitude that the British Government will take in this matter."

Right between the eyes, and where he'd expected it. Been dealing with them long enough to know that the sting was

always in the tail. Used a hard word—for the language of diplomacy, that was: "require"—nearest thing to an ultimatum
you could get; not a friendly word, not leaving much room for
maneuver. And wanting some sort of answer off the cuff.
Knew the problems just as everyone else did, but piling on
the pressure from the start, getting his foot in the door, jumping the queue for consideration. He'd done it well.

"I can assure you, and you may pass this on to your government and to your Secretary General, that it is not the intention of the British security forces and officials who are currently at Stansted that the aircraft should leave there except
as a free flight and without passengers and crew being held at
gunpoint. There is no question while the plane is under the
command of armed men that it will be refueled for onward
flight to Israel. That is a solemn guarantee." The easy section—obvious, and would satisfy nobody. The next leg
harder. "I am advised by the British Government's legal officers that the hijackers have already contravened various sections of the British criminal code—certainly illegal possession
of firearms, possibly kidnapping—and it is likely that should
they surrender they would be required to face the due process
of United Kingdom law."

"I do not wish to have to report to my government that in
my opinion the British would use minor charges to protect
these three criminals from the Soviet courts. Perhaps I have
not made myself clear, Mr. Foreign Secretary: we want these
people back. We want them quickly. We would take procras-
tination on this point as a most serious matter."

"Threats will not be conducive to settling our problems."
Quietly said by the Foreign Secretary, but with the acting and
the politeness vanishing from the soft-lit room.

"It is not a threat."

"Then I misunderstood your choice of words. We must be
most careful in the choice of words that we use; otherwise we
will have misunderstandings, which would be unfortunate."

"What, then, should I inform my government concerning
the extradition of these people?" A fractional retreat, but tac-
tical only, and the Foreign Secretary knew it would mean as
little at the end of the day as his answer.

"You should tell your government that the British Foreign
Secretary has undertaken to pass on the details of this conversation personally to the Prime Minister. You should also

say that the first priority of the British Government is to ensure the safe release of all the passengers and crew of the
plane; in the short term, we regard that as the more important issue."

The Soviet Ambassador rose, smile back on his face, firm
grip in his handshake, a word about future meetings, and he
was through the door and into the anteroom. Had time as he
walked across the Isfahan carpet to recognize the short and
stubbed presence, buried in an easy chair, of the Israeli Ambassador, now waiting for his appointment.

There was no greeting, no acknowledgment from either.

From where he sat, Charlie Webster had as good a view as
any of the Ilyushin.

Static and immobilized, swathed in light from the portable
floodlights that the military had put in place within a hundred
yards of its towering crablike form. Lowering in its discon-
tent, heavy with dissatisfaction. Penned and chained to the
emptiness of the tarmac. Unmoving, unresponding.

Behind Charlie were the Emergency Committee, who
would dictate his replies once the hijackers chose to begin
transmissions on the radio. The Home Secretary, there at the
Prime Minister's request to assume overall political control of
the affair, with the covey of civil servants hovering near him,
to advise and to caution. The Assistant Chief Constable,
spruced and neat and boasting the thin multicolored ribbons
of war service and police work on his chest. Two army officers who had made a separate journey from London, coming
from Ministry of Defense.

One civilian, as different from the rest of them in his own
right as was Charlie. Checked shirt and the collar stiffeners
bent in too many washes, so that they rode up his sports-coat
lapels. A tie that had shields on it that were lost and disfig-
ured by the many times it had been knotted. Hair that was
long and had not known the benefit of comb and brush and
water and grease and that hung loosely from the body of his
head. Baggy brown corduroy trousers and scuffed brown
shoes. Not a man who was kept; not a man who owed alle-
giance to conformity. Stiff, bold cheekbones and a ferret
nose that poked and pried into the conversations around him.
Not accepted but tolerated, because he as the psychiatrist in
the team had a role to play. Experience of psychopaths, of

the deranged, of the desperate. Had advised on the siege of the Provos at Balcombe Street, and the Spaghetti House stakeout in London's West End. The Dutch, with their knowledge of the prison and train hostage-taking operations, had proved the value of a medical man on the team, and the Home Office had drafted Anthony Clitheroe into its game plans, placing him on call so that he could be summoned from his Wimpole Street practice when the need arose. Three appointments with tired businessmen who yearned for the satisfaction of the "nervous breakdown" diagnosis had been canceled that he might come to Stansted.

Later the group would disperse to the hastily cleared offices of airport management, but at that moment all wanted to be witness to the initial contact, sought to hear the timbre of the voices of the opposition still hidden from them by the sleek, wind-wiped walls of the Ilyushin's fuselage.

In front of him Charlie had placed the three photographs that he had been given in London; spread them out so that he could see the faces, study them, learn from them. Farther to his right, as if of lesser importance, he had laid the cutout diagram of the interior of the 11 18V. He felt nervous, tensed in his stomach, waiting for them to begin, wishing them to start. But had to let them take the initiative—that was the procedure: the young people should not be hurried; all the privileges of the bride.

It was the girl who spoke first.

"To the authorities, do you hear us . . . do you hear us?"

"We hear you very clearly."

"Do you hear us . . ." Stupid cow, forgotten, or never knew, that she had to take her finger off the button when she'd finished speaking, otherwise couldn't hear the replies.

"We hear you very clearly."

Her memory of the technicalities jolted, or someone had told her, but now she had mastered the equipment. "We call ourselves the Kingfisher group. We wish to talk to the responsible persons. Have they come yet?"

Not bad English. Out of the classroom—like your Russian, Charlie. Speaking too close to the microphone, so that she distorted, and he could not gauge the strength of her spirits, her morale.

"Hello, Kingfisher group." Where had they dug that one up? Out of the norm. Black September, Black June, First of

April movement, Struggle group of any wet November Thursday—that was what they'd come to expect. "My name is Webster, Charlie Webster. We can talk in Russian or English, whichever you prefer. If you want to talk in Russian, you must accept that there will be pauses while I translate what you are saying to the people who are with me."

Silence, while they work it out. Decide whether the big man in the group wants to do the talking for himself, which means Russian, or whether they delegate to the girl. Handwritten note passed in front of him. Charlie should not let it be known that the Emergency Committee had already assembled at the airport. Going for the stall game and delay; Clitheroe's advice was clear on this, adamant.

In Russian, and a man speaking. Sounded an age away, farther than the girl, subdued, unsure; perhaps just the angle to the microphone.

"My name is David. I wish to speak to the persons who are in charge."

Charlie in Russian too. Couldn't match his dialect: softer, less cruel to the ear than the harsher speech of the North, of Moscow. Wouldn't try to ape him, just speak the way he had been taught in "I" Corps, where it was assumed that any Russian they would need to interrogate had done his secondary school in the Kremlin's shadows. Not easy, not at first. Seemed a long time since he'd spoken the language conversationally. One thing to read newspapers and official reports, even to write it, but quite another to chatter in the tongue and summon the persuasiveness to win confidence.

"Webster, Charlie Webster here. I'm the Russian-language speaker. As I explained to your colleague, there will be delays while I tell my colleagues what you are saying and what I am telling you." Take all night at this rate. He flicked the transmission switch to Off on the console in front of him, told the men who stood behind him what he had said. Back to On. Live again.

"We should say who we are. The Kingfisher group is Jewish. We are of a people who have long been oppressed and persecuted. We are political persons. We have flown out of the Soviet Union because we seek to arrive in Israel, and now we need fuel to continue our journey. We mean no harm to anyone, but we demand the fuel. Have you understood that?"

"I have understood that, David." All on his shoulders now—entire bloody committee, dogs in the desert round carrion. "I am going to tell my colleagues what you have said." Charlie repeated the drill on the console, turned in the swing chair and explained the message.

The Home Secretary said, "You know, Mr. Webster, that there is no possibility of their having fuel. The question is, do they find that out now or later?"

Anthony Clitheroe was an eminent man in his field, accustomed to delivering detailed and lengthy speeches to his professional colleagues; had a considerable list of major studies to his name and a quarter of a column of *Who's Who* to back up his claims to be heard out. But he had learned from his two previous encounters with security forces handling similar situations that they required brevity of response from him.

"Find an excuse; put him off; tell him the people necessary to make such a decision are not here, won't be till the morning."

Finger back to the console, Charlie speaking again to the flight deck.

"David, this is a very important request that you are making, and one that would have to be considered very carefully by the British Government. The problem is that we're in the middle of the holiday season here; many of the most senior men are away on their vacations. There is no one here who could give that sort of authorization. Probably we won't be able to get a decision till the morning."

"Don't make a fool of me." The inanimate, detached voice cracked back from the loudspeaker high on the back wall of the control tower. Pitch rising and hostility communicated.

"I'm not making a fool of you, David."

"Don't take me for an idiot. The Germans were able to make a decision that we should not land. The Dutch were able to offer us impossible conditions knowing that we would not accept. We are not peasants, not Cossacks, not animals. Your people facilitated this landing; that was not authorized by a junior official. Do not tell me that the responsible people cannot now be contacted. Do not play a game with me. We are very tired; we are impatient now. Do you know why I say that?"

"Of course you are tired, and that is the more reason why you should sleep now, and the pilot too must have a chance to sleep, and then we can talk in the morning."

"Not in the morning. We want the fuel tonight. In the morning we fly."

"It is not possible—"

"It must be possible. Tell your people that, whoever they are. Tell them."

Clocks ticking, a subdued cough, shuffling of feet. Charlie sighed, loosened his collar further and turned once more to his audience. Didn't need him—not to give them the bones, at any rate; picked that from the voices, David's anger, Charlie's wheedling. But he went through the drama and the explanation.

The Assistant Chief Constable had maneuvered to the Home Secretary's shoulder. "With respect, sir, and I acknowledge that there are others better qualified in these matters than myself, but it's dangerous this way round, coddling them along. I suggest we make it plain, right from the start, that they are not flying on, that it's not negotiable."

"I want to lead them to the realization gradually." Clitheroe held his ground, did not seek proximity to their political master; aloof and with his hands in his pockets. "You have heard the man's voice; you didn't need Mr. Webster's translation to tell you he's near hysterical, hypersensitive. He is exhausted and may become totally irrational. If you push him you could have a suicide situation. At best, a collapse; at worst, mayhem amongst the passengers."

First conflict, Charlie thought. Haven't been here forty-five minutes and they're swapping already. Always the bloody same when you try and do things by committee.

"You have to take a firm line—"

"Not for its own sake; only if that helps the end result."

Speedy with his oil on the stormy waters, the Home Secretary looked beyond the antagonists. Went to the man who had impressed him in London, who seemed to know and who had the humility of caution in his assessments.

"Mr. Webster. Stall them, or give it to them straight?"

Charlie closed his eyes, tried to think, tried to see his way into the minds of the young people. Just photographs and distant voices. How in God's name did you answer that one.

"I think I'd go with the doctor," he said. He saw the anticipation of the Assistant Chief Constable blend into his set, uniformed, clipped-moustache face. "With respect to all who
might disagree with me, we should not underestimate what
they've been through, to put it crudely. The stress they've
been under, the strain . . ." What do you know about strain,
Charlie? Well, more than any of these buggers. "They could
go half bloody mad if we wrapped them down right now."

Clitheroe didn't acknowledge his support; just walked away
and jangled at the coins in his pocket. The policeman was
gazing through the windows.

"Stall them, Mr. Webster," said the Home Secretary.
Looked hard at Charlie, seeking rapport, trying to share the
loneliness of taking decisions on conflicting advice. Sorry,
can't help you, sir. You say what happens; I just march up
and down and do as I'm told.

"David, it's Charlie here. Now, you're to listen to me."
Trying to get colloquial, trying to find the phrases to create
understanding, forge the bond. "David, listen. We've spoken
to London by telephone, and we are told that the Ministers
of the British Government will be meeting later tonight or in
the early hours of the morning. They have to talk about this
thing, David. You have to believe me there, they must be
allowed some time. We'll have an answer by dawn. That's the
best I can offer you, David. It's a very important matter, this,
David. They must have time to talk about it. They promise
an answer by the morning." They'll have an answer by the
time you've had a good night's sleep, by the time you've
calmed yourself, by the time the SAS boys have it all worked
out.

"You are trying to confuse us, Charlie. You do not think
that we are serious people." But the doubt was registering, the
dike was weakening; clear from the inflection. Don't know
what to do, what to say. Had the set speech worked out for
the "yes" or "no" answer, and they're thrown by the "wait
and see."

"I'm not trying to confuse you, David. Just explaining
things the way they are."

"You do not deceive me?"

"I don't deceive you, David. You'll have the answer in the
morning, good and early." Like pinching the pocket money

out of the blind school. First-timers, no briefing, no plan; just showed up and hoped for the best.

"Good night, Charlie. And you will tell us early the reply of your government. Tell us about the fuel and the onward flight to Israel."

"Good night, David. We'll talk in the morning."

Believe that lot and you'll believe anything. Charlie tucked the console switch back to the Off position, stretched up out of his chair, braced his legs, which were stiff from the long period crouched at his desk.

To no one in particular he said, "I thought they'd be better than that."

9

The Foreign Secretary would dearly have appreciated another of his PPS's mixtures from the cabinet, but not the suitable occasion, not with the night stretching ahead and the artillery ranging, the threat increasing. Not a time to find comfort in the alcohol level. Damn it.

For this senior politician with a lifetime of maneuvering and negotiating in the fraught and deceptive world of diplomacy, the problem was totally straightforward. Black-and-white, with no tolerance for the shades of gray that marked difficulty and contention. So clear-cut that the area for compromise was reduced. He had a fair idea of the appeal that the Israeli Ambassador would make to him, knew it would be impassioned and emotional and difficult to deflect. Yet his role would not be easy—carrying the burden of the onetime superpower, onetime member of the Big Five. The world had moved on, the wind had blown and the weight in affairs abroad of the government he now represented had diminished to a startling degree in the previous two decades; the cloth had shrunk, and so had the muscle of the wearer. Circumspection was required if he was to avoid provoking the hostility of those who had usurped the influence that had once been Britain's. Forget the principle, take the practical; and why not, with these silly children to concern himself with? The Russians would want them back; the Israelis would accept just about anything other than that. Three idiot children, and because of them he wrestled with a dilemma that should not have existed: whom to offend, whom to hurt—the monolith of the Soviet Union? the massive voice of the Jewish lobby across the Free World? Damned ridiculous. And both of them, Russians and Israelis alike, would be wanting one thing from him that evening: a binding commitment on a

course of action. Only card he held, and he'd see that both
went home without it.

He'd stayed in his armchair after the Russian had gone,
musing, turning the matter slowly in his mind, chewing the
cud of his problem. When he rose to greet the Israeli Ambassador it was with awkwardness, legacy of the wartime shrap-
nel embedded in his hip. Not usual for the Foreign Secretary
himself to greet ambassadors, not when the issue at stake was
the future of three juveniles, delinquents, killers. But then,
the situation was not usual; no point on an evening such as
this in sticking to the protection of protocol. Another circumspect bottom sinking into the comfort of the settee's soft
cushions, a moment's pleasantries, and then the starting gun.

"Our position is sensitive, Mr. Foreign Secretary, in that
we do not have any direct connection with these people; we
knew nothing of them before their action became public
knowledge. I begin with that, but my government believes it
carries a responsibility to all the Jewish people, not just to
those who reside in the state of Israel; a responsibility that we
must discharge within the boundaries of acceptable international conduct."

The Ambassador was leaning forward, and having difficulty
making his point with the emphasis he strove for, as his small
body had sufficiently depressed the cushions to deny him the
height and stature that were more suitable for his address.
"That these young people have committed crimes we accept;
serious crimes: we accept that also. In our country there have
been no executions since the mass murderer Eichmann was
put to death; in Great Britain there have been none for close
to fifteen years. We have both abolished the death penalty for
humanitarian reasons. Neither of us believe in judicial
killings."

The Foreign Secretary quizzically raised an eyebrow—an
art he had: only the right eyebrow—and its intention, in
which he invariably succeeded, was to signify skepticism. A
popular vote in either Britain or Israel would, he thought,
have endorsed with enthusiasm a return of capital punishment if directed against the IRA men who bombed the British cities, or the Black September gangs that assaulted the
northern Israeli settlements.

The Ambassador was not to be deterred by the movement

of a hair line. "In the Soviet Union these three will face the supreme penalty" . . . and that would be so wrong? . . . "I would suggest that you could assume with near certainty that these three will be put to death if they are returned to Russia" . . . and would the world be a poorer place in their absence? . . . "My government could not countenance the sending of these three young people to a death they would not have faced if their crimes had been committed in your territory or in ours" . . . serve the little blighters right . . . "I am instructed by my Prime Minister to ask of you an immediate guarantee that these people will not be returned to Kiev."

"What would you suggest happen to them?"

"I am instructed by my government that we would accept their appearance before British courts, and that should they be convicted, they would serve terms of imprisonment inside the United Kingdom."

"And what charges would they face in Britain?"

"They would face the charges that would have been laid against them in Kiev."

The Foreign Secretary drew a long breath. An audacious approach, but then, that was to be expected. Same as the damned Russians, seeking the propaganda coup: that amount clear to him, even through the pain that meant tiredness and that the fragments of metal still bit and snapped at the encasing gristle deep in his body. Concern for advantage, paramount; concern for the lives at stake, nonexistent. "I am reminded, though I do not have the exact text at hand, of the eloquent statement made recently by your Ambassador to the United Nations General Assembly. It was a call, if I recollect, for a rule of law to combat aerial piracy, a demand that nations band together to stamp out this contemporary evil. Are we to assume that the religious faith of these three young people excludes them from the type of justice you would wish to see exacted upon men of other creeds?"

The Ambassador did not answer him. No surprise to the Foreign Secretary. Diplomats seldom replied to each other's points of debate; bogged them down and failed to get them anywhere if they did.

"As you know, with the cooperation of your government, we are sending a personal representative of the Government of Israel to Britain. This man is a fighter; he holds a substantive rank in those units of our armed forces which deal exclusively with the terrorist threat. If you were to find it possible to commit your government not to return the young people to their deaths, then we would order the officer to use his utmost influence to persuade them to surrender without further bloodshed. We have chosen this man with care. It is not accidental that he is the one who has been sent. A fighter, a lion. In our society, could his name and his achievements be published, he would be a hero among us. We believe he is the man to appeal to these youngsters, to gain much from them—more than you can achieve."

No longer audacious; damned arrogant now.

"What makes you think we need help—"

"We have the experience."

"And no one else?"

"To the same degree, no. Ask the Germans who were responsible at Munich; ask your friend the President of Uganda."

"You know, of course, that the Government of the United Kingdom does not have an extradition treaty with the Soviet Union."

"I know that military aircraft can take off under cover of darkness, and that politicians can justify their actions at a later date."

"The Ambassador of the Soviet Union has just departed after telling me *his* government required an immediate answer on the same question that you ask. I told him that we were considering the situation."

"From which he would have assumed," said the Israeli Ambassador, "that the British require time."

"If that was his assumption, then it would have been a correct one. Your officer will indeed be taken to Stansted, but whether there is any part for him to play, while conditions are attached to his presence, remains a matter of debate."

Termination of the conversation, the pain growing and the more pressing need to speak with the Prime Minister. Worthless and predictable this, a mere swapping of words now that the battle lines had been drawn.

Alone, while the PPS led the Ambassador through outer offices and empty corridors, the Foreign Secretary sat still in his chair. One drip of water nagging at his concentration, splattering on the bedrock of his concentration: what if they were not his concern; what if the ministry of another country were in turmoil over the problem; what if he were exonerated of anxiety? Would his feelings on the fate of three young people who had taken a plane out of Russia be different then? How many speeches had he made in the constituency . . . the Russian threat . . . the need for vigilance . . . not to lower our guard . . . persecution . . . the tanks of the Warsaw pact . . . how many warplanes, how many missiles, divisions, chemical-gas batteries of artillery . . . always went down damn well, those speeches, particularly at the mid-July garden fete. Three children had taken the system to battle— thrown a tatty, unlined glove at it, and looked for a champion to ride to their rescue. Have to look elsewhere, wouldn't they, silly little blighters.

Wouldn't bother the switchboard, dial it himself, the number that was personal and restricted of the Prime Minister's holiday home.

In the forward corridor of the aircraft, where they could achieve privacy, straddled between the cockpit and the passenger cabin, David and Isaac and Rebecca talked of the radio conversation with the man who called himself Charlie. None had ever met an Enlgishman before, which made their attempts at assessing what had been told them difficult, close to impossible. There had been English students on the campus whom both Isaac and Rebecca had seen since they had started their studies at the Kiev State University, but they had not been in their classes; there had been no point of contact.

David had said it was better to wait till the morning before talking again. Isaac had not challenged him; realized the depth of bone-wearying exhaustion to which his friend succumbed; saw that the man needed a lengthy sleep and an assurance of trust that he could cuddle and hold to. Get no sense out of David, not till he was rested. Wished he'd been there, in the cockpit, to hear at first hand the message for them from the ground; but his persistent, clinging anxiety about their security at the hands of the passengers following the incident with Rebecca had prevented that. Hovering in the doorway of the cabin, while David was talking behind him in the flight deck, attention bound to his charges, watching them, eyeing them, a hen with her brood when the fox is close to the coop. When he had been told later of the germ of the conversation, he had laughed to himself, amused at David's faith, convinced in his own suspicions.

Many hours now since either had lain in a bed; the last sleep reduced to a few tossing and restless minutes of oblivion on the floor of the forest hut. Both unshaven, and the new growth tickling and irritating at the inside of their collars, and their eyes large and reddened and rimmed; slowed and sluggish in their movements. The girl worse than both of them; hardly able to keep her lids from closing, and vague in what she said when they spoke to her. Had to sleep, all of them; had to devise a rotation for resting. And now circling, aimlessly and without direction, around the conversation that David had made with the tower, and he defensive about what he had said, and the girl comprehending and repeating only that the man they had spoken to was called Charlie, and he had promised. Had to get them to sleep, both of them, and summon for himself the strength to outlast and outfight his own great weariness. A few more minutes, then they could go; could be excused; could seek the deliverance they needed. But first the passengers, the currency—valuable, without price; first he should concern himself with the passengers. Voice a little hoarse now, but clear, and to those who listened, these were the words of a man who has usurped command, filled the vacuum of leadership.

"We have requested that the English give us fuel. We are told that their government is meeting in London tonight to discuss our request. They will tell us their answer by the early morning. In the meantime, we will all sleep on the aircraft." He paused, and there was the vaguest of smiles—a suspicion—and he corrected himself. "In the meantime you will all sleep on the aircraft. There is no food for you, and there will be no drinks. You must not talk, and nobody on any pretext may leave his seat. The lights will remain on through the night, and all of you who sit at the windows must draw your blinds. We will shoot if anyone moves. That must be understood. When I say we will shoot, you should not take it just as a threat. You should not seek to prove me."

Isaac walked halfway down the aisle to where the legroom was greatest, to the seats in front of which was the passage to

the emergency doors with their escape route onto the wings.
Luigi Franconi and Aldo Genti on his right, three of the
schoolchildren from Lvov to the left. Beckoned to them with
his gun barrel, the motioning gesture of the fore sight drawing them from their seats as if he had discarded immediately
the possibility that they would understand his speech. The
children were simple, absorbed immediately among their
friends, but the Italians harder, and he had to lead them
down the aisle to where there were vacant places and stifled
protests from those who were comfortable and settled. Both
climbing over knees and bags and passengers who were unyielding and heavy with hostility at the disturbance—Franconi two rows in front of Genti, separated from their camara-
derie and nervous and fiddling with their eyeglasses.

Isaac checked the doors till he was satisfied that they had
not been tampered with, were as secure as they had been
when the plane was airborne. He walked on down the aisle,
the submachine gun swinging easily in his hand, turning to
neither right nor left, as if ignoring those who sat at either
side of him. Walked to where the drinks trolley still blocked
the rear passageway to the far exit, and bent down to rum-
mage under the final row of seats till his hands emerged with
two life jackets, brilliant orange and with their straps sagging.
A few moments' work and he had lashed the trolley to the
nearest seat legs, pulling on the knots he had made with the
straps till he was satisfied that they would hold. A slight and
primitive barricade, an obstruction between the body of the
plane and the back exit. Came back up the aisle, now staring
his way through the passengers, as if his whim had changed
and he sought to force his personality blanket wide over
them, and there were no takers, no challengers, no heroes
seeking a dangerous laugh at his expense. Even the American
not talking, even the baby stifled from its incessant howl. And
the headmaster looking straight ahead even when Isaac
brushed his hip against the shoulder of the sitting man.

Isaac came past David and Rebecca, not stopping, and
went on to the cockpit. Again the gesture with the gun, and
the pilot officer and the navigator unfastened their harnesses,
climbed up from their seats and moved back toward the main
cabin. As she came through the passage entrance, Anna
Tashova let slip the mask, dropped the facade of security and

competence and seriousness and grinned. Giving way to her youth and her girlishness, meeting the eyes in front of her, identifying the heads and faces, seeing on them the broad lines of gratitude and thanks. Had heard the clapping when she had landed the Ilyushin, and it had warmed her, a sweetening and sustaining gesture; now she saw again from these people the trust and regard in which they held her.

But too frightened to speak, and who was she to call them cowards? Knew what it was like in the Former Times, as the elderly referred to them, when Josef Stalin, who was now a "nonperson," had ruled; when the Secret Police were rampant; when the prisons were full and the firing squads busy. When people did not speak, when all was said with the eyes, because they believed they would not be punished for the movements of their face muscles, only for the tripping of words from the tongue. She knew why they were quiet and wondered what more she might do to protect them. Near the front of the plane she found a seat; the navigator took one farther back.

Isaac lingered near her, interrupting for a moment his continuous movement. Seemed to want her to speak to him, as if he believed she was a part of their plan in a confused and abstract way. Twice was about to move on with his mission of bedding down the passengers, and faltered, stayed close, inviting conversation that she was not prepared to offer.

"Are you comfortable, Miss Tashova?" Almost a request for her acquiescence.

"As comfortable as any of the passengers."

"I hope you can sleep there, that you will be rested."

The soft, derisive snort in response. "It is hard to sleep when watched by a gun, difficult to rest."

"It is not of our making, Miss Tashova. We had not believed we would still be on the aircraft tonight. We had thought to sleep in beds. . . ."

"And Yuri, you had thought for him to sleep in a coffin?"

"It was not as we intended."

"Go tell him that." Fast, cruel and hurting with her words, spoken low so that those around her could barely hear. "Go tell him, and whisper it in his ear."

"I tell you it was not intended." Hardening, cooling in his respect.

"I tell you go and speak that message to him. Let Yuri know that."

"You must sleep, Miss Tashova, so that you can fly in the morning."

"There will be no flight from here. Your friend knows it. Have you seen him? Have you looked at him, peered into him, dissected him? He knows. He knows the penalty for the death of Yuri. Only when the jets were with us, when he had so much to think of, only then could he forget our captain. And now he remembers him. Have you not watched your leader? Perhaps you should; perhaps you should study him and absorb what you see."

She spoke slowly, certain in her words, deep in her malice, comforted by the knowledge that he listened.

Her confidence rising, she spoke again, with the same hushed persistence. "It is a trivial, pathetic little army that you have. Banal, insignificant beyond its guns. A leader who is frightened because he kills, a girl who is unsure and does not know her role and who you hide at the back lest she should be a part of this and fail you. . . ."

"But we have the guns, Miss Tashova. We have the guns and we will use them." And there was that in his voice which quieted her, as if at last she believed him. Nothing more to say, and his interest in her now lost, and she responded no further, tempted and taunted him no longer.

Isaac moved away. Checked the foward doors, then slipped back into the cockpit. Closed the door behind him, creating a darkness that he would need to see beyond the steeply tilted windows. Would take him time to see through the brilliance of the searchlights that played against the body of the aircraft. Sat himself at the back, where the navigator had been, outside the orbit of the light they could throw onto the flight deck.

He kept very close, still, head motionless, body relaxed and even comfortable in the crewman's seat, steeling himself all the time to resist the tugging and clawing of drowsiness. Would not stay, not more than a few minutes. Had to go back into the passage and relieve David and Rebecca; couldn't last, not the way they were, and he must take the burden of the night watch. Not enough of them, that was the fault: not enough for a shift system of watching and guarding. But nowhere would you have found more, Isaac. Not a member of a group, of an organization, with a hydra of cells sprouting, with a recruiting belt in motion, delivering those who could stand and take their positions while others slept. Didn't even know whether others would have followed if they had disseminated their message, whom they could have trusted, approached, confided in. Just four in the world that encompassed their horizons; and now three.

Movement out there. In the space between the searchlights to the left of the cockpit. Shadows at play, flitting and diving and disappearing, but he had seen the men move. And dimmed headlights approaching, and rear lights that were reddened and departing.

A field full of evening rabbits. The lights coming cautiously, perhaps to within two hundred meters of the plane, and he wondered if the men were closer. Watched the lights turn as if unwilling to test whatever strength he possessed with too close a contact—and instantly he was aware of the two soldiers, saw the tripod of the machine gun and the reflection from the ammunition belt. One man behind the weapon, the other crouched at the side of the barrel. Saw it and lost it as the vehicle continued its traverse. Of course there would be soldiers out there, but how many and how close? Another with the silhouette of the rifle at the trail running across the front of the moving lights, hurrying and bent low so that he would be only minimally visible. Thought of the precautions he'd taken inside the aircraft; inadequate, hopelessly inadequate if they came. And David believing when the man told him to sleep, told him the message would come in the morning . . . What would their orders be? Take them alive, or kill them? David, the stupid bastard, the one whom they followed, and he had drunk in the syrup, taken it right down into the pit of his guts, believed what he had been told because he was tired and wanted to sleep and did not understand the gin trap that had been prepared for them, the mincing machine that would grind them.

No relaxation now, hunched in the seat, and with his back muscles taut and his eyes hurting as he strained into the darkness seeking more evidence of the perimeter they had placed around the plane. Lights farther back this time, on and off, perhaps a couple of seconds, but time enough for him to perceive the gaunt outline of two parked armored cars. Faintly amused him: all the precautions they would be taking to ensure that watchers from the plane saw nothing of their preparations, and he had outsmarted them. Had seen the machine gun, and the soldier who ran, and now the armored cars. What did they want the killing apparatus for? Why did they need it if they would supply the fuel in the morning? A mirthless smile, something secret and personal to himself. And two fools behind him oblivious in their exhaustion and their innocence of the broth they would sup at.

As Isaac sat alone with his thoughts in the shadowed cockpit, his resolve hardened. An ingot of steel that is taken soft from the furnace and that cools into something unmalleable. He would fight them, fight them all, do battle with the heavy guns and with the tanks that they would send, and his hand was steady on the stock of the gun that nestled in his lap. Better here, he thought, than in the cellars with the militiamen around him. What did they do to you, Moses? What did the pigs do to you? And how did you keep your silence? How did you win us the time to fly out? The pigs are here too, Moses, different only in their clothes and the voices; they are here, where we did not expect them to have their friends.

"If they had told me it would be like this, Moses, I would not have believed them." None to hear his words, none for company but the captain. It was an accident, it was not intended, old man. Join the ranks of the casualties; there are many of them, enough to keep you brave company. And there will be more; the crossfire will fiercen; the uninvolved who stand between the guns will be many. You will not be alone, old man; you will have friends.

Isaac came out of the cockpit and moved quietly to where David stood leaning against the wall of the far end of the corridor beyond the closet doors.

"Sleep, David. Rebecca and I will watch the first part of the night; then Rebecca can sleep when the passengers are quiet."

David nodded, numb, unthinking, and slouched away toward the open cockpit door. They heard him sink into the seat, still warm, where Isaac had sat, and they heard him wriggling and turning till he found the position he wanted; then nothing. Farther back in the corridor, beside the plane's front exit, were the seats that the cabin crew used for takeoff and landing and when the plane was in turbulence. Isaac and Rebecca sat there—the girl on the inside, nearer the door; he leaning outward so that his vision encompassed the whole of the cabin.

She said quietly, and she was close to his shoulder, "Some of the old ones, and the children, they want to use the toilet, Isaac."

"They can't."

"But there are old people here, Isaac; they must—"

"The Jews grow old. They too have wanted to pee and to shit, Rebecca. Are there flush toilets at Potma and Perm, and basins to wash their hands in and make themselves clean when they are locked in the huts at night? They lie in their filth."

"David said it was for you to decide. They asked him, and he would not say himself; he said it was for you to decide."

"And you, Rebecca, what would you do, how much are you softened, how much have they weakened you?"

"I would let them go to the toilet, because they must have dignity. If you prevent them from going, if they mess themselves, then they have no dignity. We should not take that from them, whatever they have done to our people. We must show we are different from them. If we are the same, the animal same, then there is no salvation for us."

Isaac stood up, abruptly, without further comment, and walked forward to the entrance of the cabin.

"There is a toilet here. You may come to it one at a time. You have to be quick, and you have to know what will happen if you exploit the kindness that we show you." He spoke savagely, soured and resentful at the concession that had been wrung from him. "And while you are squatting, think of the Jews in your camps, the ones you call 'dissidents,' whose crime in your eyes is that they want a new life in Israel. Think of them; wonder how they are crapping tonight. Think of their spoiled blankets. One at a time you come, and do not forget that the gun is loaded, is cocked."

For a full hour there was a crawling procession of passengers moving from their seats to the toilet and back again. Isaac insisted that only one person be out of his seat at a time, and the process was pained and slow. Some thanked

him for his consideration, others ignored him, and he saw
those who had not lasted and had already fouled themselves,
staining their trousers and dresses, and who were ashamed
and hated him. They will dance on my body should they kill
me, he thought. Dance and sing as if it were a holiday. From
the farthest row at the end of the plane came the one who
seemed the farmer—he would be the last. As he passed Isaac,
he summoned the spittle in his mouth and spat noisily and
with rare force onto the carpet. One at last with balls to him,
and Isaac laughed loudly and smacked the old man on the
back, and saw his face twist in astonishment that the gesture
he had spent many minutes thinking on and mulling over and
which was the only protest he could muster should be taken
so lightly.

When the man went back, with his bowed shoulders and
his worn summer coat and the boots that were heavy and
foreign to the aisle carpet and that carried the gray-brown
clay of the Ukraine, Isaac returned again to his seat. Could
hear David sleeping noisily. What a mercy sleep was. The
time of safety, when all is forgotten, when the dreads and
fears are shut out, excluded. Lucky bastard. The one who
brought us here, and who does not know the cold and the
chill and the death that surround him. Lucky bastard, David.
Dream yourself away; put your fist in your pants; conjure the
wide streets of Israel, the sunshine, green trees that carry
oranges, people who laugh and would make you welcome.
Lucky, David, always the lucky one, with the dreamy skill
that made us follow you. And the escape is yours, not ours.
You sleep, content in your warmth and your fingers; and we
are left behind with the stink of our own bodies and of another sixty, and the odor of the lavatory.

"What will happen tomorrow?" She was drowsy, eyes half
closed, shoulder against his chest, head against his cheek.

"We will ask for the fuel for the plane."

"And they will give it to us." Faint voice, and he could not
recognize whether she asked a question of him or made a
statement.

"No." Saw her start and stiffen, her mind turning, hopelessly competing with the need for sleep.

"The fuel—will they give it to us?" A question now, no
room for doubt.

"No."

"But we must have fuel to reach Israel."

"They will not give us the fuel. They will not give it to us just because we ask."

"But—"

"But nothing, Rebecca. They are all around our plane. They have machine guns that I have seen, and there are soldiers and light tanks. They are not waiting there to see the fuel loaded at dawn. They are waiting for us to break, Rebecca. They are waiting for our will to snap, fracture, so that they can take us."

"What can we do?" Trying to wake herself, trying to throw off the sleep that had nearly engulfed her; bright wide eyes. "What can we do?"

"We have to surprise them; convince them that we are hard, that we are serious, that we are not easily deflected." Bored with the sound of his own words, attempting to communicate on a different level. Not something that you can express, only that you can feel. She had no comprehension; the words meant nothing to her. "They have given in before. They sent the Arab girl back. Leila, Leila something . . . I do not remember her name. They sent her back to her people. If the threat is great enough, they will bend."

"Have we the power to make the threat great enough?"

"Too many questions, Rebecca, and past time you were sleeping."

Impatience cutting through, and too many questions. Too many questions that Isaac could not summon the answers to.

From behind the barricade of petrol tankers, Davies watched the unloading of the equipment that had been brought to him from Science and Forensics, Scotland Yard. Four metal-encased crates, with warnings of "Fragile" and "This Way Up" stenciled on their tops and sides—boxes that were handled gingerly and with respect as they were carried from the rear doors of the van. The SAS unit crowded round the cargo, noted the crudely drawn eye with grotesque lashes that had been painted on the smallest box with the title of "Cyclops." Seen it all on exercise, never in the buff, the altogether. Had been at the Spaghetti House and Balcombe Street, but the SAS hadn't been called for, had left it on both

occasions to the police. But they'd seen the results and reckoned it would make their job way easier if the storm order
came.

The Yard had sent its own operators—senior-grade men
from the civil service union: gray-flannel-trousers brigade,
with buttoned collars and ties that carried the emblem of the
single piercing eye, out of place among the denimed soldiers.
No contact, no common ground and a mutual suspicion between those who would operate the equipment and those
who would take the risks of placing it in position where its
best advantage could be utilized. Some among the new arrivals sought out Davies and closeted with him over diagrams of
the Ilyushin interior, fingers stabbing at the cockpit area, at
the porthole sections on the flanks of the replica, at the windows set into the rear of the aircraft.

They had brought from London three pieces of equipment.
Primary among them, preeminent, was the "cyclops," the
fish-eye lens with its 180-degree visual capability. Relegated to
secondary importance by those who now unwrapped the
components from their padded cells were the suction-adhe-
sive audio devices. It was "cyclops" that the experts swore by:
a lens no bigger than the nail of a man's little finger, triggered
to a camera via a flexible-fiber cable. Had introduced it into
the sealed basement of Spaghetti House, down the ventila-
tion shaft, clandestine and silent to provide the crystal-bright
pictures of the siege room; removed the incessant anxiety because you knew what was happening live behind the locked
and bolted doors. But a greater problem here, and that was
the root of the discussion between Davies and the men from
London: where to place it, where to gain maximum advantage, where it could be secreted against the outer glass of a
window and face the minimum chance of detection. Couldn't
just plaster it across the center of a porthole. And had to go
in soon, before the summer night ebbed into dawn.

"We don't know the scene inside," said Davies. "They've
pulled all the blinds . . . what I'd have done in their boat; but
I'd hazard that their central area is toward the front, close to
the cockpit."

"You can have it for the cockpit or the forward cabin, one
or the other," said the Yard man testily. "We don't have a
dozen of them."

Davies ignored the edge, the spaniel snap. "What's the

lighting factor, if we have it forward, outside corner of a window?"

Happier ground for the technician. "Pretty fair with video. You'll see the faces clear enough. Not into the cockpit, just the passengers and the aisle—most of that."

They compromised. "Cyclops" and one audio circuit at the front of the passenger cabin, the second audio for the cockpit. Further briefings for the soldiers, reminders of how to fasten the suction pads, the angle the camera required, how the cables should be laid, as if the troops hadn't handled the gear before.

"Pretty useless the audio will be," said one who loathed to see the apparatus out of his immediate and personal control. "With the doors closed you'll hear fuck all. And the pictures not much better, not going to show through for you; it's not bloody magic." And the sergeant to whom he spoke was patient and explained that though the blinds were drawn now, they would probably be raised during the daylight hours. That the people inside weren't fools; that the blinds were down because they needed the lights on in the cabin, and it would be different in daylight, wouldn't it?

Past two in the morning when Davies and four NCOs began their slow and time-totaling leopard crawl out across the smooth surface of the tarmac. Davies leading; his sergeant the work donkey with the canvas bag that held the fish-eye and the audios and the lightweight nine-foot aluminum ladder; the other three in close fire support. Coordinated advance, with the searchlights tilting their beams to new elevations, playing on the windows to dazzle and blind any who might look out.

They felt no excitement when they rose to their feet at the belly of the fuselage beneath the various indecipherable words of the Cyrillic alphabet that were printed on the hatches: professional soldiers, with the emotion and fervor of their youth before they were admitted to the Regiment long dissipated. Calm and efficient, master artisans, working the practiced procedures. Ladder in position, foam-rubber upper protection denying the sound of scratch or scrape against the metal of the fuselage. The sergeant climbing, and as he went, bending the fiber attachment, molding it to the curve of the plane's exterior; planting the lens itself, upper right corner, third porthole starboard; suction pad, and beyond it the shallow protuberance of the cobra head; the lens in place, reaching over the lip of the window fitting; need to be searched for; cursory look insufficient for discovery. The audio close to the next window forward, but reservations there: waste of bloody time till the doors were opened. Second audio at the cockpit windows, low down and wrapped among the arms of the rain wipers.

They ran the cables quickly and with discretion across the fuselage, bringing them together where the starboard wheel rested, camera case fastened in the interior of the undercarriage flap. Began to pay out the cables away from the plane, running them in the cracks that separated the concrete segments of the taxi area. Thirty-five minutes it took them till they were back to the cover of the tankers' shadows. David had slept through their visit; Rebecca too; and Isaac, who struggled to stay awake, had heard no sounds that could have aroused him from his vigil with the passengers. An intensive-care patient, the Ilyushin, with the drip feeds entering the veins.

"Bugs nicely in place, ready to bite," Davies told the scientist. Not a matter for boasting of; just the communication of necessary information.

Receivers had been moved into the cement hut behind the tankers. Three men busying themselves with screwdrivers and transistor-circuit diagrams. "Get a move on, lads. I want you out of here by sparrow fart, all tucked up in your beds by morning," said the major. The civilians worked fast, knew that he was joking, knew they were relegated to spend the next day, or two, or three, in the hut. When they had finished their adjustments, they returned to the van, unloaded camp beds. One carried a thermos flask, and another spoke of overtime, or bubble at time and a half, as he called it. "Not a bloody holiday camp" was Davies' parting thrust. He walked out into the night again. Dependent now on the boffins to get the kit into shape; but he'd met them before, believed in them and their equipment. Tantamount was the secrecy of the fish-eye; the buggers inside wouldn't know of it, wouldn't look for it.

Davies eased himself into the small gap between cabin and tail of two tankers, where the plane was flush to him. Shouldn't be difficult, not if there's only three of them, and all youngsters. Be in there in no time, if that was what the gods on high decreed. Always the problem, though, always the chance that one of the buggers won't see the reason of it, won't want to live; will take his last five seconds on earth blasting all and sundry round him. Plenty of plaudits for the rescue team if he doesn't, if the civvies come out of it in one piece, but sparse on thanks and short on medals for the chaps that pull out twenty stiffs and another fifteen in the ambulances with the sirens going full blast. All a matter of luck, whether one man stands his ground and wants to take people with him before he coughs. Same operation, same tactics, same drills and you end up either a hero or a miserable bloody failure. Israelis understood that; wouldn't have taken thirty doctors to Entebbe if they hadn't; but Davies' masters, would they understand it? Not a bloody chance.

Behind him the voice said, "There's nothing to see yet, and no one talking on the inside loud enough for the mikes, but everything seems to be operational. Should be able to start the peep show once they lift the curtain."

Proud and bold, the battleship at her moorings, Aeroflot 927 rode out the night hours. No movement inside her visible to the army of watchers, no sound that was detectable. Splendid and serene and masking her secrets, defying the onlookers to penetrate her inner thoughts. With the darkness had come the dew damp, which caused the soldiers sprawled in the grass to curse and fidget and envy those who owned at least the warmth and dryness of the aircraft seats in which to rest. Over all, the turgid throb of the generators for the lights, beating out their own discordant rhythm, sending messages far beyond the circle of men who cradled their rifles and waited.

Charlie would have liked to go down from the tower, out into the air, and walk close to the plane, sniff at the atmosphere and aura that surrounded it. But his place was by the radio; his need was for sleep. No point being knackered in the morning, not when the hard work would start. Wondered how they'd take it, how they'd react, when they realized the time was up. Come in, 927, show's over. Go ape, or take it calmly? Never could say with these people.

Past two when he came to terms with his camp bed. Not long till dawn, till the time to talk to the plane again.

Endless repetition of the same thought. How good would

they be? What caliber? Brave, and if they were, how would they use it?

Remembered the kid in Sheikh Othman—little bastard, with his shirttails flapping, and his futah loosened from the drive of his knees as he sought to clear the soldiers' cordon, and how they'd brought him down and laughed and sat on him, and you'd heard him scream, Charlie, scream for his father, and the captain had come, and the fist had lost itself in the kid's hair and they'd walked him to the corner. One shot you'd heard, you and all the others in the coffee shop, you with the ointment on your face that made you local, made you one of them. And you'd wanted to heave, and had looked around for guidance and for a lead. Not an eyebrow flickering, not a mouth cracking, not a breath drawn in. Called him a grenadier in the communiqué, and the little bugger should have been at school. Defense of the Empire, Charlie, defense of Law and Order. Shook you, Charlie, and you supposed to be a hard man.

Never could sleep without a pillow. Remember the night in the officers' mess, infantry battalion down at Plymouth, and some bright sod had suggested you go down and talk to a few of the chaps before you went to Dublin the first time. Not that they said anything, anything that might be useful, but crowed like fucking cockerels. How we killed young Paddy, young Sean, young Mickey. Terrorists all of them—seventeen years, eighteen years, nineteen years old. Bloody kids. Chased them around the alleys, up the back entries, closed the net. One shot to slow, one shot to fell, one shot to finish, and get the Saracen up fast and over the body so Dad doesn't come out and whip the Armalite for the next pig-thick ignorant kid with holes in his shoes through to his socks and one pair of jeans to his name who wants burying and thinks he's a freedom fucking fighter.

Wrap it, Charlie, time for bloody sleep. Time to kill three more kids. Little bright eyes all waiting for you, waiting for you in the morning, Charlie, and with a bit of luck the sun will be shining.

Long time coming, the sleep—not that a pillow would have helped.

10

It was now many hours that the group had been meeting. Beyond the closing of the cafés and pubs, beyond the concluding Anthem of the television stations, beyond the gradual whittling of the drumming traffic noise on the Bayswater streets. At any time of concern this was where they always gathered; not because the cramped flat was in any way suitable for their deliberations, but because its tenant was the General Secretary of their movement—in charge of their proud pile of headed notepaper and the petty cash.

At times, as many as twenty had been present, but the group fluctuated in size. Some leaving and hurrying away; others coming, fretful that they had delayed too long. Enough to fill all the chairs in the room and the stools that had been brought from the kitchenette, and the pillows pressed into service from the bedroom. They drank coffee, sharp and gritty, swilled down with tap water and sweetened by spoonfuls of sugar, and they nibbled at supermarket biscuits, and struggled to stay awake in order not to miss the hourly news bulletins that could be found on the World Service of the BBC and the more atmosphere-laden Voice of America.

They had many things in common. All born inside the confines of the Soviet Union. All tarred with the same stroke—"refugees," "exiles." All Jewish. All contributing and active members of the London-based Committee for Freedom of Soviet Jewry. All worried, all anxious, all frustrated that the strand of involvement was stretched so loose. All attempting to focus their minds and thoughts on a lone aircraft that was far away and at an airport none had been to. All willing their intellect to transport them across the miles of cityscape and countryside and deposit them close to the sharply shined hull of the Ilyushin airliner.

The shared tiredness had long since dulled the clarity of their conversation and analysis, so that for long spells the silence hung weighty and burdening upon the little room. Caused some to feel unequal to the moment, others to experience the anger of helplessness and a very few to doze comforted in the knowledge that they would be awakened by their friends at the chime of signature music that would herald the next bulletin. Just a standing lamp in a corner with a low-wattage, and therefore inexpensive, bulb to throw shadows in the room and hide the sunken and subdued faces that waited and whiled away the slow minutes. These were kicked and pummeled people. Had experienced the soaring upsurge of spirit that comes from the first breathing of liberation and freedom at stepping outside their rejected homeland, and now had realized that life was crueler, more savage; that the visions clouded in the bed-sit land where they lived and in the hotel kitchens where they thought themselves fortunate to find work. Little people whose escape had been quiet and with a whimper and devoid of fanfare, and who now fidgeted with their necklaces and their silver-chain-dangled Stars of David, and who searched their watch faces that the next news program might be hastened, and coughed hesitantly, and pulled at their cigarettes and expelled the smoke into the saturated air.

Most Sundays they gathered in a puny tight knot on the grass of Hyde Park. Took their regular turns at making and listening to the familiar speeches, and clapped and cheered, and wondered why the great herd was so uncaring and so indifferent that it passed them by without the consideration of a pause to hear the stark message of oppression and violation and humiliation. Most Wednesdays they came to the General Secretary's flat and talked and discussed and argued and made the trifling arrangements for their next public meeting. Always the culmination of the gathering as the official's wife drew a single sheet of headed notepaper from the folder and with flourish and pride wrote the requisite and formal letter to Scotland Yard (Public Meetings Section) requesting the necessary permission.

All easy, all clean; absence of blurring obstructions. And if they had not yet roused dormant British public opinion, then there was tomorrow and next year and a lifetime. But falling

on them now was a cold gust that was foreign and carried in
its wind many leaves of fear and confusion.

Of course, the evening had started well.

Backslapping and jokes, and wide and excited faces. Those
who came first had brought the last editions of the afternoon
papers with their glaring headlines, and they had stayed cemented beside the television set and the radio. Their people
were coming out—a flight out of Egypt; the great Mother
Russia had opened her thighs and raised her knees and
voiced the pangs of labor; the children were coming forth.
Escape on the grandest and most eloquent scale. Initially
they had discussed a press statement that would be phoned to
the news agencies as an expression of solidarity with young
people who were brave and of their faith. . . . Would not
their next public meeting be crowded and packed; would not
the masses at last awake to their cause and struggle because of
the action of these youths! Later had come the flesh that
covered the skeleton of the story, the news that the refugees
could bite, and subsidence of elation. A girl flying a plane at
gunpoint. Her captain, who had carried no weapon, dead
beside her. A party of schoolchildren whose lives were in
danger. Damning, and deadening to their short-lived pleasure.

When the General Secretary had telephoned to the Labour
Member of Parliament who championed their people in the
House of Commons, his wife had answered the call. Yes, she
would bring him to the phone, and there had been the
scraped sound of a hand placed over the mouthpiece and
blurred and indistinct words. He was not at home, she had
said. She was sorry. Perhaps later. Was there a number she
should take down? Another MP—not Jewish, but long sympathetic, and familiar to the head table at their Annual General
Meeting—was braver and less anxious to salve their sensibilities.

"It's aerial piracy and it's murder," he'd said with a gruff-
ness that startled the General Secretary. "You cannot dress it
up any other way. They've killed a defenseless man, imper-
iled a planeload of people. I'm sorry, but that's the way I see
it. I'm bloody sorry. Of course I'm sympathetic to you, and to
the fight, but this is a different scene. Take my advice. Stay
quiet; don't get involved."

They had followed the advice. The drafted statement to

the press was now a torn shambles of paper squares in the wastebasket.

Past four in the morning. Time for the trucks to start their trail into the city with the daily load of market fruit and vegetables, and for the street-cleaning vehicles to be out on their business. None in the group able to leave now; held and magnetized by the radio reports. Fresh fiddling with the dials: away from World Service, seeking again Voice of America. "Behind the News" reports. Read from the studio, taken from the dispatches of the Associated Press bureau in Moscow. A voice in a cracked, staccato rush, so that all in the room had to strain and alert themselves to follow the words. The bureau had been checking for reaction from those Soviet Jews who were at liberty in the Russian capital but whose opposition to the regime was known. A denial of all connection with and knowledge of those who had taken the plane out of Kiev; a condemnation of violence from whatever source. In silence they heard the message, heard the door slammed on any suggestion, however guarded, of complicity. Next a short voice track from the network's correspondent in Jerusalem. The Israeli Government had no comment, on the record or off the record, on the hijacking of the Aeroflot flight. No government official was prepared to speak on the matter. The stance of the Cabinet was well known on both terrorism and the plight of Soviet Jewry, the reporter had intoned, and it was the belief of observers in the capital that it was gravely embarrassed by what had happened. From Washington also, no authorized comment; room only for journalistic speculation, and the expressed belief that the United States Government would not seek to influence the British as to the course of action they might decide on. This incident was regarded as divorced from the President's often-repeated attitude on human rights inside. . . .

Savagely one of the listeners, galvanized now from his weariness, switched off the set. Plunged the room for a moment into an abyss of quiet; then shouted, "The cowards! Damned cowards! Stinking politicians . . ."

An avalanche of contradiction fell on him.

"And what are the people who took the plane; what are they?"

"For years we have suffered in dignity that we might win support, and now that we have succeeded . . ."

"They have betrayed the brave ones, these terrorists . . ."

"In the Kremlin they will be drinking champagne, toasting one another."

"They can justify anything now. Pogroms, show trials, roundups, arrests. Anything they want to do they can do now. Those three have given it all to them."

A girl was crying, smearing a handkerchief across her eyes, her voice broken and frail. "Why did they kill the man? Why did they shoot the pilot? There can have been no need to. If they had not killed the pilot . . ."

"Who are we to speak of what they have done, and what their motives are?" said the General Secretary slowly and with deliberation. "Who are we? We did not even make the journey to Israel. We are not a part of that place. We are the Jews who remain outside the family, and we are shocked now because a life has been cut short in the name of Israel—perhaps in cold blood, perhaps in heat. We do not know anything of these people . . ."

Interruption from above. The battered protest of an umbrella handle pounding at the ceiling. The upstairs tenants' only recourse to quell the surge of noise and argument.

". . . whether they have been stupid or wise, brave or cowardly, they are of our people. They have stretched us, tested us. Perhaps they have already shamed us, and perhaps they will also destroy us. But they are of our people and they are alone, and they have a right to our prayers."

Setting aside their weariness, those on the chairs and stools came down to kneel; those on the carpet and the pillows rose awkwardly so that they could share the moment. As he shuffled his aged legs and felt the pain in the tightness of his joints, the General Secretary murmured, "It would have been better for us if they had not come. But they are here, and they are few, and it should not be we who cast the stones. There will be many others for that task."

Each in his own form, and in silence, the members of the group prayed.

Body strength waning, muscles aching, head throbbing, limbs contorted in the limitations of her resting place, Rebecca sought sleep.

Elusive, though; hard to touch and take hold of. Too many images pursuing one another across the spectrum, denying her the comfort of oblivion. The things that Isaac had spoken of. Tanks. Machine guns. Soldiers. Cold, metallic, functional killing machines that had come for a purpose, that did not wait out there beyond the arc lights unless their value had been assessed and decided on as necessary.

There because of you, Rebecca. There to watch you, pry into you, examine you, and there to eliminate you, Rebecca. Eliminate, if that should be the instruction passed to them.

Subdued gray shadow in the fuselage, and the fidgeting quiet of the passengers. The only movement the sporadic prowling guard that Isaac maintained. Far from home, little one. Far from things familiar. Gone the games that were played in the hut, and the dreams of triumph they had all concocted and mixed and shaken together.

Love, Rebecca?

Was that the sensation and the addiction which had brought her this far with the boys, with David and Isaac? Love of one, or love of both? Was that where the answer lay?

And what was love? Not something physical, not body to body, not flesh to flesh, not with the muscles straining and the warmth soft and moist. Had not felt their hands perusing her, wanting her, searching the secret intimacy that she thought of as love.

If not love, then why are you here, Rebecca; what is your purpose?

How can I know? Whom now may I ask the question of, that I may find the answer?

An ordinary girl, Rebecca. Ordinary as cheese and mice, buses and queues, work shifts and rubles. . . . Ordinary, predictable. But there are not tanks and machine guns and soldiers deployed through the slow night hours watching and waiting on an ordinary girl, to see what her thoughts and actions will be when the light comes and when she has rested herself.

So easy in the hut. So facile when the battle was just of words. No doubts that the cause was right; certainty. Not in dispute, Rebecca. But if the cause is right, then someone must stand and defend it . . . but why you, Rebecca? Persecution, humiliation, spoliation, all these things have been visited on our people, and they have not stepped forward, have not armed themselves in their own defense. So why you, Rebecca? What was different, unique, that made this girl, this ordinary girl, stand up and plan and conspire? Not enough now, too late, to call to the soldiers of the darkness with their armor and guns and bullets that you were just a follower, that it was not of your willing, not of your choice. Too many questions, Isaac had said, and Isaac was right, always right.

All the talk of killing. All the preparations for the death of another. All the plotting, all the reconnaissance. All the hours in the hut used to make ready for the struggle that would be launched against the oppression that sat on their people. All that time, and no thought of this moment, incarceration. Brave talk it had been, and Rebecca in the thick of it. Remember? Remember the calling for the choice, by chance and not by merit, that determined that Moses should be the one?

Why, Rebecca?

God, how do I know?

Would David have loved you then, if you had drawn the short straw?

Perhaps.

If you had killed a man, would that have fired, stiffened, strengthened him?

Perhaps.

Did you have to kill a man to win David's love?

But he never came to me, never came to me as a woman. Only as a friend, a colleague . . . an adjunct; never as a woman.

His fault or your fault, Rebecca?

I don't know. God knows it's the truth, but I don't know.

Is it that he cannot, Rebecca? Is it that he is not man enough . . . ?

Let me sleep, please, please.

Did we have to come to this place for your answer, Rebecca, and have we now found it?

I have to sleep. I must sleep.

Is that your answer, Rebecca?

If that is the truth, better never to have known, better never to have come. Better to have stayed the ordinary girl. Brave, ignorant and happy.

There was a grayness in the dawn and a brush of salmon pink in the low cloud haze when Charlie woke.

Cold in the tower, and he shivered as he recalled where he

was and why. A policeman grinned down at him from the chair in front of the console that he had occupied while Charlie slept, guarding the radio but without cause to disturb the Foreign Office man. Long time since Charlie had slept rough; not since the family camping holiday outside Aberystwyth when they'd packed it in after four days, conceding second best to the weather, and he'd vowed never again, no more holidays for the mob without confirmed hotel bookings.

Have to get ready for when they opened the radio circuit. Should wash his socks through first, though; not that anyone else would have, but a standing privilege of a desk job was that a man had the right to clean socks. Quit the rubbish, Charlie, get up and concentrate.

Charlie dressed quickly, just his trousers and shirt, and felt a moment of distaste at the darkened rim of his collar.

"Any chance of a cup of tea and a half minute with a battery razor?"

The policeman was happy to vacate the chair; said he'd go and look, and that the Committee was dossing down below in the Airport Manager's office. All except the Home Secretary, of course: found him a billet down in the Fire Chief's house— a bit away, but inside the perimeter.

"Tell them I'm on the seat, my compliments, and remind them that the plane's due to come through any time now."

Going to have to be careful with this one. The crucial conversation; that much had been decided last night before dispersal. Should be left in no doubt they'd get no petrol, fly nowhere else. Clitheroe had given his sanction: all right once they'd rested to give them the pill. But didn't really matter how freshened they were, how much they could think things out, labor with the logic; always unpredictable when they flatten into a brick wall for the first time, realize they haven't a safety belt on. Getting old, Charlie, talking to yourself next. Shut up, Charlie, shut up and wait for the tea to come.

But the radio call came before the tea.

"Kingfisher here, Kingfisher here. The man we spoke to last night, is he there?"

Charlie waved behind him, the fantasies scattered; alert, in control. The beckoning gesture, and there was a shout that

echoed away down the stairs, and then the drumming of running feet that were taking the stairs two at a time.

"Charlie to Kingfisher." Humor the silly apes. "Charlie
here. Please identify who is calling. Is that David?" Keep it
simple to start with while you tune into the language scene,
while the heavies get their trousers on. What a time in the
morning to be fluent in Russian. "Have you slept well inside
the plane; did you get your heads down?"

"It is immaterial. We are waiting for the answer. We want
the fuel. Do you have the authorization for that?" He'd slept,
all right, the bastard; didn't sound as if he were back on the
ropes like last night; fresher, keener, more determined, and
rejecting the request for identification. Tapping on Charlie's
shoulder. Assistant Chief Constable there, looking as though
they'd pulled him backward through a hedge and still combing what hair he had, and Clitheroe in his braces and short of
his jacket and tie and still heaving from the race up the stairs.

"Don't worry about the translation now, Mr. Webster. Give
it to them hard and straight."

Finger to the console, switch to transmission. Deep breath;
steeled himself.

"David, this is Charlie. I have a very important statement
for you from the British Government. I want you to hear it
right through, and I don't think you should interrupt me, not
till I've finished. Is that understood?"

"We will hear what you have to say." Concession and the
fragment of subservience.

"David, this is the reply of the British Government. You
are ready to listen? There will be no refueling of the aircraft.
There is no possibility, whatever your reaction, that the plane
will be refueled in order that you can fly to Israel . . ."

There was a fast and angry explosion of shouting that
boomed out from the loudspeaker—explanatory, aggressive,
yet difficult for Charlie to follow in detail.

"You said you'd hear me out. Shut up and listen. There will
be no fuel; there will be no negotiation about flying this or
any other plane to Israel. The journey is over, David. Your
plane is surrounded by a military force that includes specialist
troops of the highest caliber. There are two ways that you can
leave the aircraft. You can come off dead, or you can come
off alive with your hands over your heads, unarmed and after

you've released the passengers. There are no other options. We will sit here as long as you need to make up your minds, but we think that you are all intelligent people, we think you will realize that there is no point in continuing, that you will understand your situation. Look out of any of the windows and you will see the armored cars. There is nowhere for you to run to, David. That is what the British Government says."

Charlie sat back in his seat; heaved his chest in relief that he'd shed the load, tipped off the weight; half-spun in the chair and gave the men who waited behind him a précis of what had passed.

Swung back and was writing hard on his pad. New voice, different accent, devoid of subservience.

"That is all you have to say to us?" Like meeting a pen pal for the first time. Had to be Isaac, and Charlie pointed without comment to the photograph for the benefit of those who watched.

"Yes, Isaac, that is all. There is no room for negotiation, no scope for it. Your position is a hopeless one from any military or physical point of view, and you must surrender unconditionally. If you do that, and have first released the passengers and crew, then I guarantee that no harm will come to you when you give yourselves up."

"You know what the consequences will be?" Too fast a reply for him to relay an English translation of what he had said; had to hang on, keep up the momentum; hopeless if he broke the spell now.

"There are no consequences, as you put it, Isaac, that will alter the decision of the British Government."

"You believe that?"

"I know it, Isaac. They will not change their stance."

"Wait till ten o'clock, ten this morning. Then tell me again."

"Isaac, there is no point in threats. There is nothing to be gained from them, only the worsening of your situation. . . ."

No one listening. The empty, unresponsive echo of discarded headphones and microphone far away. Switched off, the little bastards, cut him dead. Charlie looked up at the digital clock immediately above, saw the numeral flip over. Four fifty-two. Five hours till Isaac turned his words of consequences into action. More explanations to the men behind and a graveness in their faces as they heard the detail of the final stages of the exchange.

Assistant Chief Constable put it with the bluntness that was needed to knife through the veneer with which others would have preferred to coat the ultimatum. "They're threatening to start shooting passengers, executing their hostages, murdering . . ."

"That's about it," said Charlie, matter-of-fact, a man to whom the baldness of such a statement was not exceptional. "And it's Isaac who's coming across as the hard boy. Moved on from the one we have as David. Had the heave, didn't he? The other boy is the toughie there."

"Military won't want to be messing about," the Assistant Chief Constable went on, as if in ignorance of the interruption, "not in the light, and that's what we'll have in twenty minutes. Wouldn't have mattered an hour ago, when they had some cover. But they have to have cover, cover or it's bloody difficult for them and dangerous for the passengers. If we'd played it straight last night, and said what we meant, and they'd reacted this way, then we could have put the military in . . ." In full flow, the staff officer of Agincourt, of Waterloo, or Paschendaele, and back from the front with his gunpowder burns.

"The decision was taken by everybody." Clitheroe rising to his own defense. "We agreed that they would be more susceptible to the logical working out of their situation and position if they had had some sleep. The first one who spoke, David, he's obviously rested. But his sleep had to be paid for. Presumably the man Isaac has not slept; therefore he is exhausted, and temporarily he is the irrational one, but there is much time for the others to work on him and for him to reflect on the measures that he has blurted out to us."

It was not a new problem for Clitheroe. Early in his working life in psychiatry he had come to accept the fact that the science was not an exact one, that the ill informed were skeptical and dubious about his expertise and the weight of his advice.

"We should not take the threat too seriously; there is much time yet."

Charlie said, and his attention was off the medical man, focused on the senior policeman, "If it's not vulgar to ask, sir, what's to happen to these people? Assuming we talk them out, or we storm and take them alive, what happens to them?"

The raw nerve. Stamped on it. Pinched it. Off-the-cuff question, and he hadn't thought it out before. Civvies from London looked away. Color at the Assistant Chief Constable's cheeks.

"I don't think it's been decided yet."

"They could ship them back—that has to be one of the options?"

"That's only your assumption, Mr. Webster."

"Bad news if they get wind of it. Not going to come waltzing down the bloody steps and into our open arms. Stands to reason they're going to try and push us about a bit first."

"Outside your province, Mr. Webster." Putting the clamps down, hiding behind the medal ribbons, climbing on the gold of his epaulets.

"If I can't put that one out of their minds, then not much chance of it all ending in sweetness and light."

"Don't extend yourself, Mr. Webster. You do an excellent job as an intermediary. Quite excellent, and be so good as to confine yourself to those limits." Bloody martinet, thought Charlie; why can't he come clean, take a dose of the honest johnnie, accept he's outside the confidential circle?

The sun was playing on the aircraft now, burnishing its sides, beating up from the desert of tarmac. Made Charlie squint his eyes together just to look at it. Lonely-looking now, sort of lost and strayed off its path, and doesn't know how to get into the air again and sniff, or whatever birds do to get the road back to where they belong. Didn't suit it as well, the daylight; not like the night, with its magnification and the floodlights; seemed to have become shrunken as the sun crept up on it. Didn't have the look of anything deadly; shorn of the melodrama; just another bloody plane sitting on its wheels, waiting for its orders. Blinds were up, and some of those behind him had binoculars and gazed intently at the portholes and pointed and passed the glasses from hand to hand, but Charlie couldn't see anything beyond the darkened regularly spaced shapes of the windows; nothing living, nothing moving.

More movement at the back of the Control area. Men with cables and a portable television set, the type used by industry, with the innards gaping and not cased, as they would be in a

domestic set. It was placed on a bench close enough for
Charlie to see the screen, far enough for others to watch
without disturbing him from his communications on the
radio. Farther along the controller's workbench they fitted
the tape recorders with their attendant headsets, and the
floor was a net of crazily scribbled wires and junction boxes.

Some twenty seconds of frosting and snowstorm as they
tuned the set before the clear image came. Not bad, not bad
at all, and Charlie joined the others who pressed shoulder to
shoulder to identify the grayed, soft-shaded shapes of the
heads of men and women and children: some lolling as if still
in sleep; others alert and darting their eyes around them.
Could see some of the children, and across the aisle and in a
solid-colored suit a man who sat with them and whose face
was set and steady and did not waver.

Behind Charlie someone asked, "What's the sound
quality?"

"Not good—very muzzy, indistinct. We'd hear something
loud—shouting or a shot, at that pitch; ordinary voice levels
won't be satisfactory. Might be better when we put the tapes
through the cleaner, wash the backgrounds out a bit, don't
count on it." They let the audio man get on with it; sound
was second best. That picture was sensational was the general
consensus; a new toy, and they were reveling in its versatility.

"That's Isaac," Charlie broke in. "The one in the front.
The girl's behind him, Rebecca."

Total attention on the screen now, and hazy in the middle
distance from the minute camera was the figure of Isaac with
his chin low on his chest and his hair messed and tangled,
shirt creased and floppy and the tail out of his trousers.
Watchful and suspicious and minding his charges. Two hands
on the gun—World War Two, and Charlie wondered where
they'd dug that one up from. Looked clean enough; took an
extended magazine—thirty shots, enough. Didn't really look
at the girl, didn't know anything about her to convince himself that she wasn't there just for the ride; saw that she kept
close, not more than half a pace behind the man, and that
her dress was torn, and that her cheekbone showed the dis-
coloration of bruising. A long way up the aisle the fish-eye
followed them before they were lost, cut off by the thick lip of
the window's casing.

"That's the one you have to concern yourselves with," said

Charlie to anyone who cared to listen. "If you can persuade him to walk out with his hands up, when there's half a chance he'll be shipped back to Kiev, then it'll be champagne all round, and on me."

Pushing your luck, Charlie; only a cog, and a little one at that, and it's a big wheel you're working in. Steady down, sunshine—not that anyone was listening to you anyway.

The Foreign Secretary had not slept well. Never did in the Club beds. But the Party had been in office only four months, and the Prime Minister talked so frequently of the impossibility of continuing with so slight a majority and of his wish for a snap election that it had seemed pointless to make the expensive investment in a Central London home. Better to wait and see whether the future was in the chauffeur-driven Foreign Office limousines or the wife-piloted mini of Opposition. The Club was adequate and useful after the welter of official dinners that the Foreign Secretary was obliged to host, and at least it was quiet, with a code of ethics in the smoking lounge that would not tolerate his being accosted by other members and quizzed on government intentions.

In his pajamas he ate the scrambled eggs that the venerable servant had brought him at five. Glanced fitfully at the morning's screaming headlines. Milking it dry, pulling the udders down, but could hardly blame them: height of the silly season, with Parliament not sitting; damn all going on, and now a hijack into the back garden. Teams of reporters and teams of photographers, all with their credits above the stories and under the pictures. Even a photograph of himself leaving the Foreign Office by the side entrance that he favored; shouldn't have smiled, wasn't right for the occasion, but the little devils were everywhere and you never saw them in the dark, only felt the flash against your face. Past midnight when he'd abandoned his desk. Three long telephone sessions with the Prime Minister and not much to chew on as a result of them. Usual story. "You're the man who knows the implications of it all, as far as foreigns go. You're the man in charge; Home Office will work to you. You act and we'll be behind you." How far behind? Inside knifing range or out? How many years back was it that that socialist chap had called his ministry "a bed of nails"? Only had Labour and Industrial Relations to worry about; should have tried Foreign Office for a week.

A barely audible knock, and the entry of the PPS. Shaved, suited, clean and bringing more coffee. Thoughtful lad; good choice.

"Before your solicitations, I slept damned badly, feel washed out and would give almost anything to exchange my desk today for a decent morning's fishing." Smiles all around. "What have you brought me?"

"Transcripts from the late-night radio and television in Moscow. Going very hard on the meeting the Ambassador had with you last night, spelling out their demands; internal-consumption stuff, but still a very tough stance."

"And the Israelis?" Mouthful of toast, and a smear of marmalade to go with it. Beds might be lumpy, but the Club at least maintained a standard with the breakfasts.

"Nothing direct from them, and no commentary on the tail of their bulletins. They're taking it very straight."

"State Department and White House—anything there?"

"Secretary of State's office called. Said they didn't want to wake you—I said you'd be in the office by six fifteen. The Secretary will call you fifteen minutes later; they asked me to say he would be coming out of a function to do so. They describe it as a confidential and clarification matter."

The Foreign Secretary bit hard into the crisped toast. The lobby getting to work, all its power and all its tentacles beginning to weave into the scene. To be anticipated.

"There was a demonstration outside the British Embassy in Washington late last night their time, a couple of hours ago. Few rocks over the fence and the police broke it up. Fairly Rent-a-Mob, but the law went a bit heavy, so there will be pictures that won't be friendly. Banners about not sending them back to their deaths, that sort of thing."

"Trifle premature, but they don't waste time." Reached for the new supply of coffee, poured it himself, and the PPS noticed that the hand was not steady; sloshed into his saucer. Never at his best in the mornings, not till he'd put himself together. "What do you think, my young friend? Give me an opinion."

"You can view the question from three angles. From emotion. From principle. From pragmatism. Take the first and last. If emotion wins the day, then we'll find a reason not to return them. If it's the pragmatic we're after, then we ship them home, because sizable though the Jewish-stroke-Zionist scene is, it does not compare with the importance of our enjoying the continuing goodwill of the Soviet Union. Leaves only the principle of the matter. We're signatories to the Hague Aerial Piracy Convention. It's old now and it's gathering dust, but we and everyone else said at the time that we wanted a firm stand taken against hijacking. The firmest stand you can take is to send these people back."

"That's making it all very simple."

The Foreign Secretary headed toward the bathroom and turned on the spurting taps, leaving the PPS to compete with the half-closed door and the running water.

"As our chaplain at school used to say, where principle is involved there can be no leeway."

"And the limit of his concern was you little blighters' smoking behind the physics lab and trying to deflower the art master's daughter."

"If you take those three points, you must come out two to one in favor of freighting them. It would only be emotion that would guide you to keep them here."

"And votes"—a distant reply echoing from the tiled walls of the bathroom—"and your seat in the House and mine."

"All it comes down to is a selling matter. News Department can handle that. It's what they're paid for."

"And if I were to extract a public promise from the Soviet authorities that in view of the youth of these three persons the death sentence would not be exacted should they be found guilty, how would that affect matters?"

"If you pulled that, sir, I'd say you'd wrapped it all very neatly."

More water running, from the hot-water faucet; seemed to ease the pain. "Get the Russian chappie in for half seven, and my car here for six." Would be very tidy if it worked—solve many problems; not wound too many consciences. Israelis wouldn't like it, but then they didn't like anything—so damned prickly; but it would be a fair solution. It was one that he was pleased with as he soaped his toes.

An RAF staff car had brought Lt. Colonel Arie Benitz from Brize Norton. A shortage of serviced helicopters was the excuse for the change of transport he had been given on landing. That they were not ready to have him at Stansted was immediately apparent by the initial niggling delays. It was insisted that he should eat something after his long overnight flight; not just a sandwich, but something hot, and the mess would soon be open, the cooks on duty. There was the problem of the civilian clothes that had to be mustered—surprise to Benitz, because he was of medium height with unexceptional contours. It was suggested that he might care to telephone his embassy, and more time consumed first while they found the keys to a private office and then again while the call was routed through the Ambassador's home.

"The British have a dilemma, Colonel," the Ambassador had said. "If they bow to the Soviet pressure, then your journey will have been wasted. If they stand up for themselves, and it might be the first time in many years, then there is a role for you. But do not count on it; remember the spare parts for the Centurions in the time of Yom Kippur. At the moment, their decision has not been made. I suggest you let the air force bring you to London, to the Embassy. There is not the great hurry that we had feared earlier, and the British are showing they are in no rush to throw their apple to either side of the fence."

Two and a half hours it had taken him, first winding and turning on the country roads, then powering along the empty M4, until finally they were catacombed among the half-lit streets of the capital. First visit to London, first to England, and nothing to do but stare at the fleeting sights from the window and with only a taciturn driver for company. When he reached the embassy, he was not one who felt surprise at its fortress protection. A private road, and a message sent ahead by telephone from the Kensington end gates to warn of his arrival. Floodlights at the front of the building, a remote camera on an arm jutting above him, steel-faced door, an age of identification and explanation before the bolts withdrew, the lock turned.

Taken to the Ambassador's office to read the latest decoded communications from Jerusalem, to hear the most updated reports from Stansted, to study the photographs and biographies that the Russians had supplied to the Foreign Office and which had been passed on to the Israelis in confidence. Said little as he paced his way through the folder of documents, needing to scour the typed words only once: a man who assimilated information without hardship. When he closed the file, signifying that the contents were digested, the Ambassador spoke, quietly and with concern.

"You have a detestable job, Colonel; not one that should be given to an officer of your experience and ability. If there is a role for you in this matter, it will be to talk these people into a surrender and will be both wounding and hurtful to many of the Jews of the world.

"The position as we see it is this, and you must forgive any repetition of what you may have been told before you left Israel, but I understand the briefing time was short. The position is this. There is little to no chance that the British will provide fuel for the onward flight of the aircraft. The young people's escape has ended at Stansted, and it is their future there that concerns us. If they defy the British calls for surrender, if there is more bloodshed, more killing, then, and I do not have to stress this to you, there will be a grave embarrassment to our government. We want them out of that plane before they have done more damage, before they have had more opportunity to fuel the propaganda machine of the Soviets.

"But how, Colonel Benitz, can we wash our hands of them? Jewish students, fighting an oppression that we loudly and frequently condemn. We cannot abandon them. We cannot permit them to be returned to the Soviet Union. Our Defense Minister spoke in the Cabinet last night of our country's shame if they were to be sent back to their deaths. It is a dreadful dilemma that we face.

"That is my speech, Colonel, but it was necessary that all should understand the position we find ourselves in. We have offered your services to the British because we believe that the three will hear you; because you are a fighter, and that is how they see themselves. But we make one fundamental precondition for the use of your good offices. Should you help them win this surrender, then the British must guarantee that there will be no question of their extradition."

"Are the British likely to accede to our request?"

"No; it is unlikely, in my opinion."

"And if they do not?"

"I think we have not yet arrived at that point."

"Most of the men we fight against in the Antiterrorist Unit, those who come into our country, have come to terms with the price of their struggle . . . understand that there can be no return . . . know that we will kill them." Not articulate; trying to find the words he wanted and disappointed in himself that he could not match the fluency of the diplomat. "These will be different, without the training, without the discipline . . . their fear and confusion will be great by this time. Yet on their own scale they will believe they have achieved much." A smile slowly forming on his face. "Perhaps to them they have won their own Entebbe. . . ."

"I said to you, Colonel Benitz, that it was a detestable job that you have been chosen to perform."

"And there is no chance, no hope whatsoever, that they will be allowed to come to Israel?"

"How can there be? With the pilot dead, it is impossible. And even should the British allow it, could we receive them? When you are unpopular and alone as we are, and you wish to fight back, then your hands must be scrubbed clean. If we falter now, because our kith are involved, then we will have forfeited the right forever to speak out against the terrorism that you know better than I. If we accept that these three can become the heroes of Zionism, then we have borrowed the language of the Palestinians."

With a shrug, Benitz said, "The killing of the pilot has destroyed them."

"It has critically affected the matter."

"And would have been the action of a moment."

"You are charitable, Colonel."

"Not charitable, just realistic." Seemed to go far away, beyond the horizons of the room, to have lost interest in the conversation. "It's so fast, so rushed, there is not time for thinking—not in the moment of assault, not in the seconds that count if you are to succeed."

Before they parted, the colonel wrote down a series of telephone numbers—some that ran through the switchboard, others that were connected to direct outside lines.

"We asked," said the Ambassador with a pleasant smile on his face, one that was rarely revealed, "we asked that we could send our own communications system to Stansted, to enable you to report to us directly. The British indicated that there would be so much radio traffic that it was impossible for them to accommodate us; they said they regretted this. It would hinder their operations. We are used to these affairs; the British are not, and therefore they are tense and anxious and concerned that they emerge well from this matter at the conclusion."

They had shaken hands, and Benitz had returned to the waiting staff car. He dozed for much of the way out of London—not that he was particularly tired, but simply that he was used to taking his rest where he could find it. With the car halted and the sound of voices, he woke in the half-light at the outer-perimeter roadblock and was aware of the policeman with his flashlight scanning the travel authorization. Three miles farther and another enforced stop, and again the production of the magic paper, and salutes from men in uniform for the huddled figure sprawled on the car's back seat.

They took him to the control-tower building, men gesturing to his driver the direction he should take, which entrance he should report to. Conscious of the military as he stepped out of the car, bracing himself against the freshness of the morning: howl of an armored car accelerating in low gear, medley of chatter and static on a soldier's radio set, tire tracks that had gouged at the dried-out summer lawn. Familiar sounds and sights that he was accustomed to.

Twin pips on the officer's shoulder, but Benitz unimpressed with the lieutenant's deference as he was ushered into the hallway, ground floor, of the tower; perhaps a curl of amusement at his mouth at the flamboyance of the fusilier's cockade with the hackles of red and white set to the front of the beret. They had allocated him an office, he was told. First, perhaps, he would care to come to the control room, where the Emergency Committee had its Operational Center. Seemed quite proud, this young man, that they had things so sorted out. But it took more than titles and labels and dog tags, that was what Benitz had learned.

It had been slack in the tower, their anxieties unrewarded, since the day's only communication with the Ilyushin, and Charlie had felt free to leave his chair at the console desk and walk around the confines. Never more than a few feet from the microphone that beckoned him and held him in its orbit, but still something of an opportunity to stretch the perpetual

stiffness from his legs, flex his cracked muscles. He was close
to the door when the army officer brought in the visitor.
Something in the complexion, the tan of the Mediterranean,
and the close, quiet confidence of his eyes; Charlie knew
from his instinct the origin and homeland of the stranger.

He hung back as the introductions started. Assistant Chief
Constable had his hand out; Clitheroe examining and looking
on with interest—new species; Home Office team in a line
waiting for the exchange of names and rank.

"Someone to see how things are going. Colonel Arie Benitz
of the . . ." The lieutenant tailed away, conscious of the radio
and television equipment operators, anxious to avoid indis-
cretion.

"I think we call it Dixie, don't we? In these circumstances,"
Charlie said. "Colonel Benitz from Dixie." The usual way of
covering embarrassment. Confused Clitheroe, though, hadn't
an idea what was meant; but the policeman had the message.
Mutual caution in the greetings until it was Charlie's turn.
Men of a kind in a way. Charlie still without his wash and
brushup, stubble on his chin and the tired faraway looseness
of the eyes, and the trousers that had forgotten their creases
and the shoes that had scuffed their shine. Benitz wary and
with the jut of his jaw showing that he was not prepared to be
pushed and jolted, and aggressive because he knew that the
clothes for which he had exchanged his battle dress were a
poor fit, and a man in clothes that are not his own is seldom
at ease.

"It's been quiet overnight, but it's freshening up a bit out
there right now. They have been told this morning that
there's no petrol for the onward flight, that they won't see
Dixie this afternoon. They're not happy about it, and the one
of them who stands out from the mob is threatening dire
things for ten hundred this morning. You've seen the pictures
the Russians have sent us?" Charlie motioned to the indifferent snapshots, taking them one at a time.

"This one we know as David. Doesn't seem to have much
left in him; morale's all over the place. We can talk to him,
and work at him. This one's Isaac, and he's the headache; we
think he stood watch through the night and is therefore tired,
but he's the strong boy, and he's the one who's throwing his
weight about. Leaves us the girl, Rebecca; unknown quantity,

quality as well. We can't say yet which way she'll fall if the two fellows start arguing. We don't expect them to hold together that long—too few of them, too exhausted, and it's spelled out that there's no future in it for them. David might see reason. Isaac looks as though he's going to try and elbow us."

Charlie directed Benitz toward the television screen, read the hostility in the other faces at the interloper in the pen, the germ in the bloodstream. Carried on, screw them. "I don't know whether you've seen these things before, but they take the pain out of sieges, cut out the sweat. It's a fish-eye lens with a one-hundred-and-eighty-degree arc. Means you can watch them and they're blissfully unaware of it. Lets you know when things are heating up and gives you an idea of where everybody is. We haven't seen Isaac for around thirty minutes, hence the assumption he's sleeping. Both David and Rebecca are out of sight at the moment, one at each end of the passenger cabin where they watch from—watch us and the passengers."

"I heard that similar equipment is being prepared for us; we don't have it yet."

Charlie noted the hint, though fractional and disguised, of envy.

"We rely in these times on the skill of the manpower, not of the equipment." What you'd expect him to say, a man who did real soldiering, knew what a front line was about and an enemy that hit and slugged with you; not going to be publicly impressed, not by gadgetry. Remembered when he'd been young and his people had taken him out to Christmas-morning drinks and his own present that day had been a secondhand bike that worked but was short of paint and full of rust, and the kids of the house they'd gone to had shown off their new ones, wheeling them round, bright and shiny and pricey, and he hadn't spoken of his own present. Knew how the Israeli felt.

Charlie said, "We know it's not the end of the world, but it's useful."

The Israeli wasn't listening—not giving the appearance of it, anyway—and Charlie saw that his cheeks were drawn in and his shoulders hunched low, and turned himself to the screen. The one they called David, walking in the picture; the

girl wasn't with him, and his head was down, and he cradled
the snub-nosed gun as a mother might a newborn baby,
trying to win strength for herself from the child. In the brief
moments that the camera showed the young Jew, caught his
expression, he gave to his watchers the impression of deep
misery, an expiration of hope, the caged and caught rat in
the trap in the barn that knows that when morning and the
farmer come it will drown in the rain barrel.

Still watching the set, Arie Benitz said quietly, "Do you
expect their surrender soon?"

"They're still talking hard, giving us a rough line. There's
the ultimatum at ten, and they hint of bad things to the passengers. They're not on the boil yet, but far from cooled
down"—Charlie at his shoulder.

"And the tough one, the fighter, the one who makes the
threats, you say he is resting?"

"We think so."

Arie Benitz straightened, looked around the room, said out
loud so that all could hear and none could misinterpret, the
surgeon who had examined and would not pronounce his diagnosis, "Why don't you go in there and take them, put them
out of their shame?"

"What do you mean?" the Assistant Chief Constable spun
toward him, pirouetting in his polished shoes, smarting that
none had informed him of the Israeli's arrival and his role.

"I mean, why don't you go and finish the thing?"

"And have half the passengers shot up, have a bloodbath
on our hands?"

"If that one is anything to go by, it would be over in ten
seconds, and you have solved your problem."

"You can't attack in daylight . . ."

"Rubbish. We had daylight in Tel Aviv when we freed the
passengers of the Sabena jet. Even the Egyptians can do it—
Luxor two years ago when they took out the Libyans. At Tel
Aviv we had four to cope with, grown-ups compared with
these, and the hard one, by your own admission, is sleeping.
Of course it can be done."

The Assistant Chief Constable fastened on the luckless
lieutenant who was Arie Benitz's escort. Fighting for self-con-
trol, Charlie saw, hating the eyes that were on him. "I think
we should see if Colonel Benitz has been allocated an office

in the building. Certainly he would not want to impede our work in this already crowded space." Embarrassment, and plenty to spare; hands masking faces; discreet coughs as the Israeli left. Smiling, wasn't he? And a half wink at Charlie.

"What does he think we are, a load of butchers, that we get kicks out of turning machine guns on people?" The policeman had waited till the door was closed tight against further intervention.

"Shortens the agony if all we're going to do is send them back where they came from at the end of it," Clitheroe said, playing the marionette, exasperating and knowing it. "If all we're here for is to talk them into facing a Russian firing squad . . ."

"It's a politician's decision, not ours, what happens to them." The Assistant Chief Constable cut short the argument, preventing further contagious growth.

Charlie slid back into his seat. Nothing moving out at the plane. Not a vestige of life, and the sun was climbing and the plane shadow diminishing, and soon the tarmac would glaze and shimmer in the heat.

From behind, and the sure sign they didn't take to the waiting: "Is there any way we can start talking to them on the radio again?"

Charlie shook his head. "No way at all. It's their privilege, and we have to be patient."

From his room in the Moskva Hotel, Freddie Smyth was shouting at top volume into the telephone that was connected with the office of the Commercial Attaché of the British Embassy.

Four days he'd been hanging around to sign that contract; worth three and a half million quid, didn't they know? Jobs of five hundred men depending on it. He'd a bloody good export record behind him, and a CBE from the Queen to prove it, and he'd done bloody well to get this order, and no thanks to the bloody embassy. So what happens this morning, when he's all dressed up and ready to head to the ministry with Sales and Technical? Had the phone call, hadn't he? All off, wasn't it? Not using those words, course not—"need for further analysis of the project."

Could cut through that lot, couldn't he? Being fucked

about, and they'd gone as far as telling him why. Because of some planeload of bloody hijackers. The Attaché should get off his arse and get in to the Ambassador and tell him to get talking with whoever was responsible in London. Tell him that Freddie Smyth, Managing Director, Coventry Cables, stood to have wasted four bloody days in Moscow, and if the factory went broke with half a thousand guys on the dole, then Freddie Smyth would make sure every bloody newspaper in Britain knew the reason why.

The Commercial Attaché avoided the Ambassador's office, but went instead to the First Secretary's office on the same floor. Freddie Smyth's outburst that morning was not unique, only the most vivid. Three other relatively prominent British businessmen had telephoned to report cancellation of morning meetings with Russian officials.

"Just the start of it," said the First Secretary, flashing the sad smile of a diplomat who has already served two long years in the Russian capital and knows its ways, and has another twelve months of his sentence to run in which to learn them better. "There'll be a few more of them, too. Broad enough hints dropped by their people at the Cuban reception last night; found us out and bashed our ears, and played it coy about the Chancellor's visit, and that doesn't even have a firm date on it. But the factory ought to know about it, and we'll sling them a cable."

Long time since the Kremlin had publicly shown its displeasure with Britain, he reflected. Back to the Lyalin defection and the expulsion from Britain of all the KGB chaps, all the trade men and the chauffeurs, and that was a fair few years back. Taken their time about thawing that one out. Difficult enough to work here, even when relations were comparatively normal, but damned near impossible when you made them angry.

He would put a "priority" on the cable to Whitehall.

11

With a sharp, spruce step the Russian Ambassador emerged into the sunlight from the darkness of the Foreign Office corridors. His immense black limousine was at the curb, door held open for him by the discreetly uniformed chauffeur. A uniformed policeman and a detective from Special Branch Protection Group in the background, watching, relaxed and comfortable, in the gentle heat. Be a pig of a day later. The Ambassador looked about him and saw the television crew and the reporter struggling to get clear of the camera car in which they had awaited his exit. The cameraman and sound man jogged across the street, connecting the cables as they went, the reporter faster and more anxious lest the quarry elude him and disappear into the fastness of the car. The Ambassador slowed, then stopped and saw the gratitude of the reporter. Lens focused and the sound man asking for a level, and the reporter explaining the need for it, as if the Ambassador had never seen a camera before and had never previously been interviewed. The diplomat smiled, was unruffled, sensing his opportunity. Cameraman called, "Running. Go in five."

Q. How would you describe your meeting with the Foreign Secretary?
A. Very fruitful, and I think we have a large measure of agreement on a mutual policy of what our reaction should be to these murderous criminals.
Q. The Russian Government has demanded that the hijackers be returned to Russia if they're captured. What are the British saying?
A. The British Government and the Soviet Government are both determined to put an end to the evil of aerial piracy. I have the impression that the Brit-

ish would wish to return these three to the courts of the Ukraine, where they would stand trial for their crimes committed before and after they took over the Aeroflot flight.

Q. If they were returned to Russia, would they face the death penalty?

A. In your country there is no death penalty, and we are most sympathetic to the emotion that the subject arouses. In the Soviet Union we have the death penalty, but it is rarely applied and then only to hardened criminals. I was able to assure the Foreign Secretary that people as young as those concerned in the hijacking would be most unlikely to face the supreme penalty of the law.

Q. Are you saying that you have given a guarantee that if these people are returned they will not be executed?

A. We discussed this matter at some length. It was not a guarantee that I gave, because sentence is a matter for the courts. But I was able to indicate that my government would look with great sympathy at this matter. And now you will excuse me. Thank you.

The reporter was astonished at his good fortune, and because of his inexperience unable to assess the extent to which his microphone had been used as a bludgeon upon the Foreign Secretary, now sitting in his second-floor office and weighing the results of his most recent conversation beside the transcript of his talk with the American Secretary of State and the latest digests of world opinion on the issue being fed to the Foreign Office from British embassies abroad.

Though the television crew had what they regarded as a minor scoop, they had no outlet to broadcast it before the midday news bulletin, but standing beside the interviewer had been a young journalist from a news agency, the Press Association. Recently arrived in the capital from a Midlands evening paper, he had felt too shy to intervene and ask his own questions. He had contented himself instead with taking verbatim notes of questions and answers, and within minutes he had found an unvandalized telephone booth and had read his copy to his news editor in Fleet Street. The subeditors quickly packed the story into shape and context, prepared it for the teleprinters. All the big-selling newspapers in Britain, television and radio studios, the foreign agencies—Reuters, Associated Press and United Press International—all had received it before the young man stepped from his taxi at the door of his offices. The quotes he had taken down were recorded as of major significance, an indication of the British policy line on the matter.

By telephone the contents of the interview with the Russian Ambassador were conveyed from the Foreign Ministry in Jerusalem to the Prime Minister's office.

And by messenger a photocopy of the nine-inch-long text was taken from News Department to the Foreign Secretary.

Seemed to stun him, the flimsy sheet of paper—crudity of a coiled fist striking his aging solar plexus. Those around him had to wait, unwilling to badger him for the contents. In his own good time he would tell them. The undersecretary nearest heard him muttering as if on a loop of tape, "the swine . . . the swine . . . the swine . . . the swine." He threw the paper, half crumpled, across his desk, available to whoever wished to smooth out and read it. "They've taken us for a big ride, those damned people. You have a private conversation. Leave it at a delicate point, nuance and innuendo, nothing signed and sealed, and he walks out and tells the whole damned world about it. Read that and you'll think the British are hand in glove with them; makes a nonsense of what I told the Secretary of State."

"Aren't we hand in glove with them, sir?" queried the undersecretary currently in possession of the text.

"Not till they were safely in the air. After that we could be hand in hand, arm in arm, whatever cliché you want, but not till then. That was the deal and they've reneged . . ."

"And reduced your freedom of action, sir. Difficult now to change tack. Would seem very strange."

Realized he'd been outwitted, outthought, and that all around him knew it.

The "freedom of action" so beloved by Foreign Secretary and undersecretary alike was to be further eroded in the following hour. Home Office press desk telephoning their opposite numbers in News Department. Thought you'd like to know, old boy, that we've had the press chaps on from the Street. Seems they have transcripts of tower-to-cockpit conversations, have translated the Russian and are asking us for reaction on a hijackers' ultimatum scheduled to expire at ten in the morning. Didn't take a brain to work that one out. Threats meant government had to respond with the hard line; hard line meant send them back, as the Soviets wanted. Cannot go soft on little blighters who're throwing their weight about.

Can't you have them under Wireless Telegraphy—criminal offense tapping authorized radio channels? asked News Department. Tried it, old boy, responded Press Desk. Told us to get stuffed—more politely, of course, but that's the gist of it.

Explicit instructions had been given: corral the journalists and photographers somewhere where they see nothing, hear nothing; give them a view of the plane and nothing else. The order had been carried out to the letter. A pen was provided, but in such a position that the Ilyushin blocked any view of the SAS command post, and there was an ill-briefed press officer who could in honesty report nothing of substance to the hungry observers. But a farm backed onto that section of the perimeter where the press was held, and at dawn the owner's wife, out of a sense of charity and pity, had sent her eldest son with three full thermos flasks of coffee and a plastic bag of sandwiches to the newsmen. The boy brought with him his radio set, an advanced Japanese model and purchased as his last birthday gift and on which he was in the habit of tuning to the conversations between the tower and incoming aircraft—a hobby that he shared with hundreds of other youths who lived close to the noise of the country's major airports.

When the farmer's son returned home with the empty flasks and plastic bag, he was without the radio, but in his hip pocket were five newly printed five-pound notes and a promise of the same for each day that the worn, sleep-short men borrowed the set. The family themselves had listened to the talk-down of the Ilyushin the previous night, and the tuning had not been altered. Disappointment at first when it was realized that the early-morning exchange was to be conducted in Russian, but these were men paid their monthly salaries for enterprise. Their conversation was recorded on a casette tape recorder and the spool sent back to London by courier to await the services of a translator.

A somber gathering they had become in the Foreign Secretary's office. Some standing, some sitting, some watching the window and the crowded sidewalk, some waiting for the next intervention of the telephone. And the old man in their midst, paled face in the bone-ribbed hands. Poor devil, thought the PPS. Too old for learning new tricks; should have been out to pasture years ago and togged up in his waders and dumped in some river with a hat full of flies to keep him warm. Days that started badly didn't get better, and it would be a long one and a bitter and brutal one, and carefully compiled reputations could be demolished by the late-summer dusk. And all because of three little bastards from the other side of Europe. Made him want to weep—but there'd be enough tears to be mopped up; enough without him adding to the flood.

The light that poured into the cockpit did not disturb the sleep that Isaac had found. He had curled his sparse body into the seat that had been Anna Tashova's and settled his legs with care so that they would not brush against the floor pedals or the instrument switches of the flight deck. His sleep was dreamless, his mind a darkened vacuum, the exhaustion permitting neither the pleasure of fantasy nor the horror of nightmare. He had checked the safety catch of his gun, made sure that the weapon could not fire if he lurched or reached in a spasm of movement, and now held it tight across his chest. The brightness of his tortured eyes was extinguished, and the seared lines of tension around his mouth and on his forehead had disintegrated as if he had discovered a desperate peace and understanding with himself. He had pulled his knees close to his stomach—classic fetal position—and his breathing was calm and regular, marred only by the trace of catarrh in his sinuses from the passing summer cold that had dogged him the last week in Kiev. Not a dangerous-looking creature, not a rabid dog, not a psychopath or a manic-depressive; just a youth who badly needed rest and who tried now to regain his strength, recharge the batteries that powered him.

Slight and ineffective he would have seemed if the fish-eye could have found him, far from worthy of the circus and paraphernalia that his actions had brought to Stansted. His stomach rumbled in its desire for food, but even the aching far down behind the stomach wall was insufficient to break the hold of his sleep. First traces of a beard showing through—a shadowed mess on the whiteness of his skin and reaching under his tucked chin. Shirt that was dirty now and creased from his own sweat, sleeves carelessly rolled; hands dirty, where they were visible, from the oil of the gun that had not left his grip; fingernails too short and clipped to retain the filth that otherwise would have been theirs. Difficult to see as a figure who had created fear, even terror; difficult to take seriously, this boy who had spat his threat into the microphone now idle and propped on the back of his seat.

Two hours he'd promised himself; then David should wake him. Terrified of not sleeping, of not resting and being found inadequate when he had to be at his best, right from the days of Secondary examinations and of the tests and interviews for the University place. Had to sleep so that he would not go pallid and yawning before the tutors. David had promised to wake him. Would rouse him at eight, long before the deadline. Could rely on David. Not yesterday, not last night, not when he had sagged; but today he could rely on him.

That had been Isaac's last thought before sleep overtook him.

It was the stench that woke Rebecca.

The heavy, permeating, all-invading stench of the forward toilet. The wall of the lavatory was behind the crew seats on which she had slept, small enough to make a bed of them, an arm becoming a makeshift pillow. The toilet line had formed again, but not like the one that Isaac had controlled: people standing up from their seats, and in a line in the center of the cabin—something different, and less of the fear that there had been the night before. She lay still, head motionless, one eye half open, acclimatizing. She had dreamed, she could remember that: images of her home and of her mother and the family—nothing vicious in the images she had conjured, soft and safe and warming; and then the harshness of the smell had forced the sleep from her.

Difficult at first to realize where she was and why, a kaleidoscope of varying thoughts till she recalled the plane, its traplike compactness, its arched prison walls. The passengers walked to the lavatory, heads erect as if the tumbrils delivered them, and behind her came the repetition and routine of sounds, punctuated by the flushing of the toilet and the squirting of water into the basin. One after another they came, edging their way past David as he stood at the entrance of the cabin, some five feet in front of her, showing him deference. He held the gun lightly in his right hand, and that was the termination of her rest; that was reality—the gun and the asymmetry of its magazine from which the old paint had worn away and which still showed the oil slicks of its preservation. David did not see that she was awake, concentrating on the passengers and every minute or so breaking away to move to the portholes and peer out, searching for a sign, like someone who looks through the windows of his home when a guest is expected but is late.

David, the warmth of a winter's fire. Sustaining and comforting, giving strength and help, repelling the dangers, keeping the wolves clear from the encampment. Ever since she had known him, the bigger boy in the higher class and their only point of contact and togetherness the faith that bound and identified them. Always the bond. From when he was in short trousers and she in short dresses with white ankle socks and they had gone to the Pioneer camps, and he had sought her out, protective and all-knowing, the source of an answer. With maturity had come the cementing of the friendship— brother and sister, colleague and comrade. Different from Moses and Isaac—outsiders who had joined; they were the nucleus and the kernel. Always a shoulder to lean on, a chest to rest against, an ear for confidences. Should have loved him, now that he was a man and she a woman. No lack of opportunity; occasions that were frequent; didn't understand why it had never happened. Seemed to spill through her, the nausea of the awful primitive groping of the fool Yevsei. Thirty-six hours, just a day and a half, nothing in time, and on her back in the grass with the stupid, oafish idiot. Could have been David.

The rounded walls of the cabin pressed in on her, restricting, tightening the space available, a lowered and squat hori-

zon. Rebecca was not one to weep, not unless there was a
sudden pain, but a great and deep depression swamped her as
she lay on her side on the hardened seats: the knowledge that
this was alien to the hut in the woods outside Kiev, foreign to
their forays onto the streets in search of the solitary policemen. Always there had been a forest path or a side alley that
was good for escape; and now nothing but the barricaded
doors with their pressurized locks and the tiny windows with
their reinforced glass. A fearsome place they had come to,
that encroached on her, grew smaller till she could imagine
the moment when the roof and walls would close around her,
suffocating her, squashing the breath from her lungs.

She called to David, "Have you talked with them? Have
you talked with the British?"

"You were sleeping and we didn't want to wake you. We
have talked to them." Had seen only his back since she had
awakened, and now he turned his face to her. The night had
not rested him. Haggard and unshaven, eyes dulled and dead-
ened, only the sympathy at his mouth that is the hallmark of
news that is difficult to tell.

"What did they say about the fuel?"

"They said there would be none. That we should surrender. We would fly no farther, they said."

"What do we do, David?" Simple, quiet, oblivious of the
passenger behind him who made his way to the lavatory, little
more than a whisper.

"Isaac says we fight them."

"He said the same to me last night, before I went to sleep,
while you were resting. What does that mean?"

"Isaac says we must make them listen to us, that we must
show our strength."

"What strength do we have?"

"Only the passengers. The guns are nothing; against us
they have an army. There are only the passengers."

"Isaac said last night that if we were hard with the passengers, the British would bend. He said they have done that in
the past."

"That's what Isaac believes." David, remote and lost to her,
listening to her questions, replies mechanical, machine-
tooled. They have destroyed you, castrated, automated you.

"What do you believe, David? Not what Isaac says, but

what is your thought?" Those who are caught in the winter snows, hikers and climbers and those whose cars fail them, and who lose the will to go on, and cannot maintain the fight, want only to sleep, which is the sure and certain way to death. David, uncaring, uninvolved. Had to raise him again before he was lost. The trace of anger. "You have to know what you want, David. You have your own mind."

"I don't know. Believe me, I don't know. It was Isaac who thought of the plane as a way of escape. We all agreed, and now we must stand with him."

"And they will kill us here, kill us in the plane." Understanding the options, a cold draft across her shoulders.

"Isaac thinks we can make them surrender to us. He has told them they have till ten o'clock. It is that on your watch now, but you haven't changed for the time difference. They have two more hours."

"If they don't surrender by the time you have given?"

"Then we will shoot a passenger, where they can see it, where they will understand." He motioned to another to come forward in the line. Discussing the passengers as would the collective manager and the responsible person from the abattoir. Rebecca sitting up and reaching forward so that her fingers were on the hand that held the submachine gun, pressing into the fine-drawn hairs above the skin.

"And if we shoot one and still they do not surrender?"

"We shoot another. Isaac doesn't believe it will be easy. He has changed, our Isaac, changed in the last days; has turned to steel. He is the fighter. The last night we were in the hut I was angry, aroused at him because he thought it was easy. He has veered around. He knows now what we face. A few days back, if you had asked me about Isaac, I would have said he was not capable of this strength. He alone is our salvation now; he alone has the power . . ."

"And you, David, where is your strength?"

"Perhaps I never had it; perhaps it was just a figment, something we created. Remember when we were in the woods, when we talked, when we planned. It's different here, Rebecca. When we talked, did you know it would end like this? Do you believe that I knew that it could end like this? Think about it, Rebecca; think about it and tell me if I knew the road that I was leading you on. Think about it and tell me truthfully what your answer is."

"You told us we must fight them . . ."

"And that was words, nothing but words, and slogans and phrases, tripping off the tongue, brave and elegant, romantic. But there was no reality there, nothing of the soldiers, and the guns, and what has happened to Moses."

"Why are you saying this to me?"

"Because this is no time for deception. Past and gone, that moment. I talked us here, Rebecca. I talked and you listened. You and Isaac and Moses, you all listened to me. And that is why we are here."

"And now that we are here, you will fight?"

He didn't answer her, as if the tiredness had come again, the tide running over him that she could not stem. Just looked at her, as if she were new to him, and a stranger. Then the shrug and the smile, and the pushing of his fingers in his hair. "Take your gun, arm it and go to the back. Check that the seat belts are fastened, that the passengers not in the line are strapped in."

She walked down the aisle, briskly and trying to show confidence, putting a swing into her hips that she told herself was the hallmark of command; face set; measured stride; pistol gripped. Find something to do, occupy yourself, make work and business, that it might hasten the clock hands, cut out the awfulness they had so casually discussed. Right to the back of the aircraft. Check the fastenings that Isaac had made last night and that held the trolley across the aisle; check them and recheck them; absorb time; use it and waste it, bury it and destroy it. What does a man or a woman . . . why think of a man?—think of a woman, or a girl not yet an adult, not yet opened, penetrated, known . . . what does she do in the basement cells in the hours before they take her out and kneel her in the yard and place the policeman's pistol at the nape of her neck? Tortured, agonized, revolving mind, and how to occupy it, must find something to blot out the passing of time. Straps secure. Begin on the passengers. Some still with their hands raised because the order had never been rescinded. Others ignoring the dictum now that it was not demanded and sitting with their arms folded and fists clenched on their knees. Some seeking comfort from the gesture, some defiance, some just to hide the stains on their trousers and skirts, those for whom the snail speed of the toilet line had been intolerable.

How few of them she knew; how few she would recognize if she passed them on a sidewalk tomorrow. The American? Yes, she would remember him. The Italians? Perhaps, but not because of who they were, what they stood for; only the ornaments, the cut of the clothes, the whispered conspiracy of their chatter. The schoolmasters and the headmaster? They would not fade, because she had a knowledge and an experience of such people. Would she know the pilot, sitting far away at the front, never speaking since she had been ordered back from the flight deck; know her if they bumped in the street at a bus stop, disputed the right to a purchase of stockings in the store, collided laden with bags at a street crossing? Did not know. Yet a choice must be made among them: that was what Isaac had told David, and he had not disagreed. Academic problem; should have taken it to the professor; perhaps he would have helped them, talked it over at a seminar. The tall one or the thin one, the fat one or the fidgeter, the foreigner or the . . . Pressed her lids tight shut, blocking the sight of the domed head rising above the seat rest. That was the one who had been chosen.

It was the American whose voice she heard.

"Not much going on out there, miss, just tanks and soldiers. Not much action from the fuel trucks. Not as if they're about to refuel you."

Never had been able to stare him down, she thought; not from the first time, and not now. Couldn't muster the scorn and the indifference, not from the time she'd first been aware of his presence, and the foreign brightness and ebullience of his clothing. Handkerchief still around his head; not needed now, but worn proudly as a trophy, stain showing and somewhat awry so that the wound it was supposed to hide was partly visible. Wife's hand on his arm, counseling caution, and ignored.

"Nearly a dozen hours since we touched down. They'd have fueled you by now if they were going to. Don't you think so, miss?"

A frosted, splintered-ice smile, and even with the strangeness of the language and the difficulties she had in following his words, she could touch the changing mood, the spirit of aggression and attack. "They've screwed you, miss, screwed you proper. I'll lay a wager with you, make a bet with you, in any money you have, and give you odds, if you know what that means—they're saying the glory ride is over, right? Time to come out with your hands high. Do I have it right, miss? Time to give up; the party's over."

Couldn't draw away from him, couldn't detach herself from the hydra tentacles that kept her listening.

"You're all fucked up, miss, if you and Felicity Ann will excuse me. Up the creek without a paddle. Listen to me, now. I don't give a damn what you've done back home, what you think your grievances are if you have any. You have a nice face and you're a good-looking girl, and when you're my age you notice these things. I'd like to give you some advice, miss."

The pistol in her hand, foolish little appendage, nowhere to put it, nowhere to hide it; felt like a man with his wife's handbag and loath to be seen carrying it; a silly, awkward little machine, but it was her lifeline and her survival rope.

"My advice is this, miss. Find out what the British are going to do with you. I'm an old man, and Felicity Ann's no chicken, and no one gives a damn about us in the States; don't read a word I write; only hire me for the lecture circuit because I'm off season and cheap; so we're not that interested in how we come out of all this. I'm telling you, and I mean it, it's in your interest—find out what they're going to do to you, and if it doesn't seem too bad, then chuck it, throw in the towel. Don't go playing the martyr, because if you give them half a chance they'll cut you down, and it won't be fun, it won't be glorious and you won't be around to see if anyone weeps over your coffin. That's what I wanted to say to you, miss, and it's meant kindly; and while you're asking them, see if you can talk the Brits into sending some food up. People are hungry in here."

Sent her off on his errand. Rebecca checked none of the other passengers to see if their straps were fastened, just buffeted the length of the plane, tumbling against the armrests of seats, unaware of the impediments, needing to get to where David was standing, his back to her in the forward corridor and looking out through the cockpit windscreen.

"Is Isaac still sleeping?"

Obvious when she saw him, slumped in front of her in the pilot seat, but she sought confirmation and reassurance. David nodded; he was watching the stationary armored cars and the soldiers who lolled beside the mountings for the

heavy machine guns. Two hundred yards of open ground separating her from the men the American had said would kill
her; sitting casually in their floppy denims, one day's work not
much different from another.

"We have to talk to them, you and I, David. We have to
know whether it's necessary, what Isaac wants. Not when
he's awake, but now, when he's sleeping."

Maddening, driving her to fury, David not reacting. "We
can speak to them again when Isaac wakes up. We can wait
till then."

Only served to drive her forward, egg her deeper into the
swamp she had set herself to cross. "We have to know what
will happen to us, what they would do to us."

"Time enough when Isaac is with us."

"Can't you see it, David, that you've abdicated to him?
There are three of us. He alone doesn't have a monopoly of
negotiation. If we are together, then any of us can talk . . ."

"But not behind his back, not when he's sleeping." And the
doubt showed on his high, line-woven forehead, furrowed
with indecision as he hissed his replies, calculated not to disturb the sleep of their colleague.

"Ask them, David. Ask them what they would do with us."

He wavered, hesitated—the child who deliberates, then
puts his hand inside his mother's purse. Reached forward,
weight rocked onto the balls of his feet; lifted the headset
from the back of the pilot's seat and drew it back into the
corridor till the cable attachment was bouncing and taut. Rebecca could hear only the questions that David asked.

"Kingfisher. Kingfisher. Do you hear us? The one called
Charlie, do you hear us?"

Rebecca listening to David, a draining, sweat-soaked relief
overwhelming her. Contact with the outside world, lifting of
the horizon, breaching of the capsule wall.

"It is David who is here. . . . Isaac is sleeping. . . . There
are questions that we have for you." Pause and silence, and
both watching over Isaac, furtive and anxious lest he should
open his eyes, show an awareness of what they were doing.

"The question is this. If we were to surrender, what would
you do to us? What would happen to us?"

The words had been said, the Judas sign was fashioned;
faces turned away, the shame not shared.

• •

Charlie had stiffened and sat rigid, pencil alert, from the first moment that the call sign had been given. Conversation in the tower had been broken by the staccato identification over the loudspeaker.

"They say Isaac's sleeping . . . they want clarification on some points." Intent and peering down at his papers. Then the mirthless smile. "They want to know what happens to them if they surrender." Charlie pushed the microphone switch to the Off position. "What do you want me to say?"

The Home Secretary was four paces behind the console, summoned late from the bed in which he had slept. Had had time to wash himself and run a cursory wet shave, but showed no benefit from it. Was experienced enough to know that this was the first crisis of morale, fretful lest his instructions to Charlie affect it. "First repeat the conditions of surrender." He moved back, the pilot-fish formation of aides at his shoulder.

Charlie addressed the microphone. "The British Government is not prepared to enter into negotiations over surrender. That has been made clear to you earlier. The situation remains the same: You must first release all the passengers. When that is completed, you must leave the plane disarmed and with your hands on your heads. I repeat the guarantee that was given to you earlier. You will not be harmed by the British Security Forces."

Kids out after dark, he thought, babes in the bloody woods. Three frightened brats—two, anyway—out of their league and wanting to end it all, get back onto dry land. He swung around in his chair and said to the policy huddle, "They say they know the terms of surrender. They want to know what happens to them after that."

Clitheroe away from the main group, at the Home Secretary's shoulder; a moment of whispered talk, nodded acquiescence from the politician, and he was hurrying to Charlie's side. "Tell them that you want to speak to them direct . . . that it's difficult over the radio. More you can say if you come to the plane. Tell them it's a very sensitive matter, too many people in the tower, how much better it will be when you talk at the plane—face-to-face stuff."

Getting like the old days, Charlie. Calling for volunteers.

Repeated the message in Russian. Not that they'll buy that one, never in a month of Sundays. First basic of the hijacker's bible. Book One, Chapter One, Verse One. Never let the opposition near you; keep them at arm's length.

"Keep the pressure on them," snapped Clitheroe. "Tell them you're going to come out of the control tower and that you'll be walking to the plane. They'll see you all the way. They'll know there's no trick. But I want to get you to them, face to face, so we can start the confidence phase." Seemed excited at the prospect. And too bloody right he should be. Wasn't his bloody arse that was going on show. "See it this way: they've called us up because they're anxious, they want to do some talking. The whole thing is about this answer, this question—the crucial one to them. They want out, and they have to trust somebody, follow someone's guidance. It has to be you, because of the language, Charlie. They won't hurt you, not unless you take them bad news, and you're not going to do that."

Broke off, allowed Charlie to talk again to the aircraft. "Don't discuss it with them; don't debate. Just say you're coming." Charlie speaking, trying to sound calm, organized, casual, efficient, and half the bloody room chuntering in his right ear. Finished, thwacked the transmission button away from him.

"So what do you want me to tell them when I get there? What's the answer?"

"There is no answer," Clitheroe said. "Vague and general, that's how you play it. You're a little man; you don't have that sort of authority. You're not going out there to talk to them; you're going to show yourself, that's all. Most likely you'll be the first Englishman they've ever spoken to. You'll show them that you don't represent a threat; they'll have nothing to fear from you."

"But what if they want an answer?" Fair enough for these bastards, sitting behind the glass with binoculars. "If they want the answer, what do I say then?"

"Cover it over, Mr. Webster." The Home Secretary, authoritative, on home territory, used to plowing through the arguments of committees. "You've heard the news bulletins, and you know what the Russians are saying. Gives you an idea what's being said in London. Not possible for you to be

in any way specific, but your own mind can be at rest. Soviets
say there's no question of the death penalty for these people,
and anyway, I wouldn't put too much store by the diplomatic
optimism of Moscow at this stage. More likely these people
will spend a period in British prisons if no more damage is
done."

Charlie turned to face him, but was denied the politician's
features. Had walked away, toward the far windows, mean-
dering apparently without purpose. The Home Secretary
knew his limitations, knew deceit fell fairly in that field.

"You'll need some equipment," chimed in the Assistant
Chief Constable. With a meekness that was not usually evident, Charlie followed him through the door.

David hung the headset back onto the top of the pilot seat.
Felt the lead weight clutching at him, numbing, and Rebecca
pestering and pulling at his sleeve and whispering her demand for their final answer, the people in the tower. Isaac
still sleeping, innocent of what they had done, unaware—a
calmed, stubble-strewn baby at rest.

"He's coming to the plane, the one called Charlie. He says
the matter is sensitive, that he wants to talk to us face to face,
on the question of what they will do with us if we . . ." Surrender. Capitulation. Couldn't say it, couldn't vomit the
words.

"When will he come?"

"In a few minutes, very soon; he will walk alone to the
plane."

"Is there danger from this?"

"If one man comes there can be no danger." And what did
it matter, how could it concern them? What further danger
could there be at the moment of defeat? But he didn't know,
had not thought through the possibilities, untuned to the
technicalities of defense that had obsessed the sleeping Isaac.

"Will you wake him?"

Seemed to shake his head—not a definite movement, just
the imperceptible wave of the eyebrows, the flick of the hair
across the forehead. They clung together a long time, arms
around each other, cheek to cheek, and Rebecca stretching
upward to match her height with his. Many times David said,
with the tears running on his face, "I'm sorry. I'm sorry."

Rebecca crying too and choking in her throat, unable to reply.

It was a pleasant enough office that had been set aside for Colonel Arie Benitz.

Calendars on the walls, gifts of aviation companies that showed a combination of light aircraft and bikini-clad girls draped on their wings. Photographs, too, of the first airliners that had used Stansted, sepia-toned and looking frail and historic. Flowers on the window ledge. Easy chairs and a desk with a telephone.

When the call came, he let the phone ring several seconds before answering—time to summon his caution and prepare himself. He did not identify himself with either rank or name; was wary till he heard the Hebrew language that was used.

The embassy in London. He should know that the Soviet Ambassador had been received at the Foreign Office that morning, that he had made a statement to the press, had spoken of agreement with the British that the three should be returned to Russia. He also should know that there were journalists' reports that an ultimatum had been set aboard the aircraft, due to expire at ten hundred hours, and that it was the opinion of advice available to the Ambassador that further violence on the part of the three would only strengthen the resolve of the British to fulfill their arrangement with the Soviets.

He should find a public telephone booth and should immediately call those designated as his contacts in London; the number was the first one that had been given him in the small hours. The Foreign Ministry in Jerusalem wished to clarify his instructions in view of the new circumstances.

Arie Benitz let himself out of the office. There were many civilians and policemen and soldiers who hurried purposefully about their business and who passed him in the corridors and passages, and none had cause to notice him. A cleaning woman, with time on her hands because many of the rooms she normally tidied at this time were occupied, directed him to a telephone in the staff canteen in the building's basement. Even changed his fifty-pence piece into the range of coins he would require to make the connection.

As he walked down the stairs, Benitz felt the irritation ris-

ing in him—fueled by the clothes that were ill shaped and ill
fitting; ignited by the problems of the mission that he had
been given. Ill at ease, unwanted, a stranger amid the bustle
of those who had a task and work that could not wait. Unac-
customed to being a watcher on the sidelines.

This was a man steeped in the history of the State of Israel,
committed to the defense of its people, who had experienced
moments when protection came only from the hammering of
his Uzi and the cries of pain from his enemies. A man who
was treated with respect in his own country, called by his
given name when spoken to in conference by his Chief of
Staff. And these people here declined his help, ignored him.

As he walked into the canteen he was thinking of the three
young ones, frightened and alone, in the Ilyushin. And he
had been told on the telephone that they would be returned,
but that he would not be required by the British to assist in
their surrender. Arie Benitz had to fight against the thought
that surged in his mind. Willing them, willing the children, to
hit back, attack, show their defiance. Had to suppress it, because that was contrary to his country's interests and he was a
servant of his country.

The hard one, the one they called Isaac, the one who led
them now—he was the material of Squad 101; he was fashioned for the Antiterrorist Unit. Do not lose your courage,
thought Arie Benitz. There can be no help, there can be no
rescue, but do not lose your courage.

Unwatched, unobserved, he dialed the London code.

12

The soldier inclined his rifle and stepped back to allow Charlie room to pass. Out through the frosted-glass door of the control tower, onto the tarmac. The heat saturated him from the moment he was clear of the protective air-conditioned blanket; he could feel it wrap about him, carrying an instant clamminess to his chest and legs. The staircase had been darkened with venetian blinds, and the brightness reflecting up from the open concrete of the apron wounded his eyes. Had left his jacket on the back of the seat, forsaken his tie; Clitheroe had wanted that. Let them see from the start that you have nothing concealed on you: those were the psychiatrist's instructions. Only the radio transmitter and receiver that bumped against his hip, swinging from the strap he had hooked over his shoulder. His shoes squelched as he moved, suffering from the time he'd worn them, and his toes were uncomfortable, irritated, so that he was reminded of the smell and of the shave that he had wanted.

They'd given it to him very straight before they'd packed him off: just follow the line we've given; don't play hero games; don't go promising things that haven't been authorized or sanctioned.

Don't hurry it, they'd said. They will want to have a good look at you, see you, size you up, know you're not a threat. Don't want them jumpy, not now, not with ten o'clock closing. Halfway there, getting closer, Charlie. Breathing faster, be panting by the time you get there. Slow it. Remember the missus, what she says: no need to hurry, Charlie; we've all night; don't rush; don't speed up. Should have kept the gym sessions going, the ones you had when you were on active. But had thought those days were history, reckoned it was going to be pen pushing, right down to retirement and the presentation watch. Not in the shape you should be.

Close enough now to see the shadowed faces at the windows, not the expressions—just the basics of humanity: eyes and ears and mouths. And how many behind them who were masked from him, and how many in the grass and the rain ditches beside the runway? Half a bloody army out there, and all that shows is a few crappy armored cars and the men sitting on them. Hands a bit closer to the main armament than when you saw them from the tower, Charlie. All watching and wondering what the hell's going to happen. There'll be a concentrated firepower volume to support you; that was what they'd said, and he believed them, and he also believed it wouldn't make a damn of difference if Isaac or David didn't take a shine to him. Bad place not to be making friends, sonny boy.

Time to start putting it together now. Walk round the nose and approach from the far side, with the petrol tankers behind you, where the heavies are, the SAS men. Still be able to see him from the tower, on the outside video camera, and the microphone button was permanently up so he could talk if he found anything to say. Colossal the plane looked, damn great predator, thirty tons of it, and the fools called it "Kingfisher." Like a bloody great carrion crow. Near now to the wing that he should skirt; should begin to angle his approach so that he would move in front of the hulk and into the empty ground beyond. Charlie didn't look up, resisted the impulse to scan the windows; wouldn't be right, might be taken as anxiety; must walk as if he were out with the dog for a Sunday-morning down to the pub.

He wiped a smear of sweat from his forehead and with his fingers instinctively tidied his hair. Thirty yards from the aircraft and level with the forward starboard door, he stopped. Cockpit to the right, passenger cabin to the left. High above him, dominating and impersonal, was the Ilyushin, expression not known, mood uncertain. Difficult to see it that way, but that was how it was, with a mind and pulse of its own.

Shuffled his feet together waiting for a response to his presence.

No point shouting—no way anyone inside would hear him through the pressure-resistant windows and doors. Charlie Webster waved, right hand high above his head, as if his wife were shopping on the other side of Woking High Street and he wanted to attract her attention.

. .

Rebecca had spotted him first and called David from his favored position between the cockpit and the passenger cabin. He hurried to where she craned forward across the lap of an unprotesting passenger, her head rammed against the window. With a calculated roughness, he pulled her back to clear the space and the vision for himself. One man walking toward them, a faint and distant figure, small against the building from which he came, coming with a directness and purpose, his shadow preceding him, running to the front. The man kept far from the armored cars and chose a path in which there were no obstacles.

"Will you wake Isaac now? Tell him that the man is coming?" Rebecca spoke from behind his head.

"I didn't think he would come so fast. I wanted to let Isaac sleep on." He did not turn from the window.

"You are afraid to wake him. It is because of fear that you have not been to him, told him what is to happen."

"There is no fear." He hissed the words from close to the window, and his spittle fragmented against the glass. "When I need to wake him, I will."

"But the man is coming now."

"I have eyes, I can see."

"But are you going to leave Isaac sleeping? Will you let him sleep while you talk with this man?"

This was a moment when both David and Rebecca could have been overpowered without difficulty—both so engrossed in Charlie Webster's approach that they had no thought for the passengers. Rebecca was close to David's back, pressing against the muscle and sinew beneath his shirt, trying to share the window with him, transfixed by the advance of the lone figure. Several of those who sat behind them were aware of the opportunity, but none had the stomach to steel himself and rise out of his seat. The long hours had dulled initiative, and the threat of the guns that now seemed so casually held was too great to encourage those who were closest to take action. Luigi Franconi was within reach, but his courage had sapped and wasted since his time in the mountains with the partisans. Aldo Genti had the advantage of an aisle seat, but was farther back. The navigator considered the question for a few seconds and then rejected the moment. The headmaster was too far to the rear to be able to offer effective intervention, and the thought of it faded from his mind when he saw the tousled, shambling, sleep-laden Isaac silhouetted in the cockpit doorway.

Rebecca said again, with greater persistence, "You will have to tell him; you have to wake him, now that their man is coming."

"But it was you who asked for the contact to be made. It was you who posed the question that had to be answered. It was you who wanted to know what they would do if we surrendered. . . ."

Nobody spoke in the control tower; all gaping at the television monitor, the flickering twelve-inch gray-blue screen.

In the center of the picture the back torsos of the ones they knew as David and Rebecca. Predictable enough that they would be at the window to watch the coming of Charlie Webster. It had been the eyes of the hostages that had drawn attention to the extreme right-hand corner of the picture, as they switched from their two concentrating guards and took on the nervousness and hesitancy of people who have fear and are uncertain, looking only to the entrance from the corridor to the passenger cabin.

A small figure Isaac seemed to those in the control tower, and when they first saw him his face seemed wreathed in sadness, but the change was abrupt and the chin came forward, and the face muscles tightened as the submachine gun rose to his shoulder. When the weapon was there he paused for a moment as if to adjust the comfort and stability of the extended tubular shoulder rest. He seemed to jolt back, fractionally and strangely, because it was all enacted in complete silence, and the passengers flattened themselves in their seats while David and Rebecca catapulted back into the aisle.

"We should pull Webster off," Clitheroe shouted.

"Leave him there" the sharp response from the Assistant Chief Constable.

The noise of the single shot was ear-blasting inside the confines of the cabin. It burst through the private and inner thoughts of Rebecca and David, tearing them from their vision of the solitary man who approached across the tarmac;

the screaming of the passengers dinned its way into their consciousness, and when they spun to face the center aisle it
would take them time to adjust and reconstruct the situation
for themselves.

The gun was still at Isaac's shoulder, a cold protuberation
of his shape, with his head rock-steady behind the gunsight
and his left fist clenched tight on the upper barrel, his right
index finger entwined inside the trigger guard. And there was
a depth to his eyes, far down to a blazing, molten fury. Like a
woman taken in adultery, so Rebecca sought an explanation
and sifted for the words that would justify and was unable to
find them and instead slipped back across the passenger's lap
till she stood half cowed, half defiant upright in the aisle.
David was slower; it took more effort for him to disentangle
himself from among the unmoving and uncooperating legs
that held him back. Isaac waited with a humiliating patience
until David had freed himself.

The passengers wavered between the seared hole in the
cabin roof close to where the forward life raft was stored and
the man in the passageway. All realized the crisis of the moment and were afraid to permit themselves even to clear their
throats, move their feet, rustle paper. The baby too, close to
suffocation so tight was it held against its mother's breasts,
was silent. An endless, bottomless, deafening quiet as all
waited for the resolution. When Isaac spoke, his voice was
controlled, and all had to strain to hear his words—even
David and Rebecca, to whom they were directed.

"You did not wake me." Like a cat that plays with the half-
dead mouse, a limb already taken, helpless but a possible
source of a little more amusement. "You said you would wake
me at eight, and it's past that. You promised, and yet I had to
wake myself."

David let out a great sigh, the air in his lungs released in a
huge and noisy gust. "We were going to come; in a few minutes we would have come—believe me, Isaac."

But Isaac went on as if oblivious of David's words. "And I
wake myself, and I see from the cockpit window that a man is
walking close to the plane, and I come to the doorway and I
hear that the words of surrender are used." The bite of a
diamond cutter, the cold of the Arctic, the sneer and the
contempt, all scything through the frail and unprepared defenses of David. "Talk of surrender while I was sleeping, after

I stood the night watch that you might rest, because you begged for it, could last no longer. And when you are re- freshed and I take my turn for sleep, what is it you talk of? What is it you plan? The talk is of surrender."

"It was not like that, Isaac; you have to believe us—it was not as you say."

He wondered whether Isaac was about to shoot him. Al- most natural, almost logical if he were to. He was not afraid, hoping only that the termination would come fast, that he would be spared the games and the play.

"Tell me, then. If it was not like that, how was it? Tell me."

"They're sending a man to talk to us. They say they want to explain things that can't be said over the radio, that there are too many people in the tower and they want a more private negotiation with us. We asked them a question, Isaac; it is a question we have the right to know the answer to." Gabbling, believing that with each word he spoke he diminished the chances of his formal and summary execution at the hands of his friend and his comrade.

"What was the question that could be asked and answered only if I were asleep, if I were not a party to it?"

"We have to know what they would do with us if we were to release the passengers and comply with their demands. We have to know what they would plan for us, where they would send us . . ."

"And that is not talk of surrender? Submission, craven and pathetic—isn't that what you're talking of? Humiliating, ab- ject, crawling surrender, but don't hurt us, don't kick us, don't punch us in the cells, don't pitch us down the steps, and please, please don't send us back where we came from. That is the substance of your negotiation? And all this while I was to be asleep."

"It's finished, Isaac." Rebecca pushed her way in front of David as if to protect him, save him from the threat, provide a shield behind which he might shelter. "You know that. You know we aren't going any farther. You told me yourself last night that there would be no fuel for the engines, and this morning they've proved you right. They will not let us leave. There will be only killing, killing that leads to nothing, that can't achieve anything. More blood, Isaac. That is what we are talking of, and whether more deaths would advance us."

Isaac took a firm step forward—only one necessary till he

stood a foot from the girl. With his free left hand he swung
hard and sharply to her cheek. The blow was short and took
her without warning, cuffing her semistunned to the floor.
Had he not had on his grandmother's ring, probably he
would not have broken the soft skin, but the metal caught
against her, and by the time she had recovered to stumble
upright again, the bright crimson rivulet was welling and
flowing a path toward her neck.

"It is not finished. Not for many more hours; not till we
have tested our will against theirs. You understand? It should
be simple and clear, and there must be no more talk of submission. Our destination is Israel. That is where we go, and
we do not permit a deflection. Were we stupid and ignorant
and useless, we would have been permitted to go, thrown
onto the train for Vienna, propped on the flight for Tel Aviv;
no difficulties would have obstructed us. But we are the people whom they want inside Mother Russia, because we are
the technicians from whom the giant needs to fuel herself.
Who with higher education is allowed to leave? We are the
people whom they obstruct, whom they imprison, who lan-
guish on the trumped-up charges at Potma and Perm. We
have rejected their system, rejected it with blood, because we
did not want to be a part of their way. It is not a time to talk
of capitulation. We have come a long way. But if this were to
be the end, the destination, then it would have been better
that we had never started at all."

Isaac saw the tight, mirthless smile of Anna Tashova as she
sat three rows in front of where he stood, and ignored it.
Witnessed the confusion of the Italian who was closest to
him, and who did not understand what was said and looked
vaguely for an indication from among their gestures and who
was to remain uninformed and nervously puzzled. Saw the
headmaster, who turned away to look through the window at
the moment their eyes met. Many faces for Isaac to see. Old
and young; neat and unclean, educated and stupid, brave and
fearful. All he possessed with which to fight, humanity his
ammunition. But effective, that he knew—better than the
tanks and the machine guns and the infantry that waited in
ambush for him beyond the pressure walls. These were the
shells that would carry the weight when the battle was joined,
would push back the soldiers and their guns. The lives of the

men and the women and the children. They would bend, the
Britishers, the Westerners—after ten o'clock they would
bend. They had lost the will to fight: that was what he had
read; that was what he believed.

As if to acknowledge that the episode was over, completed,
that recrimination should not continue, Isaac said, "The man
is close to the plane now. Who is he? What have you
arranged?"

"It's the one from the tower. The Russian speaker. They
want him to talk to us."

"I have your word, Rebecca, and yours too, David, that
there will be no more talk of surrender? An oath that we fight
together?"

He did not hear their replies, mumbled from far down in
their throats, but the movement of the lips was sufficient.
The dose of contrition was swallowed.

Went into the cockpit, the vantage point, from which he
could observe the man who had broken the invisible thread
laid across the tarmac and who had entered their territory,
forsaking the safety of the armaments of his own people.
Isaac looked down at him, hard and piercingly; noticed that
the other never glanced at the windows, as if keeping his own
counsel, biding his time till the moment for contact was
right. Could recognize the mold of experience on his face.

A deep man, Isaac thought, not a bureaucrat; someone
from Security, and to be treated with care and wariness;
someone who came because the persons in authority believed
there was advantage to be gained from it, and the fools behind him trusted the promises that had been made, had faith
in the words spoken over the radio link. Unarmed; no reason
for him to carry a weapon—nothing gained. His weapons
would be in his words which would be designed to lull and
win confidence, and in his eyes which would report back to
his masters sheltering in the tower. He had shown weakness
in letting this man come close, Isaac knew that, and weakness was dangerous, because much had to be sacrificed if the
initiative was to be rewon.

Not that Isaac had studied the history and tactics of hijacking—there had been no opportunity for that in Kiev; but his
sensibilities told him that the man in his shirt sleeves and the
baggy, unpressed trousers represented a threat and a risk. Yet

he knew he wanted to hear what the man had to say, wanted an excuse to break the eighteen long hours of isolation in the aircraft, needed some release and freedom from the confines of the closed walls. But this was a man to be watched, however innocent his eyes, however honeyed his words.

A swelling buzz of talk permeated the aircraft. Bees in a rose garden. The subdued drone of activity as the passengers with window seats reported to their neighbors the news that a man had come close to the Ilyushin. Stifled thoughts of bulging bladders and stomachs that craved food overcame the awareness of the smell of sweating bodies. It was an event, and being the first of the day that offered the possibility of outside interference in their position, it was welcome. The children talked louder than their elders, and pointed to the man and pushed those with the best view aside, that the experience might be shared. The teachers tried to quiet them, but realized they couldn't. A long time they had been marooned in the plane, with little to look at beyond the brightness of the morning and the motionless armored cars and their crews and the occasional speeding airport car in the hazed distance.

Huge lenses—"thousand mill," the photographers called them—mounted on cameras and tripods of weight and security, had followed Charlie Webster's walk. The uniformed policemen who were present to prevent the unlikeliness of a surge forward by the cameramen and journalists from their corral obligingly squatted on their haunches so as not to obstruct the view of the solitary man, barely visible to the naked eye at that range but greatly magnified by film. The static armored personnel carriers and the resting soldiers had long been exhausted as a source of pictures, and this was recognized as something different, and therefore there was a hush and a cessation of jokes and anecdotes and histories of what had happened on similar previous occasions.

There were many suggestions as to the role of the man who had stridden toward the aircraft. He was "SAS"; he was "the leading government negotiator"; he was "a ranking police chief." Endless scope for supposition.

"The bastard's going round the far side."

"Same at Tunis with the BOAC VC-10; never saw a damn thing."

"Shut up. You'll wreck the bloody sound track."

"Fat lot of bloody sound you're getting at a thousand yards."

"He's gone, the bastard. Lost him round the nose."

The advance of Charlie Webster had promised much to the cameramen, and they had been cheated and were angry and bickered among themselves as the film they had taken was canned and labeled and handed to the waiting motorcyclists.

"Always the bloody same; never let you see a damn thing."

When Colonel Arie Benitz dialed the number he had been given the previous night and forced a welter of coins into the slot, the response in London was almost immediate. Two rings and the connection. He was not told to whom he was speaking, nor did he introduce himself. The conversation was brief.

"We have tried to arrange a meeting this morning at the Foreign Office, and we have been put off," he was told. "The British Foreign Secretary is in continuous session with his advisers, they say. We are being shut out, and we need to take our own course."

The soldier of another army would have laughed derisively at that moment, questioning immediately what initiative was possible, where lay the opportunity for the influencing of events. But other armies did not fly two thousand miles across hostile airspace to land at Entebbe; did not take their commando squads into territory as hostile as Beirut for the elimination of the men who fought against them; did not force down foreign airliners on scheduled routes because they were thought to be carrying the men who directed and controlled the war against Israel. If a suggestion was made, there would be no ridicule of its feasibility from Colonel Arie Benitz. He would listen, evaluate and decide on the best plan available to ensure the possibility, however remote, of success.

"Is there a chance you might get to the plane and talk to those who are holding it?" Curt, abrupt, to the point.

"It would be difficult. They are suspicious of me, the British, as I was told they would be."

"We would like a message passed to the plane, to the young people. But it is difficult if we work through the British. They are possessive of this matter . . ."

"They are possessive because they are nervous. It is to be expected. What is the message?"

"I have used the wrong word. It is less a message, more a suggestion. Perhaps . . . if they were to offer surrender now, no more killing, but conditional on their not being sent back . . . They have asked in Jerusalem that I say this to you . . . but it cannot be with the knowledge of the British. I ask again, is it possible that you can reach the plane?"

Patiently and without rancor Benitz said into the phone, "They have an army around the aircraft. I cannot just walk into it . . . you understand. And there is little time now. They have set an ultimatum—you yourself told me that. And you must see that it is difficult for the British to bend at this moment, with the pilot dead and when they are under duress from threats. If we don't have the cooperation of Security here, it would be difficult for me to reach the aircraft." Not one to use the word "impossible," but there was that in his voice which spoke it. "I will try, but you must send the reply to the Crisis Committee that I can offer little hope that I will be able to talk with our people."

"It is understood, Colonel; it is understood what circumstances you find yourself in. Call us, please, should the position change, but I fear it will not. From London we are still trying for a meeting with the Foreign Secretary, but as I have told you, they are not responsive."

Arie Benitz hung the phone back on its hook and cursed the noise from the jukebox and the babble of conversation among the airport staff, reveling in their enforced idleness, who gathered for breakfast and cups of tea and chatter of shop prices and household budgets.

Yearned to be back with his own, back with the squad, back at the training school, back near Ashdod. Skirted the tables and chairs and walked slowly toward the door, not caring to glance at the mass of cheerful, laughing, stupid humanity about him. Dull, boring, miserable little people, who understood nothing and would be frightened and craven when their livers or their kidneys failed them and they were close to death. Understood nothing, or now they would be hushed and passive, thinking of the three and of a planeful of people and what might be their fate.

Out through the door and moving briskly toward his as-

signed office; where else to go? What would have triggered
them? he thought. An incident, a single episode? Unlikely.
Was never straightforward, not with these people—never as
simple as the outsider believed it. Did not take a kicking, or a
rape, or injustice to fashion the guerrilla. Just an accumula-
tion of circumstances, a construction of despair, a fabrication
of hatred. Not a sudden thing, not a momentary decision, but
a slow-burning, stoked loathing. And courage. Nothing without courage. Even the Palestinians . . .

Flopped himself at the desk. A sad and hurt man he would
have seemed had any of those who passed his door stopped to
look at the hunched figure.

Seventy yards behind Charlie were the fuel tankers, their
considerable forward and rear heavy-duty tires providing the
dark, shadowed concealment for the SAS marksmen. Two
handled the old Lee-Enfield bolt-action rifle mounted with
the tubular telescopic sight now trained on the door of the
Ilyushin. Another pair lay beside the standard NATO General Purpose Machine Gun, belt-fed. The rifles would provide
accurate and aimed shot protection; the GPMG trained on
the same target was the fallback precaution—concentration
of fire. Behind the central tanker were men with smoke canisters fitted to the barrel tips of FNs. He was unaware of all this
and stood feeling a peculiar loneliness as he waved to the
windows and door. Bloody stupid way to be carrying on,
Charlie.

Seemed to take an age before the door began to move.
Slight shuddering action at first, as if someone were operating
the mechanism who had not handled it before. Sort of stut-
tered, not quite sure whether it was sensible to breach the
defenses, and then the sweeping movement, coming away on
its arms from the fuselage and swinging out before coming to
rest, leaving the vacant, gaping hole it had protected. It took
Charlie time to get his eyes attuned to the gray artificial light
of the interior, and then the girl was standing there looking
down on him, more with curiosity than with anything else,
and holding with her left hand to the edge of the doorway.
Least of her problems, falling out of the bloody thing. Pistol
in her right hand. Prided himself that he knew most makes,
but this wasn't one that he recognized; half hidden anyway

among the folds of her dress. He smiled at her, big and open and friendly—the smile Parker Smith said would sell sand to the Saudis, ice to the Eskimos; the smile his wife always giggled at.

"Hello, it's Charlie Webster. You're Rebecca?" Daft really, like a pickup at a YWCA hop. Had to be some sort of formality. "I've come to speak with David and Isaac . . . and with you." Don't count her out—silly, that—at least not till you've looked at the scene a fair bit closer.

"You can talk to me; they're listening. They would prefer we talk in Russian. If you speak loudly they can hear what you say, and they will tell me what to reply."

Good thinking, and Charlie always admired that; didn't matter whether it was from the friendlies or the opposition. If they were thinking well, they should be respected. Keeping out of sight, where the guns weren't on them. Particularly Isaac: drop him and the whole thing could be wrapped up, and with all the hardware lying about, no way that he would show if he had any sense. Seemed the boy was working it out.

"What I've come here to do is explain the situation as it stands at this moment." Time for the big speech; time to calm them down, because it gets serious right now if you get them excited. "The position is very clear, really, and since you are all intelligent people, we think you will see the only option that is open to you. Your plane has no fuel, and we have said that while the aircraft and the passengers are under your control it will get none. While you are on board, the plane goes no further. That is the decision of the British Government, and it is irreversible."

Working at each sentence before he spoke it, considering the most appropriate Russian words from his comprehensive but rust-worn vocabulary. Made him slow, but gave an impression of deliberation and authority.

"The aircraft is surrounded by troops who have orders to shoot to kill should there be any attempt to break through our perimeter using the hostages as a shield. There is no escape from the aircraft. You will only leave it when you have disarmed yourselves, when all the passengers have been released. I am instructed to repeat the solemn guarantee of the British Government that you will not be harmed by our security forces."

Clipped to the open neck of his shirt where it was clearly visible was a small black microphone. What was not visible was the thin, colorless connection that had been threaded from the radio set underneath his shirt and that ran up his shirt to his collar, where it merged with his hair before blending into a molded plastic earpiece.

"Keep it going, Charlie"—Clitheroe, slightly distorted, but directing and controlling him—"tough stuff first, then onto the message they've put over to the world, and next the freeing of the hostages." Made him lose his concentration for a moment, the other voice; threw him fractionally, and he felt a flush on his face as he watched the girl stare back at him, not responding, merely waiting for him to finish.

"We want you to know that your flight out of Russia has been widely reported by the international news media. If it was a protest you were seeking against any grievances you may feel you have, then you have been widely heard. If publicity was your aim, then you have achieved it. We think that any aggressive action you may be considering will only alienate the many millions of people all over the world who are currently sympathetic to you."

Crap, Charlie, but what else to say? How do you get a conversation going at thirty yards? No known way. Bound to stand there exchanging speeches. But it's a load of rubbish you're talking and you bloody well know it.

Wondered how they knew what he was talking about in the tower; must have brought some of the FO girls down, or one from the Department. Spoke Russian better than he spoke English. Boot-faced ladies with heavy rings on their fingers, gold in their teeth, who'd made it out in the thirties and started to work for the British in the war, and were in their sixties now and had to keep going till pension day if they were to afford the bed-sitters of retirement. Hated the Soviets like shit, which gave them high security clearance.

"You have many women and children on board. We understand there is a party of schoolchildren. There is no need for you to keep them; all of them could be released now and it would make a great impression on all those people who are following this action." The girl still looked down at him. He could see her ankles, a little fat, and the solid and muscular shins before the hem of her dress denied him a further view.

Face devoid of expression, and Charlie wondered which of them was screwing her; wouldn't get much for his efforts. "That's what I came to say. There is no point in talking about ultimatums. It's nonsense, and it won't work."

She had a thin, reedy voice, and he had to strain to hear her. "That is all?"

"If there is anything you want me to answer, then I will try to help you."

She ducked back inside the aircraft, lost to him, and the doorway was emptied. Time for him to see the faces of the passengers at their portholes. Poor bastards, going through the familiar hoop, and with their hopes raised now because there was a contact.

Charlie said quietly into the microphone, speaking in English, "That's the first chat over; they're talking about it now."

"They're all on the monitor," he was told. "The open door drives them into the passenger cabin—that's where the three of them are—but the girl seems out of it. It's the two fellows who are involved. Seem calm enough, no arms flying about. Now that the door is open we are getting some sort of sound, but we can't read it right now, only the girl when she spoke to you. They've probably dropped their voices to avoid being overheard by the passengers."

"Right," said Charlie. The girl was back in the doorway.

"When you said you would come, it was because you wanted to talk to us about our request for information. The question that we asked was what would happen to us if we followed your instructions. What is the answer?"

"I have said that you will not be harmed."

"That is not an answer. I repeat, what will happen to us?"

"If you have committed offenses, you will be charged and will face a fair and impartial trial."

"That is not the answer. Where would the trial be?"

"If you have committed offenses inside the United Kingdom," you will stand trial in the United Kingdom." Not much longer, thought Charlie; not much longer this bloody nonsense can go on.

"You are not helpful; you are seeking to deceive us. Will we be sent back to Russia?—is that your plan?"

"I know of no plan to send you back to Russia." Lying sod, Charlie, but what else to say? And anyway, remember the parting shot of the big political gaffer: nothing sewn up at this stage. And what right have these three to know the truth? Forfeited that, hadn't they, when they took the guns on board. "I have not heard of such a plan." Never could lie well—not that many people who can. Only a few, and they're the exceptions. The girl didn't believe him—agitated, and leaning back into the dimness from the doorway to be told what to say.

"My friends say that this is a trick, that you will send us back to Kiev. We don't trust you. If you had been able to promise, if there had been a document, then we would have believed you, but there has been nothing. Only you, and you are a little person with no authority."

Now she tells me, thought Charlie. There was a light breeze which fastened to the moisture of his skin and cooled it, giving comfort from the extreme of the heat. A great clear sky, cloudless, peopled only by the curving sea gulls, far off course . . .

"Charlie, Charlie, keep your bloody wits about you," the message beating through his earpiece. "The two men have gone halfway down the cabin . . . pulling one of the passengers out . . . down the corridor . . . from amongst the kids; must be one of the staff traveling with them. . . . There are hands trying to stop it . . . Not a bloody hope, and the guy himself isn't fighting it. . . . Off the monitor . . ."

The girl was gone, pulled by an arm, roughly and without explanation; replaced by a man, thinly woven gray suit, masking the shape of another, whose left arm was gripped around his throat and whose right held the snub nose of a submachine gun to the captive's jaw. The face of the man in the suit was ashen, the color of ceramic bathroom tiles, and his eyes saw Charlie and were pleading and helpless and without fight. The knees shook and trembled, running eddies down the lower length of his trousers. Charlie could see the summit of black curled hair above the man's shoulder. Knew the answer. Isaac was out, Isaac was at the door. Had to break the moment, pacify him, calm him, couldn't shout—not with the barrel an inch from the man's face; not with the finger inside the trigger guard.

"Isaac, it's Charlie Webster. We've been speaking on the radio. You have to understand that we're here to help you.

We understand your problems, and there is much sympathy throughout the world for the fate of your people. Nothing, nothing can be gained from further bloodshed, only the loss of sympathy you have already won."

All the men whom Charlie had hunted when he was active had been young—the common factor, characteristic. No terrorist or urban guerrilla or freedom fighter makes it to middle age. Either dead, locked up or in love with life by then. Youth was the necessity to see things with the clarity needed to topple the windmills, struggle against the spongy depth of society.

"My friends called to you when I was sleeping. They wanted to surrender. They would have, if you had said to them that they would not have been sent back. But you could not say that, Charlie Webster. Perhaps you could not tell them the untruth that would have made you the victor. But that part of them you have destroyed now—you have made them fighters; you have lost them, Charlie Webster. Perhaps you do not know the Jews. Perhaps you do not know that we have been turned aside many times, pushed and manipulated and tricked and bent. We know what it is to be trampled over, squashed and obliterated, to be a stinking second class of man. Go to the Ukraine one day, Charlie Webster; go to the great synagogue in Kiev. Look at the people there, people who have been lied to, deceived and duped. Look at their misery; look at the agony of their lives, at their fear. Go and look for yourself and then come back and tell me that you expect a Jew to believe you when you say, 'I have not heard of such a plan.' "

No breath left, lungs drained, Isaac paused.

Charlie trying to hide the flowing anxiety, trying to communicate courage to the man held in the vise lock that Isaac had around his throat. "Isaac, we have to talk about this sensibly. . . ."

"The talk of surrender is over, forgotten. We have told you that we want the fuel to fly to Israel. That is what we came here for, that is what we will leave with. This man is the headmaster who is traveling with the schoolchildren; he is the one who will die at ten o'clock if the fuel is not loaded. He will stay in this doorway where you can watch him, Charlie Webster. You have your radio, so you can tell your people what we have decided. You can stay where you are, you can watch and you can think for yourself who has the will, your people or ourselves." The headmaster limp in his hold, almost as if he needed Isaac to prop him upright, and all the time the eyes fastened on Charlie's aging face, seeking a sign, a reassurance that was not his to give.

"Isaac, you must understand—"

"I understand everything. I want fuel; you at the moment do not wish me to have it. You are playing with the lives of many people on the aircraft; tell your authorities that."

Clitheroe on Charlie's earpiece: "Don't move away, Charlie. Stay put and keep quiet. Leave it a few minutes; then try to resume the dialogue. We have to keep the conversation moving if we're to save this fellow's life. From what you've seen of Isaac, from his voice—our pickup is not that good here—is this a real threat or will he soften nearer the time?"

Charlie thought of the partial face that he had seen, sharper and with a reality because it was now freed from the flatness of the photographs and the television tube. Conjured together the strength and the ferocity of the grip on the headmaster. He tilted his head till his mouth was directly above the microphone. "He means it. The way he is now, he'll shoot others afterwards if nothing happens to satisfy him. Right through the whole bloody lot he'll go." So it would be a killing job, a hard, messy, blood-spattered killing job, and carcasses to be picked up and thrown onto stretchers.

He eased himself onto the tarmac and sat cross-legged, the hot surface penetrating the fabric of his trousers. They had taken the man back from the doorway and he stood now, blurred and indistinct, against the far wall of the aircraft. Charlie fancied the girl would be watching him, but could not be certain. Had a headache, not rampant but nagging, chewing at him; always did when he was tired. Looked at his watch; time ebbing away. Hadn't felt it when they were talking, but was aware of it now. Half an hour to go—or maybe a little more, because his watch usually ran fast. Should have bought a new one, wife had told him often enough. Thirty minutes to see what Isaac was made of; but you already know, Charlie—can sense it, smell it.

13

An interloper in their affairs, the unwelcome guest who kept them from the familiar and therefore friendlier work that would be piling up on their desks, a problem whose solution would bring no credit, a deceptive, camouflaged and horrible entity—that was how the Ilyushin seemed to those who watched from the tower. Easy now with the aid of the black-and-white television picture to imagine the agonies of the man with the submachine gun at his head, who had been sentenced to die and who was waiting out the minutes till his execution on the far side of the gleaming, clean-cut fuselage.

The "No Smoking" signs in the room had long been ignored, and the fierce pall of smoke was unnoticed as the cigarette butts burned on the edges of tables and in saucers amid the debris of coffee cartons and sandwich wrappings. Voices were subdued, as if the men there were inside a great and famous cathedral where noise would be deemed offensive, irreverent.

The Home Secretary had alternated through the morning between his room below and the operational center, but since Charlie Webster had walked out on the tarmac he had remained upstairs. Now he talked by telephone to the Prime Minister. Clarification was what he sought, suggested by his aides because they were employed to protect the back and reputation of their master. Could there be any flexibility in the official stance that government had taken, now that a life was at immediate risk? Not possible, especially at this moment—not after the Soviet statement; not after the leaking by the press that an ultimatum was due to expire. There was to be no smear of compromise and weakness under threat. While he listened he pulled at his collar, as if trying to free himself from a constriction to his breathing, and those who looked to him for some indication of the burden of the con-

versation saw only an anxiety that welled in his forehead and
the slackness at his mouth that spelled dilemma and irresolu-
tion. He made his farewells to the Prime Minister and quietly
put back the receiver before turning to those around him.

"The Prime Minister has said what I think we all expected
him to say. There will be no alteration in our position. The
fate of this unfortunate does not affect or change the decision
we have taken. He wants me to pass on to you all that he has
the greatest faith in our judgment. He leaves it to us to decide
whether the aircraft should be stormed before the expiration
of the ultimatum. We do not have very long, gentlemen, and
we need to know the options."

His voice tailed away, reflecting a mood that came as no
surprise to those who knew him well. His reign at Home Office had been characterized by a humanity and sympathy that
were not always traditional. The newspaper columnists spoke
of him as a man of compassion. His concern now was for the
passenger they knew only as the "headmaster," whom he had
seen brought to the doorway of the aircraft with the soft focus
and anonymous face set inside the squared television frame.
A man in a gray suit about whom nothing else was known
except that his chin quivered and his hands clenched and
straightened again continually.

"What are the options, gentlemen?"

Clitheroe rose from the stool on which he sat, and slowly
paced the length of the tower—a few feet only, but a space
that gave him room to consider what he might say. There
was a diffidence about him that had not been seen since they
had gathered the previous evening.

"It's Webster's opinion—his opinion only on the killing of
this man—it is just his assessment that they will go through
with it, go the limit of their threat. Webster is in a very exposed position, probably nervous, perhaps not the best judge.
I don't wish to patronize the man, not in any way at all, but
we have to remember where he is. He is unarmed, he is
within clear range of their guns, he has been close to the
intended victim. It is his judgment that they will shoot, but
he may not—"

"Who is in a better position?" the Home Secretary said.

"I don't know. None of us, I think. All I'm trying to do is
remind you of the circumstances Webster finds himself in—

we should not follow his judgment blindly." But he too had seen the fish-eye pictures, the man pulled from his seat, the hands that rose to his assistance thrust aside. "I just don't know. Perhaps they will kill, perhaps not. It is impossible to be certain. And if they kill once, it does not follow that Webster is right and they will begin a wholesale slaughter. The effect of one killing might be to break these three—that has to be considered. We are dealing with the intangible; we cannot draw up a blueprint and say that because one thing has happened then a logical process will ensue. There is another aspect: these people are Jews, but not Israelis; that may color the will they talk so much of." Clitheroe sat down again, aware of his own limitations, that he could not supply the answer they sought from him.

"If Mr. Webster is right, and they intend to kill the man, is it possible to take physical action to preempt it? What is the feasibility of attacking the aircraft?" The Home Secretary directed the question without enthusiasm to the Assistant Chief Constable.

"The military would not be happy about it. There are obvious difficulties—open ground; the need to get ladders to the plane. The SAS estimate they would need a minimum of fifteen seconds from the time they leave the tanker till they are entering the cabin. Even with far-side diversions it's hazardous and dangerous. A risk to the troops and to the passengers. At night they could manage it, but by daylight . . . What it comes down to, sir, is this: do we endanger many lives at this stage in the hope of saving one?"

"It would be difficult to sit here and watch a man die and know we have so much strength and not utilize it."

The politician had expressed the fear that swamped them all. The challenge to their very virility, to their professions, that they should stand on the sidelines, acknowledge their inadequacy. Men on a beach who know that a far-out swimmer will drown but have not the power to confront the waves.

"The Dutch did it," the policeman intoned, "at the train siege at Beilen, when the Moluccan group took hostages. A passenger was executed, and they took a decision not to storm because conditions were unfavorable. They backed off and relied on negotiations. No more passengers were—"

"We are not the Dutch," the Home Secretary rasped. "Because they have taken a course of action, it does not mean we follow. We cannot hide from responsibilities behind precedent."

He paused, seemed to stumble in his words, lose the track of his theme; there was age and unhappiness on his face, and there was a stoop in his back that was usually thrown back and athletic. He could not have held this high office twenty years earlier, when capital punishment was still exercised as the judicial retribution for various categories of murder. Would not have had the strength and the commitment to sign the final authorizations; would not have surmounted the mountain of conscience and refused to recommend that the monarch use her prerogative of reprieve.

"There has to be something that can be done. We cannot just sit here and idle the time away."

"At times, sir, we are not given the freedom of action. Options are not always open to us." The policeman was chastened; spoke with respect, understanding the sense of failure that pervaded all in the room. "We just have to hope that Webster is wrong."

Rebecca had been left to guard the headmaster.

He remained erect and tall, breath coming fast and in slight gasps, but with his head still and his eyes stretching out beyond the middle distance toward the fields and trees, and the farther perimeter fence, and the farm with the white-painted walls and the embossed and dark-stained beams, following the swooping movement of a bird that hunted for food amid the migrating swarms of summer insects. When he looked straight ahead he could not see the girl and was aware of her presence only by the occasional shuffling movements as she eased her body into less contorted positions, leaning all the time against the coat-closet wall beside him.

His thoughts were of classrooms, clean and ordered and poster-and-chart-covered, where his rule held sway. Of the management of his pupils. His work for the Party. The Party required of him a discipline that he welcomed, that provided an outlet for the enthusiasms he had harbored since his release from the army at the end of the war. The comradeship of the Party, the sense of achievement and accomplishment in the work that could be fashioned. Frustrations, yes, but nothing when set against the successes that could be attained. Could take a pride in the way the children had reacted and behaved since the taking of the plane, a tribute to his responsibility, and he had not been betrayed by the little ones. Calm and collected and without panic, the children had behaved impeccably, even with the hunger in their bellies, their fear of the guns. Should be recognized, and reported back to those in authority, whatever became of him; should not be forgotten that they were children under his tutelage and they had not disgraced themselves.

He knew what time the men would come for him, when he would pass out of the care of the girl and into their hands, but did not look at his watch. Did not value the indulgence of weakness and sought to shut out the terror that would accompany the movement of the hands toward the hour. Could hear the voices of the two men, behind him and to his left; talking to each other, but faintly, and he could not make out their words; positioned where they could see past him and down the passenger cabin. Leaving him to what peace he might find.

The headmaster saw the man who sat on the tarmac shift his body, bend his knees and settle on his toes, squatting as if mounted on a flattened toilet. A man of his own age. The one who had been sent to talk, and who had been rejected, and who now showed an emptiness of initiative. He had tried, discernible from his voice, to plead with all the reasonableness that he could muster, had tried to save him, and for that the headmaster was grateful; but he was not dealing with people who were reasonable, only with savages and beasts and animals. There was almost a warmth for this stranger with the desk pallor who had escaped the heat of summer. The stranger no longer looked about him, and the headmaster drifted into the awareness that the steeled and concentrated gaze was fixed on his own person. First the eyes straining for understanding and comprehension and communication, and then the lips moving as if with a message. Seemed to say one word, one word alone, again and again, from the rhythm of the way the mouth moved. The headmaster felt again the weakening of his legs, the trembling of his hands clasped before him.

One word in his own tongue, one word only, shouted and deafening so that it split into his consciousness: an order, a demand of him. He fought to follow, struggled to relate the bellowed voice to his movements.

"Jump!"

The noise had been soaring inside Charlie for minutes before he could summon himself to howl the command. Fearful when the moment came that his voice would desert him, that it would come as a feeble croak without the incisiveness he needed. From deep in his lungs, far down, reaching for a depth and volume that would make the bastard up there react from instinct.

Charlie saw the headmaster lurch toward the open void of the Ilyushin's doorway, saw him move into the pitching fall with all the expertise of the trainee parachutist who leaves the balloon basket for the first time. Heard the single shot that was an age late. Charlie was on his feet and sprinting. Haze of bloody confusion as the man landed. Awkwardly, agility destroyed by the years. Saw his face rise from the tarmac, eyes harrowed and frantic, desperate for the path to safety, crying for new instructions. Had regained his feet, pain at his mouth, neck and shoulders, slumped low and angled from the fall, starting to stagger forward.

"Run, you bugger, run!"

Crazy, slow-motion, broken trot, and Charlie was closing with him, and then the first crescendo of gunfire. Ricochets impacting from the tarmac, and exploding pockets of dust to trace the bullets that could not find the wavering shamble of the headmaster. Saw Isaac standing there, indecision, and then the gun at his shoulder again, steadying, aiming. Stupid bastard, had fired from the hip the first time.

Charlie plunged forward, felt his chest buffet into the other man and swept him to the right toward the shelt.r and haven of the wing structure. Had to push him when they were together on the ground, like a bloody sack, and whimpering all the time: like he can't believe it; like he thinks they'll still come for him, with clubs, sledgehammers; pulp him, mash him. Together they rolled and spun across the abrasive ground, bucking and confused and together.

"It's all right," Charlie whispered. "It's over." Checked

himself, surprised in a way that he'd spoken in Russian. Spread-eagled over the man's body, protecting it; could see only his head, pale, with the skin stretched drum-tight, and the reflection where the tears ran.

"You walk at my speed," Charlie said, louder, and pulled the man up, arms round the flabbiness of his waist. Didn't know whether they'd made the shelter of the wing or not; thought of the gun up there in the doorway burning a hole in his back, aimed foursquare at him, needle and V sight together. Hell of a weight the bugger was; had to carry him, really; pulled Charlie down, made him use muscles he'd forgotten. In step, an exhausted dance routine, they moved in unison. Just a few more seconds and they'd be clear of the hurting range of the submachine gun.

Charlie didn't look back, kept his eyes unwavering on the pole in the perimeter fence that he had chosen. Didn't know whether they were visible again, if the wing still shielded them.

"Not long now," Charlie said. "Just a few more yards. Then it's over."

And endlessly beating through his mind the memory of the hunched and coiled figure in the doorway, the gun clamped to his shoulder, the saucer eyes expanded behind the sight. Be a bloody killing job now. Have to cut you down, Isaac; have to, won't we? Because you're not offering another way.

Isaac had not lingered in the doorway.

One fierce and uncontrolled burst of gunfire, with the barrel pulling high and left, and he had realized that the opportunity to cut down the fugitive was lost. Perhaps he could have taken the Briton with an aimed shot, but it would have been a lucky one, and the wing was looming into his orbit. Understood that his reactions had been slow, dulled by lack of sleep, but still slow and sufficient to endanger them all. And the girl had again failed. Pity, really, because she was a part of them, from the same blood, but she had failed when they had needed her. Not all her fault, partly his own; had underestimated the man who came, and had been tricked and would suffer for it. It was a calm evaluation that he made, stemming from the same calmness that immediately took him away from the open space, where the rifles that were trained on him could have exacted a revenge.

Could no longer rely on the girl. Obvious, and should have been seen earlier, but proved now. Whom could he lean on? Burned and gnawed at him as he crouched close to the wall and near to the door. Which of them could be relied on? Rebecca, slumped and feeble on the carpet, holding the pistol in her two hands as if the shock of firing had toppled her. David, quiet and without comment, apart from them, taking refuge at the far end of the aircraft where he could make believe that his work was to watch the passengers. They have lost their faith, the two of them; do not believe anymore in escapé from the cabin of steel with the sunken roof, and the window-pitted walls, and the crowded seats, and the pressure doors, and the empty fuel tanks.

Along the length of the plane he shouted to David, "There is still time till ten o'clock, and we will do then as we have promised."

There was no reply and he expected none; did not even bother to gaze down the aisle to witness David's reaction. Like sheep they would follow him. Like sheep they would scatter if he faltered.

On his stomach, George Davies lay beside the sniper behind the forward wheel of the central tanker.

"Could you have had him?"

"The one with the curly hair, with the SMG? No problem."

"There was no instruction; you were right not to fire."

"Three, four seconds I had him."

"They haven't clarified on it yet. Up till now it's been not to shoot unless we can get the two men, both of them together. And I have to call in and ask."

"Take a bloody year, that; they won't hang about for us."

"Always the same when you bring a coach trip down from London to handle it."

"Any talk of us going in and busting it open?"

"Not at the moment. Can be done if they want it, but it's not ideal."

"Make any difference, what the civvie did, pulling that chap out?" The marksman spoke from the side of his mouth, conversationally and with the absence of deference to rank that was the characteristic of so small a force. Head never moving, steady on a line down the rifle barrel, searching the grayness of the door's opening.

"Shouldn't think so; there was nothing on the net about it first. Reckon he acted off his own bat, didn't think out the consequences; just couldn't sit there and watch it all in glorious Technicolor."

"Had a point there."

"We'll have to see."

All the years they'd trained for this, exercises and practices and rehearsal runs, sometimes thinking it was for real, usually knowing it wasn't. All the alerts, all the false alarms. Living and sleeping the problem for four years since the squad had been formed, and he didn't know the answers. Bloody expert he was supposed to be, and he didn't know. Nobody did, for that matter, but it didn't make the pill any sweeter.

The television camera with the long lens showed the committee in the tower that Charlie Webster had reached the safety of the cropped grass at the side of the runway. He was on his knees beside the man whom he had rescued. The episode was completed. They waited for him to call in on the radio, and when there had been no transmission they presumed that his equipment was broken.

The Assistant Chief Constable gave rapid orders, content that he was again able to perform a function and separated from the tiresome world of conjecture and interpretation. A civilian ambulance should be sent to the pair. Under no circumstances should they be allowed to take cover behind the petrol tankers some fifty yards to their left. No reason for those in the plane to get a half glimpse of the troops, to lose the belief that the vehicles were abandoned, empty. Clitheroe mentioned to anyone who cared to listen that a major breakthrough had been achieved: they now had in their possession an eyewitness from the aircraft who would be able to furnish an up-to-the minute description of the state of mind of both hijacker and hostage.

The Home Secretary remained by the monitor that showed the interior of the aircraft recorded by the fish-eye. Isaac occasionally obliging in view; David staying at the far end of the aircraft and not seen. The girl passing the length of the aisle as if communicating messages. Still no sound from the microphones that were serviced by sheepish and frustrated technicians.

"Has Mr. Webster's action helped or hindered us?"

He spoke to the room in general, not turning from the set, his hands clamped on the sides of his cheeks, elbows firmly on the table, feeling the weight of tiredness that was common to all who had spent the last five and a half hours in the tower—a tiredness that came not from lack of sleep but from the frustration of constantly playing the part of voyeurs, unable to alter significantly the course of events, shackled.

The Assistant Chief Constable had finished his delivery of instructions.

"It's not yet ten, seven minutes or so to go, and there's sixty more they can pick from. What Mr. Webster did may have had the opposite effect to that which we have been hoping for. In effect, he may have warmed them up." The policeman knew that his words were not welcome; but time he was listened to, heard out and his experience and knowledge realized. "It's not the sort of thing that is likely to weaken them; quite the reverse. It's a slap in the face for them. I would expect them to try to hit back."

"I think you're wrong," said the Home Secretary quietly. "I hope so. We were all prepared to sit here, flabby in our inability, and watch that poor man die. We had reconciled ourselves to it, justified our noninterference in a way we would have done with an interministerial memorandum. We had passed the buck. That man is now alive because a decisive step was taken. We have a little dignity now. Not much, because it was not we who authorized Mr. Webster's action. But we have some, and dignity is important. . . ."

"Sir, by the time the day's over we may have some dignity and we may have three or six dead passengers. The two don't equate on my scales." Neck reddening where it met, clean-shaven, with the white laundered shirt above the pressed collar of his tunic. "I don't give a damn about dignity. I don't give a damn if the whole British Cabinet has to crawl on their bended knees to that plane. I don't give a damn whether Mr. Webster is the hero of the hour. I want those passengers out, and I want them out safely. When we've done that, then we may be able to talk of dignity."

The Home Secretary came awkwardly to his feet and turned square to the policeman. "I'm in your way, and you have work to do. I will be below if you have need of me." He stopped, as if uncertain as to the wisdom of his gesture; then said quietly and without hurry, "I apologize for wasting your time, gentlemen. It's an alien world to me, and not one that I relish, nor have any great understanding for. If you think there is need of my presence, please do not hesitate to call for me."

"I really don't think, sir . . ." The aides were around him, edging forward, concerned.

"Sir, there is no need . . ."

"It would not be wise . . ."

He smiled to them all and made his way to the door, walked through, and closed it afterward, with care that it should not bang.

"Dignity, my Christ," muttered the policeman savagely. "What does he think we're at, winning a bloody election?"

He scanned the room for support and found it lacking— faces averted; studying the monitors; drawing from the coffee urn; unparceling the food. Made a bloody mistake, hadn't he? But what did they want? Easy answers, everything's rosy, pound's doing well, balance of payments sensational, exports record-breaking? Did they want that? Or the bloody truth? That the boat's been rocked. That we're in a new situation, and it's four minutes to bloody ten o'clock.

And they'd remember that, the smart little arse lickers who burrowed in the files and said who was right for promotion to Chief Constable. They'd remember that, and have a little titter behind their hands before they went out to lunch, and a damn good meal they'd have before coming back to pencil out his name. But nothing to kick, no one to abuse; just the second hand of the wall clock to look at, remorseless and relentless in its progress.

Luigi Franconi had long been a dreamer.

Back at Party headquarters, the drab, poster-daubed red brick block behind the Piazza Venezia where he occupied a third-floor office, the secretaries and his colleagues had become used to seeing the drift of his concentration away from their expositions and briefings. Almost a joke to those who knew him well, the way he was present and then absent, merely moving his head in agreement or dissent, whichever way the argument led. When he was corrected, exposed with much laughing and with irritation from those who were not his friends; he would assume pained apology and shake himself and indicate that surely it was time for lunch in the trattoria that graced the small square close by.

In truth, Franconi was a private person, seldom willing to share his meanders and not convinced that the word of others carried any great importance. He worked from paper, from pile upon pile of accumulated, mounting, typed and printed paper. Only when confronted with the written word or figure did he give evidence of the ability of which his superiors in the Party hierarchy were convinced. They had realized the value of this man. Not a person to be influenced by suavity and glibness and fluency. The word and statistic had to stand on their own, without extraneous support. They laughed about him in the office, but only to his face, never behind his back, and told him he must have the blood of the Germans in his veins, because no Italian could put such reliance on silence. Even Party Secretary Berlinguer, even little Enrico could raise his voice in debate, and he of the cold temperament of the island people, from Sardinia. Franconi would smile with them, and try to please, and think them fools, and relish their comradeship till there was the moment to slip away and return to the quiet of his desk.

No papers to read now. Hadn't brought a book with him—not a Garzanti classic, nor a pamphlet draft that needed tidying; not a notebook in which to jot his more casual impressions of the Soviet Union for the report they would be awaiting back in Rome. Nothing in the pouch in front of him except the bag into which he could vomit if the aircraft bucked in turbulence, and the folder that described the Ilyushin safety procedures and which was not written in any language that he understood.

The choosing of the headmaster had made little impression on him: a brief flurry of tensed excitement and apprehension as the man had disappeared from the doorway in the moment before the firing of a machine gun. He had not aped the other passengers who had first stared through the windows and then subsided in their seats seeking anonymity as the eyes of Isaac had swept them; the mood of the moment had been quickly lost on him. He had not offended; he was divorced from their struggle; they had no quarrel with him.

Before, he had been nervous—he would admit that to himself—when they had separated him from his friend, from Aldo. The same sort of fear of the unknown and the unfamiliar that he had known in the hills thirty-five years earlier, and it had passed now as it had then. He had barely glanced from the aircraft porthole to see what was the fate of the headmaster.

He phased away the exterior world with the dreams of his home. When this was all over, and it would not take much time—the youth and desperation of his captors told him that—when they climbed down the ladder that would be brought, he would bypass the journalists and television crews. There were enough in the delegation who would be queuing, indeed jumping, forward to satisfy the needs of the RAI interviewers or whoever else wanted their opinions. He'd stand alone at the side, with the half grin on his face, and shrug his shoulders and be polite and shake his head. Wait till his colleagues had said their fill.

They'd send them home by Alitalia; right to travel on the national airline, and an Italian ought to—a gesture to salve an infinitesimal percentage from the annual deficit. Overmanning the central problem; always had been. . . . No better at Party headquarters, where they preached organization and control of the work force and distribution of labor, but still suffered, equally with the capitalists, the same malady. Adriana, Maria, Cristina: all in the typing pool, all with time for knitting and gossip; any one of them could have looked after the needs of the section, but how to sack one—didn't bear thinking of, the squabbling, the arguing, the challenge over the pension rights.

He'd go home on Alitalia. The wife would be there to meet him. Tears on his shoulder, arms around his neck, lipstick on his collar, mascara on his cheek, sobbing in his ear. He'd have to endure all that. They'd drive in from Fiumicino and take the Raccordo Anulare and he'd see the girls beside the bushes and pretend he wasn't looking, and his wife would be firmly coping with the traffic. Be able to drink them in, the girls. Miniskirts and unbuttoned blouses, thighs and breasts and invitations, and he'd be left to his privacy to consider on it while nodding and agreeing with all his wife said.

Often the cars pulled up sharply: a warning flash of brake

lights and a man would jump from the driver's seat and the
girls were already hurrying for the sanctuary of the undergrowth. Luigi had always wondered what it would be like, just
what was said before the removal of the sparse strips of necessary clothing. When did you pay, before or after? And what
would there be afterward—a thanks, an acknowledgment, a
wordless wave, or just a grin? Epitaph of an experience: a
Fiat's motor starting up? Didn't even know how much it cost,
how long it took. He had spent an adult lifetime traveling the
Raccordo—seen them, wanted them, lusted in his eunuched
way after them, hovered his foot near the brake pedal—and
never dared.

The wife would drive him home, park the car expansively
in the street, and he'd comment on it and she'd dismiss the
matter and lead him like an exhibit, a celebrity brought back
from the fair, to their fourth-floor home, where the gathering
would be waiting. Kisses and hugs and backslaps now, a mul-
titude of voices, a swill of chilled wine, a pasta bowl of welcome. All would ask him to relate his experiences, but in
concert, so that even should he want to speak, none would be
listening and all talking, chattering, demanding, crying.
They'd be there for hours, the fools—filling his home, taking
his time, impressing their friendship when all he would seek
would be the solace of his wife's arms.

Drawn curtains and extinguished lights, the cosmetics to
make her no different from the girls still plying their trade at
the roadside. Moving, performing, functioning—that would
be his bedroom task on the night of his return. Have full run
of his domain that night; later would come the denials and
the tiredness and the excuses. Not the first night, though.

The hand sank into the roof of his jacket collar, gripped at
the well-woven material, took a fistful and pulled him upright,
splintering the reverie of his fantasies. It was an irresistible
strength that drew him from the seat, dragging him with impatience and without explanation from the safety of his fellow
passengers. Fleetingly he saw the faces around him, saw
them twist and turn and glide away; was aware of their shame
and degradation.

The one with the curly hair, the short one, that was the
one who held him, propelled him out into the aisle, and now
there was the thrust of a tight circle of steel against the snake

of his backbone. The dreams were losing ground, the warmth of the flesh receding; the softened arms on him no longer gave hope.

A cry came, hoarse and splitting into his consciousness; his name shouted at the pitch of hysteria, and the voice was Aldo's. Just his name, and an agony in the voice, and the sound of it hammered him till his knees buckled and his bowels weakened, till his eyes glazed to a mist and he was blinded by the flood and knew not where he was going, only reacting to the pressure at his nape that drove him forward.

It came late, but there was a moment of all-seeing clarity before the brightness of the intruding sun through the opened aircraft door obliterated all images in front of him. And there was the memory of the face of the headmaster, who had taken the similar path minutes before, as he had been led down the route that separated him from the rest, from the accepting bovine herd. Had Luigi Franconi looked like that? Had he shown the broken fear, the collapsed chin, the nerveless sagged cheeks, the faltering walk? Had he screamed inside without sound as the other must have?

Gone, lost for a moment, giving the fractional hope of salvation, before he found it again; found it where he knew he must; found the chill and symmetry of the gun barrel against the tender skin that slid back from his earlobe toward the base of his neck.

All heard the single, echoing refrain of the shot.

The reverberations were fierce inside the aircraft, quieting the frenzied shouting from the remaining members of the PCI delegation.

An empty, hollowed thud where Charlie Webster lay on the shortened grass, which caused the man he still protected to shudder underneath him and squirm as if trying to bury himself in the hardened soil.

A faint popping noise, a distant car door slammed, to those immured inside the plate glass of the control-tower windows.

Inside the press corral, where the journalists were screened from the open door of the Ilyushin, the solitary report was noted. Quizzical eyes; a margin of excitement; a switching on of cameras so that their synchronized sound systems would record any further shots; scribbling in notebooks.

"What time do you make it?" a man from the press agencies asked the reporter who stood next to him; he was required to log the day's events with accuracy.

The other kept his eyes fastened on the irrelevance of that flank of the aircraft which was visible. "Just on ten o'clock."

"Not much we can say, then. 'At ten o'clock a single shot was heard from the far side of Aeroflot 927.' That's it. Nothing else we can say."

With more powerful binoculars than they possessed, the journalists and cameramen might have been able to distinguish the lifeless body of Luigi Franconi where it rested close to the starboard undercarriage wheels. But at the distance between where they stood and the Ilyushin, the wheels only merged, shimmering in their stillness, with the unnoticed corpse.

A sound technician, a large man who prided himself equally on his wit and the perfection of his trimmed beard, made a joke. To those who heard it, it was weak, but his own laughter was picked up by all in the pen—a palliative to the suppressed tension caused by the unexplained shot. The zephyr of laughter swept out across the scorched concrete, rippling its way toward the aircraft and the control tower, till it settled on the faraway ears of those who lay in the grass with their rifles and machine guns.

There were a score of impotent obscenities from the troops who had watched the small Italian die.

14

Charlie had not looked back toward the shadowed tarmac dwarfed by the swollen impression of the aircraft.

He knew what he would see if he turned his head; could picture the exact position in which the body would by lying. Close to the wheels, directly under the cavity of the doorway, and now a confused form from which the humanity and control had been exorcised by the single shot. No need to look—not when death no longer held a fascination, when the desperate attractiveness of the peep show had forgone its uniqueness. He'd seen many before. The corpses of men who had died well; who had died badly, whatever that meant; of men who had been killed judicially, and those who had gone without the solace of legality; of men who had screamed and of men who had prayed. Made little difference to the poor bastards—not now, not when it was over.

Didn't concern himself with the way the man from the plane had died; unimportant. But why that one, that nameless one down by the wheels—why had he taken the trip? Pretty straightforward, when you think about it, Charlie. One was going to go, those were the rules they were playing by; take a mouse from a cat and she'll go find another. That's what it's about, Charlie. Took their fun from them when you talked this one into jumping. But they've a stockpile of spare parts, and you don't stop this engine by removing just one of the components; sixty-odd replacements they've tucked away in there. Saved one to kill another. Made you wonder, Charlie, whether it was worth it, worth all the adrenaline surge, and the scream and the gunfire. Can't play heroics sixty times, Charlie.

He could hear the approach of the ambulance's engine, creeping carefully forward, low gear, on the outer perimeter road. Stopped a full hundred yards from him, as if nobody had told the driver the range of an SMG. Couldn't blame him; couldn't blame anybody who didn't want his head blasted, wanted to go home to the little woman in the evening and eat his supper and talk about the sort of day he'd had at work. Not an ambulance driver's quarrel. Jews and Israelis and Russians, so where did a driver from Bishop's Stortford, on forty-five pounds a week and struggling, fit into that pattern? Charlie raised his right hand, gave the thumbs-up signal—put the poor blighter out of his misery and let him know he didn't have to come closer.

Gently Charlie pulled the Russian to his feet. Eased him into the old position where his own body still afforded protection from the direction of the aircraft. Together they shuffled forward, slowly and without precision because the headmaster's legs were still weak and unresponsive.

"We're well clear of range. We'll just get to the truck; then you can forget it."

Without turning, the Russian said through the tremor of his voice, "The last shot. They have killed another?"

"I think so." Charlie knew the inadequacy of his answer. Brusquely and with a suggestion of authority, he said, "There's nothing we can do. Not our problem anymore."

"They have killed him because you have taken me from them."

"Perhaps."

"I had not thought it would be that way."

Close to the ambulance now, a few more steps, and the moment for Charlie to button it down, conceal his impatience. But he led with his tongue, lashing and aggressive.

"Well, what do you want to bloody well do? Do you want to go and stand by the door and shout, 'Hey, there, I'm sorry I escaped. I've come back to ask you to forgive me. I didn't want the other bugger killed. It was all a big mistake, and if you shoot me can we have the other guy back, give him his life again, because I want to play the bloody hero'? Cut the crap out and get down on your knees and thank whatever God you have in uptown Kiev that an idiot like Charlie Webster, Charlie bloody nobody Webster, was sitting on his arse on the tarmac with nothing better to do on a sunny morning than stick his fucking neck on the block so that if anyone had to go into the box it wouldn't be you. Course you didn't know it would happen·like this; no bugger did. The whole lot may go on that plane, every last one of them. You may be the only one who walks out of it, and if that happens don't be in a corner and blubbering that you wanted to share it with them."

Charlie loosened his grip around the waist of the Russian as they reached the twin rear doors of the ambulance, and the other man turned and faced him and there was the sadness of apology in his face.

"I am sorry, truly sorry. I have to thank you because of what you have done for me. But it is a frightening and a fearful thing for a man to know that he has lived and then another . . . In the war—"

"Get in and shut up," Charlie said.

"In the war there were endless columns of men who went to their deaths, with no hope of rescue, nothing to help them beyond the comradeship of dying together."

Charlie opened the doors and pushed him into the interior, so that he stumbled and tripped forward across a red-blanketed stretcher.

"Shut up; forget it," he said as he followed him.

The ambulance swung through one hundred and eighty degrees, causing Charlie to grab at a wall-attached oxygen cylinder; then he leaned out to pull together the two flapping doors. Before he fastened them he saw again the bright and unsullied lines of the Ilyushin, the neatness of its airframe broken only by the opened hatch. In the half-light of the ambulance interior, shaded by the smoked glass, he held out his hand.

"I'm Charlie Webster."

"Dovrobyn, Nikita Dovrobyn, and I am grateful." Their hands locked together, and Charlie could feel the bony, clasping pressure of the grip.

"Like I said, forget it. Can't ever be as bad again." They spoke no more on the brief journey to the control tower.

When the ambulance stopped, he unfastened the doors and helped the Russian back down into the sunlight. There were other hands now to help, and uniformed arms that linked under Dovrobyn's armpits, and one that carried a blanket to drape over his back. Bloody stupid, that, thought Charlie, with the temperature where it was. All getting in on the act, and milling and fussing and flurrying round the star turn of the day. Cat-with-the-cream satisfaction on the driver's face, the man who had driven out to the aircraft; who'd done nothing, and who would revel his way through a line of pints in the canteen bar at lunchtime on the strength of it.

There was a quiet voice in Charlie's ear.

"What sort of condition is he in, Mr. Webster?" Bit of bloody deference there, and not before time.

"He's fine," Charlie said, looking at the pink-faced, clean-shaven police inspector with his uniform and neatly knotted half-windsor black tie.

"Will he be able to sustain a debrief? They're anxious—"

"God's sake, how do I bloody know? He's not dead, is he? Not been shot?"

Kill it, Charlie, you're shouting and they're staring at you. Doesn't fit the proper image, not of a hero. Supposed to be calm and collected and organized, and above all modest. Not yelling because an earnest little prig asks a sensible question.

"He'll be fine; just find him some tea and a drop of brandy."

"There's a great deal of admiration for what you did, Mr. Webster."

Charlie nodded. Would they only leave him alone, stop humiliating him! What did they think it was, a conscious bloody decision? Didn't they know, any of these people, that there weren't risk appraisals and evaluations? You just jumped off your backside and ran. If you were lucky you were a hero; if you were unlucky they'd be scraping you up and wondering how you could have been so bloody stupid.

They formed a little cavalcade up the stairs. The Russian in his ridiculous blanket at the front, with the retinue around him, and Charlie at the tail. As they climbed, he leaned forward and tapped the inspector on the shoulder and said, "I'm sorry, I didn't mean to shout."

"That's all right, Mr. Webster," said the policeman. "I know how you must feel."

An unmarked, gray-painted Transit van brought George Davies to the control tower. It had driven slowly around the outer road in full view of the aircraft, maintaining a regular speed, so that those who watched it from the cockpit and the passenger cabin would not be aroused and concerned at its progress. For a few seconds it disappeared behind the barricade of tankers, and it was during those moments that the back doors were flung open and the SAS commander had boarded. When the van emerged again, there was nothing to indicate to those on the plane that it had added a passenger to its load; nothing to tell them of the army presence still hidden near the Ilyushin.

As he sat on the metal floor of the van, Davies could reflect that there could be only one reason why he had been summoned for a conference. The decision must have been taken, the die cast; the politicians were steeling themselves for the military option.

Inside the control-tower area, there had formed a reception line of grave-faced men with whom Nikita Dovrobyn shook hands.

The Home Secretary had emerged from his lower-floor office to greet the Russian with a public smile and a word of congratulation that was lost on the survivor because Charlie was still trapped by the throng in the doorway and unable to translate the remark. The tight grip of the Assistant Chief Constable, the unwavering gaze into his eyes, the impression of the medal ribbons, all caused Dovrobyn to flinch away— his instinctive reaction to security-force authority. By contrast, Clitheroe limply took the proffered hand and led the Russian to a chair that was functional and not comfortable and for which he apologized. Others called him "sir," some lightly slapped his back and he wondered why they presumed that he had of his own volition achieved something that made him so worthy of attention. Then, in their impatience, they were all talking to him, a Babel of voices that were strange and unknown, and he looked past their heads for the one called Charlie Webster and strained to see him beyond the scrubbed faces and the buttoned collars and the uniforms and the city suits. Just wanted to sleep, wanted an escape from these people. The voice of Charlie Webster cut through his confusion—the same voice of authority that had demanded he jump when his legs were leaden, and which he had obeyed.

"Leave the man alone. He doesn't understand a bloody word you're saying. Pack it in, and give him some room to breathe."

There was a parting of the seas around the chair, and Dovrobyn found the one face, the familiar face, that he sought.

Charlie spoke in Russian, gently and without haste, as if there were suddenly time, as if the panic for speed were forgotten. "We're going to get you some coffee; then we have to talk to you. You must understand that we have to know as much as you can tell us about the interior of the aircraft. We have to know everything that you can remember, every detail. If we are to save other people's lives, you must tell us all you can. We'll hold the questions till we have the coffee, give you time to think and to remember. . . ." Charlie broke off and spoke again in English. "We should get him some coffee. He's dead tired, scared out of his mind and totally disoriented. It's worth waiting."

They stood in a circle around the Russian, watching him, staring, peering, stripping the man, so that he avoided them and focused on his hands, which he held together lest they see the trembling of his fingers. Once when he looked up he saw a soldier in camouflage denims with a webbing belt at his waist and a pistol holster fastened to it, who had not been present when he had first come, and he knew from the murmur of their voices and the way they softened and remained low till he turned his head that he was the subject of their talk.

Arrival of the coffee. A single cup set in a chipped white saucer with a steel spoon and paper packet of sugar. Carried to him by a woman who wore black with a little white cloth fixed in her hair and a white apron that showed stains. A panic consumed him as she stretched forward with the cup and saucer: would the shaking of his hands betray him; could he even hold it, would he spill and slop the drink? Then Charlie Webster was speaking to her, and taking it from her, holding the saucer himself and shielding him from the gaze of the crowd so that he could grasp the cup with both hands, so that they would not see how much dribbled to the floor and fell across his shirt and the jacket of his suit. When he had finished, Webster took the cup from him and with his other hand fiddled in a trouser pocket for a handkerchief that had once been white and neatly wiped the Russian's chin and coat.

"We need to start now, Nikita. I'll translate the questions

for you. If you don't know the answers, then say so. Don't make anything up, just to please us. You must be very exact. That's important, terribly important."

For ninety minutes Dovrobyn answered their questions. Pausing every few seconds for Charlie to speak, while he found himself steadily growing in confidence. First the narrative of the hijacking, then to his own action, and through to his assessment of the personality of the Jews. On into the dispositions inside the aircraft. Where were the various groups of passengers? Where did Isaac stand when he was not in the main cabin, out of the range of the fish-eye? Where did David stand at the rear? Where did the girl stand? Who had slept the night before, and for how long? Where had they slept? What weapons had he seen? Did they have grenades? Were there explosives? How had they protected the doors of the aircraft? How was the trolley barrier fastened? What was the morale of the three? Who was the leader now?

The schoolmaster from Lvov was no fool. Not a man used to the world of strike and counterstrike, and of government ministers and ranking policemen and troops. But he was aware of his purpose in the room. The killing ground was being prepared; the markers and the pegs and the tapes were being laid. He saw it in the face of the soldier, the one with the gun at his waist, who said nothing, wrote nothing, only listened intently. There would be more men like that, hard and cold-faced men, who did not smile, whose attention was held by the task that confronted them. And he thought of his children who sat still and strapped in their upholstered seats, who had no defenses and who would hold the middle territory between the troops and David and Isaac and Rebecca. Acceptable that he should die, and the man who had followed him, but the children . . .

Could remember now the laughing and the shouting and the waving as the parents had brought them to the school, behind the old theater where the bus had been parked, and all of them in their best and neatest clothes, with the mothers around the girls combing and brushing yet again at their hair, and the fathers reaching in their pockets for kopeks for the boys and telling them not to buy candy, not to fidget at the ballet and to do as they were told. Twenty hours now they had sat as their mothers and fathers would have wished, in the smell and stench of the plane, stomachs heaving for lack of food, covered by the guns. Their ordeal would be as nothing compared with that which they would now face, the ordeal when the troops swarmed inside the aircraft.

"You cannot . . . you cannot . . . What will happen to the children? You will kill the children. On the plane these people will not hurt the children; they are correct to them. But if you go there, and you have to shoot, what will happen to my children?"

Not that any except Charlie understood what he said; just a gist and theme of acute worry, and they moved away from him. It is not pleasant to look on a man who has broken, who can sustain nothing more, who is convulsed in weeping, who has gone beyond his own unexplored limits.

"Nobody will hurt the children," Charlie said.

"If you attack the plane and they resist, if Isaac and David resist, then there must be shooting . . . then the children will be hurt. They are in my charge and I am not there."

"Nobody will hurt the children. All of them will be saved. There is a science in these things, and if we know where they are there is no risk."

"You confirm my fear. You will attack. There is no other reason for the questions you have asked me."

Charlie did not reply. Nothing to say. Had seen the children on the television screen, their meekness and their submission. Knew the hopelessness of giving the sort of guarantee he had just delivered. A used Ford and you don't need to service it for twenty years, bullshit. A science in these matters: crap and you know it, Charlie. Knew that when the troops went in the only thing that mattered was luck, a bloody great piece of luck. One good burst of gunfire, that's all they have to get off, and what do you have—fiasco, catastrophe, disaster. Put the army in and what becomes the priority? Kill the holding mob, or save the hostages, or can you even differentiate? Intertwined, the whole damn thing. All depends on whether they fight. Isaac, the little bugger, he'll fight; perhaps David too if he's caged in; and the girl, she might shoot if the hero boys are still standing. So how many lucky bullets do you need to hit those three and no one else? And how many from the opposition to screw the whole damned thing?

Charlie straightened up, rested his hand on the Russian's shoulder; tears still running, the fight and challenge dried up.

"I think he's had enough. You should find him a bed and keep him on ice."

"Express our thanks to him, please, Mr. Webster," the Home Secretary said. Dejected, oppressed by the knowledge that the decision for action was his and could be passed to neither senior nor subordinate. The circle broke and formed an aisle, through which Charlie led Dovrobyn. "Keep him warm," he told the Inspector, "and don't let the quacks give him a shot. We have to have him on tap."

He walked back to the console and looked out through the glass at the Ilyushin. Same old bloody story: nothing moving, nothing stirring, not a damn thing—just like always. But it was all going to start; hold your hats on your heads and drop your pants. The virginity about to be broken. Going to rupture the hymen of the big, inviolate bird.

He heard the Home Secretary say to the soldier, "Well, Major Davies, can it be done, and with reasonable chance of success?"

"A reasonable chance of success, yes, sir. Shouldn't be too difficult. We know all we're going to."

"When would you attempt it?"

"First light is ideal, but if there's deterioration, we could have a go at dusk tonight. We could get in during daylight, but the risk all round is greater."

A moment of consideration, as if the Home Secretary were rehearsing the sentence; then he blurted, "Make the preparations that you deem necessary, Major."

"Thank you, sir. There's a DC-6 over on the far side. Height of the doors is right, width of fuselage about the same, wing cover on approach matches. We'll do a bit of work with it, and you'll be contacted as soon as we're happy."

"Thank you, Major."

The session was concluded. Davies bustling on his way. Conversation mounting. A lightening of the atmosphere now that the crucial decision had been taken. Charlie sought out Clitheroe, tugged at his shirt sleeve and took him to the far corner, away from the crowd that now sensed blood and waited for the chase.

"It's a bit early, isn't it?" Charlie urged. "We've hardly talked to them yet, and now we're ready to plunge in."

"It wasn't my advice."

"But the tactic is to wear them down. Nag away at them, starve them out. That's the way it's done. What the Americans do, the Dutch, what we've tried in the past."

"Correct. That is the traditional way of handling these affairs. As I told you, the present course of action is not the one that I recommended."

"What are you going to do about it?"

"Mr. Webster, I'm not here to do anything. I'm here to give opinions when they are requested. My brief goes no further."

"So what's changed, what's put the balls into them?"

"You have, Mr. Webster. Your little games out on the tarmac have changed all that. Don't stop me, don't look aggressive, Mr. Webster. You asked me a question and I'll give you an answer. They were sitting in here watching Mr. Dovrobyn, believing he was about to die. They didn't like it; they didn't like the helplessness and impotence—that was a word that was flying round this room a fair bit—and they saw what you did. Probably you shamed them, Mr. Webster, shamed them into showing what they now regard as courage. They had been led to understand that there was no intervention they could make, and you demonstrated that there are occasions when a physical course of action can be both justified and successful. Now they wish to follow your example, Mr. Webster. Virility, I suppose, comes into it; they wish to match your virility.

"Don't look pained, Mr. Webster, don't regard me as an idiot. We've been through all this while you were bringing your rescued princess back from the dragon's castle; we've all had our say. Myself, the policeman, army liaison, the civil servants. Mine was a lone voice because I cannot offer exact solutions. I can only surmise what a state of mind will be, given certain deprivation factors.

"I understand a smattering of Russian, Mr. Webster—from my college days, and some of it has stayed with me. I gather you told Mr. Dovrobyn that there was a 'science in these matters'; you were referring to the question of storming the aircraft. A 'science' implies a solution if a correct procedure is followed. I cannot supply a 'science,' only an opinion, and that is why I am not listened to.

"And you must allow for the death of the second hostage. It has deeply shocked our masters; they did not expect, were not prepared for it, and therefore their anger is all the greater. And they are fearful now of seeming weak."

"It's bloody nonsense," said Charlie quietly.

"Not so much nonsense as cowardice, Mr. Webster. They are unwilling to repeat an experience. They do not have the courage. The previous two occasions when they have been confronted with this type of situation there had been no killing of hostages. Neither in Knightsbridge nor in Balcombe Street. They could afford to be patient then; there were no corpses for the world to see, to bear witness to their inability to intervene with a strong hand. You have to comprehend, and perhaps you do already, that the basis for the respect held by the Western democracies for the urban guerrilla is that so few persons can appear to ridicule the power of an established and elected government.

"By your own assessment, only one of the persons on the aircraft is, as we would say, the hard-liner and militant; the other two are his followers. Yet look around and count up the effort, the ingenuity, the technology, the striking power that have been assembled to eliminate this threat. All of this concentration was sitting on its collective backside, Mr. Webster, wondering what to do. They think now that unarmed, unprepared, you showed them a course of action."

"If they go in there shooting, there has to be risk to the children; it's like the headmaster said, and he's right. What do they want, another bloody Maalot, another fuck-up?"

"Perhaps they consider the risk to the children less substantive than the risk that they will see another man brought to the door of the aircraft, and after him another, and another after that . . ."

"But that's not your opinion. You know and I know that perhaps they will kill one more, but they're human beings in there. They're not animals; they won't be able to go on chopping like a slaughterhouse foreman. They couldn't sustain it."

"That's not what you said from the tarmac, Mr. Webster. They took great note of what you told them. They remember your every word"—Clitheroe speaking now in a tired, half-amused drawl. "As I told you, I have offered my advice and it was not accepted."

He passed Charlie a cigarette—expensive, with a gold-paper covering for the filter. Charlie took it instinctively—hadn't smoked coffin nails for years. Leaned his head for the light; blew the smoke into the murk of the room. Without giving any particular thought to it, Charlie said, "So how do we save them?"

"It depends on whom you want to save, Mr. Webster. If it's the children, I suppose they stand an equal chance, and it's a good one, whether Major Davies leads a heroic charge or whether we sit it out and people like myself give advice on a long-drawn-out standoff. The children will be safe.

"Or is it the others, my friend? If the soldiers assault the plane, then we can guarantee, I use your word, that they are unlikely to take time off for the niceties of capturing able-bodied prisoners. Shoot first, questions later is the doctrine of this type of operation. Is that what concerns you?

"Perhaps it should concern all of us: three young people who through a chain of circumstance stand condemned to die if the army takes the plane. Whether they are evil people, or misguided, or those whom in another context we would regard as courageous, they will not survive the visit of Major Davies.

"And that is not to be criticized: his men have wives and children and homes; they too will seek to come through the assault, and deserve to. If you wish these three to live, you must persuade them to surrender, and unconditionally, be-cause then they will go before the courts—perhaps here, probably in the Soviet Union—and you must believe the words of the Ambassador that were carried on the radio, that they will be unlikely to face the death penalty if indeed they are returned.

"There can be no happy outcome, yet there was no reason to expect anything else from the moment the aircraft landed. You've been very patient with me, Mr. Webster; I'm not used to such attention."

Charlie smiled and thanked him and moved without more comment back to the console.

Waste of time trying the radio unless someone was sitting

in the cockpit with the earphones on and waiting. Felt that his place was far from here, far from the green-carpeted floor, and the hum of the air conditioner and the polite laughter, and the deference to seniority. Knew he should be on the tarmac again, sitting on his backside in the sunshine, flicking the flies from his nose and wanting a drink, and waiting for something to happen. The pictures were in front of him, where he'd pinned them in the early morning, when the issues had been sharper and the gray fog hadn't blurred the outlines of his fa¹th. Three young faces, ordinary in their type to the point of boredom, and now trapped and caged and vicious and being broken on an anvil by a force they could not combat—only strike against, bloodily and irrelevantly.

Too long on the outside, Charlie; too long living and winning without the backup of name and rank and number, without legality and authority. As much a terrorist as these little bastards. Had a base camp, sure enough, to come to with the intelligence gained by deceit and stealth, but otherwise a man of his own whims, without a general to direct him and draw lines on his map. A wolf in the forest that is hated and hunted and which has no comrades beyond the brushwood.

Easy for some to hate these three, right, Charlie? Easy to label and brand and catalog them. Easier still if you had a chauffeur and a pennant and a chest of medal ribbons and a swagger stick. But harder if you knew the isolation, and the loneliness, and the fear that makes the stomach coil, as you did, Charlie. Disowned if you're caught, that was what they'd said when he went to Dublin; don't expect the FO to bail you out if the Guarda Siochana lifts you—and when you're caught, don't cough; that way you'll keep the pension and we'll see your wife doesn't have to go out to work and the kids get new shoes when they need them. All for a job, all for a way to pay the mortgage. Less motivation than those three.

Motivation, the fashionable word that meant damn all— meant you were thick and hadn't thought it out, or too young to know what went on. Motivation, the great confidence trick, the public relations target, what they told all the men who formed the starched khaki ranks and lined up to have Herself pin a cross of dulled metal on their chests and went back to barracks to shiver in a corner and wonder how they'd been so bloody stupid.

Years since Charlie had been in uniform; despised it; sneered at the sameness and the identity and the mob instinct of men who needed polished shoes and short haircuts. What did these people know of the three on the plane? How could they understand them? Called them terrorists, murderers, fanatics . . . all the usual claptrap. Getting tired, Charlie. Getting old, romantic, you silly old bugger. But they don't care, not even Clitheroe. Stuff it, Charlie, you're a raving old bore. You're not paid to think, to be the referee. Go back to counting the fag ends. Do something useful.

Charlie stood up in his chair and looked around him.

He attracted no attention; his moment of glory was past; no longer did the others wish to rub shoulders with his success. Assistant Chief Constable catnapping, Clitheroe reading. Home Secretary gone below. Nothing changed on the screen: David out of sight; Isaac and Rebecca at the forward entrance to the passenger cabin. Could read the defiance still blazoned on Isaac's face.

He walked out through the door and began the descent of the stairs, slowly, carefully, aware of the fatigue that wrapped him. Reckoned he would have about two hours at the plane before the military had satisfied themselves on the DC-6. Found his hand was out against the wall, steadying himself as he went down.

Didn't recognize him at first, the man he saw through the open door of the second landing. Seemed shed of his earlier confidence and poise that had been on display in the control tower. Charlie stopped at the entrance, hesitated a moment.

"It's the Israeli isn't it? . . . Benitz, Colonel Benitz. The one who thought our friends were about to surrender."

"That was I; I remember you too. You were very kind."

"Did they dump you in here?" Charlie looked around the room. "Looks like you've a plague or something. Not exactly in the center of things, is it?"

"It is not the intention of people here that I should be in the center."

"What were you sent for?" Charlie said, casting off the small talk.

"I was sent to help you persuade these people to surrender."

"Why you?"

"It was thought that an army man might appeal to them."

"And they just left you sitting here, kicking your heels—our crowd, I mean? They haven't talked to you since you were up in the tower first thing? Incredible."

"I sit here and I wait to be asked."

"Well, you won't be sitting here much longer. They've just dropped a hostage. . . ." Heard the Hebrew obscenity, saw Benitz clench his fist. "Didn't they tell you? Didn't anyone even tell you that? They dropped one this morning, and there'll be another this afternoon, and then they plan a shooting gallery, with one each hour. We're gearing the heavies up, to go and thump them."

"You should have gone this morning when the one you call Isaac was asleep."

"Could have had them all then. Looking back on it, that is. With hindsight we could have wrapped it all up. And saved the hostage, and whoever else gets in the way when the military attack." Charlie had exhausted his politeness, wanted to be on his way. Said as an afterthought, "You think we could still talk them down?"

Benitz forward in his seat, tensed and trying to hide his elation. Casual. "I think it would be possible. If I were at the plane and could talk to them."

"And what would you be telling them?"

"Surrender, unconditional surrender."

"Before the next deadline, before the military go in."

"Surrender, unconditional surrender."

"Could save a deal of mopping up."

"Could save lives, Charlie."

Charlie looked behind him, satisfied himself that the staircase was unused; thumb in his mouth, the nail chewed between his teeth. "I'm going to the plane now. Perhaps . . . if you wanted, you could come with me. . . . The message from your government is that there should be immediate and unconditional surrender?"

"Yes, that is the message," said Benitz, looking mesmerically hard into Charlie's wilting eyes.

"But if they surrender, then perhaps they go back to Russia."

"If they surrender there will be no more killing. No more of the passengers will be hurt, and they themselves will live. I understand that what happens to them later is not yet decided."

No opportunity for Benitz to use the telephone, to give explanations to London, to ask for fresh guidance. Prided himself that he had covered well on the hammer-blow disappointment of the news that a hostage was already dead, that his last instructions were now invalid, inappropriate. Charlie had taken his arm and was hurrying him down the steps and seemed to stagger and falter—the mark of a man, Benitz realized, who was close to the ultimate of exhaustion.

Too late now, too far gone the opportunity for them to barter the lives of the passengers for their freedom. Possible before the captain had died, possible before they had taken their hostage. But the moment now lost. Benitz searched his mind, among the briefings and the messages he had received in Tel Aviv and from London, as to what solution he might fashion that would most please those he served.

15

Waiting for nothing, passing the minutes, spanning the chasm of time, David stayed in the dully lit recess at the back of the aircraft, his body pressed hard against the fastened drinks trolley. He had not moved since the taking of the Italian from his seat to the doorway. After the impact noise of the shot, which had sent a shudder through him, involuntary and unsought, barely a muscle or a nerve had functioned. Just stood there, hearing the rhythmic sounds of his wristwatch, willing the progress of the hands. The gun was held loosely across his waist, apparently ready to be fired at a moment of crisis and quickly and expertly, giving the impression of a man who had found confidence and was his own master. David alone could plumb the deception.

The exact moment when the knowledge that all was over, that the struggle was hopeless, had come to David was not clear even to him. Perhaps it had been on the pavement in Kiev, far over the time horizon, as Moses had stumbled and shuffled through his pockets in search of the stocking cap. Perhaps it had been in the woodsman's hut when Isaac had first raised the plan for the breakout and in so doing had usurped his own rightful and accepted place as innovator and initiator. Perhaps it had been with the words, flat and unemotional, of Ground Control over Hannover when they had been ordered to fly on. Perhaps it had been as the dawn had risen, lighting the putrid atmosphere of the cabin, and he had witnessed the fear and hatred that alternated on the faces of those who were guarded by the guns. Perhaps the moment had come, the journey been completed, when he had seen the surprise and terror and comprehension merge on the face of the harmless and inoffensive little Italian as the critical truth had splashed on him that he was to be involved, auditioned and given a critical part in their drama. Which moment he did not know, but at one of them had come the knowledge that the game was completed, that he was ready for what Isaac called surrender and capitulation.

They were big and bold words, and worthy of a greater occasion.

Armies surrendered, governments capitulated. They signified momentous times—nothing as scabrous and as dirty and fetid as the collapse in morale of three youngsters who were far from home and far from orientation and far from the tangibles onto which they could hook themselves. Too far, little Kingfisher.

Babi Yar had been a great wrong. Thousands machinegunned because they were Jewish; for no other reason. A hundred times a thousand people had died in the ravine of Babi Yar. Jews, and not remembered, and the cheap belated monument made no mention of them. And those who came with flowers upon the anniversary, upon the day in late September, they were stoned and scourged and imprisoned—or "detained," as the authorities called it. Babi Yar had been the flint which ignited the torch that had welded the four of them together; a desire to avenge an evil, to tilt the balance of the wrong . . . and now the water had come in its torrent and immersed and destroyed the final flickering of that small flame. Sunk it in a stinking obsolete shell, surrounded by enemies, encircled by loathing, hemmed in by the power of tanks and automatic guns. He had liked Moses, known him better than Isaac, because he was younger and less able and more dependent, and because he laughed more. Remembered him now, untidy, confused, willing to try, willing to become a casualty and a statistic. And Moses was already taken, and had bought them time—at what cost David could not know—and for what?

The Italian should not have died for Babi Yar, nor even the schoolmaster who had jumped. Not their quarrel, not their issue. They did not wear the uniform of the authorities, did not carry the badge of office presented by the bullies who would not permit prayers to be said by the ditch where the Jews had died that had become a garbage dump. They had no blame, no right to expect involvement. Nor was it they who sent the Jews to the camps, arrested those who sought passage to Israel. They had no guilt; yet one had died, and another had been intended to fall in his place.

If that was the cost of avenging Babi Yar and all that it had

accumulated in shame, then the price was too high; that was
the feeling of David as he stood far from the others at the
rear of the cabin aisle. How to surrender, how to capitulate?
Twin words burning an aching in his person. How to con-
clude his part without destroying what Isaac sought, without
the betrayal of his friends? He had thought long and hard
behind the unmoving eyes, struggling with his tiredness till
the solution came reluctantly upon him. A brutal, desperate
solution that brought a groping chill over his body. And then
the decision was made, and there followed a calmness and a
clarity of thought that had been denied him many hours.

Often the American had looked at him, peering and twisting around in his seat, inviting conversation, still crowned
with the knotted handkerchief that he wore across his scalp.
While David had wrestled with his problem the man had kept
his silence, bided his time. Now Edward R. Jones, Jr., recognized the lightness in the face, appreciated that he could
speak.

"How long will you go on like this? You shoot one, you lose
one, but the British aren't talking; they aren't moving, not an
inch." The same nagging, grating voice, primed with aggression. David understood not a word; knew only that behind
the deference to the gun and his youth, the older man
sneered at him, was suffused with contempt. He shook
his head, shrugged his shoulders and looked on down the
aisle.

"I said, how much longer do we have to sit on our back-
sides here, waiting for you to call it quits?" David turned with
the tolerance of one who is irritated by a wasp but cannot
gather the energy to swat it, a half smile on his mouth.

"Don't you speak English? Don't you understand me? Was
it only the girl who went to school?"

David no longer cared to listen; shut himself apart again,
sensing the subsidence of the American in the face of his
inability to communicate. Heard him mutter to his wife, with
her loud clothes and rinsed hair and hands that sought to
silence her man, prevent provocation. What did that fool
know of Babi Yar; what did he know of the labor camps; what
did he know of militia headquarters, of the informers, of the
interrogations, of the humiliations? What did he know?

His eyes roved over the heads of the passengers. Through

the hours he had come to recognize some, to know which were eager for his approval and would cringe for him, which tried to hide their pent-up detestation. He had begun to acknowledge them as a myriad of individuals, had carved faces and personalities from the one solid mass that they had been on the journey. The children were still quiet—he could not say how or why; still patient. The old man with the farm boots bristled his independence as best he might from the confines of his seat belt. The pilot, Tashova, with her hair trimmed in the shop, who lofted herself above them, superior to their struggle. The navigator, cautiously interested in what happened close to him, but never speaking. The Italians who had screamed, some of whom still cried and held each other's arms. The woman halfway forward, in the widow's clothes, with the baby on her knee and a pitch of smell around her and the reddened, weather-stained face of the country, who beseeched him each time he passed for milk for the child. The man beside her, who seemed a stranger, and whispered that she should not speak lest she draw attention to herself. Those who were frightened, those who were bold, those who were indifferent, those who rested on their nerves and those who darted their eyes to accumulate each nuance of mood from their captors. He had begun to know them all, but the familiarity had won him no friendship, only served to breed the culture of their hatred. No warmth, no love, no affection, only the loathing of those who watched him now.

Abruptly David started to move the length of the aisle. His hands had tightened on the gun barrel, fingers entwined around the trigger guard, and in front of him, their faces masked in shadow, were Isaac and Rebecca. Without a victory, he thought, not even there where it had lain waiting. Should have won her by conquest; should have taken her, how many hours, weeks, months ago? Isaac had struck her, out there in the full gaze of the passengers, and now she fawned at him and played to him, and was close so that their bodies touched and their voices would be soft with the intimacy of equal conversation. Perhaps that was the defeat which hurt him above all. One could be proud and surrender to an army, capitulate to a government, but when defeat came from the hands of your friend, when the prize at stake was not great but the way between the thighs of a girl, then there was the capacity for wounding. He had struck her, and she had come back to him: the bitch that snivels at the ankle when it has been whipped.

And Isaac no better, on no higher a pedestal. He had been betrayed by her, and now he nestled his shoulder close and protectively by hers. Irrelevant now, decision taken, glove thrown down, die cast, participation in their affairs completed. Sounded strangely formal, but then, his mind could no longer pick through the labyrinth of thoughts and images. Just a child she had seemed to him, a follower, who was not worth the attention of affection or of love, and now that she was taken by his friend the surge of regret dominated him, and he fought to hold back the tears that welled and rose in his tired, sleep-lost, exhausted eyes.

As he passed her, the woman with the baby clutched his arm.

"Sir, there can be milk for the baby. That cannot hurt you."

He saw the pleading, and the screwed, torn face of the infant, and the nervousness of the man who counseled quiet.

"I don't know," he said hollowly.

"But you are the leader," she persisted. "If you tell the others to allow it, they will not prevent it. Milk can be sent to the plane."

"It is not easy . . ."

"It is just for a child. He has not been fed for many hours. A child can do you no harm."

Angrily David wrenched himself clear of the clinging hand and continued up the aisle.

If he had taken the girl, it would not have been as it was now; his stake and his commitment would have bulged with the fulfillment. Could have been in the hut, on the dry and dusty planking, or on the sacking of the window cover if they had first shaken the spiders and cobwebs loose, or in the forest among the leaves and watched by the sky and the birds. Looked at her closely now, eating into her clothes, tugging at the creased and monotonous dress; drifted his thoughts to the whiteness that would be her skin, the softness that would be her breasts, the firmness of the hips on which he would have spent himself. Why, why had it not happened? Why had there never been the moment? And when he had gone from them, would either understand that it was because he loved them, both of them, as his sister and brother?

Isaac and Rebecca had ceased to talk and watched curiously as he came awkwardly toward them, sensing in their separate ways that the control he so obviously sought to maintain was a wasted, puny thing.

There were many contrasts between the two men who walked together across the car park that had been designated for operational traffic only.

Both were trained and expert counterinsurgency operatives—CIOs in the restricted training manuals—but the methods they had learned to use and that suited their differing temperaments were hugely varied. Charlie Webster, forty-nine, married, two kids; hard put to meet the bills, keep the garden trim; done it all and seen it all, and opted out, tried to close the file. Arie Benitz, thirty-one, single, devoid of ties and personal relationships; a room at the barracks; the seven-days-a-week student, top of the tree and looking for a higher summit. Charlie, who had survived to grow old and paunchy through cunning and stealth and the ability to merge into backgrounds. Benitz, the direct, impetuous fighter, faster and dirtier than those they pitted him against. Charlie, who saw all points of argument from whatever segment of the spectrum. Benitz, under no such disadvantage, his world neatly divided into the compartments of right and wrong. Charlie, with the flesh to spare under his chin and the haunted, flickering eyes of a man who has been hunted and harried without the strength of military-unit comradeship to turn to. Benitz, muscled, vibrant, his strength undisguised by the hanging, ill-fitting clothes the Royal Air Force had dressed him in, having to chop his stride to keep pace with the other.

Charlie had never been part of a spearhead attack team. Benitz had never taken the role of the deep-sleeper infiltration agent. Out of their very diversity, the men found a respect the one for the other.

Acting without an order was Charlie, but then, there were many precedents in his career for that, and didn't give a damn for the inquiries his initiative might rain on him. Had made his decision that Benitz alone could help him avoid the mayhem that he believed was the only possible result for a storm assault by the SAS on the Ilyushin. In his conceit, and Charlie was not short of that, as befitted a man who had spent an operational life outside the barracks walls, he had told himself that he alone of the Crisis Committee, Charlie Webster, understood the capabilities and state of mind of the three young people, and the heart of it was his conviction that Isaac, the little bastard, would stand and shoot it out, and be prepared to die. Across the car park he saw it all—the crossfire, the smoke, the screaming, the children rising from their seats to escape the blasting of the automatics, the bodies cut and ripped by the tempered steel of the shells, and when it was over, just the blood and the moaning, shock and pain. Children like his, like the ones in his road, like the ones at the bus stop in the morning, the ones who chased a football across the street. And all because they'd lost their cool up in the control-tower clouds, just as Clitheroe said. The big men from London who'd seen a single stiff, and couldn't face the same humiliation again, and would hide behind their bloody outrage and find the easy exit.

So he walked with Arie Benitz to the Transit van where the driver idled with his morning paper, and toyed with the cigarette that he had tucked into the palm of his hand.

Charlie said, "It's the same drill that we've used before. Close to the aircraft are some petrol tankers, where the Special Air Service detachment are holed up. I want to talk to them first, hear their feel of it, and then we'll head out to the plane. When the van is behind the tankers, it stops and we jump for it, flick the doors and off she goes. It's what they're doing to ferry the military back and forward." Benitz listened, well satisfied.

The Israeli climbed inside, Charlie following, both squatting on the floor of the van, the closing of the door the cue for the driver.

"You have clearance to take me?" Benitz asked.

"We can do without any more paperwork on this caper."

"It would not be like this at home."

Charlie said quietly, so that his words were almost lost in the echoed motion of the engine, "Sometimes you have to kill them, but not for the sake of it, and not when you risk the innocent."

"It is a luxury that is seldom given us, to be able to decide. The tide is not often with us. It is rare for me to have the order that I have been given, that I should help your efforts toward a surrender."

The only windows in the closed rear of the van were set in the doors, throwing little light upon the two men, preventing them from seeing the army cordon that they skirted. Had they enjoyed a view of the armored cars and the machine-gun nests, neither would have been impressed; both in their ways regarded the big battalions as a distortion of strength in the minuscule close-quarters combat in which they had achieved their reputations.

Arie Benitz said with a studied casualness, "It was suggested in Tel Aviv that if I were to talk to these people, explain to them that it is the wish of my government that they surrender without further action, they would be likely to listen to me. For that I think that we will need to board the aircraft, to talk to them direct, if I am to communicate the message with the necessary emphasis."

Won't know what's hit them, thought Charlie. Shining bloody angel climbs the ladder, and then they find he's scaled and tailed and horned, and bringing the news that destroys them, kicking them in the crotch and with interest, then boots them again, just when they're getting used to it. Not a job you'd want, Charlie, not if they were your own people; not telling them it was all over, all down the drain, that they should have stayed home.

"We're just about there," the driver shouted back. "Ease the door and go the moment I stop. Don't forget to close it again, and don't stop, don't hang about."

Charlie crawled forward, brushing against the Israeli's body, scrabbling for the door handle; moved it and waited. The stop was sudden, lurching them together, and Charlie had the door open and slid clumsily, showing his stiffness, to the ground. Benitz out straight after him, and both blinking in the newfound sunshine. Charlie fastened the door, banged lightly on it and watched it pull away.

"Get yourself behind the wheels"—a command, not to be considered and questioned—and the two settled themselves against the warmed rubber of the tires that soaked up the heat. From his left side, Charlie was aware of the blur of camouflage uniform that sprinted to him. A day's growth on the face, dark and mixed with the sweeps of lotion used to banish the whiteness of skin. "Captain Howard. They didn't tell me anyone was coming out; there's been nothing about you on the radio." No suspicion, only confusion that protocol had not been observed.

"It's because of him," Charlie said quickly; "they didn't want it all over the net. This is Colonel Arie Benitz, Israel Defense Forces, flown in by the RAF. His line at home is this situation. His presence is sensitive."

Howard acknowledged the explanation; none of his business anyway.

"There's not much here at the moment. The Major and ten others are working on the DC-6 over on the far side. Leaves seven of us here, with a basic fire-cover role. The body's still out there by the wheels, and we gather there's no contact about shifting it. The camera isn't picking up much, but the tall boy had just come down towards the front, so they're all together now where the fish-eye picks them up."

No more explanation required, and they stood together, the soldier and the Israeli waiting for Charlie's lead. But he was quiet, saying nothing, trying to work at the problem that itched and scratched somewhere far back in his mind. That did not fit the pattern, that was out of place and therefore annoying and that he should clear up. That Benitz should want them to surrender, and nothing specific and categorical on their future. Wouldn't want them shipped out, couldn't, but there must be more to it; the Russian must have been shooting his mouth; must have been a deal somewhere down the line, a deal that they hadn't been told of in the tower. Had to be something that was covert, that was being kept from them. But all a bit of a bloody mystery. Nothing new in that, Charlie; when did anyone ever give you the grand picture, the big design?—just packed you off and told you to get on with it. But he'd have to clear it up, sometime, get it all sorted out; people should know where they stood. . . .

From the cement hut the half torso of a civilian emerged, sweeping his head around, searching for the army officer.

Excitement in his voice, urgency. "Captain, come and look here. On the fish-eye, they're hanging on to each other like it's good-by, hugging, kissing, shaking hands, the whole works."

Everything else erased from Charlie's thoughts. Jesus help us, not a bloody breakout, not a split for it, not a fucking slaughter inside. Captain mirroring him, barking names, and as the soldiers ducked from the hut to their appointed fire positions, the young officer was cocking his Ingham submachine gun with a single noise-laden movement.

Rebecca struggling not to cry, Isaac gruffly and distantly silent and refusing to dispute and debate, and David all the time stumbling through the explanation. All holding and clinging to one another as a last link was forged with the past they had known.

"It's treachery, it's cowardice to both of you, but I cannot last any longer. I cannot remain here, not inside here, closed in here, waiting, waiting, waiting for what will happen. It has been too long for me, and it has broken me. . . . Not any longer, not trapped in here, sitting and standing and looking and waiting through hours and days more, perhaps. There has to be a gesture for me—the only gesture I am capable of, but I cannot last any longer. I had never thought it would take so long, that time would creep so slowly, that there would be nothing but existing here, and waiting. And perhaps then we die, or we feel the shackles and the manacles on us. I cannot wait for that; I cannot wait as they did before they were taken to Babi Yar, stand in a column and walk in a line. We are doomed, Isaac, doomed and damned and finished, and I am afraid. Afraid because I do not know what will happen to us. I cannot wait any more to be answered."

He felt the fingers of the girl tight at the back of his neck, holding his shirt collar, clamped and adhesive to him, and below at his arms the pressure of Isaac, both pinioning him against the lavatory door as if wanting to strengthen him in his purpose. Neither tried to turn him, so that there was now no retreat, no backing from his course. "Isaac, it was brave and courageous, and it might have been successful. But that time is gone, and I can no longer help you. I want to leave you in my own fashion and I do not want to look back. I am only a weakness to you now. Help me, Isaac, help me. Walk away, take Rebecca and go far so that I will not see you again."

His arm around Rebecca's waist, Isaac pulled the two of them clear, extricated himself from the tentacles of involvement. Saw the deep, nut-brown, misted eyes; felt the hand join with his own; held it, gripped it. "We showed the bastards, David. We showed them what we·could do. Only four of us, and now they know of us. Moshe and you and me and Rebecca. They will remember us. We are not beaten yet, I promise you, David. We are not beaten yet. . . ."

"They will come with the guns tonight. . . . They are waiting for the darkness . . . only the darkness, when you are asleep . . ."

"On your way, David."

David smiled, and there was the freshness of his youth and the charm of his mouth and the flourish of victory that curled at his nostrils. He reached into his pocket and drew from it the straight stick magazine and tossed it easily toward Isaac, who caught it with his free hand.

"I will need only one. I have no need for another."

"We will talk of you in Israel. . . ."

David was gone from their sight, to the aircraft door—the Kingfisher flown from them. They heard the sound of his body thudding onto the concrete below.

"One out, sir. On the ground and armed."

A dismembered, disconnected voice to Charlie, who crouched by the wheel close to the booted feet of the marksman. Soldiers crawling and scuffing on the ground to gain better vision, a superior aiming point, and the captain wreathed in puzzlement.

"Just one, no hostages?"

"Just the one. Armed. He has an SMG."

A pause in time, Charlie and Benitz and the military frozen still.

"Doesn't look like a white-flag job. Gun's up now."

"We'd prefer him alive if we can have him that way. Don't drop him yet."

"At this range I can take his kneecap out. Certainty." Driplike, the leaking faucet of the intoning voice.

"Hold it, hold it."

In Charlie's ear the captain whispered, "What in Christ's name do you think he's at?"

"I don't know," Charlie answered. "I just don't know."

Never looking away, speaking from the side of his mouth and with the quiet of a man who is in church, Arie Benitz said, "It's very clear, Charlie. He has made his farewells, and now he wants to die. Better they should do it quickly, and kindly."

Charlie turned to look at the Israeli. Too late. The face averted, the eyes hidden.

Bruised, shaken, grazed at the shins where the cheap and thin cloth of his trousers had been ripped by the fall, David rose first to one knee, then more slowly edged his way upright onto his feet. Had to fight for breath, recapture the air blown from his lungs and combat the ferocity of the sun bursting into his face after the diluted grayness of the Ilyushin interior. Focusing and fastening now on the changed environment, and he had succeeded, escaped, freed himself from the cage, turned his back on the prison. A step forward, and another, testing the unfamiliarity of his surroundings, but feeling the warmth on his face, the wind at his back, the exultation at the freedom. Around to his right an armored car, and the big gun traversing and following him, locking onto his body with the sights; repetition to the left, with the crew scrambling on its surface, and to the front the immobile, precious tankers. The tankers that held their salvation, carried the fuel they needed if they were to see the coast and the orange groves and the mountains of Israel; bright, gaudy, abrasive in their paintwork. And a triumph in his eyes when he captured the half glimpse of the short stubbed barrel of the rifle deep in the darkness beside the forward wheel of the central tanker. That was where they were—hidden, covert—and he had discovered them.

Remember the bird that Timofey spoke of. Remember the Kingfisher bird, fast and darting, sure in attack, brilliant in retreat, with the colors of a prince and a victor. Remember the dream of the Kingfisher, to be carried safe to a faraway place on the wings of speed and color. But the nets had come, and the beaters, and the men with guns, and there were no longer the riverbanks and bushes of concealment. They have clipped you, my Kingfisher bird; lured you from your sanctuary; broken, violated, trampled you.

The dream would not last. The sleep would soon be lost. Only the clarity of the machine guns and the poking, prying rifle barrel would remain.

Five shots in the first burst, finger snatching at the trigger bar, feeling the throbbing pumping of the recoil against his shoulder, watching the creeping and ineffective gatherings of dust that told him he was short, that he would not reach the man behind the wheel.

A heartbreaking desperation of silence.

"Come out, you pigs. Come out and fight. Come out and shoot. I'm here for you to kill."

Fire again—whispered the instruction to himself. Dropped down to one knee. Take the aim steadily, don't hurry, there is time now—time to control the shaking of the wrist, time to hold the flight of the barrel till it steadies. Why don't they shoot? Why don't they end it? Don't they know, can they not understand, that the reserves of courage are not bottomless? They must shoot soon, the miserable twisted, cancered pigs; they must shoot soon. How long do they think the gun can be held, how long before it drops, before the hands rise in surrender of their own jurisdiction?

Aim again and fire, so that they must shoot back.

"You cannot make me grovel before you—not at the last, not now. You cannot want that, to make me surrender, crawl in capitulation to you."

Shoot, shoot; hurt the pigs, wound them, anger them. Finger sealed on the trigger, coalesced with it, melted to it, the hammering against the muscle of his shoulder. The dirt trail inching forward, creeping to the tire, hunting the pig in his sty, searching for him, sniffing for him, the long waving line of ricochets and flying bullets closing on his target.

"Find him. Find him!" David screamed.

One bullet fired in retaliation. For the marksman it was an easy shot, easier than any he had known in the lightning street exchanges in the Falls Road of Belfast when he had been with infantry before joining the SAS. Seventy yards and a static target—better odds than in a fairground gallery, and all the time in the world to line the crossed wires of the telescopic sight on the upper chest. Time to reflect, too, before the captain tapped his shoulder, time to look at the face and its contorted and twisted bedrock, time to see the heaving of the chest. Seemed to be talking to himself, the little bugger; seemed to be saying something, all the time he was firing. Too easy, really; not even worth thinking about; never get a pigeon that simple, not even a bloody rook.

David was picked off the ground, hurled a dozen feet backward; he came to rest spread-eagled, arms and legs outstretched, the gaping and quick-staining entry wound a tribute to the marksman's skill. There were no convulsions, no tremors, no useless lingering of life.

On his hands and knees, low under the chassis of the tanker, Charlie Webster saw him fall; seemed to feel himself the power and hitting thrust of the one answering blow; closed his eyes, screwed them shut. He felt the Israeli's arm swathed across his back, and the knot of the fist clamped in the shirt above his shoulder. Heard the man sigh, a low whisper of pain. So, even he feels it, thought Charlie; even he, who is hardened and tempered and has killed many—even he feels the mother's hurt. Head of the bloody storm squad, even him.

"But Isaac won't sell himself so cheap," said Charlie.

They had walked five kilometers back from the police station.

More than two hours since they had been called from the cells, expecting only another session of interrogation; instead, they had been led up the stairs and then out into the hallway of the building. Their papers had been returned to them, and the man in uniform had swung on his heel, leaving the couple to cope for themselves with the weight of the heavy swing doors and find their own way back to their home.

Hardly a word had passed between David's parents as they had trudged the length of the streets and along the pitted sidewalks. Nothing to say, nothing to communicate. Old and wise enough to know the virtue of quiet. There had been hours of questioning: first the mother on her own; then later, when the father had been brought from work, they had stood side by side. A night spent in the cells, and then more questions through the morning, stolidly enduring the repetitions of the officer behind the desk. Always the same point, no deviation from the perpetual question. Who were his friends?

Whom did he go out with? Whom did he associate with? Again and again and again.

Never a need for them to resort to threats. They were elderly, defenseless, incapable of resistance, and they had answered. Moshe . . . Isaac . . . Rebecca . . . there were no others. They had been shown the police photographs of the injured policeman; they had been told of the seizing of the airliner, of the killing of the pilot, that the aircraft had landed in Britain, which was a country too far away and inaccessible for them to conjure the necessary images. The officer had said their son would die there, in a foreign country, or if he surrendered would be brought back to face trial and execution in his own city; he seemed not to mind either course.

Then they had been permitted to go.

There had been a cluster of neighbors outside the house—some Jewish, some not—but all had drifted away as the couple approached their home. Word of plague spreads fast, and they were contaminated, this pair, dangerous to touch, unwise to associate with. They did not speak to those who backed away at their approach; there was no reason to.

David's father opened the front door and put his arm around his wife's shoulders. It had been a proud household, exemplary in the neatness of the three ground-floor rooms in which they lived. It would take them many hours to clear the debris from the floor, to shift the confusion of the search from the threadbare carpet. They had been thorough in their work: every drawer emptied, every closet spilled out, every chest upturned, every ornament split open.

Thrown into the fire grate, the glass smashed, was the large portrait photograph of their son, taken many years back on the day of Bar Mitzvah: young, radiant; close-cut washed-down hair; promise and hope. David's mother drew it from its resting place on the newspaper that in summer covered the coal and chopped wood. It should not be there when the girls returned from the home of their friend.

16

Alone among the passengers who could see from the starboard windows, Anna Tashova had sat her ground; not flinched during the hurricane of shooting; stayed close to the glass until the solitary response. Seen it all, heard it all, enjoyed and relished it all. Her hands had come up from her lap as if she were about to clap them together as David had jerked, then tumbled backward; but she had desisted, just as she had stifled the cheer of exultation that was in her throat. Kept it private, close to herself, savoring the body stretched out full in her view when she reached across the passenger who had taken the window seat back in Kiev. She felt no pity, no horror, no sadness at the snuffing out of the life; instead gloried that her captain was at last remembered and revenged.

She had noticed long ago the way that some of the passengers craved the friendship of their captors, mimicked the collaborators of the old wartime days, and this had brought no surprise to her. Despicable and foul, but to be anticipated: of course there would be those without the sinew and the guts to fight who would wheedle and smile for favors, and hope to win advantage and precedence; thought they could gain safety from their deference. They would be recalled when the affair was over; they would be named, denounced, spoken of. And this was the time of the fighters and of a moment of victory, with the spoils of war bleeding and motionless on the concrete.

But it was to be expected that some would choose to fraternize. At the seminar on hijack theory to which she had gone the last summer in Moscow, she had heard the lecturer speak of the common practice of passengers in seeking to identify with the men who held the guns. There had been a titter of laughter around the hall, but the man on the dais had stamped on that, told them this was not just to be expected, could be guaranteed.

She had talked of that among the cockpit crew with whom she had shared her next flight, and all had agreed that faced with the seizure of an aircraft by force they would never come to terms with terrorists, only play them along for the greatest benefit of their passengers. They were brave words, spoken in safety and comfort and calm. Later, she had wondered what type of person might confront her—educated or illiterate, young or old, nervous or controlled. Natural that flight deck should think of those things; but she had found no answer, had not prepared herself for the two young men who had crashed their way through her cockpit door.

For hours, interminably, she had sat upright, staring to the front, trying to shut out the events enacted round her. She had watched the headmaster taken to his death, had not seen and did not know the manner of his escape; watched again as the Italian was pulled to his execution. Now she turned her head, glancing from window to window, swinging around so that she could see behind her, alive and vital because she had seen the man fall and watched the progress of the ribbon of blood that stretched a yard or so from him, highlighted on the tarmac.

So they did not always win, these people, these vermin. The victory was not always theirs. The one who called himself Isaac, that was the one she wanted to see fractured and pulped and demolished. She could wait for that, if it took another day, another week. To hear him scream and plead and collapse with pain. She found her thighs squeezed together, a sweated dampness, shoulders hunched, her arms rigid, all for the hatred of the young one with the curly hair and the confidence who stood now at the rear of the aircraft where once his friend had been. She was hungry, thirsting, longing for a cigarette, yearning to join the sporadic lavatory queues; but she would not bend, would not ask, not of these people. Would not give them pleasure of offering her their favors.

They had not spoken since David had gone.

Isaac at the back separated by the length of the cabin from Rebecca, abandoning her, casting her adrift, keeping his own dark counsel. Neither of them had watched him die, not willing to weaken their own fiber, endanger it through seeing the performance of a comrade resolved on taking his own life because his will had sapped and crumbled. Unable to shut out the noise of the gunfire—the little staccato bursts of the sub-machine gun; the one report of the heavier, vicious killing rifle. Impossible to block that noise, curtail the fleeting images of what had happened; but no necessity to look and stare and break the peace a friend had found.

Where to run now, Isaac; where to hide now that they know that one at least among you was ordinary, human, flesh and blood? Where to go to, where to crawl to, where to dig? David had died, uselessly, stupidly and believing in the value of a gesture. For you too, Isaac? Follow the leader? Follow the Party? Shit. No. No. We fight them, and we hit them, kick their testicles, hold their windpipes, twist their arms. Fight them.

Oblivious of the passengers, he strode up the aisle, gesturing to Rebecca not to come to meet him, to hold her position, not to move from her place that guarded the open doorway. Never looked behind, never believed that any would dare to rise up against him.

"I give them one more hour. Then there will be another. Another for them to watch. One o'clock for the next, and one every hour after that. We will bring them in a line so that all can see them, all who stand out there; they will see them and they can watch their clocks for the precision with which the next will fall."

"Why, Isaac? What is there to achieve? After David? What is left for us?"

"Because David was a coward."

"How can you say that? It was he who walked out to face them."

"Because that was the fool's escape, the quickest path. He was a coward and he was beaten, and he would not stand at our shoulder. We have to show that we are not beaten. One every hour; that will show that we are not defeated."

"Then they will attack us, storm the aircraft; they will kill us, Isaac." A breathiness in her words, the gilded light in her eyes, and she clung to his arm, the little girl again, small and feminine and clinging, who has found her man and will follow, hugging at his body. "They will kill us, Isaac."

As he laughed, she saw what she took to be madness—the

insane, fanatical desire for self-immolation, the wish for martyrdom; and she felt the great force that drew her toward him as the sensation of vertigo drags a man to the cliff face. She had no strength to struggle against it, no willingness to do so.

"If we cannot go to Israel there is nothing left but to die here," she said.

Isaac broke away from her, eased himself clear and went carefully toward the open door. A sharp and darting glance around the corner and to the outside. Time to see Charlie Webster there to the front of the tankers, arms folded, as if he were prepared to wait a lifetime, would stay as long as necessity required. Another man behind him, who wore a suit and who was younger, carrying, wearing the distinctive features of his own people. A bare second Isaac had been visible, and Charlie Webster had reacted to the movement.

"We have to talk to you, Isaac." The flattened voice, drained of emotion, devoid of tone, patient and carrying across the no-man's-land of the tarmac. "We have to talk again, Isaac."

Hidden from them and close to the aircraft wall, he whispered over his shoulder to Rebecca, "Cover behind me. Really this time, without mistake." Stayed watching till he saw her rise and straighten and walk to the center of the aisle, take her position, standing where she could see all the passengers. He would miss David. Frightened, abject, pathetic David, who at least would have stood and presented a front of reliability, but the girl . . .

"There is nothing to say," he shouted. Keep back from the door, he told himself; no target, no aim for the marksmen; give the bastards nothing. "I told you we wanted the fuel for the plane by ten o'clock or we would punish you for it. The man is there for you to see. At one o'clock there will be another if we have not had the fuel; at two there will be another; at three there will be another. Every hour from one o'clock.

"What time will you have the darkness you want, Mr. Webster? What time will that come?—eight hours after we start, nine perhaps. Before it is dark and your troops can come for us, Mr. Webster, how many will you be able to count down there beside the one who waits for company? There is no reason for you to stand there. You gain nothing from it; we will not allow you to repeat what you did earlier."

The answering call, faint and hard for him to hear: "Isaac, there is much to talk about. It has been a long fight for you, and your cause has been heard. But there is nothing further to be gained for you."

"There is fuel for the aircraft—that has yet to be gained. If you do not bring it, then you must stand there and you must watch and you must discover whether you like what you see. Understand this, Mr. Webster: we have nothing against you; we want little of you; we want only the fuel. It is a small thing for you; it will not cost you much—not set against the lives you are playing with."

Isaac crawled back and away from the door and then stood up, brushed the grime from his trousers and seemed to laugh at her.

"If they shout again, you talk to them, let them hear you, let them see you. Perhaps David went too early." He walked past her, not with haste, but casually, cosseting his gun; before he reached the drinks trolley where he would again take his stance, he was whistling, a song from the Ukraine, of his people, a cheerful tune.

Behind Charlie's back, Arie said, "You told me he was the hard one, this Isaac. You knew your man."

"All over it's the same; in every group you find one."

"Can we talk to him, Charlie? Can you get him back?"

Never looking behind, steadfastly watching the windows and the door, Charlie said, "The little bastard thinks he can win. He doesn't believe in us, doesn't believe we have the will to beat him. That's where he has to be convinced."

"You must tell him I am here, Charlie. This is what I was sent for. It was for this moment."

"You feel something for the kid, right?" A slow smile at Charlie's mouth.

"As you do, Charlie."

"And what do you want of him now?"

"That he should not be shamed."

"And nothing else?"

"If he does as I ask of him, he will not be disgraced, and no more harm will come to the passengers. Your masters will be happy with you, Charlie, and will talk of a great victory. For us there can be no victory, only defeat, and if I cannot talk to Isaac there will be defeat for us, but you will share in it."

"That's a long old speech, Benitz. Let's cut the crap; let's get on with it."

Charlie walked three or four paces, isolating himself from the Israeli. Raised his voice again, once more preparing sentences in Russian.

"Isaac, you must listen to us. A man has come from Tel Aviv. He is the representative of the Israeli Government. He is a colonel of the Israel Defense Forces. You have to listen, Isaac; you have to hear what the Israeli Government says to you. You must put the past behind you, forget all this rubbish about winning and willpower and strength. You have to talk to this man, for God's sake."

Could imagine them now. Crowded round the television set, picking up his words and searching on the outer camera monitor for the Israeli; be bedlam in the bloody control tower. Who authorized it? Whose sanction? Where from the permission? Deep in now, Charlie, over the tops of your Wellies. Blown yourself, risked the lot, jeopardized the pension, threatened the job—all the same stupid bloody things that mob will be thinking of. No point in saying you didn't reckon it was going to work out like this. No point at all. Took him here yourself, and you've made it public, broadcast to the world.

Incessant in his ear, tribal drums of anger and dissent. "Come in, Webster. Come in immediately. Webster, respond to your call sign. What the hell is going on out there? Did you take him to the location? It was expressly forbidden that he should reach the plane. Answers must be given." Seemed as if they were passing the microphone from one to another. All climbing on you, Charlie, leaning on your back, pummeling you. Tell them to get stuffed.

"I have one message for you. They will start again to shoot hostages in something less than forty minutes. I repeat, the killing starts again in forty minutes. That is why I am here. I have nothing else to report. Nothing else." And then the return of the bleated demands for clarification, amplification, justification. He reached to his side for the control panel, felt with his fingers for the volume button and turned it slowly, counter-clockwise. He was aware of the gradual fading out and diminishing of the sound.

Another step forward. "Isaac, you have to listen to this

man. He comes at the direct instruction of the Israeli Government. He's no trick; he's no stooge. You have to hear him out. You have to listen to him before there is more killing."

The answering cry was a long time coming. Seemed fainter to their ears, and there was confusion and a hesitancy.

"It is Rebecca who hears you. Isaac has said that we must have the fuel. Soon he will choose which man stands at the door at one o'clock. You do not have much time to bring the fuel. After one o'clock then perhaps we should hear what your friend has to say."

Charlie shouted again, and was not heeded. Pulled with his fingers at the roots of his hair; brushed his hand across his mouth to wipe away the saliva that had collected with his shouting. They'll have your bloody neck for this, Charlie. Right up high they'll swing you, load the lot on you till you'd wish you'd kept your bloody mouth shut. Someone had to get the scene moving, didn't he? But there're ways of doing it, Charlie. Their way and your way. Your way's a loser.

George Davies was well pleased with the training session—as pleased as he would ever be. Eight men approaching the aircraft from the safe ground at the rear. Four for the rear door, and needing more time because it must be forced from the outside and they would be unfamiliar with the locking devices employed on the Ilyushin. Four more to the front where the hatch was free, and pausing for the dovetailing of the plan, the synchronization of the triple movement that would come from his direction by radio. Three stages, and all simultaneous—the opening of the rear door, attack at the front and the detonation of flash grenades coupled with sustained machine-gun fire on the port side of the aircraft.

As much noise as possible he had said he wanted: create a diversion, get their heads to the wrong windows and rely on the instinctive reaction to gunfire, take cover. He reckoned that if he could get his men inside the plane while the pair were still crouched down, or looking to the port side, orienting themselves to a new situation, then he stood a good chance. But there were imponderables. If the diversion did not drive Isaac and Rebecca down, if their attention was not drawn across the aircraft. If they were standing and shooting.

If the hostages panicked and ran from their seats. Any number of things that could screw it. But you could go only so far in preparation, take only so many precautions. They had to realize that back in the control tower, had to know that if the military went then the picnic was over. He did not give the civilians the benefit of any doubt; thought for the most part they hadn't the slightest idea of the possible consequences of what they now planned.

Timing was working well, and the movement up the ladders could not have been bettered. Reasonable diagrams of the door mechanisms to work off. Good photographs of the boy and the girl to imprint on each man's memory. The soldier who would carry the megaphone satisfactory in the Russian language commands with which he would order the passengers to remain seated—atrocious accent, but they'd understand him. Vital that, the one continual disturbing worry that obsessed him: that the passengers would start moving.

Five times they worked the maneuver; more than that and the danger of staleness would loom. Had to keep them hungry, prevent the risk of any blunting familiarity's insinuating itself into the operation. When they gathered around him, back on the tarmac after the last run, they discussed equipment. Rejected helmets and also the armor-plated flak jackets: too cumbersome; too likely to catch on the ladder, the doorway, between the seats. Peeled their webbing down to a minimum—belt and nothing else. Tennis shoes in place of boots. The short-barreled Ingham in preference to anything that was heavier, larger, whatever the loss of hitting power. Nothing to be taken that could impede the mad, desperate dash along the aisle on which all would depend.

"Remember," Davies said to the small group that was watched from a wary distance by policemen and other unit soldiers. "Remember, the slightest sign of opposition and you hammer them. Three round bursts, and angled, because we're taking both ends. They have to be bloody fast getting their hands up if they're to live through this little lot. Any chance of them shooting, blast; if you're impeded, can't see them, take the ceiling out . . ."

"When does the next ultimatum wind up?" One of the group anxious to know how soon till they might be called on to demonstrate before the live audience what they had mastered in rehearsal.

"A little over half an hour. The civvie guy, the spook, is having another go at them at the moment; if he fails, and the gaffers think they're about to start chopping again, then we go. We won't be waiting for dark."

Three men were with the Prime Minister of Israel, the meeting slotted in between his scheduled appointments of the day. Present were his Foreign Minister, the head of military intelligence and the personal adviser to his office on counterterrorism. All four in open-necked shirts and the light slacks so favored in the heat of the Jerusalem summer.

It was an inconclusive meeting, with little to report, less to comment upon. The Prime Minister was assured that the British seemed adamant that in the event of a successful outcome to the siege of the Ilyushin 11 18V, any surviving hijackers would be flown directly to the Soviet Union. It was unlikely, he was told, that the British would even bother to prefer charges for those offenses committed inside the jurisdiction of local courts. It would be, the Foreign Minister remarked, the Iranian precedent rather than the Munich one that the British would turn to. When the Prime Minister had raised his eyebrows fractionally, the signal that he wished clarification, it was explained that the Iranians had sent back a Soviet Air Force pilot who had defected in a light aircraft seeking political asylum. The Munich option referred to the West German refusal to hand over a twenty-six-year-old fugitive who had seized an internal Prague–Bratislava flight at gunpoint and flown it to Munich.

"It is very easy for the British on this occasion," remarked the Intelligence general. "If any survivors are sent back, there is hardly the likelihood of further retaliatory strikes from the same quarter against their airliners, or acts of sabotage. Different when the Palestinians were involved, when they released Leila Khaled, when they did not seek the extradition of those who took their VC-10 and destroyed it at Amsterdam. Nor, again, did they seek the rule of law when their flight went to Tunis. Circumstances are different, sir; they have nothing to fear for the future if they acquiesce."

And the Americans had not helped, thought the Prime

Minister. Promises of covert and exploratory pressure from the State Department that had never ignited, only fizzled briefly before being doused in the brush-off from London. The matter had been abandoned.

"I had hoped for more from the Americans," said the Prime Minister, turning to the army reserve general—an old friend, one who could be trusted and whom he had brought out of retirement to sit close by his office. "I had hoped that their influence on the British would be greater."

"The taste of this business has not been palatable to them. They will stand by us when the danger is greatest, when they believe we are without defenses. But they do not like to think of us, or our people, as having a will of our own. The three have shown their claws and their teeth; they have killed with them. It does not fit the image that our friends have of us."

"With the hostage dead, with the Americans asleep and unwilling to wake up, then we have lost. They will go back, these two, and there is nothing that we can . . ." He broke off, as if reminded of something distant. Clutched at the straw. "The man whom we sent—Benitz. Has there been communication from him?"

"He spoke to the relevant people by telephone this morning. But his opportunities are limited. The British offer him nothing."

"They have not used him because they wish to send these people back."

"But he is a resourceful man."

"A lion, one of the best we have. But there are impossibilities even for such a man as this."

"He has made no contact for some time now—none that has been reported by London."

"Which means nothing. In these circumstances, nothing."

So often like this, the helpless, ill-informed back seat, while the pursuit of policy remained in the hands of the soldiers. Many times the scene had been enacted: the directions given, the orders made clear, the aspirations pointed to, and then the waiting for the cipher cable, the telex, the radio message, always the same men in the room—the identical frustration.

Abruptly the Prime Minister curtailed the meeting. Nothing to be gained from further dallying, talking around a situation they no longer directly influenced. The delegation of the

Histadrut had been waiting more than twenty minutes in the anteroom outside his office. He should not delay them longer. The problems of the trade unions would be with him long after the affair of the taking of the Ilyushin to Stansted was forgotten.

That he should have closed and refastened the door Isaac knew. Should have shut them in again, sealed the breach, barricaded the gate, prepared his defenses. But he could not bring himself to come again to the bright hole through which the sunlight dazzled and the clean air flowed; kept back from it, nervous of the danger and of reverting to their isolation and their incarceration. But it was weakness not to go to the big lever, plunge it downward through the semicircle of its locking mechanism; it was a sapping of his will that he could recognize but felt hopeless to correct. Not many hours since he had slept—four perhaps, and not much more—but the passing of time had been concentrated and had ravaged his strength and his thinking ability: the escape of the teacher, the killing at his own hands of the Italian, the death of his friend. Great and cataclysmic events, all far beyond the extremity of any previous experience he had known, each demeaning the importance of the others, till they had taken a toll of him that he would not have believed possible, sown the weed of lethargy in his mind and his legs and his arms.

Should have fastened the door, Isaac, if you mean to fight on. The door must be locked and bolted, Isaac. Their entry point. Through there that they will come with the machine guns and the rifles. They'll be laughing, unable to believe their luck: a door left open, an entry point signposted. But the tiredness swept over him, compelling, overwhelming. Just wanted to permit the closing of his eyes. The sleep without dreams, without the desperate fear of watching and waiting, and hoping. They'd be laughing as they squatted on the roofs of the armored cars, helpless, collapsing themselves, hysterical.

But the door must be open for one o'clock, right, Isaac? That was when you told the man Charlie to be watching and waiting if there was no fuel. Allowed himself a slow smile as he remembered the fever in the voice of the Englishman, the anxiety that he sought to suppress. Brought a quiet and cracked grin at the side of Isaac's mouth. That was why the door should be left open: so that they could see it, and regard it, and count the minutes that passed on their clocks.

Strange not seeing David at the far end of the aisle, not following his bowed silhouette the length of the aircraft as he had hovered in the cockpit. Had made an abscess in their group, his going. Gone, blasted, carved on the tarmac. And what for? What for any of it? The policeman back in Kiev, the captain in his cockpit seat, the passenger misshapen on the tarmac—didn't even know their names, so what for? The path on which David had led them, the road that he had shown them. A road that was safe and secure with the darkened shadows of escape—no blocks, no armed men, no uniformed sentries. David had told them of Babi Yar, and of Potma and Perm; lectured them on the diet of seventy-five grams of black bread a day and cabbage soup to wash it down with; harangued them on the young men of their faith who languished in the cells, the injustices, the cruelties, the interrogations. A blow for freedom, David had promised, and where was freedom?—where was the land he had told them of? Not here, not in this stinking cell, not with these animals to be watched and guarded and shepherded. You ran well, David, ran early, and you left us, you little bastard, left us to face the wrath you had brought down. Bastard coward; fucking, fucking bastard; ran out on us, ditched us. Holding your leaking condom, holding your bastard baby. But what if there can be no survival for the fighter? What if he is made for martyrdom; what if that can be the only writing on his gravestone?

Isaac seemed to be laughing to himself, and there was the slow, gentle, smiling shake of his head. Not what you came for, Isaac. Not why you bought the tickets, not just to purchase a grave plot. Good enough for David, but not for Isaac.

Rambling, you fool, deep in your self-pity. Wondered what they'd said that morning in the lecture hall as they gathered for the first class of the day, the ones he had studied with. Would they know now where was the one who always sat in the fifth row, three seats in from the door, the one with the spidery writing, good at practical and poor at theory, who asked no questions and took the "B" marks, and who was quiet and had nothing to say in the canteen line at morning break? Would they know; and if they did, what would they say? Those who liked him, what would they say if they had stood beside him at ten and watched his finger tighten on the trigger bar, seen the disintegration of a man's skull, the way he wiped the spattered bone and brain tissue from his arm? Would they have embraced him; would they have cowered beyond his reach?

His hands gripped the narrow barrel of the gun. Whitened at the knuckles. Hurting yourself, Isaac, wounding yourself. But you have to decide now, cannot stall and study your cards longer. Have to close the door if you're going to fight them, Isaac. It's your guts that are fleeing you—draining through the open door, spilling out, splashing on the tarmac; ripening the time for surrender.

Cut the crap, finish it, Isaac. He pulled himself up from the floor, hanging from the trolley for leverage. So damned tired, his legs. And the baby still crying. No one trying to stop the little thing's fury, letting it scream and yowl as if to batter at him. And all watching for his reaction to the droning noise, waiting for him to burst into protest . . . or to capitulate and ask for milk to be sent. Eyes watching him, waiting for the sign, letting the child pierce and pummel at him. They would not wait much longer; but for now the bastards could wait, sit on their asses, sit on their shit and wait. Even the American quiet now, even he of the homilies to Rebecca and the arrogance. Should have chosen him, the American, not the little frightened man he had dragged to the doorway; should have been the damned American. Not that it would have changed anything, only greater satisfaction.

Down the aisle again, Isaac. Damned cat in a cage, with a circumscribed path inside the bars. Down the carpet, eyes to the right, eyes to the left, and watch the pigs squirm, watch them look away, and wriggle and try to hide and lose themselves. Came to Rebecca, and his arm was around her shoulder—carelessly, not with emotion; more to offer a faint degree of comfort.

They should not have brought her.

Chilled him to think what would happen to Rebecca. Perhaps he was strong enough to face the bullets; perhaps. But the girl, never. Without the muscle, without the mind. Should not have permitted her to come. Late in the day,

Isaac. In their eyes she'll be as culpable as the men, will be judged with equality, the same hurtful fate. A fucking mess, fucking chaos. And how far from where it had started, and what had it started for? A heap of cretins sitting in their excreta, in their urine, that Babi Yar should be remembered. Babi where? Babi damned Yar. Isaac laughed to himself, out loud, pealing inside the confines of the aircraft.

Rebecca said, "What you said to the man, Isaac, did you mean that? It is close to one o'clock; do we kill one more then? Do we have to?"

"If we believe that we are going to Israel, then we must kill another, and another, till we have the fuel." Steady voice, calm and without anxiety; the pupil talking of how much he must do in the evenings if he is to pass his examination with credit.

"Are we going to Israel, Isaac?"

"Questions, Rebecca, questions."

"But now there must be answers, Isaac. David is dead, the Italian is dead, the captain is dead. There have to be answers."

"What do you want to hear me say, Rebecca?"

"I have to know what you think. I have the right to know what you will do. Again, Isaac, are we going to Israel?"

"And you, Rebecca, what do you think? Do you believe we will fly from here?"

"Don't play with me, Isaac. Not now. We have been here too long for games that amuse you. Too much blood, too much hurting. We have to have honesty now."

"So what do I have to say for you? Do I crawl to you and beg for your forgiveness?" He spat the words at her, and the hate was there again. The loathing not for her but for the great sponge that hemmed in on them which they could kick against, but not hurt—not inflict pain. "Do you want me to plead to you, plead with you to forgive me and to forget where I have taken you?

"Of course we will not see Israel. . . . There, it's the first time that I've said it. . . . Again, and this time louder, so that all these pigs can hear me . . . we will not see Israel. We will never see Israel. We are like the herd of our people, the masses of the camps and the prison cells. No better than they, no worse than they. We are as ineffective as they are.

We will never see Israel, Rebecca. You wanted me to say it, and I've satisfied you. It was for nothing, Rebecca. Nothing."

"So there will be no more killing?" A small voice, a whisper, flattened by the enormity of what she had drawn from him. She pushed the hair back from his forehead—a quick movement of her hand, so that he barely felt the texture of her fingers against his skin.

"No more of the passengers will die." The smile regained, promising a girl a present, something she would like and be pleased to accept.

"Who else—who else other than the passengers? The soldiers, if they come . . . who else?"

"They will send us back, Rebecca. You remember when you and David talked to them, when he was defeated, when he wanted to end it, and they couldn't answer you. Remember that: they could not answer the question you asked. They will want to send us back. You understand that; you know what that means. It is not for me, Rebecca, and you could not go alone. We will go back, Rebecca—not together, not singly. They will not take us."

"That was why David went?" Couldn't use the words that swarmed to her tongue—a betrayal of David as great as if she'd gone to the window and stared down at his broken body. "That was why David went. Because he knew. That was why you called him a coward. . . ."

"Because he could not do it by his own hand. He needed others. We will ask no help. Ourselves, together, we will do it."

He felt her stiffen against him, driving her body closer to his, pressing with a ferocity as if to mold their two persons into one. "I will be frightened, Isaac. I will need you." He kissed her softly, full on the pale and grayed lips, stifling her words.

"We must hear what the man from Tel Aviv has to say to us. First we must hear that."

He went to the doorway, for a moment was visible to the outside watchers before the instinctive caution won through and he backed again to the side and shelter.

"Charlie, Charlie," he shouted. "You can come now. Bring the man from Israel."

Strong and clear and strident, his voice across the emptiness of the tarmac. The burden thrown off, discarded. There were many rifles aimed at the general direction of his body till the hands that held them relaxed and the barrels were dropped. Charlie Webster and Arie Benitz started to walk toward the Ilyushin—a slow and careful step, and all the time the Englishman talking into the microphone close to his chin.

Seemed a great distance they had to go, a chasm to be bridged.

Summoned again from his exile on the lower floor, the Home Secretary read the transcript of Charlie Webster's radio message.

> There has been a substantial change of mood on the part of both Isaac and Rebecca. After threatening that executions would recommence at thirteen hundred local if they were denied fuel for the onward flight to Israel, they have now invited me to bring to the aircraft Col. Arie Benitz of the IDF. They want to hear what message for them he brings from the Israeli Government. The message will be that they should surrender. My assessment is that this represents a considerable weakening of Isaac's position. For personal guidance, is it likely that on surrender they will be returned to face Soviet courts? Over. Webster.

The Home Secretary edged his glasses farther down his nose. "Has someone answered Mr. Webster's query?"

"Yes." The Assistant Chief Constable spoke with caution.

"What was the answer?"

"He was given guidance, not specific information."

"Which way did you guide him?"

"We said that the position was not clear, but—"

"In heaven's name, man, what did you tell him?"

"He seemed to need some sort of answer, something that would help during the difficult negotiation stage he is embarking on."

"Don't fool with me."

"We told Mr. Webster that there had been a change of

approach by Foreign Office; we told him they were unlikely
to be returned to the Soviet Union."

"Who told him that?"

"I did." The Assistant Chief Constable stood his ground,
aware the worst was over, confronting now only the puzzlement and confusion of the politician. "On my own authority.
I judged that the belief that this was the case would only help
Mr. Webster at this moment."

"It's not true—simply not true."

"Behind them they have a man shot in Kiev; the pilot of
the aircraft is dead in the cockpit; a passenger is dead on the
tarmac. More stand to die as the afternoon goes on. The
truth of what Webster tells these people is, frankly, unimportant. They've forfeited the right to truth." He'd carried the
day; saw the retreat, the change of tack, the Home Secretary
backing from confrontation. Stupid bloody man, and what
did he know of the scene anyway; better off downstairs and
out of the way than holding inquests over a half-truth.

"I hadn't thought it would cave in quite like this." Had to
assert himself in some way; had to say something, and let
bloody Clitheroe answer him, the Assistant Chief Constable
thought with rare magnanimity.

"They end with a whimper, these things; that's the experience." The psychiatrist had joined the group. "On other occasions we've noted there's an intensification of demands in
the final hours before surrender. These two people are
undergoing most severe nervous strain, loss of sleep, lack of
food; they are in a hostile environment, isolated from communication. When they raised their demands, it was because
they acknowledged that their earlier threats had failed. Mr.
Webster has now confronted them with the Israeli. They're
bewildered at the moment, and they will want to know what
he has to say. The combination of persuasion by Mr. Webster
and Benitz should be too much for them. I would predict it
will be all over today—shorten that, in fact, to this
afternoon."

"Extraordinary behavior of this fellow Webster." The politician still perturbed, recognizing that his hand was far from
the helm. "Just going off, no instructions, no authorization,
taking the Israeli . . ."

"It's quite simple. The last time Mr. Webster was present,

we were engaged in the debrief of the Russian. We were preparing for an attack. Mr. Webster was anxious to avoid the necessity of an assault."

"So are we all." The Home Secretary bridled. "The last thing any of us want."

"If the military assault the plane, Mr. Webster believes there would be an inherent risk to the children who are amongst the passengers; harm a large proportion of them. If I may be indiscreet, I think he also believes that it is not necessary to kill the two young people. He would like them to survive. If he is to save them, he will be all the better equipped to do so in the knowledge that they will serve a few years in a British jail before release. He's a complex fellow, Mr. Webster; his experiences are outside our own, and I think he's bored with ushering young people to their Maker. The only relief I feel at the moment is that it will not be myself who disabuses him of the destination of his Isaac and his Rebecca should he prove successful."

Clitheroe let the words die in the silence; saw the awkwardness and embarrassment that were his creation. Let them suffer, he thought; let them writhe. And make a damn good tale, too, at his dinner table.

Both in their shirt sleeves, Charlie encumbered only by his radio set, Benitz with the lightweight aluminum ladder that would reach to the bottom of the doorway. Around them a terrible, icy, deafening stillness. Benitz steadied the ladder against the fuselage of the aircraft; noticed its age, the dents of unknown mechanics, the flashes of rust from the vents in the bodywork, the peeling of the weather-worn paintwork of its livery. He put his foot on the bottom step to calm its vibrations.

Charlie began to climb toward the doorway.

17

Isaac was back again in his lair, hugged to the drinks trolley, ignoring now the sights with which he had lived the hours: the coats and possessions stuffed into the racks; the printed flower patterns on the walls; the fabric covering of the seats; the bobbing and moving heads. Rebecca huddled in the cockpit doorway, shunning the sight of the body of the captain, unmoved and whitened by the pallor of death. Both from their different positions could see the top of the ladder, saw it buckle and heave and shake as it took the weight before there was Charlie's shoulder for them to fasten on, and his growing height as he climbed with effort into their view. He seemed to them to pause for a moment, hesitate and look about him, nostrils dilating to the smell of the interior which both had long since been accustomed to. His eyes roved about him, and there was a smile of recognition on his face, hasty but still evident, when he saw the girl, followed by a slight inclination of his head and then the faint twist of protest at his mouth, unspoken, at the pistol leveled at his chest. He turned his head back toward the place he had come from, the world beyond the hatch, and called in English, so that only Rebecca understood him, "It's fine, Arie. Come on up; the party's ready."

Squinting down the length of the aisle, trying to penetrate the face, assess the man; the enemy or the ally; Isaac demanding an answer. Didn't fit the image of the enemy. Too old, too sagging, too careworn, too gross about the waist. An ordinary man such as he would have seen in Kiev, such as would work at the railroad station, would occupy an office in the Bureau of State Pensions. Didn't wear the hostility to be an enemy; moved with neither the suspicion nor the aggression of a man who would do them harm.

But this was the man who had broken them, who was the

spokesman for the great force on the outside, who had not
acceded to their demand for fuel. And his weapon had been
placid, unyielding reasonableness, the faucet that dripped on,
beating out a message of logic and persuasion in endless repetition. Rebecca beaten from the time they had first heard his
voice; David following her; and now himself, now Isaac, joining his colleagues in defeat.

How many times had he said there would be no fuel before
the message had slowly and inexorably won through? Not an
enemy, but not an ally, not this man with the dirt-stained
shirt and the crumpled, baggy trousers. Nothing he had said
that carried friendship, sympathy or understanding. Could
not be an ally. A functionary, that was what the man Charlie
was. The one who had been sent to do the work.

Different the one who followed him: sharper on his feet,
quicker in his movements, harder in the eyes. Poised, intense. He was an opponent; he should be watched. But this
was the man sent by his own people; this was the one they
had to hear before he took Rebecca past the trolley barricade
to the place of privacy in the far end corridor, beside the back
toilets, close to the rear door. Not now, Isaac; shut it out; the
time is coming fast enough.

Charlie began to walk, slowly, gently, so that there could
be no doubt about his intentions, down the aisle of the plane.
Stopped then where all could see him, reach into contact
with him, hand resting and relaxed on a seat back. Confident, friendly, assured.

The famous smile, winning friends, putting the fearful at
ease; the man who was in control, looking to the passengers
as his priority, avoiding Isaac with his pinched and sprung
intensity, and his submachine gun. Not looking back at the
drab girl with the pistol.

"Hello. My name is Charlie Webster. Just Charlie they
generally call me. I'm with the British Foreign Office and I've
come to take you off the plane. It won't be immediately, but
it'll be very soon. You just have to be patient for a while
longer; I know you've been that already—fantastic—but just a
little bit longer while we sort some things out with the gentle-
man and the lady. Please stay in your seats—don't move at
all—and remember that it won't be long now."

There were some who found his Russian difficult to follow,

so there was a chorus of explanation as the word was passed
back through the rows of seats till all comprehended. The
applause came suddenly and spontaneously—sixty men and
women and children hammering their hands together and
shouting their support. Charlie blushed and smiled again, and
put up his hand without avail to halt the flood tide of gratitude sweeping down the cabin, engulfing him. Looked for
someone to speak to, and was grateful for the presence of the
pilot, still staring to the front, hands moving in rhythm with
the others', tears on her cheeks, losing the fight with her
emotions.

Charlie said, "You are Miss Tashova. I want you to know
that everyone in the control tower, all the authorities who are
gathered there, have expressed their great admiration for
your achievement last night. The landing was brilliant, abso-
lutely bloody brilliant, if you'll excuse me. They are looking
forward to congratulating you personally." Just once she
slipped a glance to him, without commitment, without dropping her reserve, her defenses, and then was gazing again
into the dour material of the seat back in front of her.

Keep it going, Charlie; keep it moving around, gentle and
natural. Make the two of them believe it's all over, that it's
finished, out of their control. No negotiation, no concession,
just that the game's gone, the whistle's blown. Taking the
initiative, the boffins would call it, and holding it so that Isaac
couldn't wrest it back. Silly little bugger, should have known
his bible: rule one, "Never let the bastards with the open
faces and the empty hands on board." Curtains after that,
Isaac, old sunshine.

He moved forward two more rows. Closer to Isaac, closer
than he had ever been, where he could see the twisted, confused and shadowed face with its sheen of sweat. Able to
focus on the gun, understand its cooling system, its front
needle sight, its age and peeled paintwork. Shouldn't dwell on
it, though, Charlie; shouldn't show apprehension; like a
policeman who edges along the windowsill toward the man
determined on suicide, and who must talk with a calmness
and be mundane and boring and matter-of-fact.

As he turned to the baby's mother, the style of the gun was
imprinted on his mind, the knowledge that a flick of the trigger, casual and involuntary or meditated, and the magazine

would be unloading in a cascade of shells hurtling through the trimmed airspace between him and the squat, tensed, curly-haired boy. Tapped the baby's head with his left hand, trying not to draw away from the stench of the unchanged clothes, attempting to weave the web of normality. Just keeping it going, Charlie, ever so slow, ever so gradual.

In front of him the children, the school kids, still tidy, still quiet, and waiting for you, Charlie. Had to get beyond them, had to impose himself between the boy with the gun and their soft flesh that would be ripped and carved by a single volley. Winked at a couple of the little brats. Eight or nine more rows, that would be enough. Then he'd be a shield for the kids; then he could talk of who left the plane first; then he could believe that it was finished.

All the time moving, edging closer to the boy with the gun; soft voice, controlled smile; creeping nearer, insidious, eroding the distance; and deep inside, his heart pounding, and his muscles taut and stretched, and his eyes on the gun. Don't lose sight of that gun, Charlie; don't take your bloody eyes off it.

Gently Charlie spoke to Isaac, spanning the few feet of carpet with his words, making the contact. "I've brought Colonel Benitz to see you, Isaac. He's from the Israel Defense Forces, and he's a fighter; he's like you. His enemies are your enemies. Listen to him, Isaac. Listen to what he tells you."

It took Charlie time to realize that Benitz had begun to speak behind him. A different voice and words that he could not understand, a language that was strange to him and incomprehensible.

Benitz turned back toward the open door and the cockpit entrance. Gazed down the length of the aisle toward the girl. "Come here, Rebecca. Come close to us where you can hear what I say." A cool, spring voice; an instruction in the Yiddish tongue. "Come nearer, so that I do not shout." Looking into her eyes, absorbing the creased lines of her tiredness and her faltering step. The girl who wanted to come to Israel; who wanted to take her place among his people, bear her children there, in the dream of his country. "Keep coming, Rebecca, keep coming; you have nothing to fear from me."

Saw the way she looked at him, as if the floodgates of her misery might now be broken down; saw the relief catch at the curls of her mouth that now, after all the hideousness and pain, she had finally found her friend. And they had told him on the telephone that these young ones would be sent back, would be returned to the land of oppression, and to cells, and to death and to the quicklime pits. Wondered as she came toward him where she had started, where she had begun the journey that had brought her here. In the arms of one of the boys? Or something more rare? Had there been the inner driving commitment, the force that sharpened the men whom he led, the men of the storm squad? And he would not know, would never know, because now there was no time.

When she reached him, Benitz put his arm around her shoulder, draped loosely and carelessly; glanced once at the pistol held in her hand and mingled with the folds of her dress; worked his fingers into the muscle of her shoulder—the gesture of reassurance—and saw Isaac straighten as if his fear too were waning.

"We know what you sought; we know what you have accomplished." Arie Benitz spoke with simplicity, with the humility of the funeral oration at the graveside of a soldier of Squad 101. "We know of it and we marvel, and are proud. We understand what brought you here, and we understand the depth of despair, the pain and the agony that will have been yours when the welcome was of guns and armed men and tanks. We understand why you felt driven to take the life of a man who now lies outside and dead. We understand." Both of them looking to him, both watching, and Isaac's gun barrel lowered so that the muzzle aimed at the slight space between his feet.

"In many ways we can struggle against our opponents. The battle may be offensive, it may be passive. There are those who fight in the front line, those who are far to the rear. There are sudden victories that can be won, and there are those which are secret and quiet and without garlands." Tore into him, ripping at the hardness of the assault soldier, the sight of their faces that were calmed now and at peace.

"There are times when the victory must be purchased, times when great sacrifice is demanded. Those are the sad times, the times when our people weep upon the coffins. . . .

The tank forces who held the Golan at Yom Kippur, when the Syrians came: for them there could be no relief, no reinforcement, no supply. They were pitifully few, and they fought till their shells were expended, and then they fought with their machine guns, and when the magazines were empty then they threw their grenades. And they died by their broken tanks. Died because it was required of them. And there was no fear, no terror, no panic. They died because Israel needed their lives, needed them as currency to pay for the ultimate victory. They won us time, and when we returned, we stood in awe and understood what those few had achieved for us, and we buried them in the military cemetery that is on a hill outside Jerusalem, and there are flowers there, and men come with their women and children to stand in silence beside the stones."

Only Isaac and Rebecca comprehending his words, but the plane hushed and still, as if all felt a sensitivity to the moment.

"We do not share our fight. We do not rely on allies. We stand by ourselves and expect favors from none. It is a hostile, friendless world." Arie Benitz smiled, not with humor, but from a deep sympathy. "You have found that; you know it as I know it. When you were in the air over Hannover, that was when you would have known it, and when you woke to the dawn this morning and found the guns that circled you. It is a hard and savage place that you have come to."

His hand slipped from the girl's shoulder, and his fingers played now with the sun-dried skin of her upper arm where it was bared beneath her sleeve; pulled gently and squeezed it, and played patterns with his nails. Winning her, comforting her, steeling her, and all the time edging down toward the limply held pistol. "The British have told you that you will not fly from here. If they say that I believe them, and I have no power to alter their decision. And if you surrender the British will send you back—back to Kiev, back to the courts . . ."

Felt the girl stiffen at his side, and his hand now gripped her arm, tight, pinioning, pressing it against her body, denying her movement.

"What do you want of us?" The peace passing from Isaac's face as if a cloud had moved across the sun. "What is the message that you bring us?"

"There is only one course for you, only one that you can

contemplate, and I have come to help you." Said firmly, with a resolution: the man who has loved his dog, which now is in pain and must be destroyed. "I will help you. It will be at the hands of a friend." Benitz' hand had sunk far on her arm, below the boned elbow, and his fingers brushed at her wrist and close to the butt end of her pistol.

"That is what you came to tell us?" Isaac laughed, threw back his head. "That was the message which they flew you here to deliver? Be good little boys, kill yourselves nicely, and we'll send a man to do it with you, to hold your hand, make certain it's a nice clean shot, that it's not messy . . ."

"You cannot go back, Isaac. Neither of you can go back."

Isaac now sank to a crouch, the barrel up, the passengers fidgeting in their seats.

"There is no other way, Isaac." Benitz shouting down the aisle.

"From these people, yes: from the British we could expect this. From the Russians, yes: we could expect them to send a killer to us. But that it should be you, of our own people, who can offer us nothing . . ."

"There is nothing else." The calmness gone, the soldier in uniform. Benitz' fragile patience diminishing.

Slowly and with emphasis, pointing each word, Isaac said, "But that it should be you."

"I said it was a hard and savage place that you had come to. I offer you the best, the only way." And there was a shame in his voice, a humiliation. And banging in his ears the words of the Ambassador. A detestable job. "I was not ordered to bring you this message, not by my government. They wanted to save you, but you have destroyed yourselves. When you took the man to the doorway, that was when you died, Isaac. Whether at my hand, your hand or a Russian hand, that was when you died, Isaac. I come only to make it easier. I can give nothing more. When you took the man to the door, you went beyond our reach."

One hand at the pistol, jerking it from the girl's grasp; the other jackknifing her arm behind her back, so that she shuddered from the pain of the movement. Pulled her across in front of him, protection against Isaac's submachine gun which was now at his shoulder, aimed clear and straight down the length of the aisle.

The urgency scything over the heads of the passengers,

Charlie shouted, "What are you saying, Benitz? What are you telling them?"

"What I have to say. What is obvious to a fool."

"What is it? Tell me." The rare anger that Charlie was unused to.

"Keep out, Charlie. This is not your quarrel; you are the stranger. You should stay out."

A rabid dog, that was what Benitz had made of Isaac. Fashioned the monster with his words, molded the danger of the raised gun, the twisted desperation of the boy's face.

It was Rebecca who told Charlie the message that Benitz had carried. Shrieking the words: the sound of a bitch in labor, of a saw that finds a sunken nail. "We have to die for him, Charlie. And he is the friend who will help us. We go no farther, he says, and if we surrender we are sent back to Kiev. So we must die here, and from his kindness he will help us. That is the kindness of the state of Israel. Did he not tell you, Charlie Webster? Has he betrayed you as he betrays us . . ."

Charlie yelling back at her, "It's not true. Just not true. They are not sending you back. From the tower they told me—"

"Shut up, Charlie. You don't know what you talk of. It's delusion, stupidity; you only hurt them." A whipcrack from Benitz.

". . . Throughout the Jewry of Russia there is one dream"—Rebecca ignoring the two men, as if their dispute were irrelevance. "It is the dream of going, at a time however far in the future, to the country we know as Israel. How many try as hard as we have tried to reach that place? He has broken the dream, this man whom you brought to us."

"Come back, Charlie; come back to behind me."

A command, spoken with unarguable authority, and he edged his way down the aisle, all the time watching the face of Isaac, watching for the steeling of the eyes that would mean he was preparing to shoot. Backed past the children, past the woman and the baby, away from the American, away from the pilot officer. Benitz' arm came to meet him, grabbed his collar and half-guided, half-hurled him sidewise among the legs of the passengers. As he stumbled, tried to regain his balance, pressing into a lap for support, Benitz was past him, and the girl was his protection as he advanced with a slow and strange circumspection toward Isaac.

In step the two of them moved.

Arie Benitz forcing his thighs and knees into the back of the girl's legs, melting their movements into one, compressing his body against hers, and all the time talking in the language that Charlie did not know. Softer now, and using the tactic of persuasion, the same message and theme all the time, till Charlie had no doubts. Wanted the submachine gun, wanted it thrown down, wanted it abandoned and harmless. Had the pistol that would be the weapon of execution, raised and cocked and ready. Two shots all that he would require.

How long, Charlie, since you've seen anyone killed, shot down, seen the explosion of a bullet rip through the clothing, seen them jump and sag, pulled the puppet strings, watched the marionette dance? How long, Charlie?

Ten paces from Isaac now, the Israeli and the slight Jewish girl. Ten paces and closing. Charlie could anticipate the way Benitz' mind would work. Work himself close enough to propel the girl against the boy, and in the melee and confusion hope for the chance to snatch at the submachine gun, or just simply shoot into the chaos he would have created. Still closing on Isaac, and staring him down all the while with piercing ferret eyes above the tangled stream of her dark hair. The advance of the predator on the rabbit, and no bolt-hole for Isaac.

One sentence Rebecca shouted.

"Shoot him, Isaac; shoot him!"

Banal, silly, pathetic, postcard words. Not those she would have chosen for her epitaph; not the final words she would have wanted to speak to Isaac, the last she would say in her life to the boy who had kissed her lips.

A single drumming cacophony of noise. Breaking through Charlie's images as he was thinking out the technique of approach that Benitz was using. Endless bleating of the machine gun, spitting out the bullets, the glutton at the feast, on and on, continuous, the unbroken rhythm of the flashes at the barrel end.

It was a low-velocity weapon, and the first shots struck only the girl, beating at her body, hitting, wracking, breaking her till she pitched forward.

Still the gun fired as Benitz made a last and forlorn gesture toward the saving of his life. Alone now and without the hu-

man wall for security, he seemed to try to aim the girl's pistol
at the source of his pain. There was a half face for Charlie to
see, a face bemused and irritated and disgusted that he had
been found out in such trivial company. A man of Entebbe,
and the Savoy Hotel, and of Maalot and Kyryat Shmona; a
man who had fought with the storm squad against the best of
the Palestinians, and now was undone by a boy and a girl
who knew nothing but the dream of a country they would not
see.

Benitz was a long time falling. Even as the bullets struck
him he sought to steady himself, holding grimly to a seat.
Raising his right hand, the fist that held the pistol, as each
succeeding shell threw back his resolution, forced him to begin again; a man who fights the tide and cannot win. When
he was still, on the rumpled carpet of the aisle that his feet
had rucked and that soon would be stained by the coursing of
his blood, then Isaac pulled his finger from the trigger and
lowered the gun barrel.

Scrambling along the aisle, Charlie reached Benitz; knelt
by his head, Isaac forgotten; lifted him at the back of the
neck as he had been taught to do. Precaution against a man's
drowning in his own blood; standard and automatic reaction
however grave the wounds, however destitute the hope of
survival.

The dusk was spreading on the sun-drawn complexion of
Arie Benitz, as a cloud passes over a hillside, shadowing and
discoloring, exchanging the vitality for gunmetal.

"They had to die here; we would not let them be sent back.
It was rubbish you talked, Charlie; silly, deceitful rubbish.
They go back, and you know that." A gurgling, panting
chant. Charlie's hands under his head, tilting it. "The little
fools did not know, did not know which was the easy way.
Dead whatever they do, better at my hand . . . better at the
hand of a friend." The death of Arie Benitz came in a last
shaking spasm that lifted his head sharply; the cough was
barely complete before the life fled him. Charlie eased the
weight back onto the carpet and looked up at Isaac, still stationary, still motionless, the gun at his knees.

The baby was crying.

"I prefer to believe him, Charlie. Not your newfound
promise for us. And we were going to do as he wanted; we did

not need to be told. Not by the man you brought to us, not by anyone. We knew, Charlie. But it was to be in our own time—not with these bastards sitting around us, counting us out. Can you understand, Charlie?—the girl and I, Rebecca and I, we were going to do it. We trusted you, and you brought this animal to kill us and gut us and hang us up by the ankles. You brought him, Charlie, and because he was with you, because of what you said, we wanted to hear him. He came to execute us, here among the crowd. Not even in Kiev is the firing squad public, Charlie."

Isaac started to come forward. Lightly, almost with delicacy, slightly built and on the balls of his feet. Had acknowledged that the struggle was lost, that the forces against him outnumbered and overwhelmed him. He swung his arm in a lackadaisical way so that the gun arced in the air, was close to brushing against the roof of the passenger cabin before, in its hushed descent, Charlie caught it. No pain now with Isaac, only the great calmness.

"Do it for me, Charlie. Do it quickly."

In three fast and automatic and trained movements Charlie disarmed the gun. Magazine removed, shell in the breech ejected so that it flew from the weapon sidewise, falling on a passenger's trousers; pulled the trigger with the barrel aimed at the ceiling. Contented himself that the thing was harmless, the teeth had been drawn, the wings clipped.

"No, Charlie, no." Isaac curious that his request had not been observed. "You have to do it. You owe it to me, Charlie."

He had stopped seven, eight feet away, separated from Charlie by the mingled blockade of bodies of Rebecca and Arie Benitz. He did not look down, fastened his haunting eyes on Charlie. Like nothing he'd ever known before: a man who was ready, had made peace with himself.

"Charlie, you have to do it." Faintly, hard to hear, but certainty, the first trace of anxiety winning through the trance that had becalmed him since he had killed Rebecca and the Israeli. "Charlie, you cannot leave me to them. I'm not strong enough—not to be sent back, not to do it here . . . not without Rebecca. Charlie . . ."

Animals they called them in the pub where he went at lunchtime from the Department. Swine. Murderers. Com-

munists. Fanatics. Should come and face one of their animals, see him at three paces.

"Just keep coming, Isaac. It's all over. You need some food,
some sleep; you need to rest. You're not going back; they told
me that. Just keep walking." Nothing else to say, Charlie
thought; away from what he knew, away from the papers that
would be piling up on his desk high in the tower block half a
day's drive away.

Now the scream.

"Charlie, you're lying to me. You have to shoot, you have
to. You cannot send me back there. Charlie, we believed in
you. You were the one we trusted . . ."

There was a scuffling sound of movement far behind him,
and Charlie spun to see the first of the SAS troopers emerge
from the doorway into the interior of the plane. A fast,
trained man whose speed was electric, and fear-inspiring
from the way he brooked no hesitation; the line of the little
gun, the Ingham, up to his face traversing with his body.
More noise, louder and closer, and Charlie turned back to
see the wheeling of the door behind Isaac and the flood of
men intervening, scrambling aboard in their broken-pattern
camouflage uniforms.

The lead man of the group that came from the rear of the
Ilyushin was half over the bound and fastened drinks trolley
when the implications of the moment swirled through Isaac's
dulled comprehension. He seemed to launch himself forward, not at Charlie, but at the space beside the body of the
Israeli, the few vacant inches of carpet where lay, alone and
inviting possession, the gun that had been wrested from
Rebecca.

Charlie knew the meaning of that last gesture of defiance;
could have swung his foot toward the pistol, kicked it clear or
trapped it beneath his shoe, and he did nothing. All of the
alternatives were there, available to him at the flywheel speed
of his brain when confronted with the sharpness of Isaac's
jump. But he stayed back, rooted and detached.

Edward R. Jones, Jr., had understood not a word of the
screaming appeal that Isaac addressed to the pale, drawn Englishman who had boarded the aircraft. His ears still sang
from the explosion of the killing bullets, and he had seen the
entry of the troops from the forward door, was unaware of

those who moved behind him. To his own mind the situation was clear-cut, crystal-bright. Elbowing his wife hard in her ample stomach so that she would make way for him, he heaved his considerable frame out of the seat and pitched himself at Isaac. Much of his weight landed on the back of the young Jew—sufficient to arrest his momentum, cause him to flinch from his target, lose sight for the fractional and vital second of the gun that he was reaching for. The American and the Jew wrestled on the floor, and then, as if a signal had been given, the passengers who flanked them rose from their seats and threw themselves into the melee.

Charlie lost sight of Isaac. Saw the face again that held terror and shock and surprise, then could not find it. Fists from the teachers; the dark, flying boot of the man who dressed as a farmer; the pummeling of a straight arm that wore a suit that was well cut and had buttons at the cuffs. He was brushed aside—a quick, fast push—and his view of the writhing and shouting scrum was obscured by the trim blue uniform that he knew was worn by Anna Tashova. Her flat-soled shoe in her hand, beating without aim, without direction, into the melee. He made a feeble attempt to pull the bodies clear, achieved no result and felt the exhaustion trampling over him till he sagged back on the plastic-coated armrest of a seat.

The SAS men cleared the aisle. One bellowing into a megaphone that all should stay in their places, the rehearsed drill; others dragging and tearing at the passengers—Russians, Italians, and last, the American.

His face blooming with a mouth-breaking smile, Edward R. Jones, Jr., held out his great fist to Charlie. Enveloped in it was the pistol.

"I think I was just about in time for you. Perhaps you'd like to look after it."

Charlie took the gun without response and looked past the American, who was maneuvering himself back over his wife's legs while she reached up and clung with linked hands around his throat. Isaac was there, uncovered now, visible and violated. Angry blotches on his temples, weals where there would soon be blood at his cheeks, shirt ripped open to expose the reddened patches of impact against his ribs, trousers at his knees to expose the particular vengeance of one.

But he was alive, and he was conscious, and his chest heaved as he struggled to replace the air lost from his lungs.

Nausea rising through him, welling from his stomach. Charlie wanted to heave his load to the winds. Couldn't take his eyes off the boy, like all the others he'd ever seen; strained to hear what the kid tried to say.

"Charlie, the last time, you have to do it. Don't let them send me back. Please, Charlie, please."

"It's not like that, Isaac. You're not going back; that's what they told me."

The boy tried to laugh, bitter, destroyed, shrill, till the sounds merged with his tears which melted the bravery, stripped his strength.

"Don't give me that crap load, Charlie. Shoot me; for fuck's sake do it!"

The last cry, the last plea, the last moment of faith in a stranger. Charlie felt the pressure of the gun handle where it rested against the softness of his palm, where his fingers twined around the trigger guard. Tried to think back to what the tower had told him, the way the response had been phrased, the words of the policeman, whether they had been specific and definite, whether there was room for interpretation—all the bloody double-talk the bureaucrats had laid on. Couldn't seem to remember the exact words, the phrasing, but the impression had been there, that they wouldn't send them back. Or was that just what you wanted to hear, Charlie? And the little bastard didn't believe him anyway. So what now, Charlie Webster?

He saw that Isaac had closed his eyes, pinched and clamped his lids together. It's what he wants; begging you, cringing to you, because he thinks that you amongst all the army of enemies can succor him, rescue him. Believes in you, Charlie, believes you can do it. Don't hide—not behind what the tower told you. Don't shelter there; they'll leave you naked, those bastards. Do you kill him or not? Can't pass the buck anymore; no one else to catch it. Do you kill him, Charlie?

Seemed to see a boy in handcuffs pulled by the troops toward a prison wagon and the death cell of Nicosia Central: same height, same youth, same hopelessness; and you'd fingered him, Charlie. And another in Aden who was dead in the gutter with the rubbish, shot in the temple and quivering, and you fingered him, Charlie, told the squaddies where to look. And there are more who are pushing the weeds up so that you could make a living, earn your shilling. Haven't there been enough, Charlie; haven't you finished sending the bright-eyed kids on their way?

But if it isn't Charlie Webster, it will be someone else, a bloody Russian, and that only after all he'll go through first. Don't know, do you, Charlie? And you've no time to find out. The gun was at his side, held loosely, unmoving.

The SAS hauled Isaac to his feet, one on each arm, not unkindly and with only the amount of force that was required to shift him, unprotesting, to the back of the aircraft. He looked back once at Charlie before the caged little face was gone, replaced by the matted black hair highlighted by a trickle of blood.

A set of motorized steps was driven to the forward door of the Ilyushin. There was thoughtful improvisation among those who planned these things, because by the time the first of the passengers clambered uneasily and with unsure legs down to the oil-streaked concrete, supported by a line of soldiers, their rifles slung, the corpses of David and Luigi Franconi had been covered with the scarlet blankets of the ambulance stretchers.

Anna Tashova, her right shoe still adrift, hobbled the first few steps on the tarmac on the arm of her navigator, then seemed to collect herself and disengaged and walked unaided.

The teachers, like worried sheep dogs, penned the children together in a single cohesive group, which stood and watched with fascination the bulging heaps that were covered all except the footwear: one of polished leather, still shining and immaculate; the other a tainted, dirty, torn canvas.

The Italian delegation of the Party subdued their traditional ideology and made the gesture of the cross over their chests as they recognized what the blankets hid.

Edward R. Jones, Jr., had his arm around Felicity Ann and had readjusted his handkerchief bandage so that the coagulation of the scalp blood showed clearly to all who might wish to see. He remembered to adjust their camera to compensate for the sunshine of the exterior.

The baby still cried.

The man who might be a farmer was triumphant.

As best they might, they scrambled onto an airport apron bus, and one of the Foreign Office interpreters told them there would be hot meals and beds and baths at a nearby hotel, and that an official from the Russian Embassy in London was waiting there to greet them. There was no shouting, no cheering as the bus pulled away; none believed there were grounds for self-congratulation, and the very smell and filth of their bodies humiliated them.

A Saracen armored car replaced the bus, but drove closer to the steps. On stretchers, the bodies of Arie Benitz, Rebecca and the pilot were moved awkwardly down the steps by men who sweated but bore the load in silence, and were pushed far into the recesses of the vehicle so that they lay amid the welter of CS gas-canister boxes, and the coils of machine-gun ammunition, and the entrenching tools and the emptied cigarette packs and coffee cartons. On top of the Israeli and the girl the soldiers laid David and the Italian, who to those who handled him seemed unmarked except for the scratch on his face from his headlong fall to the ground.

Then Isaac's turn.

Handcuffed now, his arms locked across the front of his body, seeming not to be a worthy opponent to the troops who ushered him from the plane and onto the ramp at the top of the steps. But he intrigued them—a boy who fought without a uniform, in the absence of a commander, and received no pay for it—and they permitted him for a moment to pause there, as if to drink in the freedom of the air, accepting and assimilating the surroundings to which he had brought the Ilyushin. Then he saw, deep in the Saracen, the body of David, uncovered, grotesque in the angle of fallen head, and seemed to wilt, as a flower will that has been denied water after its plucking. He did not travel with David; another armored car was designated to carry him, and the soldiers hustled Isaac to it, hands under his armpits so that he was almost lifted into the back, and then with his escort he was sat upon a cool iron seat. The great, thickened, high-velocity-proof doors were closed on him, exchanging for the boy one tomb prison for another.

From the Foreign Secretary's office overlooking the lunchtime crowds that surged across Horse Guards parade ground seeking the grass of St. James's for their sandwiches and newspapers, the news of the conclusion at Stansted spread quickly. Permanent Secretaries wound up their meetings; undersecretaries canceled their lunch appointments. In News Department they prepared themselves to issue the statement that would explain the course of action being followed by Her Majesty's Government.

There was no more discussion as to whether the survivor should be returned to Kiev. That decision had been taken; News Department was concerned with drafting only the justification. There was much fetching and carrying of United Nations transcripts, Security Council and General Assembly, of debates concerning aerial piracy. From the Security Council meeting that had followed the Israeli military intervention at Entebbe in July of 1976 there was much to be taken that pleased those who would eventually fashion the Foreign Office release. The red pencils were busy underlining passages from the speech of Chaim Herzog, Israel's ambassador to the United Nations.

. . . Those countries which fail to take a clear and unequivocal stand against international terrorism for reasons of expediency or cowardice will stand damned by all the decent people in this world and despised in history. There is a time in the affairs of men when even governments must make difficult decisions guided not by considerations of expediency but by considerations of morality. . . . It is now for the nations of this world, regardless of political differences which may divide them, to unite against this common enemy which recognizes no authority, knows no borders, respects no sovereignty, ignores all basic human decencies, and places no limits on human bestialities.

Also coming down from the shelves were the transcripts of the 1970 Hague convention called to discuss the "Suppression of Unlawful Seizure of Aircraft." Article 6 was the one that most concerned the drafters.

. . . Upon being satisfied that the circumstances so warrant, any contracting state in the territory of

which the offender or the alleged offender is present
shall take him into custody and other measures shall
be as provided in the law of that state but may only
be continued for such time as is necessary to enable
any criminal or extradition proceedings to be
instituted.

It would be harder to explain the absence of an appearance
before an Essex magistrate's court, and the speed with which
it was intended the surviving hijacker should be removed
from British soil and begin his journey back to the Soviet
Union, but the press conferences at Stansted should divert
immediate attention from the one point of contention. Get
rid of him first was the priority, before the protests were mobilized, before intergovernmental relations were strained.

There were one or two in the labyrinth of Whitehall who
voiced concern at the planned culmination of the affair, but
they were not overly loud with their anxieties and were soon
muted. Closed ranks and consensus opinion. So much more
dignified that way.

Charlie came off the plane last of all.

They had let the photographers forward, and he saw them
in their broken ranks running across the ocean-wide space
between the Ilyushin and the distant perimeter fence, hus-
tling with their pronged tripods and cameras and cables.
Those who were least encumbered with equipment, and remembered him as the man who had walked out across their
lenses in the early morning, had a chance to photograph
Charlie. When he perceived their opportunity, he raised his
hand to cover his face—a reflex gesture. He would have been
horrified to know that he had provided the Fleet Street cap-
tion writers with one of the day's many bonuses. "Shy Hero"
was the title they dubbed on the picture of the shambling
figure walking away across the tarmac with his shirt-sleeved
arm raised and his trousers sagging on his hips.

18

The shadows were clawing at the late summer afternoon when they flew Isaac out of Stansted.

He had only a few feet to walk from the midnight-black police van to the stunted steps of the Hawker Siddley executive jet that carried for its markings the painted red, white and blue concentric circles of the Royal Air Force. A cluster of men, some in uniform, the majority favoring well-worn civilian suits, were there to see him on his way. No farewells—only a series of curt handshakes between those who were staying and those whose work was not yet finished. They talked around Isaac, not speaking to him, pretending to ignore him, as if to demonstrate their relief that the load was to be shed, the burden passed on.

No more defiance from the boy, left behind in the small cell in the basement of the airport police station where he had sat and pondered on what awaited him, whiling away the hours for the details of the flight to be arranged. A child again; no trace of the savage hostility the fish-eye had mirrored. He stumbled on the bottom step, but there were hands on his arm which prevented him from pitching backward, and the faces around him were stern and closed, as if their owners were unwilling to display their emotions, bare their thoughts to him.

Five passengers in all. A member of the Russian Embassy staff who had been the first to climb on board; they had checked his name after he had proffered it against the Foreign Office list of Soviet diplomats, found him described as a chauffeur. After him a uniformed corporal of the Royal Air Police, immaculate in his starched and pressed battle dress, who had a cap with a red ribbon around it and a webbing belt which carried the whitened holster encasing a Browning automatic pistol. Next Isaac, climbing with difficulty as he trailed his right arm, linked by handcuffs to the wrist of a second service policeman. Two Foreign Office men—both from Security, though neither would have admitted it—hurried inside the aircraft before the door was closed and the twin rear engines started.

That was the last Charlie Webster saw of Isaac, the back view of the dark-haired, pale-faced boy illuminated casually by the rotating blue lamp of the police van. Charlie still slumped in the chair in the control tower from which he had watched the departure. To some he seemed churlish in his rejection of the many congratulations that were showered on him when he was greeted by the politicians and the political aides, the senior policemen, the army officers and civil servants. But Clitheroe had moved among the offended and Charlie had heard the words, hushed and discreet, of "shock" and "terrible strain," and "it was necessary to deceive him—helped him, in fact," and "what you'd expect in the circumstances" and "exhaustion" and "be right as rain once he's had a good sleep." From where Charlie sat, he could see the Hawker Siddley taxi and then thrust forward in the gathering, closing gloom for takeoff, the flashing red lights marking its progress down the runway. He watched it all the way through lift-off; stayed with it till there was just a moving star of light which faded along with the roar of the engines under power.

He reached for a telephone and dialed his home. Told his wife that he'd be home, but late; was irritable when she asked him where he was and where he'd been and didn't he know she'd been worried; didn't answer, and heard her say that the key would be under the front-door mat if he'd forgotten to take his own yesterday morning, and there'd be some food on the kitchen table, and please to be quiet when he came in because the children had exams at school tomorrow.

He stayed a long time in the control tower, way after the others had gathered their papers together and made noisy and exultant farewells, after the cleaners had been through with the stiff brushes for the carpet, and the complaints about the stubbed cigarettes, and the big plastic bags for the rubbish that had accumulated; they worked around him, subdued in their normal exuberance and chatter and gossip by the hunched figure who held his hands over his eyes and who did not move, who had not even a nod of recognition for them.

Tried to blot it out of his mind: The thought of the small jet landing at Tempelhof, West Berlin. The waiting car and the few courtesies that would be exchanged. Bundled into the back seat of one in the convoy that would not be at the front or the back, but would be sandwiched against any intervention—not that there were men and women in that city who could even have begun to organize a rescue attempt. Play it by the book, wouldn't they? Because that was easiest, that was the simple and tried way, which said five cars for maximum security. Through undefined channels that existed for communication, word would be sent that the prisoner was on his way; a time of arrival would be given.

Half an hour, not more at the speed at which the cars would travel, and the column would be at the checkpoint. Barriers would be raised, and two groups would meet in the center of a barren, floodlit road. Brief handshakes and riddance of the package. Won't be your checkpoint, Charlie— too public; one of the remote ones. In case anyone should witness the exchange, and ask why, and have no bugger there able to answer.

Wondered whether he'd struggle, the boy Isaac; whether he'd be pleading, screaming. Didn't think so; wouldn't be the style of the kid. He'd be thinking about you, Charlie; certain, stands to reason. Thinking as he stepped forward and exchanged captors, thinking why Charlie hadn't fired, thinking of it as the new hands held him. They'd spin on their heels, and there'd be a new fleet of cars and a new airport, divided from the first by the gorge of ideology and the wall and the mines and the wire.

Should have known, shouldn't you, Charlie; should have seen through the crap they gave you; would have if you weren't so bloody stupid. And if you had known, would it have been different, would the boy have been obliged? Can't blot it out, can you, Charlie? Not the face of the boy, not the eyes and the mouth and the tight-sewn cheek that begged for a release from all that would now be inflicted.

The air-traffic controllers were less susceptible to his feelings than the cleaning women had been. Had to shift now: reopening the airport; needed the chair; all the holiday flights queuing up—Faro, Málaga, Naples, Valetta, Crete. And it was outside regulations for an unauthorized person to remain in the tower. Mustn't keep the vacationers waiting any longer, Charlie; put them to enough inconvenience as it is; shouldn't bugger them about anymore. Polite enough about it, but they wanted him out, and left him in no doubt as to their priorities. None knew who he was; different shift coming on, didn't know what he had done that day, and some reckoned after they'd seen him through the door that he'd been drunk.

Below was a police control post, in the process of being dismantled. He put his head around the door, stopping the conversations, cocking the heads inquisitively, and asked whether there was any transport going to London.

"I've been with the Foreign Office people here," he said.

There'd be a car in about fifteen minutes—Special Branch; he could go with them. He should wait in the canteen, and they'd fetch him out when they were ready to leave. So he passed the time with a cup of untasted, cooling coffee in front of him till the summons came.

They drove fast and without talk for the first hour along the All, out through Bishop's Stortford, hammering along the deserted road. It was the driver who broke the long silence.

"Did you see the little bugger?" he asked chattily, uninvolved, wanting to start the dialogue.

"Yes," said Charlie.

"Didn't look much, did he? Like we could have had him for breakfast."

"They usually are," said Charlie. Oncoming headlights lit up the faces of the driver and his companion beside him. Showed them to be relaxed, at ease and at peace with themselves.

"I saw him in the cells," the driver said. "Meek as they bloody come. Reckon I'd have been going spare if I'd been in his shoes—going back home to face the music and all that. Fair old reception he'll have when they get their hands on him."

"Yes," said Charlie.

"Wouldn't care to be in his pants. Shitting myself I'd be."

"Too right," the front passenger chimed in.

"I don't know why we didn't bump him on the plane. Would have been the easiest thing. His mate's bought it, the girl's dead; could have finished the whole bloody thing then and there. Save the old RAF a mass of trouble. Did you see what he went out in? Only a bloody executive jet, like old Onassis; the real red-carpet treatment. No, they should have shot him on board."

"You can't just do that," the front passenger said. "It's not as simple as that. We have to show we are prepared to stand up to this business. And the best way to stamp it out is to pack the blighters off home again, let them sort it out there. We don't owe the little rat anything, not a bloody thing. Cost a fortune, this business. Cost the life of the Italian, and he had damn all to do with what this mob are shouting about. Italian, right? So how does he get his pecker into the state of the Jews in Russia? Doesn't, does he? All he'd done is buy a ticket for a plane flight. You've got to sit on these people. Sit on them hard, that's the way you end it. So the Russkies give him a rough time; well, that's his problem, not the rest of the world's. Should have thought about that first."

"You're a hard man," the driver said, and they both laughed. "What did you think about sending him back then, squire?"

"I don't know," said Charlie. "I just don't know."

"Keep it tight, you Foreign Office people, don't you?"

"I don't mean that. I'm not avoiding you. I just don't know."

"Served him right," said the front passenger. "If he doesn't like it, he should have stayed at home. Should have watched his telly."

"You're right," said the driver. "Course you're right. But doesn't make it any nicer. Not sending him back there. Different if he was a Yank or something, but where he's going, then, that's different, that's something else."

The car sped on, taking Charlie back to that which he knew. His home. His family. His office and his work. Going back to all that was familiar, where his attitudes would not be cuffed by a boy half his age. Going back to all that was safe and secure. Wondered what Parker Smith would say. Probably be a sherry on the house, and a slapped back and the word that he'd done the section's name a power of good, and didn't we always know you still had your balls in the right place, and be making damn certain you don't get pinched again by "operational" after all this.

"I didn't ask you, squire: where did you see him—in the cells?" The driver bored with the quiet and resurrecting the conversation.

"I saw him on the plane," said Charlie.

"I thought it was the SAS blokes that took him off."

"I was on before them." Charlie spoke woodenly, without pride, claiming no victory.

"You were the FO guy, then?" The front passenger had turned eagerly in his seat, excited; something to tell the lads back in the pub behind the Yard if they made London before closing. "Were you the one that pulled the hostage clear, then went on board and wrapped it up?"

"I was on board when it ended."

"Jesus—that must have been something, quite something, when he blasted and all that; when all the heavy stuff was flying about. He shot the girl himself, didn't he?"

"Yes," said Charlie. He looked at his watch: another hour at least. Felt the noose tightening, felt the hopelessness of a prisoner with no escape.

"And the Israeli—he was killed then, was he? When the Jew fired on the girl?"

Where would he be now? High over the North German plains, or perhaps beginning to hear the descent of the engines, the lowering of the undercarriage, feeling the gusting turbulence as the air brakes were applied. Wonder whether they're talking to him, whether he's just a parcel of bloody freight.

"Shut up, Bill," said the driver, and as an afterthought that ignored Charlie's presence, "Pack it in. The poor sod's had enough on his plate today without having to go through it all again with us."

They talked between themselves, the two Special Branch men, for the rest of the journey into the lit streets of London. Only once did they break into Charlie's private world: when they asked him where he wanted to be dropped. He told them that Waterloo Station would do very well, and that was where they left him. They stayed in the car as he walked across the concourse fumbling in his pocket for the return stub of a ticket he had bought the previous morning. When he was past the barrier and disappeared through a door of the first carriage of the Woking train, they went on their way.

"Funny sort of blokes you find in the spooks," said the front passenger as they headed across Westminster Bridge. "You've done well. If we can find somewhere to park the motor, we should be able to get a fast one down."

The report from the Ambassador in London lay on the Prime Minister's desk. It was a clinical and well-worded document, devoid of emotion and attempting merely to set out the circumstances in which the hijacking of Aeroflot flight 927 had ended. It set forth a brief description of the death, to the degree to which the facts were known, of Lt. Col. Arie Benitz and as much information as the diplomat could muster on the thinking that had led the British to fly the one survivor of the terrorist team back to Russia. The Prime Minister was more amused than surprised that his representative had chosen the word "terrorist." He could reflect that there had been a time, less than three decades ago, when the word had held a respectability now long since discarded. Back in the days of Haganah and the Palmach, the days of Jewish struggle against the British—then there had been no stigma to the label of "terrorist."

But what was in a word, in a name, in a title? Terrorist or freedom fighter or urban guerrilla—only labels to express the international community's displeasure at or acclamation for the men who fought the hidden wars, who belonged to the lonely and unrecognized armies, who shunned the safety of the big battalions. But it was a dangerous thought, impossible beyond the privacy of his office. He could not permit himself to express such a view outside the stout wooden door, because that would mean acknowledgment of the Palestinians who in their puny groups likewise attempted to overthrow the status of accepted authority.

His last duty that night was to telephone his Minister of Information. There should be no government reaction, either attributable or nonattributable, by any of the Ministry's spokesmen about the events of the day at Stansted. It was to be regarded as an affair between Britain and the Soviet Union—that was to be the line taken; any other suggestions should be treated with noncommittal answers.

It had been a difficult and trying day for them all, he thought, and his plans, which had seemed at best difficult and at worst unfeasible, had ended without success. And lost to them was a man they could ill afford to be without. Hard to find again another like the young Benitz, with the clear eyes and the devotion and the expertise. His secretaries were long since gone, and he switched off the lights of his office and of the anteroom before walking out to where the body-guards lounged in the corridor.

At his morning meeting, the Foreign Secretary was told of the night's developments.

He was briefed on the exchange of Isaac at the least-used and least-observed checkpoint between West and East Berlin. The cipher teleprinter messages from the Foreign Office men of the transaction's being carried out without any unseen dif-ficulties and in strict accordance with the mutually agreed-on planning. He was informed that the Russian Ambassador had sent a message of congratulation to the British Government, thanking it on behalf of the Supreme Soviet for the firm stand that had been taken in the maintenance of the rule of law. There was nothing in the text to bring him to assume that the prisoner would face any penalty other than death. This did not distress him; the time for window dressing was way past, gone with the takeoff of the Hawker Siddley jet; but he knew the habits of the Soviets sufficiently to believe that the fate of the boy would be decided and executed swiftly and without recourse to the beating of drums. He had read two of the day's morning papers in his car on the way to Whitehall, and asked his private secretary if there had been hostile reac-tion to the Foreign Office statement in those which he had not yet seen.

"Not really, sir. Bit of a quibble in some about the speed of things. But nothing openly antagonistic in the leader pages. They all carried a very good wire picture from the Italian ANSA agency—showed the wife of Franconi, the Italian who was killed; she's in tears with her children round her. Difficult for Fleet Street to conjure up much of a row when they have a snap like that to use alongside. Seems to me it all went off rather well."

"I think we sometimes preoccupy ourselves too much with public reaction," the Foreign Secretary said. "Every now and then they want a good, firm decision, and that's what we gave them."

"I doubt if the Israelis are that pleased."

"Not our concern, young man. We're not elevated to these lofty climes to please the people of Jerusalem and Tel Aviv and Haifa. They've shouted long enough and loudly enough about the need to teach these people a lesson, and quite right, too; they've complained at the softness and the lack of resolution in the West to hijacking. Well, we've shown them what we can do."

"But it's not as simple as that, is it, sir?"

"Of course it isn't. Quote me and I'll fire you—too damn right I will. Of course it isn't that simple. The only thing that amazes me is that more people haven't said so."

What also surprised him was the degree, now that it was completed, to which he had enjoyed handling the crisis. True, it had not been a major one; but crises, and even the little ones, were welcomed when you sat in high office. He would miss the briefings, and the hurrying in the corridors, and the ambassadors kicking their heels with impatience outside the door. If the opinion polls were correct in their assessment of the popularity of his party, his tenure of the Foreign Office was limited in the extreme.

He would remember these last two days, remember them with affection.

For an hour now the bird had been still, motionless as a statue, perched on the dark oak root that curved out from the riverbank over the clear, fast-flowing water.

Such a small body, with its disproportionate head and the brown bill that projected with benign aggression from the brilliant mass of the blue-and-green feathering of the head and back which in turn softened to the reddened brown of the breast. Patient, and accepting no limit on the time it must spend before the unwary minnow or stickleback, held in an illusion of safety, might stray beneath the watching eyes.

When it dived, it was with a flashing, sudden movement that was too fast for the sight of the old man to follow, leaving him only with the bareness of the root and the wrinkled circling of the water that would soon be lost in the constant eddying and jockeying of the flow. Gone for a second, perhaps two, till the little lungs must have been fit to explode, and then the supreme moment of triumph as it broke the water, seemed to float for a moment before thrashing angrily clear of the frail spray and arching up toward the hold which the old man had found many months earlier and which was the reason he came to this place. Mingled with the colors of the bird was the tiny, flapping silver fish, frantic in its death throes; and they were gone, predator and victim, lost to sight under the lip of the bank that was its home and where he knew the fledglings would be waiting.

Most days he came to this spot, crawling on his hands and knees into the thicket that hid him from the kingfisher's view. Only heavy rain that made him shelter in the hut, or the needs of hunger and a hunting expedition far into the forest, would keep him away, prevent him from sharing the pleasure of the bird as she provided for her little ones. He would not see her for some minutes now while she broke up the meal before consigning it to the hungry throats.

Perhaps the male would visit; that would be value for a further wait—a heavier, larger bird, its colors more complete and deeply accented, that would swoop low over the stream as he came and call once in the shrill shriek that was the signal of his approach. The same sound that he had taught the young man, David, who was deep and serious and passionate in his beliefs in something that Timofey did not understand, and who needed the guns for his fulfillment.

Five days now since the young one had gone with the guns in their wrapping, and with the ammunition and the magazines. Each day Timofey had remembered him and felt the bolt of loneliness when he thought of their farewell that he had not experienced since the outset of his solitary hermitage.

His ears were keen to the sound of approaching footsteps, and when he first heard the breaking of twigs and the cracking of the parched leaf mold under the policemen's boots, he had hoped that it heralded the return of David. He waited for the call, silent, hidden, anxious. Waited. He had taught the boy well, till his imitation of the kingfisher call was perfect, the call of the big bird that he now expected, when it returned from its lone forays and measured its hunting success against that of its mate. But the barking of the dogs, frantic now with excitement, the scent regained from the hut, aroused him to the danger. Timofey was old, and though his senses were still keen, his agility of movement was long lost.

An age it took him to scramble to his feet; more time to recognize the source and direction of the threat; longer to plot which way he should run. There were voices now, lively with pursuit, and ever closer the yapping of the hounds.

His hands were still scrabbling at the far bank of the stream when they came to the place where he had been concealed as he watched the bird. Two dogs, large, well fed, disciplined to attack and straining and heaving at their leashes. Four men. Two of them dog handlers, the others carrying light machine guns. All wearing the dun uniform of the Kiev militia. Stupidly, because the chance of escape no longer existed, he tried to pull himself up the slippery and crumbling bank—something that was instinctive to so old a fugitive. Fighting upward and falling, rising again and subsiding, his isolation broken and rent. Destroyed by the boy who had come; nullified when he had won Timofey's friendship, when he had taken the guns. All clear to the old man as the moss and earth filled his untended fingernails and his movements became more sluggish, more tired.

He did not know of Isaac. Had no way to conjure in his mind the small hunched figure in a cell corner with the bruises refreshed and alive around his face who had denounced Timofey. The information he had bartered would purchase Isaac a few more hours before they took him from his cell for the last time. A few more hours; that was the value of the old man's life.

Four bullets they fired at him. Three to buckle him in the water, a fourth to be certain the job was completed.

Deep in her hole in the riverbank, the kingfisher and her family waited for the screams and the thunder to pass. Half a day she stayed there before hunger overtook her fear and she emerged again into the slanted light of the late afternoon and tripped to her perch to wait and to watch. The water beneath her was stained where the main current had not cleansed it, and though she remained till dusk, the fish did not come again.

main

FEB 1 8 1984

WITHDRAWN

APR 1 3 1992	**DATE DUE**	
APR 2 7 1992	SEP 0 6 2005	
MAY 1 8 1992	APR 0 9 2008	
JUL 1 0 1992		
AUG 1 4 1995		
MAR 1 6 1996		
JUN 3 0 1997		
SEP 1 6 1997		
AUG 0 6 1999		

BRO DART   PRINTED IN U.S.A.   23-521-002